SUITCASE CITY

SUITCASE CITY

Sterling
Watson

A NOVEL

This is a work of fiction. All names, characters, places, and incidents are the product of the author's imagination. Any resemblance to real events or persons, living or dead, is entirely coincidental.

©2015 Sterling Watson
ISBN: 978-1-61775-319-0
Library of Congress Control Number: 2014938700

Akashic Books
Twitter: @AkashicBooks
Facebook: AkashicBooks
E-mail: info@akashicbooks.com
Website: www.akashicbooks.com

To Mike, the best brother a guy could ever have

ACKNOWLEDGMENTS

My thanks to Jamie Gill for library research, to Judd McKean and Suzy Johnson for help with boats, and to Tom DiSalvo and Margarita Lezcano for correcting Spanish. I am indebted to Margot Hill, Dean Jollay, Bill Kelly, Dennis Lehane, Ann McArdle, Peter Meinke, Bill Miles, and Jay Nicorvo for criticism and commentary. Your insights made this book better. Thanks to Jerry Witucki for one very good line. Thanks again to the marvelous crew at Akashic Books, especially Ibrahim Ahmad, who guided me through some difficult revisions with patience, good humor, and keen intelligence. And, as always, a loving thank you to Kathy, the best reader of all.

Lay your sleeping head, my love,
Human on my faithless arm . . .

—"Lullaby," W.H. Auden

PART ONE

ONE

1978, Cedar Key, Florida

Jimmy Teach left professional football at the age of twenty-four, and his life went into a fast fall. He squandered money on bad friends and foolish business deals and the drink and drugs that went with them. He lived hard and the months passed and it became a slow suicide. He woke up one morning in a car he didn't own in the driveway of a fashionable house in Atlanta with a policeman at his window. Teach had no idea who owned the house or why he had come to it. He had passed out with the engine running. A half-open window and an empty fuel tank had probably saved him from a blue-lipped death.

Teach went home broke to Cedar Key, Florida. To start over in the old place. To remember who he had been, build a man again. One he could stand to be. People in the little towns were used to their sons and daughters coming home. The little places sent out a strong call to their own. The call was, *Come back. Come back and be small again.* And many did.

Teach looked for jobs in the local fishery, but the crabbing, oystering, and gillnetting had fallen on hard times. He worked in kitchens, then as a bartender. At first it was hard because people asked questions. As simple as: what are you doing back here? As difficult as: what happened to all that football money? But it wasn't long before Teach was one of them again. Before he was nothing special.

One night, Teach was serving a party of sun bunnies who had arrived on a big motor sailer. He was dropping the paper umbrella into a banana daiquiri when a black man said, "Hey, what you doing back here?" The question was old, the man was vaguely familiar.

The man looked over at the people he was with. They were the easy, pretty people who stopped in at the Cedar Key docks and ate in the restaurants and then sailed on to the next piña colada or planter's punch. Teach called them the Whatever People. *Whatever* was an attitude, a place where people had enough time and money to let things happen to them, things that felt good. Teach said, "Do I know you?"

"Hey, Jimmy, come on." The man's accent was local, the black version of it anyway, but the attitude was from Whatever. Teach still couldn't place him. The guy laughed, leaned close, and said, "*Delia B.*, man. Remember?"

It all came back. The *Delia B.* was a trawler Teach had piloted when he was fifteen years old. An accomplished kid with a boat, he had coasted the *Delia B.* into a secluded canal bank where she would meet a rented truck. When her cargo was off-loaded, he would take her back out again, jump into a skiff tied to her stern, and wave goodbye to his friends who would clean her out and run her back around through Key Largo and up to Homestead. The black man's name was Bloodworth Naylor. Nine years ago they had been business associates.

"Naylor," Teach said, "how you doing, man? It's been a long time."

Teach remembered it all now, the nights he'd brought the boat in, the fat envelopes of cash, the things he'd bought for his widowed mother, the secrets. Bloodworth Naylor glanced over at the Whatever People, lowered his voice. "Ah, you know. I get along one way and another. Right now I'm babysitting tourists for ten bucks an hour."

After Teach closed up that night, he let Naylor in the back door and they sat in the dark bar. Naylor was crewing on the motor sailer, running tourists up and down the coast for a couple of New Age gurus who had them meditating in string bikinis and Speedos and contemplating the Tao. "Bunch of mantra-mumbling fools," Naylor said over his third rum and lime. He stared at Teach. "You probably think it's a coincidence us running into each other like this."

Teach raised his Wild Turkey and sipped. He was supposed to smile, say yeah, he thought it was a coincidence. He glanced around the bar. A table of waitresses over in the corner counting tips and telling evil-tourist stories. The cleanup crew coming on with mops and buckets. This was Teach's life after football. Apparently, the man he had come home to build was a bartender. Bartenders know the past always comes looking for you.

Teach said, "You're doing it again, Naylor. You're back in the import business."

Blood Naylor smiled. "Not yet, but I'm thinking about it. Now that you're back in town."

The trawlers didn't come from Homestead anymore, and they didn't cross to Freeport for the product. Teach and Bloodworth Naylor were subcontractors for a consortium of Guatemalan importers. The Guatemalans owned a mother ship designed to transport yachts across the world. Its huge bow doors opened, boats were floated aboard and secured, then the seawater was pumped out. They brought the mother ship up the Florida coast at night, floated an eighty-ton shrimper named the *Santa Maria* out of her bow, and three Guatemalans named Julio, Carlos, and Esteban piloted the shrimper inside the twenty-mile limit. The shrimper's steel booms had been removed to give her a smaller radar signature and more deck space. The *Santa Maria* was loaded to the gunwales with bales of marijuana, the Guatemalans were armed to the teeth, and the night skies were full of cops.

Teach did the job he had done as kid. He ran out in a twenty-one-foot Boston Whaler, met the *Santa Maria* and the three surly Latino gangsters, brought the shrimper in, weaving her through a maze of mangrove canals to the place in the Steinhatchee game preserve where Naylor met them with a rented truck. Teach and Naylor off-loaded the bales while the three *pistoleros* stood around smoking caporal cigarettes and stroking their mustaches. Once, Teach said to the ranking Guatemalan, "Hey, Esteban, why don't you guys help us with the heavy work here? We get this done sooner, you get out quicker. It's better for everybody." Teach looked up at the sky, reminding Esteban of the DEA aircraft that patrolled this coast.

Esteban looked at Teach the way he would at a guy who'd just asked for spare change. "*Soy soldado. No soy peón.*"

Teach knew enough Spanish to get the drift. A soldier, not a laborer. "Yeah, well, we get caught here you'll be somebody's pom-

pom girl up at Raiford. They like the little brown ones up there." Teach squared himself, wiped the sweat from his eyes with his shirt sleeve, waited to see what Esteban would do. Maybe he had gone too far this time. He didn't like the guy, didn't care for any of the Guatemalans. They were Indians who had worn gaudy suits only long enough to learn how to sneer. Their eyes said they would kill without remorse, and their hands always hovered near the weapons they carried in shoulder rigs or in their waistbands.

Esteban opened his coat and showed Teach the gleaming stainless steel nine-millimeter automatic pistol. He smiled and showed some smoke-stained teeth. His eyes were not touched by the smile. He said, "Quickly, quickly," pointing a manicured finger at the work still to be done.

Teach did the work, took the cut Blood Naylor gave him, and buried his money deep in the woods. He knew enough about bank examiners, Internal Revenue Service inspectors, and human curiosity to realize that he'd better keep living on a bartender's wage until he had saved enough to leave town. He'd figure out later what a man did with half a million dollars in cash, a man who did not have paycheck stubs or Aunt Lizzie's last will and testament to show for it.

Going in, Teach and Naylor had agreed on two things. One: they would do only as many trips as it took to get each of them started in something legitimate. Two: the day either man decided to quit, they were both out of the business.

Blood Naylor took care of distribution in the university city. He knew the black community there, where the white kids went to buy. He promised Teach that no one in Gainesville would ever hear Teach's name. Teach told himself that he was just a pilot, a man who operated a boat for a couple of hours, a man who carried some harmless agricultural product to a waiting truck. When his conscience came calling late at night before he fell asleep, he called himself a maritime consultant. When he was awake, he called himself a bartender.

The day Teach had the money he needed to start a new life, he told Naylor the next trip would be his last.

They were sitting in Teach's locked-up, darkened barroom after midnight, drinking Tequila Sunrises and watching the cleanup crew mop the floors. Naylor drew hard on his cigarette, lighting his dark eyes with a red glow. "Old Esteban ain't gonna like it."

Teach thought about it. He didn't like what he'd seen in Naylor's eyes when the cigarette made them visible. He said, "Old Esteban can find two new humps. We're sticking to our deal, all right?"

Naylor raised the glass of fruit and alcohol. The next drag on the cigarette confirmed what Teach had seen. Greed.

"A deal's a deal," Naylor said. "But what if old Esteban decides he like the two humps he got? Wants to keep them. What we do then?" Naylor put out the cigarette in the sunrise.

Teach wanted to say, *That's up to you, my friend. You made the deal with Old Esteban. You promised me I'd be the ship-to-shore connection, tote a few bales, and that was all.* But Teach didn't say it. Instead: "I got what I want out of this. Next trip's our last. Cool?"

"Cool . . . cool," Naylor said. Teach was glad he could not see the man's eyes now. The voice, the regret in it, was bad enough.

Naylor came by the bar, middle of the noon rush. He drank a beer, paid for it, and wrote the loran coordinates on a bar napkin. At midnight, Teach took the Boston Whaler from a rented slip behind the house of an old woman who had known his parents. She was eighty, nearly blind, and had no idea when Teach came and went. It was late September, still hot, and there was a bright harvest moon in the sky. Teach wove the Whaler through the maze of canals with high green mangrove walls, following the pathways he had memorized from boyhood fishing in a handmade plywood boat with a three-horse kicker. He smelled the open Gulf before he saw it, punching the Whaler out through a little delta of white sand and driftwood into a low line of breakers.

The moon was high and Teach could see for miles. Off to his right, a low, scudding banner of clouds drifted south on a fresh ten-knot breeze. Teach hoped the clouds would swell and obscure the moon before he made the rendezvous point. He doubted it. Ahead of him, the sky was high and starry, and he could see the silver contrail of an airliner heading for Tallahassee. The DEA Cessna Skymasters flew without running lights, and Teach had little hope of spotting one silhouetted against the heavens before it saw him. He ran without lights too, but it wasn't much of a precaution. Anyone up there would see his wake, a mile of silver ribbon tacked to his stern.

Well, the Whaler was full of the usual fishing equipment, a lunch, a cooler of beer, and a thermos of coffee. The live bait well was stocked with shrimp, and Teach had even taken the precaution of buying some ballyhoo. If a Coast Guard or a DEA boat stopped him, he'd look like the real thing. But all of this, Teach reflected standing at the Whaler's steering station with the wind throwing his hair straight back behind him, was little protection. His best safeguard was the enormity of the Gulf of Mexico.

Twenty miles out, he saw the huge bulk of the mother ship rise like a black moon out of the horizon. Six miles away and she had seen him. Her bow doors slowly opened and she gave birth to the shrimper *Santa Maria*, a dark blot on the shimmering sea. If the timing was right, Teach would arrive just as the *Santa Maria* was powered up by Carlos, the best of the three gangsters. Carlos, Teach had learned from scraps of stray talk, had been a fisherman before he had taken up the drug trade. He understood and loved boats. Teach cut his speed, and the twin Yamahas complained a little, then settled into a five-knot idle.

He made the bow of the *Santa Maria* just as the mother ship started her slow, ponderous arc west to deeper water. She would steam a wide five-hour circle and meet the shrimper when she returned, deadheading. Teach tossed a line to Julio and scrambled over the shrimper's transom.

For the next five hours, the night would belong to Teach and Naylor. Teach had once asked Esteban why the Guatemalans didn't just let Teach and Naylor take the shrimper in, bring her back out. Why they risked going ashore, three armed illegal aliens. Esteban blew a big huff, gave Teach those *el stupido* eyes. "What if you jus take de boat? Never return? What about dat?" Esteban struggled with English but had no trouble with his sneer.

Teach had smiled, shrugged. "Hey, we're all businessmen. We honor our commitments." Again, Esteban had opened his coat, letting Teach see the big pistol.

The trip was fast and lucky. The banner of wispy clouds filled up with moisture, became a thick dark curtain, and covered the moon. Steering by the loran, Teach found the mouth of the tidal canal and eased the shrimper through a hole in the mangroves with only three feet of clearance on either side. From a hundred yards offshore, no one would even see the hole. From twenty yards off, no one would think the passage was more than three feet deep. But Teach knew a strong current flowed here from a spring not far inland, sweeping the hole deep enough for the *Santa Maria*.

From this point on, it was slow and careful going. Sometimes Teach had to cut the power so much that he almost lost steerageway. The thick green mangrove walls of the canal lashed the shrimper's rails. Leaves and torn branches rained on deck. Roosting anhingas and herons cried in the night as the boat ghosted past, her engine thumping. When Teach could take his eyes from his work, he watched Carlos and Julio moving around on deck, kicking branches and debris overboard. Sometimes the sides of the shrimper scraped the great, spidery mangrove roots, painting the boat with streaks of mud.

A half-mile inland, the canal widened and Teach breathed easier, loosening his grip on the wheel. On the foredeck, Julio and Carlos relaxed, lit cigarettes. Esteban stood in the bow like the captain he was, staring ahead into the darkness.

Teach reached down and turned on the radio, a rock station from Gainesville. The Stones singing their hearts out: all these years and still no satisfaction. The wheelhouse door opened, and Carlos's flat peasant face emerged from the darkness. Teach switched off the radio.

"No, no," said Carlos, smiling. "*Déjala encendida*. Let it go. Play it."

Teach turned the music back up. Carlos lit a cigarette, filling the little wheelhouse with the heavy stink of caporal tobacco. He shrugged, offered the gold cigarette case to Teach, who shook his head. "*No fumo.*" Teach thinking, *This little Indian with a big gun wants to be my friend. Well, we've been through a lot together.*

Teach reached into his hip pocket, pulled out a half pint of Wild Turkey. He took a swallow and offered it. Carlos took the bottle and sniffed it, then drank. Again. "*Muy bueno,*" he said. "*Gracias, amigo.*"

Teach nodded, took another bite, and put the bottle away. He saw something, some glimmer through the trees ahead. He caught a murmur of surprised talk from the deck below. Carlos slipped out of the wheelhouse, his feet rapping on the ladder. The *Santa Maria* was approaching a bend in the canal, and now Teach made out the glow of a lantern, a small boat, a man in it, glittering through the mangrove branches. They had never met anyone back here, though Teach had always known it was possible. He also knew that the only people a man would meet back here at midnight would be locals who observed the unspoken rules of silence.

Teach put the shrimper into reverse and spun her screw until she barely drifted. He went down onto the foredeck. The man in the boat was Frank Deeks. Deeks was a sometime handyman, sometime fisherman, and full-time drunk. Deeks kept his back to the men in the boat as it drifted up, pushing a heavy wave ahead of it, and Teach could see why. Deeks was poaching stone crab traps.

Teach had heard rumors about Deeks doing it. Few men would have dared. A crabber was justified, at least by local standards, in shooting anyone he caught messing with his traps. Looking down into Deeks's leaky skiff, Teach could see next to the hissing Coleman lantern a bottle of Heaven Hill bourbon and some sandwiches wrapped in wax paper. Deeks wasn't brave tonight, he was just more than normally drunk.

The three Guatemalans stood behind Teach, talking in low, urgent tones. Teach heard *cantar*. Informer. He didn't get it all, but he knew he had to improvise. He stepped to the rail and said, "What you doing out here so late, Mr. Deeks?"

Deeks looked at him out of pale, rheumy eyes. He was saintly thin and egg-bald and wore a railroad engineer's cap made of gray ticking, a khaki shirt, and old Bermuda shorts. Like a lot of thin men, he moved his limbs with exceeding slowness. His mouth was another thing. "Uh, fishing," Deeks said. "Ain't doing no good, though." There was no fishing gear in the boat. Deeks looked up at the *Santa Maria*. "What you doing out here in a boat so big, boy? You lost?"

Teach kept making it up: "Uh, Mr. Deeks, these gentlemen hired me to take this boat down to Harry Parsons's High and Dry for some repairs. I guess we a little lost." He smiled, winked at Deeks. A don't-let-on-how-lost wink.

Deeks didn't catch it. "Hell, boy, Harry Parsons's is two miles in the other direction and you know it. And . . ." Deeks's eyes left Teach's face and went to the shrimper again, the three men behind

Teach. "Who you say that boat belong to? She sure don't look like she come from around here. What's her name, anyway? What you say's wrong with her?"

Teach was about to say he hadn't said what was wrong with her. He was about to shift the conversation to the crab trap oozing mud into Frank Deeks's leaky boat, ask Deeks when he had taken up crabbing, when the pistol went off next to his right ear.

Teach grabbed the ear, screamed, and fell to his knees. His first thought was that the concussion had ruptured his eardrum, but soon he knew it hadn't, and soon there was more to worry about. All three of the Guatemalans were firing, the muzzle flashes wild and bright against the green wall of mangroves, the smoke thick and sweet, hot shell casings raining down around Teach. He crabbed backward on his knees and heard Esteban yelling, "*Paren! Basta! Se acabó!* Enough!" He had no idea how many shots they fired, just knew Carlos and Julio ignored the order, kept shooting until their magazines were empty.

Teach edged forward and peered over the rail. Frank Deeks lay in a sinking boat covered with blood and gasoline. A good-sized crab lay shot to pieces on his chest. Fragments of crab, flesh, brain, and fried egg sandwich littered the boat and the surface of the water.

Before Teach could speak, he felt Esteban's hand on his shoulder. "Get up. Take us out of here. *Rápido. Vámonos.*"

In a fog of head-hurt and shock, Teach did what he was told. When he had the boat moving, her stern abreast of the little skiff, he felt a second concussion, heard a whoosh, saw a tower of flame rising behind the *Santa Maria*. Heard Esteban call out again, "*Rápido! Rápido!*" Teach gave the shrimper more power. When he had her out in the middle of the canal, he stepped from the wheelhouse and gazed back at the shallow place near the bank where Frank Deeks lay burning in the gasoline from his outboard.

TWO

By the time they reached the off-loading site, Teach had calmed himself and treated his headache with whiskey. His first job, he knew, was to keep quiet about what he had seen. There would be plenty of time later to explain to Naylor. No telling how Naylor would react if Teach told it now.

Teach eased the *Santa Maria* as close to the canal bank as she could go. Naylor always hid in the scrub beyond the bank until Teach gave the signal to bring the truck up the last half mile. Teach idled the engine, picked up his flashlight, and shot the beam at the scrub. Naylor flashed back twice. Teach waited in the wheelhouse while Naylor threw aboard the two lines he kept secured to the trunks of cypress trees. When the boat was moored fore and aft, Naylor lowered a gangplank fixed by hinges to the base of a cypress. A block and tackle in the treetop let the gangplank down across the twenty feet of water to the shrimper's rail. It was a good and speedy arrangement. The plank was the only permanent apparatus, and when it was upright you had to be in the water directly opposite the tree to see it.

Naylor waved his flashlight to Teach and took off jogging for the truck. Teach went down to the deck. He hadn't spoken to the Guatemalans since the shooting. He found them in the stern, smoking, their heads together. They stopped talking when he approached. He stood only a few feet from them, but he and they were separated now by more than land and language. It had been crazy stupid to kill Frank Deeks. If they had given Teach the chance, he could have explained Deeks to them, told them the guy was poaching traps. Told them Deeks would have cut off his hands before admitting he'd seen the *Santa Maria*.

Teach said, "*Mi amigo va por el camión. Regresa en unos minutos.*" He could already hear in the distance the slow whine of Naylor's engine.

Esteban stepped away from the other two, looked at Teach. "It is just as it always is. Hurry with the unloading."

Teach nodded. Ordinary nights, Teach had ten bales ashore before the truck arrived. He looked at Esteban. The man was different. Teach was not sure how. Was this the way you were after you shot someone? Esteban was always tense, wired. Now he seemed relaxed, serene, satisfied. The change frightened Teach more than the pistol under Esteban's arm.

He looked at Carlos and Julio and saw it there too. Their faces settled, their eyes uncurious, decided. Maybe he saw a little sorrow in the eyes of Carlos, the fisherman. The man who knew boats.

Teach humped bales until the truck arrived. When Naylor's face loomed out of the darkness, sweating from the half-mile jog, Teach only smiled and said, "Get aboard, buddy, and put some weight on your back. Those clouds are blowing south. Pretty soon it's gonna be moon over Miami."

Naylor looked at him. He sensed it. Something was wrong, different. Teach turned back to the gangplank, hurrying for the next bale.

When the unloading was finished, Teach went to the truck cab. As he passed Esteban, who stood at the back of the truck looking at the bales with those uncurious eyes, the man said, "*Adónde vas?*"

Teach stopped. "To the truck. For a cigarette." Esteban nodded.

In the truck cab, Teach found the .38 Smith & Wesson Chief's Special that Naylor kept in the glove box. He remembered Naylor showing it to him the day they had done their dry run before the first trip. Teach laughing. "What're you gonna do, shoot it out with the DEA?"

Naylor getting sulky, his masculinity damaged. "White man, you never know when that piece might come in handy. Better safe than sorry, I always say."

"Right," Teach had said. "Don't shoot yourself in the foot."

Teach put the pistol in the back of his waistband, under his shirt. He had been thinking white hot since Frank Deeks had gone up in flames, his mind trying for some clear, certain place where he would know what he had to do. He kept seeing things: How the three Guatemalans had stopped talking when he approached them on the stern of the *Santa Maria*, some evil fog around them of what they knew and he didn't. Their eyes holding that serenity. It meant, Teach knew, that they had decided. They had made up their minds.

Teach pushed out of the cab and walked back past Esteban. "Out of cigarettes," he said.

"Take one of mine." Esteban reached into his coat pocket for the cheesy gold cigarette case all three carried.

Teach waved no and pinched his nose. "Too strong for me, man."

Esteban gave an elaborate shrug, shook his head at the weakness of gringo lungs.

When the truck was closed up and ready, Teach stood in front of Naylor. He looked over at the three Guatemalans standing together by the gangplank. "Last trip, Blood," he whispered. "Wish me luck."

Bloodworth Naylor laughed, then looked at him. "What's going on, man? Everything cool? You seem a little—"

Teach slapped him hard on the shoulder to stop his mouth. In a hearty voice he said, "See you tomorrow, man. The bar, just like always. Drinks on me."

Teach always pushed the shrimper out along the same route he had taken coming in. Only it couldn't be the same. Not this time. He knew it now: the Guatemalans wouldn't do anything until he had taken them back to the Gulf, deep water under the keel. Then, something would happen. If Teach read those satisfied eyes right, there would be another body burning in a boat. The boat would be a Boston Whaler, cut loose from the stern of the *Santa Maria*. The body would be Jimmy Teach.

So the route tonight would be different, and Teach had to hope that the three Guatemalans didn't notice. He had to hope that they trusted him, believed in his seamanship, hadn't counted the turns he always took in this maze of mangrove canals.

Teach was approaching the place where he would take the new turn when the wheelhouse door slid open. Carlos. Teach said, "Hey man. *Qué paso?* Quiet night now, huh?"

"*Sí, mi amigo. Muy quiet.*" He looked at Teach. "It is too bad about the man in the boat." He shrugged. "But it had to be. You understand, don't you?"

Teach gave back the same sad smile. Soldiers lamenting the necessities of war. "Sure," he said, "I understand. It's tough, but it had to be."

Carlos looked ahead into the night and then over at Teach again. "Amigo?" he said, a look of supplication on his face. The Indian licked his lips, smiling.

"Oh," Teach said, "sure." He pulled the Wild Turkey from his hip pocket and passed it to Carlos. The man drank and handed it back. Teach reached to put the bottle away.

Carlos said, "Have some, drink with me."

The turn was just ahead. Teach said, "Sure, buddy." He drank and returned the bottle to his pocket, drawing his fingers across the pistol butt under his shirt. At the bend, he swung the shrimper right instead of left. It was a tight turn, but so were many of them. He could feel Carlos tensing beside him. Teach didn't look at the man, just waited. Carlos's hand was on his shoulder. On the foredeck below, Esteban turned and looked not at Teach but at Carlos.

Carlos said, "*Vamos bien?* We going the right way? You sure about this?"

Teach turned to the man, smiled. "Hey, Carlos, who's the pilot here? I know what I'm doing." Teach let go of the wheel, stepped back. Let a little anger come into his voice. "You think you can do better, man, you take over."

Carlos looked out at the walls of mangroves. In seconds the *Santa Maria* would plow into the bank. Fear in his voice, Carlos said, "I am sorry, *Señor Piloto*. Take the wheel. Take it."

As he took the wheel, Teach heard Esteban call out from below. The man shouting in Spanish, pointing at the looming trees. Teach turned the shrimper back into the channel. If it was going to happen, it had to be soon. The place Teach wanted was only a few minutes away, and so was the man he would become.

Teach felt Carlos relax beside him. Keeping one hand on the wheel, Teach raised the other and stretched, yawned. "Long night," he said.

Carlos looked at him, took out a cigarette, and lit it. He offered Teach the gold case.

"I told you, man, I don't smoke. *No fumo.* I drink. We did that together." Teach lowered his right hand and scratched his back.

"Then why you tell Esteban you go to the truck for a cigarette?" Carlos dropped the cigarette and reached inside his coat.

Teach snatched the Smith from his belt, fitted it to Carlos's skull just below his ear, and pulled the trigger. This time he was ready for the noise and flash in the little wheelhouse. Carlos grunted, "Nuh!" and stiffened, exhaled, went down limp. Teach cut the engine, pocketed the key, and stepped over Carlos's twitching chest. He pulled aside the sliding door, its little glass pane painted red with blood and brains, slipped out of the wheelhouse, and slid down the ladder to the narrow passage between the deck and the rail. He crouched there, listening. Footsteps came from the stern. Julio called, "Esteban, did you do it? You did it already?"

Julio thinking it was Teach dead up there. Well, now there would be no more calm, uncurious eyes. There was going to be some serious curiosity. Moving fast, Julio appeared in front of Teach, looking up at the wheelhouse, his pistol low by his thigh. Teach fired from a crouch, his pistol barrel almost touching Julio's chest.

Julio dropped the heavy nine-millimeter at Teach's feet, then sank to his knees, blood pouring black from his mouth. "*Madre*," he gasped, his face close, his breath garlic and cigarettes and blood. He clawed at his chest, tore at his tie, fell backward, and pulled his knees up to his chin.

"She'll be waiting for you," Teach muttered.

In the dark, the quiet, with the engine stopped, the *Santa Maria* drifted toward the canal bank. Teach could hear only the breeze that rustled the tops of the mangroves, the sluicing of water against the sides of the boat, the buzz of insects, the single cry of a heron, "Scrawwk."

Teach had been lucky with the first two, and now it would be grim. He would have to hunt Esteban, find him, and kill him. Still in his crouch, Julio relaxing into his death three feet in front of him, Teach picked up the big nine-millimeter, lowered the hammer, and stuck it in his belt. He reconsidered the matter. He would not hunt Esteban. He knew the boat better, knew the mangroves. What could the man do? What option did he have but to hunt Teach? If Teach left the boat, Esteban would be stuck here until he was discovered in the morning, or he would be lost out there in those miles of swamp.

Teach slipped through the door of the lazarette beneath the wheelhouse and into the head. He lowered himself to the toilet and waited in the foul stench of thirty years of seagoing piss. His back was protected by a bulkhead, he had walls on either side, and anything that passed by the door was dead. That was how Teach figured it.

He waited, hearing what he could over the thumping of his heart and the ringing in his ears. Twice he thought there was movement, a foot scraping, the boat subtly shifting under a moving body. The *Santa Maria* would hit something soon, and Teach decided to wait until she did, to see if the collision would give him Esteban's position. He braced himself against the walls of the toilet, waited, felt first the deep scraping of the forefoot on the canal bank, then the shrimper rising as she plowed up the bank. Hearing the pop and snap and groan of the mangroves as the bow tore into them, Teach thought: *Don't drive yourself too far aground. I've got to get out of here. After.*

When the boat had shuddered to a stop, Teach waited again for what seemed a long time. Then he heard the twin Yamahas roaring to life. *Damnit,* Teach thought, *I forgot about the little boat. Damn me for leaving the keys in the ignition. He'll take the Whaler and, with any luck, find his way out of here before morning.* He tried to keep the panic down, tried to sort through the possibilities. Maybe it was better if Esteban left him here. He could do what he'd planned to do with the shrimper and then run. Get away. What could the Guatemalans do tonight? Esteban couldn't meet the mother ship for another hour. Could he even find her out there in all that water? Had he bothered to learn the loran coordinates? By morning, Teach could be long gone. Lost in a new life.

He peered out of the head into the darkness of the lazarette. The Yamahas were still running, idling now. Why hadn't Esteban gone yet? A trick. Esteban was waiting out there for him. Teach heard the Yamahas grumble as the transmission shifted into gear. Then the Whaler seemed to be moving away.

Teach remembered something: there was a hatch in the roof of the lazarette. Through it you could climb into the wheelhouse, a way to get up there in heavy weather. He went to the hatch and pulled down the ladder bolted to the ceiling. He pushed at the hatch, but Carlos was up there. Dead weight. Standing on the ladder, Teach forced his shoulder against the hatch. Warm blood dripped down onto his head.

He managed to shove the hatch open enough to get past Carlos. He slipped out of the wheelhouse and crawled back to look down at the stern. As he reached the spot where he would have to risk his face to look down, the moon came out from behind the clouds. He could see the empty Whaler fifty yards away, churning its bow into the mangroves. He lifted his face an inch more, then another, and saw Esteban below, crouched behind a big winch housing, his pistol aimed at the lazarette door.

It would be a difficult shot. From above, the available target was the top of Esteban's head and his shoulders. Teach sighted the Chief's Special, then changed his mind. He slipped the Special into his belt and pulled the nine-millimeter. He eased back the hammer, released the safety, and got to his knees. He could aim and fire better from this position. He was trading risk for effect. The advantage of position was his; the advantage of killing for a living was with Esteban. A moment of fear came, sliding cold into Teach's bowels and rising thick into his throat. He could turn and run, leap from the bow of the shrimper, and disappear into the mangroves. But no, he thought, his mind clearing, his hands ceasing to shake. They would only come for him later. Find him and kill him. This was better. The only way now.

Teach edged forward, and as he did, the Chief's Special loosed from his belt and clattered to the lazarette roof. Esteban raised his arm, aimed at Teach. The moon caught Esteban's face, and before it disappeared in noise and flash and smoke, Teach saw that smile. The smile Esteban always gave Teach when he opened his coat to show the big pistol.

THREE

Teach emptied the magazine. Fired until the pistol was hot in his hand, and the night was a hellish carnival of flash and roar. He was not sure how many times Esteban fired back. After his first trigger pull, Teach heard only his own shots and felt the rock and roll of the pistol in his hand. When it was over and he lay back again on the deck, gasping for air, his hand sweaty on the pistol grip, he felt the sting begin in his right side.

Touching himself, he found the ragged furrow that cut through the outer plane of his left pectoral muscle and passed through his armpit. He was bleeding. He took off his shirt and balled it under his arm, removed his belt, and wrapped it around his chest. He waited, counting to fifty, before going down to look for Esteban.

Any of the four wounds could have killed the man. Two in the upper chest, one just below the right eye, and one at the base of the throat. Teach found superficial wounds in Esteban's right wrist and left forearm. The winch housing and deck around Esteban's body were covered with bullet holes. The nine-millimeter's magazine held fifteen rounds.

Teach backed the shrimper off the bank, then up the canal to retrieve the Whaler. He carried the three dead men down and put them in the bilge, a fetid crawl space above the hull. It was hard, dirty work, but he took his time and did it right, stopping occasionally to reposition the bandage he had fashioned with his shirt and belt. The wound Esteban had given him hurt, but he knew it wouldn't kill him. After filling the bilge with human flesh and three weapons, he lay on his side above the dead men and poured Wild Turkey onto the shirt wadded in his armpit. Then he howled rage and pain into the belly of the boat.

Back in the wheelhouse, Teach did what he had meant to do when he had turned right and not left. A hundred yards down the canal was the deep hole where thousands of gallons of water boiled up from a spring sweeping a channel deep enough for a shrimper.

Teach crawled down into the engine compartment at the stern. The shrimper was of Central American design—even Frank Deeks had recognized her as foreign—but her engine was a Caterpillar twelve-cylinder diesel. Teach smiled, looking at the works. A truck engine modified for marine use. He found the raw-water intake and cut the hose at the intake side of the strainer.

When he stuffed the severed end of the hose under a motor mount below the waterline, saltwater poured in. There were through-hulls in the head and galley Teach could have opened, but he knew this would do the trick and do it quickly. He crawled out of the tight, hot space that held the big diesel and went topside.

Starting in the wheelhouse, he searched for anything that might identify him. He scoured the lazarette, the decks fore and aft, found nothing. Finished, he sat on the transom watching the shrimper settle. Her mast was thirty feet above her waterline, and Teach wasn't sure she'd sink far enough into the spring to be completely obscured. He would hope and wait.

When the *Santa Maria* was ready to take water over her rails, Teach jumped into the Whaler, untied her, and sat drinking the rest of his whiskey. Water poured onto the shrimper's decks, and she listed to starboard and sank with a sigh, an explosion of gases from her hot muffler and stack, and a groan of timbers taking the enormous weight of the water that pushed her down.

Teach raised the whiskey bottle to her as her mast-top slid under. "Goodbye, old witch," he whispered. Then he hovered above her on the dark surface, shining his flashlight down into the roiling spring. He could see her mast-top twenty feet down, and so would anyone else who came here. And they would come until years later she rotted and disintegrated into the mouth of the spring. But only the locals, and only a few of them, knew this place, and Teach knew that any man finding a shrimper sunk here would likely keep it to himself. Likely leave well enough alone.

Teach raced home in the Whaler, tossing Naylor's pistol on the way. At three a.m., he climbed the stairs to the room he rented in the Island Hotel. He dressed his wound, but found that he could not sleep. He walked to the bar he kept, unlocked the door, and sat in the dark, drinking whiskey and thinking. Blood Naylor would come the next night to meet him, and Teach knew what he would say. He would tell Naylor that he, Teach, was going to disappear. He would advise Naylor to do the same thing. Naylor would have to close his distribution business in Gainesville in a hurry. Time, Teach would say, was of the essence. And that was all. To Naylor's questions he would answer only that it was better not to know more. Naylor could like it or not—that was up to him.

At sunrise, Teach had drunk enough whiskey to numb the pain under his arm. He went out and stood on the Cedar Key docks looking west to the Gulf. Out there somewhere was a mother ship steaming in circles, searching for the offspring she had birthed six hours ago, a black-sided shrimper carrying a saint's name and three men with calm smiles and big pistols.

FOUR

1997, Tampa, Florida

James Teach, forty-five and feeling it, vice president of sales for Meador Pharmaceutical Company, lifted his Wild Turkey and water, peered through its amber lens at the glittering bottles across from him, and said, "God, that was a good day. That . . . maybe . . . was the best day of my life."

The man sitting next to him smiled at the mirror across the bar. A fat man with an odd name Teach had now forgotten.

It was the end of a long week, and Teach was tired. Here he was in a pretty good bar, Malone's, in an unfamiliar part of Tampa, lifting his fourth bourbon—or was it his fifth?—and talking to a stranger about the good old days. The days when Jimmy Teach, a walk-on from little Cedar Key, Florida, had quarterbacked the Gators to an SEC championship and two bowl games.

On his best day, against Auburn in Shug Jordan Stadium, Teach had thrown for three touchdowns and rushed for one. Everything had worked for Jimmy Teach that day. His feet dancing the backfield, his arm a gun firing tight spirals through the crisp fall air into the hands of his fast friends in Gator blue and orange.

He finished the story: "So, I called a quarterback sneak and just put my head down and prayed to my Jesus, and the next thing I know I'm lying in the end zone with my ears ringing, and the ref's hands are reaching straight up to heaven."

The fat man's smile applauded the story. Teach shrugged and threw in some humility. "Hell, what was it that guy said? *Half of it's just showing up?*" He grinned, noticing the man's pricey olive-green suit and tropical tie. Teach's wife, Paige, would have known the three places within a hundred miles where you could buy the suit and probably the name of the designer. Would have known. Paige had been dead a year now, and thinking of it, remembering that next week was the anniversary of her death, Teach felt guilty about the best day of his life. Why wasn't it the day of his marriage? The day of his daughter's birth? He shook his head and said, "Who was it said that thing about showing up? You remember?"

The guy smiled again, showing his teeth, a little rabbity on top, the lower jaw undershot. "No, I don't. But I do think it was a rock star." The accent was Savannah or Charleston. The man had said, *Rock stahh.*

In his present state, Teach liked the accent. It was funny. He tapped the bar with his glass for another bourbon. "Hell, enough about football. No great deed goes unpunished."

He examined his right hand, the one that had thrown the bullet passes, the one with the half-moon cleat scar on the back. The hand had been stomped by an Ole Miss linebacker, a stomp applied with purpose and glee. "I'm sorry, but I've forgotten your name."

The fat man said, "Trey McLuster."

McLustuh. Teach liked it, that old Charleston music.

McLuster looked at Teach and smiled the fan smile. That knowing, loving smile. The guy wanted to touch him. Teach knew it from years of times like this, though not so frequent anymore. The guy wanted to squeeze the arm that had thrown the high tight spiral that had settled as soft as cotton fluff into the hands of Digger Dupree in the FSU end zone with three seconds on the clock and bookies dying of cardiac arrest all over the Great Republic.

Then McLuster said, "Screw rock stars. Tell me about the time you beat Miami in that hellacious rainstorm. That must have been something."

So Teach told it. How the ball was heavy with the rain, and slick as a Suwannee River catfish, but he'd completed nineteen of twenty-three and led the Gators to a squeaker 14–13 victory over a team that bettered them in size and speed. Bettered them on paper. But football games, he told the man next to him, weren't played on paper. They were played on grass in real weather against men whose skill and courage equaled yours or didn't.

Teach lifted his glass and gazed into it. Christ, he'd had more to drink than he'd intended. More than he was used to. His companion was quiet now, appreciating what he had said. "Gentlemen," Teach whispered, including the bartender now, "it's consistency that wins, not the brilliant thing you do only once. It's doing the job day in and day out, and knowing you can do it." It was what Teach had always had, the thing that got it done. The thing you called upon when the contagion of defeat crept into other men's eyes.

And suddenly it hurt, what Teach was saying. It hurt because he was forty-five and his best days were behind him. It hurt because he had used the words he had just whispered, the truest words he knew, to sell pills to physicians all over the state of Florida for so many years now that he couldn't say them anymore without seeing himself in some family-practice doc's waiting room with a display case on his knees.

He swallowed the last of his bourbon and remembered that Dean's ballet recital would start in two hours. He closed his eyes and saw his daughter turning and toeing and sweeping her flower-petal hands in gestures so gorgeous and graceful that they brought tears to his eyes. Well, the football stories had pushed the pills that earned the money that bought the toe shoes and the tutus. Teach caught his reflection in the mirror. It was time to pee and leave.

The front door opened and sunlight slanted across the floor of Malone's Bar and a black man stepped in. He was tall and moved with an easy, athletic grace, and this made Teach watch him sit at a table near the men's room door.

Teach pushed away from the bar and stretched. "Well," he said, "time to point Percy at the pavement." He glanced at his watch. "And then off I go to perform the duties of a father." He looked at McLuster, inviting him into the age-old complicity of fathers. The man nodded, and it seemed to Teach like a good way to end this pleasant interlude.

He knew, and he supposed McLuster did too, that he could never share Teach's understanding of what it was to rise to the top of something. But any man could know the warm arms of a wife, the sweetness of a daughter's kiss, and the two of them could part in that knowledge.

As Teach started for the men's room, McLuster said, "Hell, I guess I'll bleed the monster too."

They were at the urinals when the black man came in. Teach had it out and flowing. His head thrown back, his knees flexed, he was thinking about pulling himself together for the ballet recital. He'd cinch up his tie, drive through rush-hour Tampa to the Women's Club, get the old Minolta out of the trunk of the Buick. A mint for his breath. Lord, he'd forgotten to buy film. He'd have to find a drugstore.

Paige's society friends would all be there in pearls and boutique dresses. Their faces would be made up perfectly, which meant imperceptibly, and they'd smell delicately of Chanel, and their necks and shoulders would be flushed with worry for the girls about to dance. And they would watch Teach, the widower, enter. The man not quite of their station, whose wife had been one of them. Beautiful Paige who had died so suddenly and in such an ugly way.

"Well, look at you nasty white motherfuckers."

The voice, its threat, its confidence, made Teach quickly holster his cock and turn to face the men's room door. He heard McLuster at the next urinal mutter, "What the . . . ? Oh Jesus."

Teach could see now that the black man was no man. He was tall and filled out—Teach made him at least 220 and all of it muscle—but he couldn't have been more than eighteen. That Teach had taken him for a grown man said something for the confident way the boy moved. Teach remembered giving the boy a friendly nod on his way to the men's room. And hadn't the boy nodded back?

The boy took another step into the room. There was no mistaking the threat of his stance, legs wide, arms ready at his sides.

The boy wore black jeans and a white silk shirt. He pointed at them with his left hand. "Give it up, bitches." The white shirt opened at his waist, and Teach saw it in the waistband of the black jeans—the shiny black handle of a straight razor. McLuster started to pant, and Teach thought, *Heart attack*, then McLuster moaned, "Oh no," and Teach saw the dark stain spreading around the man's clutching fingers.

The boy laughed quietly. "You bitches better give it up. I ain't gone say it again."

Teach held his eyes on the boy's face and made himself smile. His salesman's smile. The smile that ate shit if shit got the purchase order signed. He willed the boy to look at him, apply those cold, coffee-bean eyes to his. When the boy did it, Teach let his smile flow into his eyes, ten years of schmoozing receptionists, accommodating assholes in white lab coats, and closing, closing. He had to close the distance here. He reached out a careful hand and eased McLuster to his right. Teach had to talk but didn't know what to say. There was a razor in the boy's waistband.

He saw the headlines: *Local Businessman Slashed in Bar. Motive: Robbery.* But headlines were ink and there was going to be blood here. Teach imagined the boy grasping the black handle of the razor and flipping out the gleaming blade. The smallest touch of such an instrument, Teach knew, could bring forth the red gush that ended life in seconds. And for what? Some cracked-out kid wanted money.

Teach said, "What do you want? Our wallets? Is that it?"

The boy looked at him, his head tilted sideways. He held up his left fist and loosened three fingers. "That's three, bitch. I said I wasn't gone ask you again."

Teach glanced at McLuster and shrugged. "He wants us to give it up. You got any idea what he's talking about?"

When the boy looked at McLuster, Teach did it: leapt across the space between them and delivered a sweeping right forearm to the side of the boy's head. Even as Teach knew the sweet smack of contact, felt the boy's body go limp against his, heard the whack and skitter of the razor hitting the tile floor, he thought it had been too easy. Somehow too easy, too lucky. The boy's head hit the doorframe, and he slid unconscious to the floor, blood pouring from his split cheek.

Teach looked at what he had done. What he'd had to do. The thing, apparently, he was still ready to do after all these years. His right elbow ached where the shock of the blow vibrated. He turned to his companion. McLuster with his back against the wall, both hands clutching the urine stain that spread down his trouser legs. "My God," he said, "look at this. I don't *fucking* believe this."

Then the boy on the floor groaned and Teach knew this wasn't over.

He grabbed the boy's collar and dragged him facedown through the men's room door and into the middle of the bar. There he knelt beside the boy, pinning his right arm between his shoulder blades.

The bartender, a stocky bald man whose name tag said *Benny*, a man Teach had only vaguely noticed before, a man with the bartender's gift for appearing with the needed thing and then returning to the status of furniture, looked across the bar at Teach and the boy who was bleeding onto the carpet. The bartender's face said everything about the things we least expect.

Teach said, "Call the cops. This kid tried to rob us in the men's room." Then, to the man's expression of disbelief, Teach said, "He had a knife. He was going to rob us. Kill us. I don't know. Call 911."

The bartender turned for the phone, and the boy groaned again. His eyes were foggy but clearing. Teach shoved his arm up to let him know his situation.

The bartender put down the phone and came over. "They're coming." He looked at the boy's face on the carpet. "Jesus," he said, "look at the mess you're making. I gotta get Malone in here."

Malone? Malone? Teach thought. *Ah yes, this is Malone's Bar.* He looked around now, out of the bright tunnel of violent energy that, for a few moments, had included only him and the boy and what had to be done. The bartender was on the phone talking to Malone. McLuster sat at a table against the wall, a wad of paper towels pressed to his crotch. The tunnel widened even more, and Teach heard him whisper, "Christ, I don't believe this."

Teach tried to think of a comforting word for the man. It seemed right even though he had, by his lights anyway, already saved him from a cut throat. The black boy gave a long, low moan. Teach tightened his grip and glanced up at McLuster. It occurred to him that he needed the man. McLuster was his witness.

A customer came in, an old guy in white Keds, khaki Bermuda shorts, and a Tampa Bay Bucs T-shirt. Bald head, hairless limbs, and tortoiseshell sunglasses with a white plastic nose cap. He took two steps into the bar, saw Teach and the black boy on the floor, pushed his sunglasses to his face, and tiptoed out.

Teach watched the door, hoping that McLuster would not leave. And what would you do? Would you wait around like he is doing? Be a stand-up guy for the man on the floor with the bad kid, the guy who saved your ass? Or would you haul ass out of here, write this off as absurdity and rotten luck? Let the guy on the floor deal with the cops. Hell, it was an easy enough story to tell. A straightforward tale of armed robbery thwarted by the decisive action of a man who knew what to do and had the wherewithal to do it.

The door opened again and two men in sport coats and ties came in. The first was black, about six feet tall, stocky, maybe in his early forties, carrying some ribs and corn bread around his middle but carrying them well. The man behind him was white, short, and rail-thin. They stood taking in the situation. Teach on the floor holding the boy, McLuster pressing the ball of towels to his crotch, the bartender on the phone giving Malone a play-by-play.

The black cop walked over and put his hand on Teach's shoulder. There was a world of authority in the hard way the man touched him. Teach remembered this touch. He got up, stepped back, and took a deep breath because it was all over now but the talking. He took another breath and felt in his gut the dizzy ebbing of the tide of adrenaline that had started when the boy had stepped through the men's room door and said . . . What was it? Teach couldn't remember now.

The black cop knelt and slid the boy's hand down to his belt and cuffed it, and Teach remembered that rasping sound. Then the cop said in a deep, resonant baritone, "Sir, would you step back, please."

The thin white cop in JCPenney slacks and scuffed black oxfords watched with cool interest. The smell of garlic and onions came from his clothes. He smiled, nodded as a man did when he was thinking, *We've seen this a thousand times.*

The black cop turned the boy over and pulled him to a sitting position, neither roughly nor gently but with a surprising ease.

The boy looked at the cop and his eyes rocked in their sockets. The cop said, "Hello, Tyrone."

And Teach thought, *Good. They know this kid. He has a sheet. A punk they've snagged before.*

But the white cop stepped away from Teach and looked into the boy's eyes. "Jesus," he whispered in a voice Teach recognized as grit.

Teach felt the adrenaline flow again into the hungry, empty space in his belly. The place he would fill with the dinner he and Dean would have after her ballet recital. Steadying his voice, he asked,

"Uh, officer, do you know this boy? Have you arrested him before?"

The black cop led the boy to a chair, then squared himself to Teach, showing a holstered Glock and a detective's shield on a belt clip. He gave a guarded, almost whimsical smile. "Do you have any ID, sir? A driver's license?"

Teach pulled out his wallet, the thing the boy had demanded he "give up." He offered it, but the cop raised both hands and smiled. "Just the license, sir."

Teach took it out, handed it to the man who passed it to the white cop. The white cop sat at a nearby table and began writing in a notebook.

The black cop said, "Yes sir, I know the boy. His name is Tyrone Battles. He's my sister's son."

FIVE

While the boy applied ice to his cheek and the bartender finished his phone report to Malone, the black cop, Aimes, took Teach to a table near the front door. As he told the story and Aimes listened, Teach tried to read the man. All he got was an even temper, a solid self-confidence, and a concern for accuracy. Sometimes the cop challenged Teach. "The boy said, *Give up your wallets?* You *sure* that's what he said?"

Teach said, "I think so. Maybe he just said, *Give it up*, but we know what that means, don't we?"

The policeman didn't nod or write it down. He just looked steadily at Teach and waited for more.

When he could, Teach glanced at McLuster who was telling his version to the thin policeman. The wad of paper towels was gone and the urine stain was fading. Teach would bet the smell was as strong as ever. The poor cop. The things these guys had to do.

The boy, Tyrone Battles, uncuffed now, holding an iced towel to his cheek, sat watching Teach like a boxer waiting to come out of his corner. Talking to Aimes, Teach was beginning to think the boy's intentions were the least of his problems.

After Aimes made him tell the story a second time, Teach said, "Look, I've told you everything I can remember. It happened fast. I was afraid the kid was going to pull the razor. There was no way out except through him, and that's the way I went. Frankly, I think I saved two lives in there. I don't know why we have to keep . . ."

The detective raised his eyebrows as Teach unreeled his good-citizen speech, his voice rising with exasperation. Teach stopped talking when he realized he had just said, "I was afraid." *Afraid* was a word Teach hadn't used much. It changed things.

Aimes lowered his gaze, spread his big hands on the table, examined his clean, trimmed fingernails. When he looked at Teach again, his eyes were tired. "Frankly, Mr. Teach, there are two ways to look at this. One is that you just assaulted my sister's only son who's an honor student and the star running-back on his high school football team. Frankly, you busted open the face of a nice-looking young man who's never been in trouble a day in his life. That's one way."

Teach closed his eyes and there in the darkness the boy's surly face leaned into his as it had in a men's room, and he had to stop himself from shoving past Aimes and out the door. He conquered his temper and calmed his violated sense of fairness and stayed in his chair. He opened his eyes, attempted a smile, and said, "Detective, I'm trying to help you here. I've given you all the information I have." He glanced at his watch and a splash of bright stage lighting burst into his mind. *Jesus, the ballet recital. When? Oh Christ, soon.* He had to get out of here. The cop had said there were two ways to look at this.

Aimes said, "Mr. Teach, you said there was a razor. Where is it? The boy doesn't have it on him."

Teach massaged his eyes, tried to think. "It's still in there. In the men's room, I mean. I heard it hit the floor when I . . ."

Aimes looked over at the table where McLuster was unburdening himself to the white cop. "Detective Delbert," Aimes called in that low, burring baritone, "excuse yourself for a minute there and go into the men's room and find me the weapon Mr. Teach says he saw."

Teach glanced at McLuster who watched Detective Delbert walk to the men's room. He needed McLuster to look at him, give him even the smallest reassurance, but the man only stared bleakly at the place where the trouble had started.

The thin policeman returned from the bathroom, his face composed, something dark and gleaming in his hand. As he came on, Teach thought, *He found it.*

Detective Delbert put the object on the table between Teach and Aimes, and Teach saw the cops' eyes meet for an instant in certainty, gravity, and without surprise. And he saw that the shiny black thing on the table was a comb. Teach stared at its black plastic handle, his eyes straining to turn it into what he was sure he had seen. The cop's low, musical voice said, "That's not a razor, Mr. Teach. It's what the kids call a pick."

Teach searched the man's obsidian eyes, hoping to find some favor in them for the mistake he had made when he'd had only seconds to make anything at all. Aimes rose and walked across the bar to the table where McLuster and Delbert sat. When Aimes put his hand on Delbert's shoulder, Teach thought: *That hand holds the power of the state. That hand takes away a man's belt and shoelaces, handcuffs him, and leads him out of a courtroom to a holding cell, and from there to some godforsaken, sun-hammered prison where he eats beans and collards and waits for his time on the exercise yard, and watches, if he's lucky, television programs that appeal to morons.* Teach knew where a man went when that hand touched him.

The two cops moved to the bar and stood there talking. McLuster looked everywhere but at Teach, and Tyrone Battles held the bloody towel to his cheek.

When Aimes and Delbert finished, the white cop went back to sit with McLuster. Aimes approached Teach. "Mr. Teach, my colleague, Detective Delbert, tells me that Mr. McLuster over there says you just lost it in that men's room. He doesn't know why. A big overreaction thing is what he calls it."

Teach blinked, could think of nothing to say. Knew what his face must look like: some comic cartoon goof staring down in disbelief as the cliff crumbles under his feet and he begins the fall, thousands of feet to the canyon bottom. He shook his head, lifted a hand to massage his forehead. The bourbon, the wonderful, convivial bourbon, had left him with a hammering headache. He heard himself saying, "Jesus, I swear to you, I . . ." And then he knew he wasn't saying it. Was only thinking it and was glad he had kept his mouth shut.

Aimes went over to the table where McLuster sat with Delbert. He directed them to the table where the boy sat and said, "Mr. Teach . . ." and nodded at the only vacant chair.

Like a child summoned to the front of the classroom, Teach walked over and sat with them. The boy stared at him with the bleakest hatred Teach had ever seen.

Aimes cleared his throat. "I don't know what happened in there. Only you three know, and you all tell it differently. Tyrone . . ."

Teach watched closely as the two regarded each other. Would he see the family bond in their eyes? A recognition: that was all Teach could see.

"Tyrone," Aimes said, "if I take your word for what happened, I can arrest Mr. Teach here for assault."

The boy started to speak, his eyes fulminating. Aimes put his hand on Tyrone's forearm. That power again.

"Mr. Teach," Aimes said, "if I take your word, I can arrest Tyrone for attempted robbery, take him away with me."

Teach tried not to let his eyes say what they preferred. *Let this play itself out.*

Aimes continued, "Mr. McLuster here, he thinks maybe you overreacted, Mr. Teach, but mostly Mr. McLuster just wants to get out of here." The detective glanced at the fading stains in McLuster's crotch. McLuster nodded, sucking his lip to the side and biting it. "Soooo . . ." Aimes exhaled a long breath and looked at each of them in turn, his eyes stopping on Delbert. The two exchanged some tired message. "Soooo, I'm going to call this an altercation. An unfortunate encounter in a men's room. Maybe some drinking went on here . . ." He looked at McLuster and Teach. "Maybe some words were passed that shouldn't have been . . ." He looked at Tyrone who stared his rage at Teach. "I'm going to leave it there for now, with Detective Delbert's concurrence, of course." A firm nod from Delbert. "Now, what do you gentlemen think of that?"

It's over, Teach thought, *at last over.* He could get out of here. Not leave as the hero he'd thought he was (*Did I ever tell you about the time I was attacked by this kid with a knife in a damn men's room? And, buddy, I mean a small men's room!*), but leave with no more damage than the blood on his coat sleeve, a mean headache, and a lower opinion of his fellow man.

But Tyrone Battles looked at Aimes, who was his uncle, and said, low and cold, "Fuck no, man, it ain't all right with me." The kid shoved back in his chair, away from the circle of reasonableness Aimes had drawn, and said it again: "Fuck no, man. It *ain't* all right. Look what this white bitch did to my pretty face. I'm gonna get me a Polaroid and take some pictures of this face, *man.*" He pointed at Teach. "I'm gonna *get* you, man." He stuck his forefinger under his cheekbone and pushed the split flesh up in a way that must have hurt. The boy shoved his face forward, bending at the waist, show-ing it to Aimes, and Aimes was on him. A big man moving fast, he caught the boy by the front of his shirt and sat him down.

Remind me, Teach thought, *not to mess with this man.*

Aimes stood over Tyrone, staring down into his face. "Don't you ever call me *man*. You call me *uncle* when I'm eating at your mama's table, and the rest of the time you call me De-tec-tive Aimes. Those are your two options, you understand me?" He sat down and looked around the table. "Now, like I said, I'm gonna call this an altercation. Detective Delbert and I, we'll file the report. You three gentlemen think about it for a day or two, and then if anybody wants to put charges on anybody, why, we'll take it on from there, see where it goes. Now, is that all right?"

Teach tried to catch the man's eye to say, one man to another, that it was a good plan. But the cop wouldn't look at him. Teach didn't push it. Maybe the boy had embarrassed his uncle. Maybe this family thing put the cop in a place where he wasn't comfortable. Teach looked carefully at McLuster and said, "Sure. I guess so." He glanced at his watch. "My daughter's dancing in thirty minutes."

Delbert wrote something down. McLuster shook his head, dis-gusted. He examined his hands on the table, sighed. "Sure, it's all right." He looked around the bar and muttered, "Stop for a drink on a Friday afternoon and what the hell happens? Jesus."

Delbert wrote it. Aimes nodded at McLuster, then turned to Ty-rone who was smoothing his silk shirt where his uncle's fists had wrinkled it. The kid shook his head. "Fuck!" And his lean, lithe body was up and out the door.

Aimes stood and Delbert imitated him. Aimes shook his head, then looked down at Teach and McLuster. "We've got your names and addresses. I take it you gentlemen will be leaving now?"

Teach said, "Thank you, Detective Aimes."

Aimes looked back at him sharply. "Don't thank me, Mr. Teach, not yet anyway." He turned to his partner. "Just a minute . . ." He walked toward the men's room. *The fucking black hole of Calcutta*, Teach thought, watching the detective go off to pee.

When Aimes was gone, Teach rose and walked over to Delbert. He had to talk to the guy. Find out what he thought about this.

As Teach approached, Delbert's eyes hardened. Teach was about to rest a salesman's hand on the cop's shoulder but the eyes told him not to. Teach put his hands in his pockets and said, "Uh, look, Detective Delbert." Nodding at the men's room. "What's he, uh, what's he going to do about all this?"

Delbert shrugged, pursed his lips, closed the pad, and put it into his coat pocket. "I don't know what *he's* going to do, but you better hope this thing stops right here." Delbert pointed at the door Tyrone Battles had just exited. "That boy's family's a walking history of the civil rights movement in this state. Freedom rides, the St. Augustine Slave Market sit-ins, all of it."

For the third time in an hour, Teach's knees liquefied, and his vision narrowed. "But what about him?" Nodding again at the men's room door. "What's he gonna do?"

Delbert shrugged again. A cop's response to a life lived in the vortex of Tampa's troubles. The Big Shrug. Delbert said, "I don't know what he's gonna do. But I'll tell you this: with Aimes it's hard but it's fair."

Aimes came out of the men's room, and Teach watched the two cops leave. Then he turned to the bar for the bourbon he needed. For the mended view that would come with it. McLuster was already at the bar, getting a quick one for the road. Teach took a stool and said, "The same again, please." Then to McLuster, "Christ, what a day. You walk into a bar and you—"

Benny the bartender looked at Teach in a not very serving way. "Your money's no good here, buddy. Why don't you take your ass down the road. We got to make a living in this neighborhood."

Ah, Teach thought, *ah yes.* And his hand shook a little at the deferral of bourbon. *Ah yes, indeed. So speaks this minion of the unseen Malone.* Teach slid from the stool. Looked over at McLuster, who stared back at him from the bottom of the well of a fat man's unhappiness.

"Well . . ." Teach tapped his watch. The ballet recital, his daughter spinning in bright light, in impossibly unstable shoes, surrounded by a supporting cast of the young and eager, and sometimes the beautiful. His daughter a vision of gift and light and love. Teach said to McLuster, "Well . . . I'd like to stay for one more, but I've got to go."

The man's chin trembled. "You ever," McLuster said, his hand lifting a glass to his lips, spilling some of it, putting it down. "You ever tell *anyone* about this . . ."

Teach raised his hands, let them fall, shook his head. Why would he? Who did he know that would . . . ? But now he *could* see himself telling the story. The pee stain a necessary piece of the bizarre puzzle of this afternoon.

McLuster swiveled on the stool, his chin quivering, his eyes going moist. And then Teach felt for the man. He took a step forward, some notion of comfort gathering in his mind. A hand to rest on the man's shoulder. A couple of pats.

But McLuster leaned back, raised his hands, made fists. "Stay away from me, man. You got some serious aggression, you know that? You got some unresolved shit in there you need to work on. You need to *see* somebody."

McLuster tossed money on the bar and started toward the door. Teach watched him. This was not a day to let anyone get behind you. McLuster stopped at the door, his red face swollen, shaking. "You never were worth a damn in the pocket, Mr. Hot-Shit Quarterback. You had a noodle arm, and you never could pass the gut check."

The gut check? Teach thought, as McLuster opened the door, as the light, not so bright now at five thirty, shafted across the floor. The gut check. Check your guts at the door when you come to Malone's Bar. Oh, how they piled on you here in Malone's, Teach thought, and he would have laughed if his throat had not been too dry for even an exhausted croak. Benny the bartender wiped his shiny bald head with a towel and turned away.

SIX

Detective Aimes stopped beside the unmarked Crown Vic and looked at La Teresita, Tampa's best cheap Cuban restaurant. He had left a plate of trout à la rusa on the counter before crossing the street to Malone's Bar. From the other side of the Crown Vic, Detective Dwayne Delbert was watching him carefully. Delbert's eyes were full of that quiet redneck seriousness, that question: *What now, boss?*

Aimes and Delbert had been eating, Aimes having his usual, and Delbert addressing himself to a pressed Cuban sandwich with so much Louisiana pepper sauce on it, he was hissing, "Haaa!" with every bite. Some old guy rushes in, so skinny and brown he looks like bones in a leather bag, with one of those white plastic caps that protect your nose. This old guy comes in talking loud about some nigger boy and blood and trouble across the street at Malone's.

Then he sees Aimes at the bar, and he thinks, *Oh Lord, I just said, "aardvark," and there's, by God, an aardvark sitting right there at that counter.* The old guy backs out like a fiddler crab scooting for its hole. So Aimes turns to Delbert and nods and Delbert goes, "Haaa!" waving his skinny hand in front of his mouth, and walks outside to the city car.

Aimes gets two more bites of the Russian trout, savoring the crumbled egg, the sweet breading on the fish (he is suspicious of the fish, thinks it's mullet, but what the hell), loving that hot olive oil rolling around his mouth. Then Delbert is back, standing behind his stool, reaching over for another bite of Cuban sandwich. Delbert says somebody called in a disturbance over at Malone's, says, "I told dispatch me an' you'd check it out."

Aimes turns to him. "Delbert, my young friend, would you ever say, *Me would check it out?*"

Delbert considers it, about as interested in grammar as he is in Italian light opera. Aimes thinking Delbert is only taking the question seriously so he can get another bite of sandwich.

"No, I wouldn't, come to think of it. I'd say I would check it out."

"Right. So when you add *me*, what do you say?"

Delbert thinks about it. "I say you and I . . . we'd, uh, check it out."

Aimes pushes off from the stool, looks at Yolanda, who's at the cash register burying some currency. La Teresita is jumping as usual. Aimes points at his plate, mouths, *Save this for me*. Yolanda frowns, looks over at the door where several kids from the university are waiting in their Reeboks and button-downs and culottes or whatever those spread-your-legs-without-fear skirts are called. Yolanda smiles sadly. Aimes smiles too for community relations, and turns to Delbert. "All right, let's go over there."

On the way across the street, Aimes says, "How come you told them we'd take it? How come you didn't let the uniforms have it? Let them get their clothes ripped, blood on their shoes. We did that already. We are the sport coats now, Detective Delbert."

Delbert says, "I know we're the coats. But that old guy that came in, he might know it too. He might be a citizen with not enough to do. The kind that writes to the *Tribune*, calls WFLA 970 on your dial, talks about why some people disturbing the peace in a bar have to wait twenty minutes for uniforms when they's two detectives in a restaurant right across the street."

When they's? Aimes thinks. Another grammar fart. But young Dwayne Delbert is nobody's idiot child. He has a point about the geezer in the nose cap. A citizen with time on his hands.

Back outside, Aimes looked across the Crown Vic's roof at Delbert and said, "Bet Yolanda threw away my food."

Delbert put a hand delicately on his stomach where, Aimes figured, the hot sauce was warming up the man's duodenal ulcer. Delbert said, "That stuff is all waistline anyway, man." Delbert disapproved of Aimes's weight, but Delbert couldn't claim the virtue of three-minute abs. The man just had the metabolism of a gerbil.

Aimes got into the car. Delbert settled in beside him. He and

Delbert had been out knocking on doors, talking to people about the murders of some local working girls. There had been three now, and the *Trib* was warming up to the story, calling it a *string* of prostitute murders, speculating about a serial killer.

Tampa was a city with a perpetual inferiority complex. For a while, the local flacks had called it America's Next Great City. Then somebody had stumbled over the comedy of that title. Tampa had the Bucs, and that was good. Tampa had hockey, the Lightning, but hockey was a B sport in the South and always would be. Tampa had great seafood, its own branch of Cosa Nostra, too many malls, the world's best airport, and lately, Ybor City.

Ybor, the old Cuban cigar-manufacturing district, had been renovated, gentrified, and reborn as the nightclub scene. Tourists walked the Ybor streets in the hot afternoon, gazed at the beautiful wrought-iron lampposts on Seventh Avenue, ate at the Columbia, witnessed the awesome rite of the hand-making of a cigar at Ybor Square. They read the historical marker that said José Martí had lived here, and wondered what all the excitement was about. They didn't see the kids pour in for the slams and the bad poetry coffeehouses and the clubs that heated up at one a.m. That was when it got wild, and that was when it got dangerous, and that was when three prostitutes had disappeared from the streets crowded with stumbling drunks and punk ravers and university students.

The newspapers wanted a winning football team, a nightlife better than Bourbon Street or South Beach, and, Aimes figured, they wouldn't be happy until they had their own serial killer. If they couldn't have one, they were going to invent the guy. Make Tampa the next great city it had always promised to be.

Some kids playing behind a small electronics-manufacturing facility had smelled something strange, and being kids, they'd opened the lid of the dumpster and found the body of a young Vietnamese prostitute named Phuong Van Tran. The woman had been tied with curtain cord, ankles to wrists, simple square knots, slipped into two plastic bags duct taped together at her waist, and then hoisted into the dumpster. If anyone in the neighborhood Delbert and Aimes had canvassed had seen or heard anything on the night she was dumped, no one was admitting it.

The method chosen for killing Phuong Van Tran was execution-style shooting. Phuong had a single .22-caliber bullet hole in the back of her head. The ligature marks at her wrists and ankles were not deep or abraded. They came from postmortem swelling. When she was tied up, she had not struggled. She had not been beaten. She was fully dressed in panty hose and a cocktail dress with a label from one of the low-end clothing outlets in a local mall. She had been bound and shot in a way that was matter-of-fact, or maybe curiously gentle. Looking at her, Aimes remembered thinking that she must have gone along with it, must have thought it was some sex game she'd play and get paid for, must have been smiling or at least not screaming when a firing pin had struck a primer sending a bullet into her brain. However curious or gentle or playful it had been, murder was murder, and Aimes and Delbert had been out talking to people about what they might have seen or heard.

They'd finished a long afternoon of walking and knocking and talking, and then they'd gone to La Teresita for that Cuban sandwich and the dubious but delicious Russian trout. Then Malone's Bar. Now Delbert glanced over at Aimes and said, "Your sister's boy, huh?"

Aimes knew that Delbert, his new partner, wanted to hear about it. Knew Delbert wouldn't push. Knew that if he just said, *Yes, my sister's boy, and a surprisingly nasty piece of work he is,* Delbert would nod and that would be the end of it. Nobody pushed anybody in this car: that was Aimes's rule with his partners. No prying and no lying. But they would learn about each other. They would learn a lot. Some of it by inference, some of it by telling, most of it by experience. And some of the experience would not be pretty. Aimes was teaching Delbert the detective business.

Aimes didn't look at his partner. He guided the Crown Vic through the rush-hour traffic toward the police station on North Tampa Street. He said, "Yeah, he's my sister's boy. I don't know him all that well. His daddy and I didn't get along. His daddy was in the Navy. Served on a tanker. He was killed in an accident, fueling a destroyer at sea. It happened when the boy was ten. I never got close to him after his daddy died. He's supposed to be a good kid. The family hope. Straight As in school. All-state on the football field. Hell, the kid could ride his brain *or* his jockstrap to college. You don't see that too often."

Aimes looked over at Delbert as they sat at the traffic light at Fowler and 30th Street. Delbert nodded, touched his stomach, leaned to the side, and belched quietly. Aimes said, "Why do you eat that stuff, man? You know it hurts you."

"Same reason you eat that fish in a puddle of oil. It tastes good. I like it. I'm a creature of unbridled appetite."

Aimes laughed. "You're a creature of a great deal of bullshit."

Aimes had twisted one of his fingers when he'd grabbed Tyrone Battles by the front of his shirt, and it was throbbing now. He laughed again, and it felt good. Thinking: *And a creature of some particularly fucked-up grammar. And wait a minute. Where did "unbridled appetite" come from? That isn't the Delbert I know and educate.* Aimes figured it came from some soap opera or some girl or both. One of the gum-snapping, line-dancing, short-term loan officers Delbert dated. A woman who liked to watch soap operas when she and Delbert weren't two-stepping to the "Cotton-Eyed Joe" at Zichex or wherever it was they went in their snakeskin boots and up-the-crack jeans.

"So," Delbert said, looking ahead at the traffic, "the good boy was just having a bad day?"

Aimes thought about it. What in the hell was his nephew doing in that bar? Blacks didn't go into Malone's. Hell, the boy wasn't even old enough to drink. What had he been doing in the restroom with those two white men? Had the boy really said, "Give it up"? Both of the white men had said so, though the fat one had thought the boy only had to pee and was asking for a place at the porcelain. Well, something had made the fat guy piss his pants. And something had made the other one, the big handsome guy with the confidence and the aging athlete's body, thump the boy upside the head.

Aimes had never seen Tyrone in a scuffle, but he had seen the boy work on the football field. Aimes had played some football himself, enough to appreciate the boy's talent. He knew it wasn't just local. So maybe the white guy had sucker punched the boy. How else could a middle-aged pharmaceutical salesman coldcock a kid with the physical gifts of Tyrone Battles? Well, something had happened in there, something strange.

Then Aimes thought, *Wait a minute. Teach? James Teach?* He knew the guy. Knew him by reputation at least. Didn't the guy play football? Where was it, Florida? Yes, that was it. Jimmy Teach, the walk-on quarterback from some one-light town up in the Panhandle. Teach had been good, very good. It made sense now. Tyrone had met his match in that men's room.

Delbert waited until they caught the next stop light. "So," he said, "you think they gone let it go or not?"

Aimes thinking, *They gone?* He said, "Delbert, my young friend, this world is full of fools. If those two have the sense God gave a tin-dick dog, they will most certainly let it go."

"Fools will be fools." Delbert scratched the side of his face with the stubby ends of his fingers.

He bit his fingernails to the quick, another thing that endeared him to Aimes. Aimes had offered to paint the fingers with quinine, something really nasty-tasting. Said he'd bring the bottle himself and the Q-tip every day, do the painting. Help Delbert break the habit. Delbert had declined, said the women he dated didn't mind his fingers that way. Said they liked vulnerable men. Delbert said he told his women he was in a dangerous line of work, and he hoped he could be forgiven some scuffy-tuffy fingernails because in every other way he was a straight and unwavering public servant.

"You tell them that?" Aimes had asked. "That thing about straight and, what was it, unwavering?"

"Words to that effect," Delbert had told him.

Aimes: "And it works?"

Delbert: "Sure does."

Aimes thinking that no self-respecting black woman would fall for a line of bullshit like that.

They turned off North Tampa Street, drove through the gate into the parking lot at the rear of the police station. Delbert said, "Pretty weird, we go in that bar, and it's your nephew."

"We didn't need it, did we?" He wasn't going to remind Delbert that someone could have told the dispatcher to let the uniforms handle it. You didn't last long with a partner if you dealt in might-have-beens.

Aimes was going to cover his and Delbert's ass with the paper of a very carefully written report. He'd write it brief and general. It would describe an altercation in a bar. It would include the names of those involved, the names of the witnesses, the time of day. It would say that Teach had admitted drinking. It would say that both men claimed to be the victim and neither requested medical attention. It would say that Teach alleged there had been a razor which later turned out to be a comb. It would say the scene was cleared without an arrest. Period. Those were the facts, and Aimes would not move an inch beyond them.

He collected his possessions from the front seat of the car, checked the floorboards for anything he might have dropped, then turned to Delbert. "I hope that boy has sense enough to leave our man Teach alone. No good can come from those two meeting again."

Delbert nodded.

Aimes knew the people in that bar thought he had lost his temper with the boy, grabbing him by the shirt, sitting him down hard. But he hadn't lost anything, and he knew Delbert understood what he had done. Controlling the boy a little before things got out of hand again between him and Teach. It was good police work. What bothered Aimes more than having to use force, more than the finger that throbbed steadily now, was Tyrone's arrogance, the boy not knowing, apparently, what he was risking by getting into a fight with a white man in a bar.

Sure, the kid came from a different generation. He lived by different rules, some combination of hip-hop and bad-ass football bravado. But shouldn't a kid smart enough to get those good grades know how easy it is for a favored child to fall? Shouldn't he know how fast and how far that child could fall in what was still a white man's world? Even when you figured in the boy's youth and inexperience and how much he had already been petted and pampered by white coaches and teachers, it still didn't make sense. The boy being in that place, doing what he'd done, taking the attitude he'd taken with a sergeant of the Major Crimes Division of the Tampa Police Department.

SEVEN

Teach parked the Buick under a majestic banyan tree on the old redbrick drive of the Tampa Women's Club. The city of Tampa had once proudly worn miles of redbrick streets, and employed men, mostly Cuban, who knew how to grade the roadways and spread the white beach sand and nestle the rich red bricks into the sand from one granite curbstone to another. The artisans were gone now, and the red bricks survived only in the best neighborhoods, saved by the vanity of the rich.

The automobiles Teach passed as he hurried toward the old Spanish stucco and terra-cotta tile facade of the Women's Club were the thoroughbred descendants of the Packard Roadsters and Delages and Stutz Bearcats that had lined this drive when the banyan trees were sprigs, and the sky beyond the club's roof was not crowded with glass-and-steel skyscrapers. Ahead of Teach, the last arrivals, women in filmy tropical pastels and expensive shoes, towed in their bored husbands.

Teach checked the bloodstain on his coat sleeve for the tenth time since leaving Malone's Bar. He had bought film at a drugstore, then, with a few minutes to spare, he had driven to a bar on Kennedy Boulevard. The bourbon he'd tossed back while the barmaid counted out his change had steadied him, quieted the loudest voices of his headache, and sent him back out into the muggy dusk with the ramshackle house of his optimism somewhat repaired.

Teach quickened his step and prepared his smile. It was always strange for him, stepping into the opulence of the ballroom. The varnished mahogany wainscoting, the crystal chandelier shedding its pink light on the damask tapestry with its stilted scene of serene men on horseback spearing a lion that seemed to be in no particular pain. The murmur of conversation that would suddenly quiet as the lights went down and the music began to play and the first dancers appeared on stage, shy and brave and fragile.

Teach rested the old Minolta SLR on his right coat sleeve, concealing the bloodstain. He would look, he hoped, perfectly natural entering this way. A club woman gave him a program and a gentle frown for his lateness. Teach deferred the pleasure of opening the program to see Dean listed as principal dancer. He stood behind the last row of seats, imagining his wife, Paige, somewhere in the sea of organdy and silk. That she had not lived to see their daughter in this role seemed a crime of fate, a sin worse than any of Teach's own. He closed his eyes and saw Paige where he knew she would have sat, halfway down on the aisle. In his mind's eye, she lifted her head to look around for him, her shining honey-blond hair in the usual chignon. She'd had a good neck, long and smooth, and a heartbreaking wisp of hair had always escaped the chignon just under her left ear.

As he started down the aisle to find a seat, a hand took his arm, turning him. A red-faced man in a pink blazer looked petulantly at him and said, "Please."

Teach stepped aside as the man ushered a tall, fiftyish black man and his wife down the aisle to the reserved front row. *Stately* was the word that formed in Teach's mind. The way the couple moved, the way they claimed the usher's deference and the attention of this prosperous audience. The black man walked with a musical grace, and his dark suit was rakishly cut for a man of his age.

The man's wife carried herself with regal dignity. The entire ballroom watched them settle in the first row next to a couple Teach recognized as the mayor of Tampa and his wife. The two couples smiled and greeted each other comfortably, and the lights began to go down.

Teach hurried down the aisle in the half dark, excused himself across the knees of a sixtyish couple, and dropped down next to a diamond-beglittered matron. He smiled at the woman, who inclined her head toward him and sniffed. Her nose worked on the air between them, then she frowned. The bourbon. And if she could smell it, so, probably, could others. Well, what the hell? Other men had come here straight from work after a bump from the office bottle or a

stop at Eric's in the Franklin Street Mall. Teach took a good compre-
hensive whiff of himself and got it all: the musky sweat of violence
and fear, the tang of blood and whiskey.

After a brief overture, the curtain rose on a woodland scene
Teach thought must have been painted by a descendant of the tapestry maker. A line of girls flowed onto the stage in pink tutus, white
tights, and pink toe-shoes. Their hair was blond and bunned, and
each wore a white blossom on the crown of her bun. These girls,
Teach had learned, were the corps de ballet.

Several of them were pretty. They were all earnest and deeply
imbued with the seriousness of The Dance. But none of them, Teach
knew from years of these evenings, was talented. And wait a minute,
there was a new girl. A black girl. She tottered in on uncertain toes,
her movements a little too robust for the corps. Watching her, Teach
knew she was an athlete. He could see her running the hurdles or doing the Fosbury flop over a high-jump bar. A spirited girl, she seemed
trapped up there on the stage, her eyes a little panicky, her energy
too large for this subtle rite.

Sitting here amongst these complacent burghers, listening to the
lilting music, watching these daughters of wealth and privilege move
in stately patterns on the stage, Teach shuddered and thought, I could
be handcuffed in a police station, could be fumbling through the Tampa phone di-
rectory for the name and number of an attorney, could be leaving a phone message
for my daughter: "Uh, it's Dad. Sorry I didn't make it, honey. Something's happened. I'll be home as soon as possible."

And then the entire vista of disaster opened up before James
Teach: himself in prison, a lost man in a world of grinding stupidity
and violence, all because of a few seconds of bourbon-inspired her-
oism in a men's room.

And there was gorgeous Dean. She had swept onstage in a swell
of violins, turning on pointe with her arms sweetly arched above her
head, the stiff tutu flaring out to reveal the clean line of her thigh.
God, she was beautiful. God, what gifts she had given and been given.

She had inherited Teach's athletic talent, but that wasn't all of
it. She was the perfect combination of his power, reflexes, and con-
centration, and something ineffable and inexpressibly fine that was
Paige. Teach watched as Dean commanded the stage, turning and

twirling in front of the other girls. Behind her, they were no more animate than the trees and shrubs of the backdrop. When the solo was finished, Dean moved to the wing and three other girls danced in unison—wood nymphs, shepherdesses? Teach wasn't sure. He looked at the program. There would be three more moments for Dean, and one of them had to be Teach's too. He would rise in false apology, hurry, bent-backed, down the aisle, and kneel at the foot of the stage. As unobtrusively as possible, he would snap the Minolta's shutter, capturing the elusive art of Dean.

Teach pushed himself up and apologized his way to the aisle. When he got to the foot of the stage, the music was swelling for Dean's second solo. Teach knelt and the corps de ballet moved into his viewfinder. In the middle was the black girl, and, as she entered Teach's field of vision, he heard to his right a small squeal of pleasure, a whispered, "There she is. Isn't she just so sweet?"

Teach lowered the camera and looked over at the black couple. They had melted in delight at the sight of the girl. Beside them, the mayor and his wife looked on with dutiful appreciation. The black man slowly turned his head. He looked mildly annoyed to see Teach crouching in the dark. Teach lifted his chin in greeting, held up the camera, shrugged. The music swelled. The man nodded and turned back to the stage. Teach focused the camera on the dark space in the wings where Dean would enter, bringing magic.

EIGHT

Bloodworth Naylor aimed the camera and snapped the picture. "Oh yes," he said. "Oh my, my, yes. I love it. I do love it. Turn the other way. To the light. That's right. Now hold it just like that."

The boy, Tyrone, turned his pretty head to the side, that sullen, pouty look on his face. That injured-party look. The shutter clicked. The Polaroid that rolled from the camera looked like a mug shot. Bloodworth Naylor moved closer, getting the wound on the boy's cheek into clear focus. Blood liked the wound. It was lucky. More than he could have asked for if he'd written the story himself, the story of what happened in a bar between a black boy with an attitude and a white man with a bad temper. He told the boy to hold still, adjusted the light from a standing lamp so that it was harsh on the nasty, bruised-mango gash. The pictures were turning out very *True Detective*, very *National Enquirer*. Blood took the last picture, then sorted through them all. Lord, weren't they wonderful?

He put the camera on the table by the lamp. He had the boy in the warehouse behind his rent-to-own furniture store. Back here among the cardboard boxes and the packing crates and the repossessed mattresses and the bedroom suites tagged for the loading dock, nobody would bother them. Nobody would see the splash of light from the camera each time Blood Naylor took a shot of that lovely, ragged little mouth of flesh on the boy's cheek.

"And you didn't put no ice on it?" Blood asked for the second time.

"No, man. I told you. I didn't put no ice on it."

"That was smart," Blood Naylor said. Compliment the boy. Keep him in the spirit of the thing. "You know we want it to look as bad as it can look."

The boy nodded.

"And you didn't go to the emergency room because they might take some blood, and we know what they might find in it."

Tyrone nodded again, and Blood thought it would have been nice for the boy to go to the emergency room, get that medical-records thing going, but they couldn't risk it. A boy with blood like this boy had.

Tyrone had told him the story twice, but Blood wanted to hear it again, at least some of the details. "You just decided to follow those white men into the men's room—the idea just come to you, just like that?"

Tyrone nodded once more, looked at Blood with those nervous, ready eyes. Blood knew what the kid wanted. Blood's Special Reserve. And, Lord knew, he'd earned it.

Blood said, "You want to do up?"

The kid looked almost angry now, that big, scary football anger. It made Blood want to laugh, thinking about angry boys on a football field doing angry things by the rules with some referee in a striped shirt and funny pants blowing his whistle when somebody got too specifically angry at somebody else. Blood Naylor knew the real anger, the one that walked the yard at Raiford. It was specific. Someday he might show it to the boy. If he had to.

With Tyrone watching, that baby anger, that nervous impatience, Blood pulled the plastic baggie out of his pocket and stuck the blade of his penknife into it, dipping out the white powder. Bloodworth Naylor's Special Reserve. The Colombians gave it to him uncut, a small amount for his special customers. None of that baby formula mixed in this shit. Jam up your sinuses, make you shit like a goose. This was the pure extract of the coca leaf, and you had to be very careful with it. A little of it went a long way. A little of it had taken Tyrone Battles, honor student and football hero, a long way indeed.

Blood Naylor had tailed his old friend James Teach for a month, using a car he borrowed from one of the men who worked on the loading dock. Teach had no idea what was happening. What white man would notice a middle-aged nigger in a beat-up Camaro riding along behind him on Bayshore Boulevard and parking outside a doctor's office when he went in to check on his salesmen? Blood knew Teach's patterns, knew how he spent the mornings at the office, then went out in the afternoons to bird dog the sales force. How he liked to make the early afternoon pit stops in the local bars, talk some of that jock talk with the Corona-and-lime crowd.

Teach was a football hero, a guy who told a good story about the good old days. Blood sitting out in the trashy Camaro in the hot sun thinking about Teach and the good life. Hell, if one of the men who worked for Blood did two hours in the office, a two-Corona lunch in Old Hyde Park, then called it quits at three thirty, that nigger would be down the road. So Blood knew a few things about Teach, some of them from experience, some from observation, and some from research. Blood figured he even knew things about Teach that Teach didn't know.

Watching Tyrone's eager eyes, Blood bent over the glass tabletop and chopped the white powder with the single-edged razor blade. He knew about people's secret problems. Tyrone's was this powder here and Teach's was bourbon. And he knew from reading the sports pages of the long ago that Teach had a very bad temper. Oh, the guy had a reputation for cool under fire like any good quarterback, but there was a disturbing pattern of violence in his life. It was right there in the record for anybody who wanted to read it.

Blood divided the powder into two equal portions and cut them into lines. "Now, you got to take it easy with this. It ain't that high school shit you used to." Blood knew the people who supplied the shit Tyrone and his friends used, and he knew what he was talking about. Tyrone took out his wallet, removed a ten-dollar bill, and rolled it with shaking fingers. Blood let his voice go soft, made the sound of an older brother, the sound of caution, good reason. "Just do a line and wait a minute. See how it takes you."

The boy leaned over and inserted the rolled bill into his nostril. Too eager, too eager by half. Blood loved that youthful eagerness. It made the world go round. It made business run smooth and the money roll in. He watched the boy draw in the line of cocaine and then jerk back with the shock of a pure dose. Pull back like his skull had been seized from above by the talons of a giant, ravenous bird. Well, it had been seized, and so had his spinal cord. Every nerve in his strong, young body was singing the Cartagena conga. *Ta, ta, TAH . . . BOOM!* Oh my, my, yes.

Blood always cut some lines for himself. Good customer relations. But with the boy, he hadn't yet. And the boy didn't seem to notice: that eagerness, Mr. Impatience, telling the boy there was more for him if Blood didn't take any.

Two weeks ago, Blood had brought the boy back here among the boxes and the crates and told him he had a choice. He could do what Blood asked him to do with James Teach, and Blood would continue to supply him with the thing he loved most in the world, the Special Reserve, or he could go without the drug (Blood described some of the physical unpleasantness of this to the boy) and Blood would see to it that certain people were made aware of some of Tyrone Battles's activities. Blood had expected some of that phony football anger, some of that young-buck-raging-around-and-confronting thing, but the kid had just looked at him and thought about it, realized that Blood had his balls in a vise, and said, "All you want me to do is confront the guy, piss him off, and see what happens?"

"That's right, my friend," Blood had said. "You just get in his face a little like the mean little nigger you are and see what he does. He does nothing, you just walk away. No problem. But he bows up on you, gets in there eating your breath, goes dog to your dog, then you improvise, see where it goes. I told you, the guy has a history of losing his temper. But remember, we want *him* in trouble, not you."

The truth was that Blood didn't know what Teach would do, but he figured it was worth a try, this thing with Tyrone Battles. Even if Teach didn't take the bait, Blood might learn a thing or two. What had happened, the story Tyrone had just told, was righteous beyond Bloodworth Naylor's wildest dream.

Tyrone fell backward into a Barcalounger that was about to be shipped out to some whores in an apartment in Suitcase City. The football star sprawled there with his mouth gaping, his hands twitching, his eyes the size of cocktail coasters, muttering, "Oh man. Oh shit."

"I told you it was good shit." Blood didn't think the kid heard him. Whatever. The kid knew what to do next. The kid would hear him when the time came. And if he didn't, Blood would crank the vise a little tighter on those eager young balls.

It was hot back here in the storeroom, hot and private. Blood left the boy sitting in his coca-leaf hyperdrive dream and walked out to the loading dock. He rolled open the big steel door and let the evening breeze blow across his face. He looked at the two-acre fenced lot where the delivery trucks were parked, *Naylor's Rent-to-Own* painted in bold black letters on their sides. He glanced up and down the alley.

To the west, where the sun was setting now, he could see the two whores who usually stood under the jacaranda tree behind the laundromat moving into position for the night. They'd stand there under the tree in a litter of cigarette butts, fast-food wrappers, and crack vials until somebody came along and they started hollering, "Booty for sale! I got the softest mouth in Tampa." Shit like that. They were crack-addicted whores. The walking dead. Blood Naylor had invented a word for them: *zombitches*.

Blood ran whores, but he did it the smart way. His scam was neat, efficient, and safe. He ran the rent-to-own as a legitimate business, and it did all right, nothing spectacular. But the bulk of his income came from the whores whose apartments he furnished. He shipped cheap furniture out to them, kept them on the books as rent-to-own clients, and recorded his share of their take as monthly payments on the furniture. The cocaine business provided a small part of his revenue. He only dealt with upscale clients: connections in the universities and some people in the medical and legal communities who liked their recreational drugs to come from a discreet and reliable source. It never hurt to have friends in Armani suits.

The sun had gone down over the jacaranda tree, and the two whores were doing business. A white man in a van had pulled up next to them and was negotiating. The two girls strutting their pathetic, skinny butts and talking that whore trash to a redneck from across the bay in Kenneth City. Blood heard Tyrone muttering to himself inside on the Barcalounger. That Special Reserve gave a man power dreams. Blood figured he'd better get back inside before the boy wandered off to stick up a convenience store with his dick. He'd give the boy some cocaine to take with him, put the photos of the boy's face in an envelope, and stick them in his pocket, maybe tuck a couple of hundred-dollar bills into the boy's wallet for good measure. Customer relations.

Bloodworth Naylor dreamt his power dream at night, and it was always the same story, and James Teach was always in the starring role. And James Teach was always surprised, beautifully surprised, when his sweet white world turned to blood and shit all around him, and in the dream Bloodworth Naylor was always laughing. And there was someone else in the dream. She was the reason for all of this. A beautiful woman. And, oh yes, wasn't that always the story?

NINE

Teach awoke to the ache in his elbow. He rolled onto his back, wondering why it hurt. Then it all came back. The bar. The men's room, that angry ebony face, the shirttail flagging to the side for a second, showing Teach what was almost certainly the handle of a razor.

He lay staring at the ceiling, feeling the sweat of fear break on his face. How had he gotten himself into this mess? Why hadn't he waited a moment to see what the boy would do, ask him again what he meant? Then he thought: *No, damnit.*

As a kid, Teach had read about the murders of Sharon Tate and her friends in a wealthy house in the Hollywood Hills. How a band of lunatics had just walked in smiling and laughing and killed everybody. No one had sounded an alarm; no one had resisted because everyone had assumed the freaks had come for the party. The story had changed Teach. Taught him that it would always be better to trust instinct and strike when the alarms went off in your head than to wait the extra second to be sure. You could die in that second. Abigail Folger had waited. Wojciech Frykowski had waited, smiling, asking if he could help Tex Watson, who drew a pistol and shot him, then jumped on his back, stabbing him as Frykowski staggered across the lawn. Teach wasn't sure he'd done the right thing in Malone's Bar, but he was sure he'd do the same thing again.

He worked the elbow that ached because it had split a boy's cheek and wondered if Dean was awake.

She had come out to the auditorium dressed in jeans and a thigh-length T-shirt, still glowing with stage makeup and the excitement of her triumph. She'd brought two friends with her—Missy Pace, a cheerleader, and the black girl, new to ballet. Teach had nodded and smiled at the two girls and opened his arms to Dean who gave him a brief hug. He'd whispered into her warm, fragrant neck, "Beautiful tonight." When she pulled away, her eyes glittering with that energy she turned into movement on the stage, Teach said, "As usual."

"Thanks, Daddy." She smiled at some club women passing up the aisle.

Teach said, "Time to go, Deanie. I've got reservations at Bern's." Dinner at Bern's was their after-recital tradition.

Dean frowned, then smiled. "Daddy, would it be okay this once if I skip dinner? There's a party at Marty Flipper's house." The two friends watched Teach solemnly.

He tried to think of how to say no to all three of them. He could invite the friends to dinner.

Dean fired the heavy artillery. "Daddy-please-can-I?"

Unable to come up with a good no and worried about the blood-stain on his sleeve, Teach cleared his throat to summon his Stern Father voice. "No drinking at this party, young lady. And I want you home at eleven."

"Oh, Daddy," Dean groaned, mortified to have drinking (or was it coming home on time?) mentioned in front of her friends.

Teach had played golf with Harold Flipper who owned the local Volvo dealership. He was a dim but affable fellow and so, Teach reasoned, must be his son, Marty. The two girlfriends examined their fingernails and studied their Doc Martens to see if the scuffing on them was just right.

Teach abandoned Stern Father in favor of Old Guy Trying to Be Humorously Hip. "Will you girls give me your word you'll say no when the wine coolers are passed around?" Missy looked stunned, as though she did not have a word to give, but the black girl looked Teach in the eye and said, "I promise you, Mr. Teach, if Deanie tries to go the way of all flesh, I'll place my body between her and temptation."

Teach kept his jaw from dropping, but he could not keep from chuckling his appreciation.

She stepped forward and extended her hand. "Hi, I'm Tawnya. It's nice to meet you."

* * *

Teach swung his legs out of bed and sat working the aching elbow. He felt Saturday-morning sad. It was sad but not fatal that Dean had ditched their celebration dinner for the giddy delights of a party at Marty Flipper's house. Sometimes life was losing things. He had lost Paige, and he was losing Dean to the fate nature intended for young girls. (Not, please God, Marty Flipper, but someday a young man with a future.) The phone rang. Teach hurried from bed.

"Hello, I'm trying to reach James Teach. Is he there, please?"

Teach summoned his vice president's voice. Easy and affable. Ready to meet what the day brought to his door. "This is he."

"Mr. Teach, my name is Marlie Turkel. I'm a reporter at the *Trib*. Do you have a minute?"

Teach thinking: *What does a reporter want with me on a Saturday morning? Something about Dean, her dancing?* There had been a couple of pieces in the Sunday supplement. Dean's success at the American Dance Festival. Her prospects for a New York career. Teach kept his voice low, pleasant. "Sure," he said, "I've got a minute. What's this about?"

"It's about yesterday afternoon, you and a Mr. Tyrone Battles." The woman's voice changed. It went from brusque efficiency to a husky purring that couldn't hide her excitement.

Teach felt the worm of fear move in his belly. Jesus, a journalist, and a woman. How in God's own name had she gotten hold of this thing, and so soon? And what did she plan to do with it? Teach said only, "Yes?" aware that his voice had lost its affability. Aware that he was buying time without any idea what he would do with it.

The woman cleared her throat and in a low seductive throb said, "I'd like to get your side of this thing before we go to press with it."

She sounds like sex, Teach thought. Like she had known him for years and not in Sunday school. Like she had enjoyed knowing him in a way she wouldn't deny, and she knew he wouldn't either.

"Listen, uh, my daughter's asleep. I want to take this downstairs. Can you call back in a minute or two?"

The woman—what was her name, Turkey? Surely not. Turkel, that was it, said, "Fine, Mr. Teach. It's eight forty-five. I'll call at eight fifty. Will that be all right?"

"Tell you what, give me ten minutes. I'll make a cup of coffee. Wake up a little."

Marlie Turkel said ten minutes would be fine with her, but now her tone said, *You won't fuck with me if you know what's good for you.*

Downstairs, Teach put the coffee on. With a cup in his hand, warm and reassuring, he considered simply refusing to talk to the woman. She had probably seen the police report, knew what he'd told Aimes. Elaborating might get him into more trouble than letting the facts speak for themselves. And it would be easier, at least for the time being, to ignore her.

When the phone rang again, he snatched it from its cradle thinking of Dean upstairs. She'd wonder who was calling so early on a Saturday. Teach decided that elaborating a bit would serve him better than the bare bones of a police report. And he had no idea what the cop, Aimes, had written. He said, "Hello, Ms. Turkel. What can I tell you about yesterday?"

"Anything you want to tell me, Mr. Teach. I've got Mr. Battles's side of the story. I thought it was only fair to call you."

Fair? Teach thought. *Right.* He told her what had happened: the good fellowship of two men who liked football, the necessary but regrettable trip to the men's room, the boy coming in, calling them . . . Teach faltered. Should he say the word to a woman? Hell yes, he should. If she was any kind of journalist at all, she'd want the facts. So, he told it: the boy calling them *white bitches,* telling them to give it up. He told her about his certainty that the boy had a weapon, the probability that he would use it.

He told the woman he believed Tyrone Battles had planned to take their money and leave them dead in a men's room. He painted the picture vividly for her, thinking that he might appeal to a woman's fear of just such an encounter in a parking garage, on a dark street. As he talked, she murmured, "Yes, uh-huh, yes, I see," and he could hear her fingers chattering on a computer keyboard.

Teach finished with, "So you see, there wasn't much I could do. I mean, except what I did. I think any man . . . Well, I mean it seems to me to be a natural reaction to the situation. The only reaction, really." He should have stopped, but let himself say, "If you'd been there, you would have been glad I did it, Ms. Turkel."

"What about the other man? Why didn't he react like you did?"

Teach thought about it. From where he stood, the only true response was: *Who the hell knows?* He said, "He just froze, I guess. It happens." *And pissed himself.*

Should he tell her that? Teach let his answer stand. And he doubted that Mr. Pee Stain would elaborate the matter much if Marlie Turkel found him.

The woman cleared her throat again. "Mr. Teach, when you saw the boy, did you have any idea who he was?"

"Uh, no. No, I didn't." Teach thinking: *For bleeding Jesus' sake, what do I know about high school superstars?*

"I see." That purring voice, keeping him at ease, opening him up, going for the deepest part. "You'd had something to drink, is that right?"

"Yeah, sure. I had a couple of drinks. That's what you do in a bar."

"A couple? Do you mean two?"

"Two, three. I'm not sure exactly. I wasn't drunk, if that's what you're getting at."

"The bartender says you had five bourbons." The claws out now, flashing, then resheathed. "He said he remembered that pretty clearly."

Teach told her his memory was as good as a bartender's (hoping this thing didn't get to cash register tapes, records of bourbons sold), and he remembered two or three drinks.

"I see. You were a football player, weren't you, Mr. Teach, a long time ago? Weren't you a very good football player?"

A long time ago? Not so long, Teach thought. He didn't tell Marlie Turkel that he still couldn't walk into restaurants in Tampa without some stranger waving to him, calling, *Go Gators!* "Sure," he said, "I guess you could say that."

"You know, I got *interested* in you when this thing came across my desk. I looked you up in the files. You had quite a career. A conference championship and two bowl victories. Pretty impressive. And then the Atlanta Falcons." Something hard happened to her voice when she mentioned the Falcons.

"Yeah, well, I had three pretty good years in the NFL, but it ended, and . . ." Teach summoned whimsy, regret with a little sweet nostalgia, "what can I tell you? It was a great ride while it lasted."

"What about Nate Means? Can you tell me about that, Mr. Teach?"

Jesus, Nate Means. How had she, what did she . . . ?

Teach repeated what he'd told the press twenty years ago about Nate Means. It was a speech he'd memorized. "It was a clean hit. Nobody in the league ever accused me of anything illegal. It was just bad luck. If the guy with the video camera hadn't been too close to the sidelines, Means wouldn't have hit his head like that."

In his third and last year in the NFL, James Teach had been moved to special teams, a wild band of suicides who ran the length of the field on kickoffs and punt returns and collided with whatever waited at the other end. That night, Teach had hit the kickoff returner, a million-dollar, first-round draft pick out of Michigan. Nate Means was a supertalent. It had been a bone-bending, white-light explosion of a tackle, and Means had caromed into the steel frame of a TV camera dolly. His third and fourth cervical vertebrae were crushed, and Means was rendered a paraplegic.

The referee had thrown no flag that night, but the instant replay had shown that Means was inches out of bounds when Teach had hit him. The press had been divided: half calling it a late hit, even an intentional maiming by a frustrated former star, the other half saying that football was a contact sport and Teach's hit was mean but clean. Journalists said what they said, and Teach knew you just had to keep your feet under you in the storm of ink.

"But Mr. Teach, isn't there a pattern of violence in your life?"

"Football's a violent game, Ms. Turkel. You don't survive in it very long without being violent yourself. But that doesn't mean you play dirty."

"It's too bad your career ended that way."

It was her first comment. Teach wasn't sure if she meant too bad he'd gone from backup quarterback with prospects for a starting role to free safety (where he'd lacked the speed for success) to special teams, or too bad about Nate Means, or all of it. Teach considered his pro career all of a piece and all too bad. When he thought about football, he concentrated on his college days.

It occurred to him that he might try something different with this woman, maybe yet find a way out of this thing. Hadn't she said she was interested in him? "Listen," he said, "why don't we have lunch? Talk about this face-to-face." He was about to say, *Maybe have a couple of drinks, get to know each other better,* but recognized in time the stupidity of mentioning alcohol. "I'd like the chance to explain what happened a little more fully before you . . ." the phrase was cold in his mouth, "print this."

Marlie Turkel sighed. "I don't think that would be a very good idea, Mr. Teach."

He kept trying: "Look, maybe there's, you know, not really as much of a story here as you think. Maybe this thing doesn't really have to be in the paper."

"Mr. Teach, race relations have deteriorated in Tampa in the last five years. A lot of people think we're primed for something like what happened in St. Petersburg last year. It doesn't take much to touch off a riot. There's going to be a story whether we have lunch or not." The sex was gone from her voice. Now it was firm, sorry, a little righteous, the way you'd be with a kid caught breaking a rule. "I got onto this thing because I learned that Mr. Battles has already been to see Ellie Goings. He showed her some pictures of his face and said he was going to the black radio station when he finished talking to her."

The worm in Teach's empty stomach turned again. Ellie Goings was the local minority affairs reporter. In her weekly column, she alternated between inspiring stories about African American achievement on the local scene and scathing tales of lives blighted by racism. Teach could have written her Tyrone column himself. In the Ellie Goings version, Teach would be a knuckle-dragging troglodyte, and Tyrone would be a composite of Heroic Black Youth.

Teach felt his naked toes hit the bottom. The bottom was cold and slimy. "Look, Ms. Turkel, do you have to do this? I mean . . . ?" What more could he say? He was begging.

"I'm sorry, Mr. Teach, but yes, I do. It's news and the public has a right to know. And I've given you a chance to tell your side of it."

Right, Teach thought, *my side as seen by Marlie Turkel. And you aren't finished with me yet.*

"I'm surprised you don't know anything about Mr. Battles's athletic accomplishments. Don't you read the sports page?"

"Not much," Teach said, aware that his voice had gone dull, cold. "Tell me what's in the sports page." *About our saintly Tyrone.*

"A lot. He's not just a football star who's been contacted by over a dozen colleges and universities. He's an honor student. His SAT scores are good enough for a full ride to college without football. He's never been in trouble before. He's really quite a remarkable young man."

It sounded like she was reading from the screen in front of her, quoting herself. Teach thinking: *And what am I, just your common, drunken, middle-aged white householder with an attitude about black people?*

"There's one other thing, Mr. Teach. Do you know anything about Tyrone's family?"

"Only what you just told me. He does sound like an exemplary boy." But a memory was waking up, turning over in the fetid loam of Malone's Bar. What was it the cop, Delbert, had said? *That boy's family's a walking history of the civil rights movement in this state.*

"I see. Well, I guess I ought to tell you that Tyrone's uncle is Thurman Battles. He's an attorney, quite an important man here in town. His specialty is litigation involving violations of federal civil rights statutes. He's been very successful in the courts." The woman waited for a reaction. Teach not sure he could, or should, give one. Not sure what might be printed. Maybe he'd said too much already.

All Teach said was, "When?"

"Excuse me?"

"When will the article be in the paper?"

"Monday. It'll be part of longer piece on local race relations."

When Marlie Turkel said a polite goodbye, Teach sat alone in his kitchen sipping cold coffee. He could smell himself, the sweat of the last twenty-four hours heavy on him, the evil odor of bad surprises. He was confused, but one thing he knew was that he would wait as long as possible before telling Dean about his trouble. This was the morning after her triumph. He would do all he could to make it a good one, and that began with breakfast. Waffles were her favorite morning meal. He was halfway to the pantry for the batter mix when something occurred to him. He found the program for the recital on the hallway table where he had left it last night.

The names of the girls in the corps de ballet were familiar to him. Theirs were the family names engraved on the brass plaques outside the law offices and doctors' offices in the better parts of town. In the program, he found what he was looking for. The new girl in the corps, the athletic, charming black girl who could have been running a hundred-meter dash or kicking her legs out in the arc of the long jump. The girl who had promised to place her body between Dean and temptation. Her name was Tawnya Battles.

TEN

Teach put two plates of waffles topped with fresh strawberries and two glasses of orange juice on a tray and carried them to the breakfast room. Buttery sunlight streamed through the French doors that let onto the back terrace. This was his favorite room on weekend mornings. He walked to the stairs and called, "Time for breakfast, Deanie." And standing here he felt his heart rise with the remembered joy of mornings when Dean was little and it was Paige calling her down for a meal before driving her to school. The sounds and smells of those mornings flooded over him. The dizzying sweet waft of shampoo from Dean's hair as she passed through the foyer and hurried toward the breakfast room. The heat of the crown of her head as he briefly rested his hand there. The rubber scuff of Dean's sneakers on the ocher Spanish tiles. The bounce of her blond ponytail on the blue and green tartan of her Episcopal school jumper.

The radio came on upstairs, a rock station blasting the quiet morning, and over it, Dean's tired voice called down, "Okay, Dad."

Back in the kitchen, Teach poured himself a fresh cup of coffee and a glass of milk for Dean and carried these and a pair of scissors out to the breakfast room. He opened the French doors and smelled the hot, fragrant air of the garden. Paige had told him when they'd moved into this sixty-year-old Mediterranean Revival house that she wanted a walled garden like those she had seen in old St. Augustine. She wanted high, stuccoed walls bordered by shade trees. And there must be benches and oyster shell paths and a fountain. A fountain was the heart of a garden, she had said, just as the hearth was the heart of a house. She wanted to stand by the splashing waters of her fountain and look up at the Barcelona balcony letting into the bedroom she shared with her husband.

Teach had built the garden exactly to her specifications, and her only disappointment was a city ordinance limiting the height of the walls. Walking her oyster-shell paths, Paige could see into a neighbor's window, or glimpse the straw hat that floated along on the head of Angel Morales, the yardman who worked this neighborhood. These things, she had told Teach, harmed the illusion of isolation she wanted in her garden, but the rest of what she felt in it was wondrous. She had planted Spanish bayonet and bird-of-paradise under the Jerusalem thorns along the ivied walls. Terra-cotta jugs of dendrobia hung from low tree branches.

With the scissors, Teach snipped a beautiful yellow and orange bird-of-paradise blossom. Back in the kitchen, he put it in a crystal vase just as Paige would have done and sipped coffee while he waited.

And then Dean stood in the kitchen doorway rubbing her eyes. Her honey-blond hair was matted to her scalp in what she called "bed head." She wore a long T-shirt and razored jeans and was barefoot. Teach looked at her poor scarred feet. She was sixteen and her feet were forty, calloused and abraded from years of dancing. There was a scud of soap along her jawline and blond wisps framed her blurry blue eyes. Dean's eyes, people always said, belonged to Teach. The eyes of his hangovers. Had Dean been drinking at Marty Flipper's party? Better not to ask. *Better not to tilt the fragile thing we are now, father and daughter so far from those mornings when a little blond head passed under my hand on its way to a warm winter kitchen.*

Teach reached over and gently wiped the soap from her face. "I didn't think you'd want coffee."

"I do. With skim and a little sugar."

And when had she started drinking coffee? Bringing back the cup, watching his daughter sip from it, make first a face of distaste, then of bored approval, Teach saw the spot of blood on the floor beside her chair. Smeared spots of it led across the tile to the chair where Dean sat now trying a sip of orange juice. When she glanced up out of the bleary vagueness that was adolescent morning, Teach had to turn away because his eyes were full of tears.

As he walked to the kitchen, he heard Dean behind him: "Wow, Dad, these waffles look great. You're really jammin' in the kitchen this morning. Kinda reminds me of when I was a kid."

Teach took a copper mixing bowl from a cabinet, poured some medicated hand soap into it, and filled it with warm water. He found a fresh dish towel in a drawer, dried his eyes with it, and turned back to Dean. Her head was bent over the plate of waffles and strawberries. The fork dipped and rose with a mechanical rhythm. Teach walked over and knelt with the bowl and towel at his daughter's feet.

"Dad, what are you *doing*?"

Teach lifted the bleeding foot and examined it. Dean tried to pull it away. He held it, his head bent, hearing the fork settle to the plate. "Dad?"

Teach didn't answer, couldn't speak now. Not yet. In a minute. He put the bowl under her foot and began to lift warm soapy water to it. He wanted Dean back. Back from that place where adolescent girls went for a while to get away from their parents. He couldn't look up at his daughter now, couldn't show her his red eyes, couldn't say any of the necessary things he carried with him for her and for her lost mother. Well, he would say them later. To say them was the thing he wanted most. Now he would wash this poor bruised foot.

Dean did not resist his hands, but he knew that if he looked up he would see her blushing face, a daughter's eyes darting around in the improbable fear that someone was watching this. He said, "Deanie, I wish you could dance without hurting yourself so much. Look, this is infected. After I wash it, I'll have to put iodine on it."

Dean said, "DADDY, get up, will you? I don't know what you're doing down there." But Teach could hear it, her voice softening. The years slipping away. When she said, "You know, that feels kind of good, actually," he finally looked up at her.

He wished his eyes were not what they were, red and swollen, but there was nothing he could do about that.

"What's wrong, Dad?"

"Nothing, honey." Teach dried her foot and began to wash the other one. It wasn't bleeding, but it was covered with horned callouses and raw scrapes. *The cruelty*, he thought, *of the things we love*.

"Dad, are you okay? Did something happen last night?" Her voice was slow and warm now like the water that dripped from Teach's hands. The child was little again, putting her world in order. Sighting bodies in the firmament of home. *Daddy, are you okay?*

It was easy for Teach to say, "I'm okay, Deanie. Nothing happened." Drying his daughter's beautiful, skillful, wounded foot, he thought, *And I want us both to be okay. This Saturday morning is what I want.* He rose and took the bowl of soapy water to the kitchen and said, "Now don't you move. I'll be right back with the iodine."

ELEVEN

Teach sat in the Grille Room at the Terra Ceia Country Club sipping his second beer. He had purchased a pitcher. He felt rank and grubby and knew he looked it. He hoped the members who glanced at him as they passed through would conclude that his greasy hair and thirty hours of beard were simply the Saturday-morning rebellion of a successful man who'd already played a relaxing nine. The eleven o'clock beer would just have to puzzle them.

After breakfast, Dean had gone up to her room for the friend phoning that was her Saturday-morning ritual. Teach had gone out to the garage and slipped on the polo shirt he kept in the LeSabre's trunk for the times when he stopped at the driving range after work. In the club parking lot, he'd put on his golf shoes and a white visor, and walked to the Grille Room to order the beer and wait for attorney Walter Demarest.

Walter teed off at seven o' clock Saturday mornings, sun or rain, no matter what the condition of the Great Republic or the needs of his well-heeled clients. Teach knew Walter's patterns, knew he would pass through the Grille Room on his way home. He trusted Walter as much as he trusted anyone on the narrow social shelf that housed Paige's friends. Walter played good golf, didn't cheat, and had never said a word to Teach about any of his clients.

When Walter Demarest walked in, Teach was on his third beer and believed he might be looking exactly like a guy who'd played a pleasant early round. Walter went to the bar for his usual Amstel Light. With the bottle in his hand, he turned and surveyed the room. Teach waved. "Walt, join me, why don't you?"

Walter Demarest glanced around the Grille Room as though he

might get a better offer, saw nothing, smiled, and ambled over to Teach's table. He was tall, round at the middle, and as pale as the belly of a catfish. He had coffee-black hair and the sort of chinless, hook-nosed look that reminded Teach of the British royal family. He had been president of his chapter of Alpha Tau Omega at Florida, and Teach had known him in one way or another for a long time.

Walter looked Teach over, sighting down the brown barrel of the Amstel bottle. "So, Teach old buddy, you get around already? How'd it go out there? I didn't think you were an early bird." Walter lowered the bottle from a mouth that was small and too crowded with chalky-looking teeth. *Inbreeding*, Teach thought, not for the first time.

Teach considered lying about a golf game. Why bother? Walter would question him about his deportment on the evil twelfth hole, a par five that required a drive and a long iron over water to a narrow landing, and he would have to invent golf shots and be questioned with legal precision about the lie of his ball and his choice of clubs. "Actually, Walter, I didn't play this morning. I've been sitting here waiting for you. I need to talk to you about something important."

Walter put the Amstel bottle on the table and shrugged on the mantle of his profession. Clearly, he did not want to wear it: not here, not now. He examined Teach carefully, noting in his mental ledger Teach's greasy hair, the clean golf shirt, the haggard, unshaven face. His eyes lingered on the half-empty beer pitcher, then met Teach's frankly. "Rough night?"

Teach nodded, drained his glass, and poured another. "Rougher than most. In fact, the roughest I've had in a long time." He told the story, starting with the bar and Tyrone Battles and moving on to the crushing coincidence of the cop being the boy's uncle. Walter winced at that particular detail. Teach finished with his getting out of Malone's with his ass and a few tatters of his dignity intact, taking his bloody sleeve to the women's club for Dean's recital (Walter: "I saw you there. You did look a little, well, rattled, come to think of it. But Dean was wonderful as always."), and, finally, the waking up to Marlie Turkel, the woman with hot sex in her voice and a Pulitzer Prize in her icy heart.

When Teach finished, Walter whistled low and slow. "Jesus, poor old Teach."

Teach nodded, sighed, drank. He looked into Walter's clear, cool, light-green eyes. "Walt, am I well and truly fucked?"

Walter pushed back in his chair, glanced around the still mostly vacant Grille Room, raised his empty bottle, and set it down again. Teach leaned over and poured beer into Walter's bottle. Walter tasted the Budweiser and made a sour face. "You actually drink this stuff?"

Teach wanted to say that he had drunk a lot worse and liked it better, thank you very much, but he was after Walter's legal opinion.

"Well," Walter sighed, "there is of course a lot of terrain between well and truly fucked and just, say, fucked without a kiss, but I would say you are in some trouble."

"What can the kid do, Walter?"

"Well, assuming there are no criminal charges—I mean assuming the cop, the uncle, decides to leave the matter where it lies—there's still civil court. And believe me, my friend, anybody can sue anybody for anything in civil court, and the burden of proof is much less severe. It's not proof beyond a reasonable doubt; it's proof by the preponderance of the evidence. Lots of difference there, old buddy."

"What about this guy, Thurman Battles, the kid's other uncle? What's he like?"

"Oh my Christ," muttered Walter Demarest, drinking the Budweiser from his Amstel bottle. "Oh my sweet, suffering Savior, Thurman Battles is a bear. A veritable grizzly."

Walter had said, *Bay-ah*, and Teach didn't like it, but you couldn't have every good thing with a friend, and Walter was a friend. Walter was, in fact, a lifeline thrown across the wild, heaving seas of this table to the leaky rowboat of Teach's life. Teach drank the last of his beer and said, "You mean I couldn't go talk to the guy. He wouldn't listen to reason?"

Walter Demarest looked at him and slowly shook his head. Teach couldn't tell if the man was weighing the stupidity of the question or was simply at a loss for words. Finally, Walter said, "Thurman Battles is reasonable as Thurman Battles sees reason. He's reasonable as it suits him and his client. He's reasonable when his reasoning is better than yours, and the judge and the jury know it. The rest of the time he's Vlad the Impaler in an Armani suit."

Teach had saved the best and the worst for last. The thing he had come here for. "Look, Walter," he said, trying to get the man's small, clear, green eyes to meet his, remembering all the times when the two of them had played golf with a pint of Wild Turkey in the cart, "I was wondering if you'd consider representing me if this thing gets out of hand. I mean, if this kid does file a civil action."

Teach waited. Walter's eyes brightened. He put down the beer Teach had given him and pushed back in his chair. "Uh, Jim . . ." His voice was measured and a little remote, the voice he used when telling Teach to put the five iron back into the bag and go with the six because, after all, there was a breeze behind them and Teach was hitting to a sloping green. And Teach noticed, vaguely, from the thickening haze of morning beer, that *old buddy* had gone away. Teach was Jim now. "Uh, Jim, I hate to say this, but you couldn't afford me. Not for half as long as a thing like this could take if it goes the way Thurman Battles might want to take it."

Teach felt his anger rise out of the beery mist. What the hell, how did Walter Demarest know what he could afford? And just as quickly as it blossomed, Teach's anger wilted. Walter had been to Teach's house, had seen him wearing the Brooks Brothers suits he bought once a year at the Christmas sale at the Old Hyde Park store. Walter had ridden in Teach's two-year-old LeSabre once when his own Lexus was being serviced. Walter knew what he knew. Maybe this was a kindness.

"Listen, Jim," Walter said, rising and leaning forward, putting his pale, manicured hands on the table, "call my office on Monday and I'll give you the name of a young guy I know who's just getting started. He's good, and he won't charge you an arm and a leg, and I'm sure he'll do as good a job with this thing as I could. Hell," he added, "maybe better."

Walter pushed off from the table and crossed to the bar where he signed his check and left his empty bottle. As he headed for the door, Teach called out, "See you out on the course, old buddy."

Walter didn't turn or speak, just raised his left hand, giving Teach the back of it in a jaunty wave.

Teach finished the beer, feeling like a very old buddy. He got up a little unsteadily, carried the pitcher and his glass to the bar, and signed the chit. Trevor, the weekend bartender, retrieved the pen from him, did not look at the tip, and said, "Going to hit some now, Mr. Teach? It's a gorgeous day out there."

Teach smiled. "Maybe I will get a bucket."

In the parking lot, he was stowing his golf shoes in the trunk of the Buick when he saw Bama Boyd walking from the pro shop to her old Alfa Romeo. *Jesus.* Teach had completely forgotten. He was supposed to play this morning with Bama and two guys from the St. Pete club where Bama was an assistant pro.

Hiding behind the raised trunk, Teach glanced at his watch, tried to remember when they'd agreed to meet. It was eleven twenty now. His memory wouldn't give up the needed detail. Tall, willowy, grave in the way that all great golfers are, and, yes, masculine, Bama put her golf bag into the trunk of the ancient Alfa and quietly closed it. He watched her look back at the pro shop, her still-beautiful face a little leathery from years on golf courses. She looked like a tall house about to fall down. She opened the car door with a hand Teach knew well, because he had held it, kissed it in their long-ago youth. She got into the car without even removing her golf shoes.

Teach imagined the scene inside the pro shop. Bama and her two friends presenting themselves at the counter. The assistant pro, an arrogant kid named Neally, explaining to them that they could only play as guests *with* a member. Bama asking, one professional to another, for an exception. After all, Mr. Teach had meant to be here, would probably arrive a little after their tee time. Would probably catch up with them on the third or fourth hole. Bama using that Alabama charm, and maybe a little of the reputation she'd had as a college golfer, to get the kid to bend the rules. But Teach knew the kid wouldn't bend. He imagined Bama, the all-American, the college girl he had dated ardently and publicly, standing there pissed and belittled in front of two guys from her club. How could he have forgotten this date with her? Christ, who would have remembered anything after Marlie Turkel?

Teach peeked over the lid of the trunk. The two guys were nowhere in sight. Probably already gone after a long drive from St. Pete and an ego-spanking from a twenty-three-year-old assistant pro with a scratch handicap and an attitude. A guy too young, maybe, to remember the golden exploits of Bama Boyd. Teach saw the dark blue smoke blow from Bama's exhaust pipe, knew he should come out of hiding and hurry down the parking lot, stop her. Apologize. At least invite her in for a beer. But he couldn't. Not now. Not this morning. This morning too many things had happened and there was more to come. So much to come that he could not summon even common decency. Teach hid, hoping Bama would take the far exit, would not drive past the spot where he crouched over an open trunk.

They hadn't seen each other for a long time. This morning was to have been a reunion. The excuses and last-minute cancellations had all been Teach's. There was the long drive across the bay, Bama's perpetual marginal employment, the way it got difficult for him to answer her questions about his own success, the way the old stories got harder to tell about how Bama had been the Lady Gator long-drive queen, the next Nancy Lopez to his king of Gator football. The world had belonged to them for a while, and for a while it looked as though they would make a life together. And then one night in the backseat of Teach's car, Bama had confessed her secret. She liked women. She loved them, in fact. And Teach was, she had explained to him, a beard.

A what?

It meant, she had told him, a woman who married a gay man to conceal his nature. "But I'm not a woman," Teach had said, still holding Bama Boyd in his arms.

"And I'm not a man," she had replied, "but the arrangement we have . . . is the same."

Teach moved away from her then. "I wasn't aware we had . . . an arrangement. I thought we loved each other."

"We do," she said, starting to cry. "We do, but I don't love you . . . *that* way. I can't. I can only love women that way. But nobody can know it."

Teach had thought she could love him that way. She had sure acted like it. In motels across two counties, she had acted like it very well. But acting was acting, and she was right. Nobody could know it. Not in that time and place.

"You have to *promise* me," she said. "Nobody can know."

"Sure, I promise." And he had meant it. He asked her, "So do we keep on . . . ?"

"Yeah," she'd said, crying hard now. "We have to keep on . . . for a while. Then," she was sobbing so hard that he moved back to her and took her in his arms again, "then we have to break up. It'll be in all the papers. Our breakup. It'll be big news. And we, I mean, I won't date anyone after that. I'll be carrying a torch for you."

"So I'll be the reason we break up?"

"Yes. If you don't mind. Please, Jimmy, I'd like it if you'd be the reason. It would be better for me."

They both knew this meant that Teach had to find a new girl, and he had to do it publicly, and that in the public eye he would be the lout who had dumped Bama Boyd, ruining a sports-page romance.

"Okay," Teach had said, "but I'm gonna miss you." He held her hard in his arms, trying to press into his body the memory of hers forever, and hoping that as she wept and pressed back, holding him hard too, in some strange way she was not acting. And he did miss her. For a long time.

Now Bama backed up, gave the Alfa's once-furious engine a couple of rumbling revs, and rolled toward Teach. He duckwalked around to the front of the Buick, hid there, his head throbbing with shame, while she rolled past. Teach tried to form in his mind the words of the apology he would phone to Bama. He would tell her about hiding. She would know about that. And he'd tell her it wasn't her he was hiding from.

TWELVE

Meador Pharmaceuticals operated a manufacturing facility in what had once been an orange grove west of Tampa. The firm produced formulas developed by its small research division, but mostly served as an importer and distributor of offshore drugs. An anti-inflammatory from Mexico, a hypertension pill from Switzerland, and fertility drugs from France and Germany. James Teach managed the sales force, men and women who went out every day to physician's offices, clinics, and hospitals purveying Meador drugs and the perks that went with them. Teach had started with Meador on the loading dock and had risen to sales, then to sales management, and finally to a vice presidency.

He had known for a long time that he would not be considered for the presidency. Mabry Meador, the company's founding president and CEO, and his wife, Oona, had produced two daughters. One daughter had married well, the other not so well, but both had married ambition. Mabry Meador was as healthy a sixty-year-old as Teach had ever seen, and when he decided to step down, the top job would go to a son-in-law: Ambition A or Ambition B. Teach figured he'd be swept out in the housecleaning when Ambition ascended to the presidential suite.

As he got out of the LeSabre and stood stretching in the hot, muggy morning, he knew that even his present position was uncertain. Mabry Meador would have read the newspaper. If he had missed the article about Teach, then someone from the company would have called him, in the company's best interest, of course.

Mabry Meador encouraged such things. He was a Southern Baptist who believed in a heaven of cottony clouds and plucking lyres, and a hell of eternal, unbearable fire. He abhorred shady dealing or sharp practice. The Meador sales force was required to balance expense accounts to the penny and to submit to vigorous questioning by company accountants should any voucher suggest lavish tendencies. Meador insisted that all members of middle- and top-level management attend biannual retreats on the campus of a Baptist summer camp to discuss research and development, sales strategies, and the fraying moral fiber of the nation. Failure to attend the retreats was career suicide.

Teach lifted his briefcase from the front seat of the LeSabre and wondered how to play his entrance. Should he breeze in like this was just another Monday, and there was no reason for him, or anyone else, to worry about the strange but insignificant events of the previous Friday afternoon? Should he enter wearing the small, grim smile that said, *What the hell, I'm in a little trouble here, but I'm still the guy you know and respect?* Or should he stride in angry? Show them the righteous combativeness of a man unjustly accused? The trouble was that he felt all of these things at once.

As he walked from his car to the door, Teach reviewed in his mind Marlie Turkel's article. It was a masterpiece of innuendo and insinuation masquerading as objective reporting. The article followed the line of her questioning on the phone. She led her readers from Teach's narrative of his actions in the men's room (hotly disputed, of course, by Tyrone Battles), to Teach's drinking, to the "pattern of violence" in his life (she devoted nearly half the article to the Nate Means incident). Artfully and subtly, she floated the implication that James Teach was a frustrated, substance-abusing white man who had pounded the shit out of Tyrone Battles, star athlete and honor student, because Battles was to Teach, in some twisted way, a reprise of Nate Means, the million-dollar athlete who had come into the NFL just as Teach was leaving it a failure.

Opening the heavy glass front door of Meador, he became aware that his lips were moving in violent debate with Marlie Turkel. *Damn it,* he thought, *pull yourself together.* He tried to compose himself for business as usual, but the exertion of his mental argument had left a sheen of sweat on his face.

"Good morning, Mr. Teach." Celia, the receptionist with bubblegum-pink lipstick and big blond hair.

He nodded to her, smiled. She watched him carefully as he stopped for coffee, then went on down the hall. Halfway to his door, Teach realized that the building was unnaturally quiet. He could actually hear air whispering in the vents.

Inside, he stood before the desk of his secretary. Amelia Corso, an intelligent woman capable of more loyalty to her boss than to the company (an essential trait in a secretary), raised her head from the memo she was pretending to read. "Well, hello there, tough guy. Let me see those hands."

Teach held out his hands for inspection.

"Don't see any cuts. You use brass knuckles on that poor, innocent kid?"

Teach shrugged, feeling the ache in his elbow. "No, I used my elbow and only once. It still hurts."

"Well, I wouldn't go complaining about the parts of you that hurt, not today anyway."

Teach nodded. It was good advice. Good old Amelia. An Italian transplant from the Bronx. Her husband, an ex-cop on a twenty-year pension, taught martial arts in his own karate dojo in a Carrolwood strip mall. Amelia's bluntness had saved Teach from more than one dumb mistake.

She handed him a *While You Were Out* message. Bama Boyd had called. There was an X in the *Please Return Call* box. Teach winced, folded it, closed his eyes, and tried to form a few words of his apology to Bama. Not much there. Amelia made her brown eyes big and said, "*He* wants to see you, ASAP. Called first thing this morning."

He was Meador. *First thing* could only mean the worst. Meador spent the first half hour of every working day reading the Bible at his desk. It was an ancient leather-bound book, as scuffed as an old boot. He liked to tell people it recorded a hundred years of Meador family births and deaths. Teach wondered if he wrote the names of sacked executives and the dates of their departures in it too.

His stomach rolled like a fish dying in a bucket. He gave Amelia his brave-fellow-marches-to-the-fight smile and walked to Meador's suite.

After Teach was announced by Meador's secretary, Martha Grimes, Mabry Meador let him cool his heels for five minutes with nothing to look at but Martha's stumpy ankles. Teach figured Meador was searching his Bible for a verse to guide him in his trouble with Teach. Finally, a light blinked on Martha's desk. "Mr. Teach, Mr. Meador will see you now."

Teach got up and squared his lapels again. "Thank you, Martha, and, may I say, you look particularly fresh this morning in that cheery spring frock."

Actually, the dress was a shroud of Mother Hubbard design. Martha owned multiple copies in colors running the gamut from mud-brown to soot-black. Teach always complimented her appearance, and she always responded with a tightening at the corners of her mouth.

When Teach walked in, Mabry Meador undid his collar button and leaned forward in his chair. The Bible rested on a copy of the morning paper. *Jesus*, Teach thought, *the subtlety*. Meador was a fair-skinned man of sixty who had the body of a thirty-year-old pole vaulter. When he leaned forward and placed his hands on his blotter, Teach could see his biceps jump in his white shirt. No one knew what kept Meador in such good shape. No one had ever seen him exercise, or heard him talk about the delights of rowing or cycling. Yet he was hard, supple in his movements, and never winded. Teach's theory was that rectitude taken to extremes was a fat burner. He took the chair opposite Meador's desk and waited. Best to let the boss begin.

Meador looked at him for a long time. Finally, he pressed his lips together until they whitened, and shook his head. "Jim, do you know how I found out about this?"

It was a rhetorical question, but Teach answered anyway. "You read the paper?"

Meador frowned.

Teach tried again. "One of my good friends from the company called and *suggested* you read the paper?"

Meador was not a man to suspect comedy in others; nor was he equipped to deal with it. He simply shook his head. "*She* called me. At home. This woman . . ." Stabbing a forefinger at the newspaper. "This Marlie Turkel. She called Saturday morning at ten o'clock to ask me what I thought about you getting into a fistfight in a bar with some—"

"It wasn't a fistfight, Mabry. If you read the article, you know I said the boy was trying to stick up two men in a restroom. I was in that bar having a perfectly cordial drink and—"

"Having it on my time," Meador said.

Four o'clock on a Friday afternoon was no man's time, but Teach decided to let that pass. Ownership of that hour depended on what you'd accomplished, and Teach had had a good week. Maybe he should point that out to his boss.

Meador waved an impatient hand and leaned forward. His tight little eyes and wiry, short-cropped hair were the same color, a corroded gray. "Jim, I'm putting you on sick leave until we have some sort of disposition of this thing."

Meador waited, but Teach did not know what to say. *Disposition?* He tried to recall the company's sick-leave policy. What were you entitled to? *Jesus, a salary?* Had the time come for Teach to negotiate, or was he supposed to throw himself on the majesty of Meador's generosity and get the hell out of here? He took a deep breath.

"Mabry, I didn't expect this. It seems a little . . . extreme to me. I don't see why you think it's—"

"Jim, I know Thurman Battles, and I know what he's capable of doing if he gets a bee in his bonnet about this thing."

Teach thinking, *Jesus, a bee in his bonnet.* It occurred to him that he knew nothing about Thurman Battles except what he had been told by a white policeman, a golfing lawyer named Walter Demarest, and now this man, a Baptist druggist. None of what he'd heard was reassuring, but maybe there was more, or less, to this Battles character than people thought. The more, Teach hoped, might be the milk of human kindness. The less might be something Teach could use against him.

"While you're on leave and we, ah, we see how this thing works out, I want you to consider some counseling. Dan Boyle can recommend somebody, I'm sure."

Teach sat there numb and nodding. Dan Boyle was director of HR, a reformed alcoholic who gave speeches at the retreats on subjects ranging from "Courtesy in the Workplace" to "Substance Abuse and What It Costs Your Employer." Teach had wondered at first why Meador tolerated Boyle, a dullard who had no particular gift for han-

dling personnel. He had finally concluded that Meador loved nothing more than the sinner who had grasped the lifeline. Boyle was the
company's chief sinner. Maybe that was what Meador wanted from
Teach now. A vice president who could talk about "How Counseling Helped Me Overcome the Demons of Alcohol-Related Violence"
or "How I Learned to Stop Quitting Work an Hour Early on Friday
Afternoons." James Teach: Assistant Chief Sinner. Teach shook his
head, sighed. Maybe there was room for a repositioning here.

"Look, Mabry, I realize how you feel about this. It hurts the company, and it offends you personally, but I have to insist that I told the
truth about what happened in that bar. I went into the restroom, the
kid came in and demanded money or else, and I decked him. Mabry
. . ." Teach heard the note of anger in his own voice, "I saved my own
ass and the other guy's. And he, by the way, did nothing but stand
there with his dick in his hand and let the thing happen."

Meador leaned back, shook his head again, his mouth as tight
as a line of small print in a severance agreement. Teach knew he
shouldn't have said *ass*, and certainly not *dick*. As far as he knew, Bap-
tists did not acknowledge the existence of such parts.

"Jim, you know I don't like that kind of talk from people who
work for me. We run a family company here."

"Mabry, the family's not here right now. It's just you and me, and
I'm telling you this kid is a scumbag."

Meador frowned, then leaned forward and began writing in his
ledger. Meador's notebook was famous. He took notes on all conver-
sations. He wrote while people talked to him, giving the impression
that he was far more interested than he really was in what they were
saying. Sometimes, like now, he waited until the conversation was
finished and took notes while you sat there trying to remember what
the hell you'd just said, wondering if Meador was getting it down
right and how he would use it later.

When Meador finished writing, he opened his desk drawer and
took out a bottle of pills in a plastic wrapper. It was the kind of sam-
ple kit drug salesmen took to doctors' offices. "Here, Jim, I want you
to try this. It's a new antidepressant that just came in from Israel.
They've got high hopes for it in the American market. The prelimi-
nary reports indicate a significant elimination of mood swings and

elevated feelings of optimism and well-being. Take a few of these while you're out, ah, resting, and let me know what you think of them."

Jesus, thought Teach, *Jesus Halcyon Christ*. Meador had a medical degree now. He was diagnosing Teach as a manic-depressive and prescribing medication. Teach reached across the desk—across the newspaper, the Meador family Bible, and the man's doomsday notebook—and accepted the pills. "Thanks, Mabry. Uh, listen, can you tell me how long . . . you think I'm going to be out on leave?"

Meador got up, walked around, and extended the small, strong hand that Teach had shaken often, but never without surprise at its temperature: cold. "Let's just play it by ear, Jim. See how this thing goes. The important thing right now is for you to get your life back in order. Okay?"

Teach followed the script as his boss had written it. "Okay," he said, "uh, thanks, Mabry. I take it you'll call me when . . ."

Meador smiled, concerned but finished. "I'll call you."

THIRTEEN

When Teach departed Meador Pharmaceuticals, there was nowhere to go but home and, once there, nothing to do but pour himself a bourbon. He downed the first one, neat, before removing his coat and tie. He tossed the coat across a chair, put some ice in a tumbler, and poured a second sipping drink. He sat at the kitchen table, first in a brooding numbness, then feeling the whiskey trickle into his brain, knitting the severed ends of his optimism far better than any new drug from Israel or any therapist provided by Dan Boyle, Chief Sinner.

The phone rang.

Teach looked at it with dread, then said to himself, *Things cannot get worse. I can answer this phone with impunity.*

"Hello, old buddy."

"Walter? How you doing? Listen, uh, how come you didn't call me at work?"

"I did call you at work, and—"

"They told you?"

"In a roundabout way. You are at home recovering. You aren't expected to be back for a while."

"How long before I am expected to be back, Walter?"

"They wouldn't say. I should say, *she* wouldn't. Your secretary. Seems like a good sport. They've got her fielding the questions. She implies that you have worked so long and faithfully for Meador that you need a rest."

Teach raised the glass and drank until the ice rattled against his front teeth. "Walter, you didn't call to tell me what my secretary is saying."

Walter's voice kept playing that smooth legal note. "No, I didn't.

I called to say that there are, reportedly, big doings over at the law firm of Battles, Brainard, and Doohan. They're preparing a civil action against you. I thought you'd want to know."

Teach closed his eyes. Lord, was there no end to this? Was he to be hounded to hell for a mishap in a men's room, a moment's impulse lacking all malice? "Jesus," he moaned.

Walter said, "Exactly."

After a pause, while Teach tried to think, Walter continued, "Have you considered my offer? I can give you the name of an attorney. The guy is good and not too pricey."

Teach knew he'd be a fool not to take the name, but the idea of going to some stranger about this, letting another pair of eyes and ears, two more raised eyebrows, another fucking attitude, into this thing, was repugnant to him. "Walter, are you sure you won't consider representing me? I'm not a pauper, you know."

If he had to, Teach could sell the condominium in New Smyrna Beach that Paige had inherited from her parents. The property was valued at three hundred thousand dollars.

Walter said, "No, Jim, I don't think that would be best for either of us. I can explain if you like, but—"

"No, Walter, that's all right. Let's leave it where it is." Teach thinking Walter might tell him exactly how much this thing could cost. Then, hearing the phone hit the floor as Teach went into cardiac arrest, Walter could dial 911. Or, in some ways worse, Teach might learn why it would not be professionally advantageous for Walter to take on Thurman Battles. Hell, maybe the two attorneys were in bed together.

Walter said, "Well, I thought you'd want to know."

"I did and I didn't." Teach poured himself another large one.

Walter said, "Let's play a round soon. Nothing like golf to take your mind off your troubles."

Teach said, "Sure, let's do that," with as much cheer as he could muster. He was thinking about the Terra Ceia Golf and Country Club. Did the club have a ceremony for drumming scumbags out of their ranks? Did they march you down a gauntlet of golf bags, striping your bare ass with lob wedges?

"See you then," Walter said, impatient to get off. His time was billed at some outrageous rate by ten-minute slices. He had just spent money on his friend Teach.

"Right, see you. And Walter. Thanks for calling. It was good of you."

"Fairways and greens, buddy." Walter hung up.

Teach knew what he had to do now, had known it for a while, in some part of his mind. It was knowledge he had been avoiding. It was like the swollen, discolored lump you find in your armpit. You have to see the doctor, you know it, but you don't call and make the appointment. You live in fantasy and dread while the cancer grows.

Teach was going to see Thurman Battles. Today. Right now. He was going to announce himself to the man's receptionist and say he'd wait until Mr. Battles could see him. Say he'd wait all day if he had to. Come back the next day and wait again. He had to talk to the guy, see if they could be men about this, work out some compromise so that this air strike on Teach's life might be called off.

FOURTEEN

Teach told the receptionist he needed to see Thurman Battles about a very important matter, had no appointment, and would wait. She was a pretty young black woman with kind, somber eyes and red fingernails so long that when she touched the phone to announce him, she had to flatten her hand against the keypad. Teach imagined her trying to type, then surmised that her job was only to look professional in a simple black blazer and white silk blouse, to communicate good taste, and answer the phone.

Holding the phone to her ear with a padded shoulder, she said, "Mr. James Teach for Mr. Battles," then she listened, frowned, listened, smiled. "If you'd like to have a seat, Mr. Teach, Mr. Battles will be with you in a moment."

Teach, who had expected resistance, expected to have to use charm and salesmanship to get inside, was surprised. It took him a second to pull a polite smile to his lips and say, "Thank you."

He turned to the green leather sofa, but he couldn't sit: he was too full of energy. He clasped his hands behind his newest blue Brooks Brothers suit and made a slow circle of the room, inspecting the certificates and diplomas and framed memberships on the walls. Thurman Battles had more than enough of them, and they were more than extraordinary. Getting in to see the guy might be a good sign. It might mean Battles wasn't going to play lawyerly delaying games, didn't want him out here stewing in his own vitriol, coming in angry or reduced to a web of frazzled nerves so he'd give ground. It meant, Teach hoped, that the man would treat him fairly, talk to him—one decent, well-meaning soul to another.

The phone rang and the pretty receptionist said, "Mr. Battles will see you now. Through that door and all the way back to the last suite." Teach thanked her and walked.

Halfway down the hallway with the plush carpet and the framed charcoal studies of sprinting racehorses, he realized that his knees had a little rubber in them and his mouth a little lint. *Come on, man, relax. You've done this before, the corridors of corporate power, the big meeting.* But most of his experience was selling, and this wasn't selling. This was something else.

Teach tried to take himself back to football, those tense huddles of long ago when a first down wasn't enough. You needed seven points to win and you knelt and looked up at the circle of tired, battered faces, the steam of their breathing rising like they were cattle at a cold morning trough, ten strong young men whose eyes, undefeated, looked at you saying, *Lead us.* Teach drew strength from the memory as he opened the door with the brass nameplate: *Thurman Battles, Esq.*

Inside the suite, a better grade of carpet, more framed history, another pretty black woman (older, no paint on her nails, redolent of education and irony), and another closed door. The woman's smile was warm and small. "Right on through, Mr. Teach."

Teach, who had called the play in his mind, nodded, smiled, and kept walking. He planned to explain what had happened without embellishment and admit that the boy's actions and words were open to interpretation. He'd say he was sorry, not for what he had done, but for the way things had turned out, sorry because this whole thing was, apparently, a misunderstanding. He'd offer to pay Tyrone Battles's medical bills, but insist that this was not to be taken as an admission of guilt. He'd say he was willing to consider any other reasonable restitution (including an apology, private or public) if this thing could stop here, now.

Thurman Battles stood with his back to Teach gazing out the floor-to-ceiling windows at the Tampa skyline. It was a corner office on the thirty-sixth floor of the Barnett Bank building, facing south toward Tampa Bay and east toward Ybor City. The high blue sky was bisected by the towering, deep-purple column of a thunderstorm marching up the bay toward the city. Out across the tall apartment buildings along Bayshore Boulevard, Teach could see the derricks and warehouses of the port of Tampa, and, farther out, a phosphate carrier plowing the roadstead, the diesel smoke from its stack sucked toward the horizon by the undertow of the coming storm.

Watching Thurman Battles's erect, starchy back, Teach thought, *How does he get any work done in a place like this? I'd spend all my time looking out the window.* Then he thought, *No, no, a man can get used to anything. Power, riches, a crippling injury, the death of a loved one, penury and incarceration. People do it every day.*

Thurman Battles turned and observed him thoughtfully, a narrow-faced, balding man with smooth, delicate features, and Teach saw himself kneeling by the front row at the Women's Club to gather the image of his beautiful daughter into a camera lens. This was the man whose wife had said, "Isn't she just so sweet?" referring to the girl listed in the program as Tawnya Battles.

Teach remembered how Thurman Battles and his wife had passed to the front of the auditorium like a natural force, parting the humanity before them. How, when Teach had knelt with his camera, Battles had gazed down at him with the sort of bored expectancy that said he would allow his picture to be taken and he assumed Teach was the human instrument that performed such a function.

Teach was about to begin, *Mr. Battles, it's good of you to see me on such short notice,* but Battles raised a hand, pushed a flat palm toward him. "Mr. Teach, it's my duty to inform you that you shouldn't be here. Your own attorney will agree with me about that. He'll be very disappointed when he finds out you've come here. Now, if you want to leave, the course of action I recommend, I won't be the least bit offended."

The man watched him, eyebrows raised, a pleasant smile on his face. Teach searched the dark brown eyes, the handsome fifty-five-year-old face, for any hint of cruel enjoyment. He saw only a grave, close observation and the expectation that Teach would take the advice he had just been given. Advice others would pay dearly for.

Teach swallowed the lint in his throat and thought about it. He could take the advice. The message in it was clear. Battles expected him to engage counsel and defend himself in court. He had come to see the man and had seen him; maybe this was all that honor required. Teach swallowed again and decided to push ahead. He glanced around the large office—brass, gold, mahogany wainscoting along the inner walls, floor-to-ceiling glass, and open curtains along the outer ones. A single chair stood in front of Battles's desk, a desk the size of a small boat. Teach walked to the chair, stood behind it. "Mr. Battles, may I sit down?"

The attorney lowered his chin an inch, closed his eyes, opened them, and nodded not so much to say yes as to say, *So this is how it will be.* Battles cleared his throat. "By all means." He watched Teach sit, looked at his desk, then walked to a corner by a bookcase full of gilt and red legal volumes and drew up a matching chair, placing it next to Teach's in front of the desk. Some message in this, Teach thought, a big man forgoing his right to look down on a little one. *We begin as equals.* Fine, Teach thought, generous even.

He watched Battles cross his long legs, smooth the thighs of his Armani suit, and then press one forefinger to his temple as though he had just suffered the onset of a headache. "All right, Mr. Teach, what did you come here to say?"

For an instant, before Teach began talking, he wondered if there was a tape recorder running somewhere in the room, quietly making good on the threat of Battles's opening remark. *It's my duty to inform you that you shouldn't be here.*

Teach told the story as he had planned to tell it (as he was becoming, depressingly, so capable of repeating it) without embellishment. Just the facts as he saw them. Battles listened carefully, not moving except, occasionally, to smooth his long-fingered hands across the thighs of his exquisitely tailored suit. Occasionally, as Teach spoke, Battles raised an eyebrow in mild surprise or murmured, "Hmmm, I see."

Teach finished with the offer he had conceived in the car driving over here. He would pay the boy's medical bills and any other fair restitution, and apologize. He knew he had spoken well, kept his tone even and firm, his narrative clear and free of self-serving flourishes. Man-to-man, he had made his offer. It was fair, he thought. Fair.

Battles closed his eyes and seemed to consider it, the forefinger going to the temple again, the eyes squeezed tight. Then Battles armed himself up from the chair and walked to the windows again, his back to Teach. As the older man moved, Teach noticed for the first time the energy of a fading athleticism in his movements. That loose, oiled-in-the-joints, almost bouncing way he'd crossed the room. Waiting, Teach wondered if Thurman Battles had the same athletic past that promised to be Tyrone's future. If he did, then he and Teach had something in common.

Battles turned from the window and stood facing Teach, his hands clasped in front of him. "Mr. Teach, what do you know about me?"

Teach didn't know what to say, but knew the question was rigged. Should he say, *Not much*, and risk offense? Should he fake it, say that he knew the biography of an extremely accomplished local attorney and risk failing to answer any follow-up questions? He took the middle way: "I've heard you're very good at what you do, Mr. Battles."

"I see, and that's all?" Battles watched him now with some impatience. Clearly, Teach had somehow offended.

He had to say more. "I know you're committed to the cause of civil rights." Would this do?

"Ahhh." Battles threw back his head and smiled broadly. "Mr. Teach, I have devoted an entire career to trying to rid the world of the kind of KKK, vigilante impulse that made you strike down a poor, unarmed honor student who had merely stopped in a bar in the white section of this city to use the lavatory."

Oh shit, thought Teach. *Oh my Christ, here it comes.* As Battles unbuttoned his coat, warming to this thing, working himself up, Teach realized how pathetic had been what he'd quaintly thought of as his offer. He had been let into this fine, high office so quickly because the man had offers of his own.

Battles's voice was soft. "Mr. Teach, you are a contributing member of society, are you not?"

Teach was being invited into the game. He chose not to play. Only looked straight into Battles's eyes.

Battles said, "You have a good job in a decent business? Your daughter is a dancer of some talent?"

Teach stiffened, was about to say, *Leave my daughter out of this.* Battles held up a hand, blocking any objection. "Oh yes, I remember you at the recital, taking pictures. A loving father, proud of a graceful and talented child."

Teach nodded. Thinking: *All right, now what?*

"And you tell a lively story about what happened in a men's room. Some of how you see things I'll chalk up to perspective; we all see things differently. Some of it I'll peg to your being a salesman, Mr. Teach. A man with the gift of gab."

Battles smiled, more to himself than to Teach. He began to pace up and down in front of the windows, giving Teach the uneasy feeling that he was walking on purple sky, striding the air in front of a storm. He closed his eyes as he walked and still walked straight, opening them occasionally to glance at Teach as though he thought Teach might crawl away during one of his pauses.

"Oh, I know the gift of gab, Mr. Teach. I have seen what it can do in a court of law. Some have even said I possess the gift in some small measure myself, but . . ." Battles chuckled softly, "they flatter me. Oh yes, Mr. Teach, you tell a lively tale, but even as I listen to it, I am reminded of the many young black men I have known over the years who have found themselves pleading before the bar of justice. Some of them have told very compelling stories, indeed. Perhaps you have heard of the young black man who was sitting in the very electric chair itself, in a Mississippi prison, sitting there with that steel cap on his shaved head and his poor legs strapped down; sitting there with that white hood about to fall over his eyes. Sitting there knowing that a white man stood a few feet away with his hand poised above the switch that would send thousands of volts coursing and burning through his body. Do you know what that boy said, Mr. Teach? Do you know?"

Teach sat there growing numb, sweat breaking out on his forehead, the bourbon headache thumping at his temples. Battles took two steps toward him, bent at the waist, and pushed his face forward. "Do you know?"

"No, Mr. Battles."

Battles drew back, lowered his voice, and smiled. "I shall tell you, Mr. Teach. I certainly shall." He started pacing again, chin lifted, eyes closed. "That boy said, *Save me, Joe Louis. Save me, Joe Louis. Save me, Joe Louis.*" And suddenly, Battles was that boy, breathless, parched, his face twisted, his words a prayer.

Teach sat there thinking: *He's good. He's very damned good. And he's going to do this to me. In the courtroom, he will become Tyrone Battles, and Tyrone Battles will become someone I have never seen.*

Battles opened his eyes, stopped pacing, and gave him a sidelong glance that seemed to invite him into an agreement. "Imagine it, Mr. Teach. A young boy crying out to an athlete, a sports hero, for salvation in his hour of travail. Well, Mr. Teach, I am not Joe Louis." Again the dry, soft chuckle, the sound of a man in a room alone, appreciating the humor in his own thoughts. "I have very little talent in the area of sports. I am a clumsy black man, Mr. Teach. Think of it. I can fall on my face walking flat ground in broad daylight. I had to work my way through Howard University washing dishes in the cafeteria and doing yard work for the wealthy white folks of our nation's capital. I possess no athletic prowess, but I possess the law, and that is a powerful possession to have in your hands when a young black man cries out to you for justice. I can't punch like Joe Louis . . ."

Battles did a little time-step now, kicking his feet out toward Teach in a creditable imitation of the Mohammed Ali shuffle. He made a few jabs at the air and finished with a tight left hook. "No sir, I am not Joe Louis, but I can hit hard in the courtroom, and I intend to do that. You, Mr. Teach, are going to be on the hot seat, and it is going to be my hand on the switch."

Battles smiled brilliantly now, and his grin, his glittering eyes, seemed to Teach to draw their brilliance from the high white sky that poured into the windows. "Mr. Teach, you won't believe me when I say it, but there is nothing personal in this. In my own way, I wish you well. Good day to you, Mr. Teach."

Teach rose and looked at the man, trying to decide what was left here to save. Certainly, he could not renew the negotiations. They were closed. He might appeal to the man, drop to his knees right here on this plush carpet and beg for his career, his assets, his very life, throw himself on the mercy of a man who possessed more money, more wit, and an infinite and brutal resource, the law and its cost, its endless delays, and its perverse reliance on the whimsy of juries. Or Teach could simply preserve dignity, step forward, and shake the man's hand. Say goodbye and walk out.

Even as Teach chose this last alternative, his body rocking forward slightly, he stopped himself. Battles might refuse to shake his hand, and that would be too much.

Teach steadied himself and said, "Goodbye, Mr. Battles. I'm sorry we couldn't come to an agreement."

"Oh," replied Battles, lifting his chin to release that dry chuckle again, "we have an agreement. We agree to meet in court."

Teach nodded, turned on gummy legs, and walked out past the pretty, matronly secretary who did not look up from her work. In the outer office, he stopped, cleared his throat, and asked the young woman with the red fingernails where he might find the nearest restroom. She smiled, glanced at the door Teach had just come through, and then pointed at the door leading to the elevators. "Outside," she said, "then left and left again." Teach thanked her.

In the men's room, Teach bent over the sink drinking tap water, cooling his muddy throat, filling a huge and fragile hollowness. Then he vomited for a long time, a wracking chain of heaves, his only pride that they were silent.

FIFTEEN

So," Detective Delbert said, "your family in an uproar over this thing with Tyrone?"

They were parked at the edge of the county landfill under a flowering jacaranda tree. Those beautiful purple blossoms spiraling down onto the car hood like little umbrellas dropped by tiny tree people. Aimes's briefcase was open on the console between them, case files, photos of four crime scenes, and scraps of lunch spread on it. Aimes looked at the chicken wing he was eating and then at the picture of a dead Cuban prostitute, Carmelita Rojas.

"Only the boy's father's side of the family, far as I know," Aimes said. Word was getting around the city about the lawsuit cooking over at Battles, Brainard, and Doohan. Damages sought for the violation of a young man's civil rights. Compensatory and punitive. Seven figures to salve the wounds. In the crime scene photo, a young, honey-skinned woman lay, legs splayed, in a pile of garbage in the landfill. Some of the Cuban girl's pubic hair was visible in the picture and it made Aimes put down the chicken wing and wipe his mouth with a paper napkin. He cleared his throat. "Delbert, you notice anything about this guy's choice of victims? I mean, assuming the same guy did all four of them."

Delbert looked at him. Was this some kind of test? "Well . . . they were all prosties. Is that what you mean?"

"No, not really." Aimes watched the young cop patiently, letting his eyes say, *Take your time.*

Delbert thought about it, squinted hard, closed his left eye, then opened it. "The same MO—all three shot execution-style, tied up but no bruising, no sign of struggle with the cord, all dropped in dumpsters."

Aimes nodded, not because he liked Delbert's answer, but for emphasis. The idea that had come to him was a good one. He knew this because it was, once you saw it, obvious. In fact, it was plain as the balls on a tall dog. Once you saw it. "The third one, that Phuong Van Tran, was Vietnamese, right?"

"Right." Delbert scooped up a forkful of jambalaya and shook Cholula hot sauce onto it. He brought the hot sauce bottle to work with him in his briefcase every day and doused every forkful of food that went into his mouth. He hot-sauced Chinese, Cuban, even the meatball sandwiches they picked up from Mama Leone's out on North Dale Mabry.

Aimes said, "And the second one?"

Delbert chewed. "Uh, that was, I believe—"

"She was a black girl, name of Aleesha Soyar."

"Right," Delbert said, chewing, his eyes saying, *So?*

"You see anything there?"

Delbert swallowed and said he had to admit it, he saw nothing.

Aimes sighed. "Well, either it's just the bad luck of the draw, or this guy likes them in colors. And he doesn't do the same color twice."

The hot sauce bottle stopped shaking over a forkful of rice, red beans, and andouille sausage. Delbert lowered it, cleared his throat, and whistled like he was calling the dogs back to the fire. "Damn, this guy likes the foreign ladies."

"No," Aimes said, with a little more emphasis than was reasonable. "Not *foreign*. Aleesha Soyer was as domestic as your great-granddaddy, Dwayne the Third. What makes her part of the pattern is she was a woman of color." Aimes thinking he hoped nobody else got onto this, at least not too soon. He could see the headlines: *Rainbow Killer Stalks Tampa. Diversity Murders Continue in Bay Area.*

Delbert was back at the trough. Forking, sprinkling, and chomping. Aimes looked at his chicken wings and felt his stomach maneuver a little. The tuft of pubic hair that sprouted from Carmelita Rojas's bright-red underwear came to a dark, curly point that drew his eye to a pool of dried blood in her navel. Forensics said she had not been raped, although, as with the others, there was evidence of recent sexual activity. The blood came from the single gunshot wound to the crown of her head, indicating, according to forensics, that she had been shot from above and behind and had remained in an upright position long enough for blood to flow down under her clothes to her abdomen and dry there. And that, Aimes thought, was the odd detail. Had the woman been placed standing up in some kind of container for a while before she was taken to the dumpster? And there was another odd thing: analysis of skin scrapings from all of the women had revealed the presence of peanut oil.

Delbert said, "So, you think maybe some twisted character with a taste for alternative cultural experiences?"

Aimes frowned. It was possible. On the other hand, it was just as possible that the killer hated people of color for any of a dozen half-cooked reasons. Or loved them and liked to send them to their eternal reward. Or the guy was just crazy as a poothouse rat. Always a possibility, some guy with his Walkman tuned to that Crazy Station.

They sat in silence for a while, Aimes watching the purple blossoms spiral down. Most of the year, the jacaranda tree was an ugly and useless thing. It gave only patchy shade and dropped a carpet of seed pods that had to be raked and carried away. But in the spring and early summer, it put on this gorgeous lavender show. Looking out over the city from a rooftop, you could see the trees like puffs of purple smoke among the green. If you had to eat lunch in a car, and if the wind was blowing in the right direction, it was not bad under this tree at the county landfill, but it put Aimes in mind of the way of the world: beauty and ugliness cheek by jowl, all mixed up together and boiling like the water when a tarpon hit a school of mullet. Aimes had devoted his life to keeping right and wrong apart.

Delbert changed the subject: "So, the boy's other uncle, this Thurman Battles, he's going to put it hard to our Mr. Teach?"

"Apparently," Aimes said, "he's going to cut Mr. Teach long and deep."

Delbert kept bringing up the thing with Teach, a matter that Aimes considered closed, at least until something official happened that made it his concern again. And it didn't look like anything official was going to happen. The case had moved on to the civil arena. Aimes loved his sister and embraced at least some of an uncle's responsibility for her only son, but he did not like the boy's other uncle, Thurman Battles. Aimes worked for the City of Tampa and Thurman Battles was a bomb thrower. When he threw bombs, they hit the mayor, the city council, or the police department.

Aimes had learned long ago that a black man made it in a white man's world by working inside the house, not chucking rocks at it from out in the yard. There was no disputing Battles's money and success, his position in what some folks liked to call the black community. Hell, when the guy died, they'd probably erect a monument to him on the Franklin Street Mall. When Aimes bought it, he'd be lucky to afford a plot of ground in Memorial Gardens and a decent stone over his head.

But downwind from Thurman Battles, the air had a certain odor. Aimes's cop nose knew the smell, the tang of something not exactly right. He knew he probably wouldn't live long enough or well enough to learn what it was. And there was something smelly about Tyrone too. It wasn't just his big, smart mouth. Every adolescent kid had one of them nowadays. They learned to talk that trash from the rappers and the politicians who told them they were entitled to everything but a day's work. There was a bright, crazy flash in the boy's eyes—it was anger, excitement, something.

Standing in that bar, backing Tyrone off, telling him to cool it, Aimes could have sworn the boy enjoyed the scene he was making. Enjoyed being Tyrone watching Tyrone act up. Maybe the kid would get over it. He had brains, good looks, and guts. Football guts, at least. Kids grew up and found their ways in the world, just like Aimes had done.

Aimes had done well on the high school football field and in the classroom and had graduated from Florida A&M with a degree in sociology and a winning record as a quarterback. But the pro offers had not come. In those days, black men did not play quarterback in the NFL. The book on black men was that they could run and jump and hit—oh Lord, hit you like the midnight train to Valdosta—but they couldn't think. At least not well enough to lead white men in the NFL. It didn't matter that Aimes had called his own plays for three winning seasons at A&M. None of that hand-waving, aircraft-carrier-landing thing from the sidelines.

After college, he had gone into the Marine Corps. It was one way a black man could get respect and security. And the military was a good background for a career in law enforcement. He hoped by the time he finished his hitch in the Corps that the Tampa Police Department would be open to the ambitions of a smart black man. And that was the way it worked out. Aimes had come along too early for a professional football career, but just in time for the Corps, and he'd been a groundbreaker in Tampa law enforcement.

Delbert was running his finger around the edges of the empty jambalaya plate, wiping up all that sausage fat, licking it. Aimes watched a purple blossom land on the windshield in front of him. The good and the ugly. You had to keep them apart, especially in your own head.

"Detective Delbert, how come you keep returning to this thing with my nephew and our Mr. Teach?"

Delbert pulled his finger out of his mouth and touched his temple, squinted, closed his left eye. "Something about Mr. Teach. Ever since I saw him, I keep thinking I'm gone remember it."

"It's the football," Aimes said, yawning, already feeling that after-lunch heaviness setting in. "He's a football star, quarterbacked the Gators."

"Naw." Delbert never seemed to get that after-lunch slump. The guy ate like three tapeworms in a Great Dane and still had the energy of a hummingbird on crystal meth. "Naw, it ain't—excuse me—it *isn't* that. It's something else. It'll come to me. It always does."

Aimes chuckled at Delbert correcting his own grammar. It was like a guy splitting his foot with an ax, then buying steel-toed shoes. "The same thing?"

"The what?" Delbert looked at him, lost.

"You said it always comes to you. I asked if it's always the same thing. You know, that comes to you?"

Delbert's face slowly opened into a smile of recognition. "All right," he said, "go ahead and make fun of old Dwayne, but you gone see. It's gone come to me. There's something about that guy and it ain't—*isn't*—football."

SIXTEEN

Teach sat in his study waiting for Dean to come home. He had to tell her about his troubles. Had to prepare her for what people would say.

A car entered the driveway with a little squeal of tires and a blast of rock music. The radio stopped, and Teach heard the car door open and Dean's familiar giggle, then the raw throb of an adolescent baritone. He looked at his watch. It was nine thirty, late for Dean to be getting home. He had no idea where she'd been. He wanted to go to the window and see who was out there with her. He looked at the empty glass on his desk next to a pile of sales projections. He poured himself another bourbon and tried not to think about Dean out in the night with her friends and everything else that was out there. Hurtling automobiles piloted by drunks, soulless thugs with guns, men who sold drugs to children. Or worse, children who handed other children drugs with the wise smile that said, *It's all right, everybody's doing it.*

What he feared most for Dean was out there in the driveway. The throb of that baritone that still broke from time to time, returning to its prepubescent yawp. That voice held the power that would someday call her away from him, promising a world far from the father who had carried her in his arms. Teach knew it had to happen. He had no desire to stand in the way of Dean's dating, all the rest of it. But he wanted it to be right for her. He wished that he could somehow save her the pain of learning what a woman had to learn.

The quiet outside his study window was broken by the boy's voice. "Cool, Deanie. See you second period." Then Teach heard his daughter's voice, not the high giggle, but a lower, more confident tone. The warm music women played deep in their throats to make slaves of men. Listening, Teach knew there was already a terrain of Dean's he could not enter.

The front door burst open and her shoes slapped the tile in the foyer, then boomed on the stairs. Above him, her bedroom door closed. Teach had time to raise the bourbon to his lips before rock music shook the timbers of the old house. The door opened again up there, pouring the screech of heavy metal down the stairwell. Then the music stopped, and Dean's bare feet descended.

She stood in the study doorway. "Daddy, I wish you wouldn't drink so much."

It was not what Teach had expected. "How much do I drink?"

"Too much."

"How much is that?"

"You have at least two bourbons before dinner, and then you drink two or three glasses of wine. In driver's ed, they said that makes you legally drunk."

"And I seem to come and go safe and sound."

Dean frowned. They both knew she was right. She was wearing a short pleated skirt, almost a mini, and thick white cotton socks. Her T-shirt said, *Animals Have Rights Too*, beneath a drawing of a rabbit holding out its right foot which was a key ring. Her gorgeous face— in the genetic raffle, she'd drawn the best features from him and Paige—was a little flushed and her hair, usually fresh and lustrous, looked dirty.

"What have you been up to?" Teach asked her.

"Cheerleading practice at Missy Pace's house."

Teach nodded. Charlie Pace was a prominent ob-gyn, and Paige had considered their daughter Missy a desirable friend for Dean. But cheerleading had been a matter of contention in the Teach household. The dance teachers said it would ruin Dean for ballet. Teach loved her dancing, but had never promoted it. She would dance if she wanted to. So far, she had shown a remarkable fire. She rehearsed long hours, endured injury and fatigue, and gave up some of the social life other kids enjoyed. Dancing burned time and energy. At Dean's age both were dangerous, and it gave her an identity beyond being pretty or living in a wealthy neighborhood. Now, apparently, she was practic- ing for cheerleading tryouts in spite of her dance teachers' warnings.

Teach wanted to ask how the boy who had brought her home fit into cheerleading at Missy Pace's house. Was the kid an ogler? Had he (and other boys) been invited there? In Teach's own youth, girls would have stoned any male who attempted to watch them hopping like martyrs in the fire of cheerleading practice.

Dean moved into the room, her hips swaying like her mother's had, just enough. Her head bowed, she walked around the study, picking up things (Teach's putter, a sleeve of Titleist golf balls, a trophy he had won in a club tournament with Walter Demarest). She examined these things thoughtfully. Teach glanced at the bourbon glass on the desk, wanted some, but didn't pick it up. She made the circuit of the room and settled on the sofa under the casement windows that let onto Paige's garden. The sweet odor of jasmine flowed in on the night air.

"Daddy, what's going on? The kids at school are talking about you. Over at Missy's tonight, Lisa Dupuy said you were in trouble with the law."

Lisa Dupuy, Teach thought. *The fat little cow.* A gossip just like her mother. He looked at Dean, and she stared back at him, ready to hear what he had to say, ready to believe him. Teach, who, by any standard, had been through hell the last few days, saw the pain in his daughter's eyes and felt like crying. He fought it, could not show her the man she depended on for love and money dissolving into rheumy tears. "What else did Lisa Dupuy say?"

"Well . . ." Dean shot those blue eyes at him, then crossed her legs and dug earnestly at a cuticle with her thumb. "She was whispering to Missy and they stopped when I came over to see what the big secret was, so I said, *Look, would you two like to tell me the big secret here? I mean, like, we're supposed to be friends and all, and . . .*"

Her eyes were misting now. Teach wanted the bourbon, wanted to rise and take her in his arms. Wanted to run like hell to someplace far away where his daughter would never have to see him again. He said, "Go on. Tell me the rest of it."

"So, Lisa goes, *Don't you read the papers, girl?* and I go, *Not lately. What's in the papers I'd want to read?* and she goes, *Your dad, that's what.* After that, I wouldn't talk to her anymore."

Teach sighed and shook his head. It had come to this. Dean,

whose life should be, at least for a little while longer, like the dances she did: fantastic and colorful and loosed from the bonds of earth. She had been dragged into this dirty thing that had followed her father home from a bar.

"Deanie, I was going to tell you about it tonight."

He told her the story. Told her he still believed he had been right, even though things had turned out badly and might get worse. Told her he was sorry this thing had touched her life, that he would have given just about anything to keep that from happening.

She listened in a grave calm. Teach waited. He thought she might complain about the cruelty of things or speculate about how the life she lived, the life of a daughter of wealth, might change, but she said, "Daddy, Tommy, he's the boy that brought me home tonight, he's on the football team. He knows Tyrone Battles pretty well, and . . ."

Teach thought, *Of course, of course my daughter knows Tyrone. All of her friends must know him.*

"And he told me something you ought to know."

Teach considered stopping this father-daughter talk. He could say that he appreciated her wanting to tell him about Tyrone Battles but thought it best for her to stay out of this mess. But his daughter's eyes told him, sternly, to listen. They watched him carefully, and Teach saw something he had never seen before. It was not her love; he had seen that. Her love for him was one of the blessings of the good life that might now be passing. He saw this in his daughter's eyes: she wanted to help him.

"Go on, Dean. Tell me what Tommy said."

"He said Tyrone isn't the kid people think he is."

"Did he tell you what he meant by that? What Tyrone did that—"

"No, he wouldn't go on about it. Those football jocks! They stick together. I had to work pretty hard just to get that out of him." She glanced up at him from the cuticle she was surgically removing with a thumbnail. "Oh, sorry, Dad. I didn't—"

"Forget it, sweetie, I haven't been a jock for a lot of years, and there's nobody much I stick together with but you." He smiled. "Really, it's okay."

She bowed her head, then looked up at him from under her unruly honey-blond hair.

Teach said, "So this Tommy character wouldn't tell you what's not right about the honor student?"

"Nuh-uh," Dean said, "so I asked Tawnya Battles."

Teach sat up straight in his chair. "You *what*?"

"Dad, we're friends. She's a cool girl. You met her at the recital. Anyway, Tawnya, she doesn't like Tyrone because he only dates white girls. And he tells the other black kids she's acting white because she wants to be a ballerina. She told me he's into some stuff that's gonna get him in trouble."

"What stuff, Dean?"

She looked at him, her eyes asking permission to cross some barrier, go to a place from which they would both look back at a lost world. Teach gave her a smile of careful encouragement. "Dean?"

"Drugs. Tawnya says Mr. Tyrone Football Star, Mr. Big-Deal SAT Scores, has a major crack jones."

And that was when Teach saw it, and knew that Dean had seen it way ahead of him. "Go on, Dean, what else?"

"Tawnya says Tyrone hangs with the kids who go out on the causeway at night. You know, they do the bonfires and sit on their car hoods, jamming and playing tunes."

Teach got the gist of it. It was the same in every place, every time. Reckless youth out on the edge of the town, the city, the village. Out where the wild river ran, the cops didn't go, and parents didn't see what happened. There was always that place. Out there.

"Tyrone smokes crack with that crowd, and Tawnya told you about it because he dates white girls? She told you this about her own cousin?"

Dean drew in her chin, held her hand up, and examined the cuticle. "Us chicks hang together, Dad. Don't you know that yet?"

His daughter watched him, a smile that was pure irony, pure woman, purely inscrutable, playing at the corners of her mouth.

All right, Teach thought, *maybe this does wash*. Maybe an allegiance of sex across racial lines is stronger than a bond between cousins. But, Teach reminded himself, Tawnya Battles was telling secrets about her father's client. Maybe she didn't get along with her father either. Or maybe she just didn't give a damn about advancing the cause of civil rights by ruining the father of a friend. The thing was difficult to credit entirely, but right now it was all Teach had.

Dean watched him. Everything was different. This was no little girl. There was plenty left for Teach to protect and guide, but there was something else now. Something wise and, yes, by God, a little cunning.

She said, "You're going out there, aren't you, Daddy." It wasn't a question.

"Oh yes," said Teach, "I'm going out there."

She got up a little wearily, lifted herself from the sofa like a grown woman finishing a long, hard day. She walked over to the credenza where she had stood moments ago looking at her father's mementos. She knelt and opened the cabinet, reached into it, and took out a bourbon bottle. She held it up by the neck with two fingers like it was a decomposing fish, turned to him, and shook her head. She reached into the cabinet again, rising with Teach's Minolta in her hand. She walked over and put the camera on the desk in front of him. "Take this with you."

Teach looked at the camera, then at his daughter, a grin shaping his lips. "You mean tonight? They'll be there tonight?"

"That's what Tawnya said."

"Come here, baby."

Dean stepped into his arms and he held her like some Crusoe coming in to land.

SEVENTEEN

Twice, Teach had driven past the group of teenagers gathered around a circle of cars on the Gandy Causeway. There was no bonfire tonight, just the light from the poles along the four-lane, the headlights of passing cars, not so many this late at night, and a glow in the west from the grandstand of the Derby Lane greyhound racetrack. Overhead, a half-moon dodged the storm clouds riding a fresh wind up the bay. On his third pass, Teach saw the spot, behind an abandoned radio station, where he would park the Buick.

Wearing Levi's and a black shirt, he got out of the car with the Minolta and stood at the water's edge, looking north toward the lights on the Courtney Campbell Causeway, torturing himself with possibilities. What if a cruising cop saw the Buick, the guy thinking Teach was breaking into the abandoned radio station or dumping a body in Tampa Bay (a thing done with depressing regularity lately)? What if one of the kids two hundred yards back up the road recognized him? Was he risking more by doing this than he stood to gain?

Shit, he thought, *stop it. You've got to do this.*

He started back up the causeway, slipping between the mangroves and the surf. It was slow going in the muck, and there were stretches where Teach sank ankle-deep, releasing a reeking marsh gas. He had walked for ten minutes when he heard the murmur of voices and music rising and fading on the night wind. He saw a pathway through the clotted roots of the mangroves and started up the gentle slope, feeling the sand grow firm under his feet.

Sweating, he had stopped to free the camera strap from a branch when he heard, close by, "What's that?" The whisper was young and female, frightened and urgent. Teach sank to his knees, making his profile small against the lights on the Courtney Campbell five miles north.

A second voice, a boy's, said, "I don't know. Maybe a raccoon. They got a lot of 'em out here, but hey . . . they're harmless."

A rustling sound, then the boy pleading, "Hey, come on. Don't put those back on."

The girl: "I don't like this. There's something out there. I don't know what the hell I'm doing here anyway."

"Well, if *that's* the way you feel about it."

The two rose only thirty feet in front of Teach, slim, pale shapes against a dark background. The girl slid her pants up her bare legs, disappearing from the waist down. She put on a shirt and was completely gone.

The boy stood naked in front of her, pale legs and a torso. "Come on, Jenny," he pleaded. "It wasn't nothing. Don't be like that."

The girl's voice was hoarse with fear: "I heard something, Earl. Stay if you want, but I'm getting the fuck out of here."

Teach knelt, rigid, his breathing measured. The boy flung his white arms in a violent shrug, grunting as he put on his clothes. Then he lifted a blanket from the sand and followed the girl.

Lord, Teach thought, *it takes a powerful, skinny need to make love in the mangroves at night. Such is youth.*

He followed the lovers' footprints up a winding path to a spot where he could watch the midnight gathering of outlaw teenagers.

There were about twenty of them, and about half as many cars. The cars were mostly new, and many were upmarket rides. He counted two BMWs, a Benz, and a big Range Rover. In groups, the kids drank beer and talked. Couples embraced leaning against cars, or in backseats. Radios and tape decks played what was to Teach's ears a hellish mixture of noise and garble. The words were a philosophy of loneliness, breaking things, and *want you, baby, baby, baby.*

Though a three-hundred-millimeter telephoto lens, Teach found Tyrone Battles surrounded by friends, white and black, most of them half his size. Teach would have to get closer. He would have to sprint from the mangroves to the nearest vacant car. It would take luck to cross thirty yards of open sand without being seen. He was about to try it when the white Bronco arrived.

The night warriors turned to watch the Bronco roll to a stop near the group where Tyrone Battles held sway. The football player separated from his fans and sauntered over, leaning into the window. Teach aimed the Minolta and fired. He did not know what he could get at this distance, in this light, but something told him he'd need coverage, a complete picture.

He ran to the closest empty car and crouched behind it. The Bronco pulled away, heading back up the causeway toward Tampa. Teach dodged to another car and then to another only twenty-five yards from where Tyrone Battles stood surrounded by young people. The kids wore slashed jeans and Doc Martens and T-shirts emblazoned with logos of bands. Beers or wine coolers hung from their fingers. They were all well on their way to falling-down drunk.

As Teach watched through the lens, Tyrone Battles produced an object from his pocket and moved it to his lips. He raised his other hand and Teach saw the sudden flame of a lighter sucked into the bowl of a glass crack pipe, saw Tyrone's cheeks swell, his face go rigid as he held the hot smoke in for all of its power. Then he lowered the pipe and blew a long gray stream into the night air, following it with a sigh and a shout. "Man, what a brainfuck!" He surveyed the group. "Who's next, man? Step right up here."

Two of the kids staggered away from the group. One knelt to vomit not far from Teach. A girl—by her voice, Teach thought she might be the one whose tryst he had spoiled in the mangroves—said, "Not me, dude. That shit'll kill you."

Tyrone laughed. "Chickenshit white bitch. It ain't killing me."

A skinny, bare-chested white boy with long, matted dreadlocks stepped forward, scratching his upper arm. "Lemme try a hit, man."

Tyrone shoved his hand into his pocket, lurching from the power of the drug, and pulled out another rock. He unwrapped it, tinfoil glinting. He held the pipe to the boy's lips and lit the rock. The butane flame danced as the boy dragged on the pipe. Teach clicked the Minolta's shutter. Tyrone turned away from the boy and looked with deadened eyes at the spot where Teach crouched, then wandered off toward the mangroves. "Pay me later, man," he said. "Right now, I got to enjoy my ride."

Teach kept firing the shutter until the tall football star was gone, staggering among the branches. Then he moved away from the Tyrone circle and shot the other groups, shot all the cars, shot their license tags.

Ten minutes later, sweating and filthy, Teach retraced his steps up the muddy shoreline to his car.

EIGHTEEN

Teach stood in the vestibule of Thurman Battles's office for the second time in as many days. When he told the pretty woman with the long red fingernails he wanted to see Mr. Battles, her mask of cool professionalism slipped. What was the crazy white man doing back here? Hadn't the first visit hurt him enough?

She told Teach that Mr. Battles had a full morning calendar. She doubted that she could work him in, but she would speak with his secretary. He could have a seat.

Teach kept standing. "I have to see Mr. Battles right away." The woman gave him a look of suspicion (would he slip the paperweight from her desk into his pocket while she was gone?) and walked through the door to deliver his message. Teach moved to the wall of Battles's framed accomplishments and opened the manila envelope.

In the little dark room he had built for himself at the back of the garage, he had developed the photos the same night he'd taken them. They had turned out well. The best one, and Teach's best hope for a return to the life he had lived before meeting Tyrone Battles in a men's room, showed the football player sucking flame into the bowl of the crack pipe.

By lucky accident, the boy's head was framed in a corona of light from a streetlamp a hundred yards away. The look on Tyrone's face was priceless. His eyes were closed, his cheeks were hollowed as he sucked the smoke, and his head was thrown back in chemical beatification. His religion was rock cocaine, and its message turned a web of nerves into an incandescent lamp. It was, apparently, a rush more powerful than anything a boy could get toting a pigskin into the end zone.

Teach put the photo back into the envelope with the others

he had chosen—Tyrone holding the pipe to the lips of the skinny, bare-chested white boy, lighting it, holding the flame to the rock.

The young woman returned with a disappointed expression on her face. The door opened behind her. Thurman Battles's secretary stood in the doorway. She was a woman of bearing and dignity who, in a better world, Teach thought, would have been a lawyer herself. She said, "Mr. Teach," and stepped aside, holding the door open for him.

Teach walked into the hallway lined with charcoal sketches of racehorses. He was moving toward Battles's office when the woman put a hand gently on his arm. "Mr. Battles asked me to tell you he can't see you. He said to remind you of his advice." She smiled sadly and looked a question at him.

Teach said, "I remember his advice." He was touched by this. She had taken him inside. She had chosen not to banish him in front of her younger colleague. Teach handed her the envelope. "Please give this to Mr. Battles . . . and tell him I'm waiting."

The woman took the envelope and examined his face with confused, careful eyes. Was she dealing with some kind of lunatic? Was this a letter bomb? Was it a bribe, some pathetic flailing by a man about to sink into a maelstrom of legal catastrophe? She said, finally, "All right, Mr. Teach. I'll give it to him, but . . . as I told you, he's very busy."

Teach waited until she turned and took a step before he said, "Should I wait here or return to the outer room?"

The woman stopped, turned back, smiled. "Please wait here, Mr. Teach. I'm sure this won't take long."

He had examined two of the charcoal studies, a mare grazing under a willow tree with her foal, and a stallion extending his head across a fence toward a woman standing beside an open roadster, when Battles's secretary returned. "Please follow me," was all she said. Her face gave nothing away. Teach guessed she knew only that something unusual was afoot. Good. The next few minutes had to be handled with the greatest care, and the fewer people who knew about it, the better.

When Teach entered and quietly closed the door, Battles was seated, his head bowed over the photos spread across the desk. His elbows rested on the blotter and his slender hands were clasped in front of him. Teach took the chair in front of the desk. The curtains were closed; today there would be no vista of Tampa Bay. This was a dark room meeting. When Battles looked up, he made no attempt to hide his disgust. "So, Mr. Teach, you turn out to be a blackmailer."

Teach had anticipated this, had thought long and carefully about what to say. "No, Mr. Battles, I am not. I'm a man who wants you to know that your nephew, a boy you seem to care a great deal about, is in a lot of trouble. He's a boy with enormous potential. You yourself pointed that out to me. He's throwing his life away on crack cocaine." Teach stopped for a breath, aware that his words sounded memorized. They were. He wouldn't apologize for that. Yesterday, he had sat here in silent, terrified humility while Thurman Battles had delivered his own speech.

Teach went on: "I see myself as a man who is offering you an opportunity that I, as a father, would want for my daughter if she were in such a situation. I'm offering you a chance to intervene in this boy's life before it's too late. To handle this quietly before it breaks into the open. A chance to get him back on the path that people who know him, except of course the kids he does drugs with, believe he's on. I think I'm offering you the boy's life, his future, Mr. Battles. I think I'm making amends for what I did to the boy. I hurt him, I split open his cheek and gave him a scar he'll have for the rest of his life, and I'm sorry for that. But now I'm giving the boy and you something much bigger than that, a chance to heal this wound of drugs. You and I both know it's a wound that can kill.

"You wanted me to be a symbol of white racism, and you wanted to punish that symbol. You wanted to use Tyrone as a symbol of—to use your phrase—*the young black man crying out for justice.* Well, neither of us is a symbol. I'm a man, and Tyrone is a boy, and we've both made mistakes. I thought he had a knife, and he didn't. He's a good football player and a good student and he's using crack. I think you should put your love for a boy above your need for a symbol and get on with the business of saving his life. You've got the money to put him in treatment if that's what he needs. Spend your money and your time on that rather than on ruining me."

Teach considered saying that this was his advice to Battles, remembering how ready the man had been to give advice to him, but he kept this inside. Let him draw the inference if he would.

Battles started to speak but Teach allowed himself the same gesture Battles had used in this office the day before. He held up his hand and stopped the man's words. "You're about to ask me what I want in return. Well, I've already told you I'm making amends for what I did. That's something I want. You can believe me or not about that, Mr. Battles. I suspect you'll think my talking about making amends is a load of crap. You're entitled to your opinion. But I want this on the record. I want to be a good man, just like you do, and I want to live in a good world, and I think what I'm doing here can make good things happen. It can make my daughter able to continue living without all the hell you planned to bring down on our heads. It can make Tyrone a better boy and maybe someday a better man. All you have to do for me is drop this lawsuit. And I think you can find a way to do it without hurting anyone."

While he spoke, Teach watched Battles's eyes, the softening planes of his face, the sinking stillness of his body behind the desk. He watched for signs. Of rising anger, of a stubborn refusal to listen. He saw none of these, only a slow, gathering acknowledgment of the power of Teach's position. "Please, Mr. Battles, let me know what you think. Am I a blackmailer?"

Battles smiled, and Teach knew they were in a courtroom again. Battles had won too many cases, had prospered too well in the law, and had suffered, Teach guessed, too many setbacks in it too. With all of this behind him, how could he answer a simple question simply?

Battles leaned back in his chair and laced his fingers behind his balding head. "Let's say, Mr. Teach, that I see the strength of your position." He waved a sinuous hand. "Oh, don't think I contest the sincerity of your interpretation of things. And I told you I admire your gift of gab."

Teach wanted to say this wasn't about performances, it was about lives. But he'd made his speech. It was Battles's turn to talk.

"But I believe the good life you and your daughter live is built on a foundation that would collapse were it not for the brick-and-mortar of racism. That makes your protestations of your own goodness seem a little silly to me, Mr. Teach. But we live in a practical world, and the practical fact is that you have my nephew by his short and curly hair. I wanted very much to show you up to the city of Tampa for the racist I still believe you are, but it appears that practical concerns eliminate that possibility." Battles collected the pictures, stacked them, slipped them back into the envelope. He opened the desk drawer in front of him and put the envelope inside. "All right, Mr. Teach. I shall do as you suggest."

Teach contained his joy. He nodded and said, "At the risk of presumption, I suggest that you tell the newspapers you've investigated the matter further and you're convinced I made . . . an honest mistake."

Teach saw the danger in suggesting strategy to the better general, but he knew something about damage control. He wanted to help write the history of this sorry event. After all, he was the villain of the pageant. From now on, no matter what Battles said to the papers, he'd be known as Teach, the guy who got into a racial scrape in a men's room.

Battles smiled. "And, of course, you'll give me the negatives."

"Of course," Teach said, thinking, *And I'll surrender my copies of them when pigs fly across the moon at midnight in perfect formation.* He stood and extended his hand to Battles, certain that the man would not refuse to shake it. Battles's grip was firm and brief.

Teach turned and moved toward the door. Battles said to his back, "I underestimated you, Mr. Teach. You've taught me something."

With his hand on the doorknob, Teach turned back. "I had to protect my daughter. You should have known I'd do whatever I could." There had been other times and places when Teach had done what he'd had to do. He'd thought he was doing just that in Malone's Bar, and some part of him still thought so. He still believed it was better not to wait and see if Charlie Manson had come for the pinot noir and the canapés.

As Teach walked the gauntlet of charcoal horses, he found that he was full of joy and a little sad too. Maybe this thing was, after all, more about winning and losing than about right and wrong. He said goodbye to the kind woman who had thought enough of his feelings to invite him into a hallway before dismissing him. He nodded to the lovely lady with the very red fingernails. Then something, call it superstition, made him stop in the men's room to drink again the water of his recent humiliation.

His thirst abated, he turned to the toilet where he had vomited and then to the mirror. He whispered to his own glad face something he remembered from a college class, "History is the story told by the winners."

PART TWO

NINETEEN

In his white Bronco, Bloodworth Naylor followed the delivery truck out to Suitcase City, a neighborhood of cinder-block houses, duplexes, and cheap apartments baking in the sun. He was setting up three girls in a house with a rent-to-own account that would launder what they earned with their ankles behind their ears.

The house in Suitcase City was near enough to the university for the girls to pick up college boys in the bars and clubs. It was close enough to Busch Gardens so they could troll for horny dads who left the wife and kiddies asleep in the motel room after a long day of adorable animals. Those deprived husbands out on the streets letting the real animal out of the cage. Blood Naylor loved the stories his girls told about the johns. Guys with their faces sunburned from waiting in line all day for Wet and Wild with little Susie and little Freddie and mama Mary Beth. Enough energy left to get the wild thing wet. Guys who said they wanted something special and were willing to pay for it. Guys who could always be convinced they'd gotten it.

One of the new girls, Terri, a cute little blonde with six toes on both feet and skulls tattooed on her tits, was riding in the delivery truck, sitting up there like a pit bull terrier between Mook, the driver, and Soldier, the kid who helped Mook move the furniture. The truck was weaving a little and Blood figured maybe the new girl was giving Mook head for twenty bucks. He admired her enthusiasm, and, what the hell, he'd get his cut. He'd been in the life long enough to know the girls who would pay out, the ones who would burn out, and the ones who would get sick of the life and get out.

Terri was a star. She would burn high and hard and then drop like a dead cold rock. She was shooting methedrine into the veins under her tongue. One of the other girls had caught her licking blood from her lips in the ladies' room at the Celebrity Club and asked her what happened. *Some guy get rough with you? Nothing,* she replied. *Nothing happened.* Smiling that gone-from-here smile. Blood Naylor would get what he could out of her and watch her closely. She was the kind who could get him into trouble.

At the house, Blood supervised the unloading while the girls watched, Terri and Marie and Severiana, the Colombian. The girls pranced around trying out the chairs and mattresses and flirting with Mook and Soldier. They told Blood they liked the Barcalounger with the built-in tray table and the early-American dining room set and the two Louis XIV bedroom suites. All of it was recently removed from a house nearby where two of Blood's girls had lived. Redheads, twin sisters from Des Moines, a cheerleader and a majorette who had come to try out for the Busch Gardens Ice Capades show and didn't make the cut.

When the unloading was finished, Blood tipped the two muscle-heads twenty each and went into the kitchen for a beer. Severiana was in there on her hands and knees cleaning out the oven. She had on thick rubber gloves and an apron and was spraying that foul-smelling lye shit people used to clean ovens. Blood admired her ass for a while, watching her shove her head into the oven, breathing hard as she reached way back for that grime. Finally, he said, "Girl, cut that out. You keep breathing that stuff, you won't be able to work. You want, I'll send over a new oven. Have old Mook take that one to the landfill."

She wiggled out and met him with those serious butterscotch eyes. She looked like a good girl, a village girl, somebody's sister. Guys liked that look, thought they were corrupting the woman, turning her away from the path of righteousness for their dick's sake. One of a hundred easy turn-ons. Severiana had been a steady earner for two years, and she didn't do drugs. One of the girls had told him Severiana was sending half her money home to a sister in Cartagena who took care of her kids. When the sister got enough cash together, she was going to bribe Severiana's husband out of prison. Then Severiana was going to bring him to the *Estados Unidos* and set him up in the restaurant business. Blood had told her if the guy came to the

States, she better make sure he wasn't one of those hotblooded Latinos, one of those guys with a butterfly knife who thought his wife was sending home a thousand bucks a month on a maid's wages. None of that shit.

Severiana got to her feet, pulled off the rubber gloves, and dropped them in the sink, massaging her knees. "It's okay. It's clean now. You want to replace something, get me a new dresser. That one you brought me got roach poop in it."

Blood said sure, sure, he'd see to it. Anything to make her happy. He wanted his girls to be happy. Happy and afraid of him and clean enough, quiet enough here in the neighborhood to do business without any trouble. They brought trouble down on Blood, he returned it to them tenfold. That was the deal. It was what they knew.

Severiana had left the newspaper open on the table, some of it lying on the floor where she'd used it to wipe up that evil shit she sprayed in the oven. Blood drank the cold Corona Severiana put in front of him and looked at the sports page, then the city section.

Holy shit, there it was! Thurman Battles dropping the lawsuit against James Teach. Saying the racial situation in the city was too volatile. A long, what was that word, *contentious* trial could take things over the top. Saying the facts of the case were ambiguous. (Why couldn't the guy talk English?) They didn't, in Battles's judgment, merit the time and expense of a trial. And blah, blah, on it went. Lawyer bullshit for the simple fact that Battles was quitting. Blood and Tyrone had handed the guy a perfect opportunity for the kind of grandstanding he loved, and he was letting it slip out of his hands. *What the fuck is going on here?*

Blood tossed the newspaper onto the floor and walked away from the stink of the oven cleaner, the spicy sweat of Severiana, the funky musk of the house (strong despite the air-conditioning he was paying for), and went out to the Bronco. Mook and Soldier had left with the truck. Blood sat in the Bronco with the engine running. It still had that factory-clean smell that reminded him of good hotel lobbies and jewelry stores. He had to think about this thing. Review his options.

He opened the glove box and put his hand on the Smith stainless steel .357. It was clean, unregistered. He kept it near to hand, had

never used it. He did his job without violence or hired out the physical stuff to the dime-a-dozen thumpers you could find in College
Park. What he wanted to do right now was drive over to Teach's
house, knock on the door, screw the barrel of the Smith right into
Teach's upper lip, right up his big fat white-man nose, and pull the
trigger. Keep pulling it until there was nothing in front of him but a
fine red mist.

Blood's hand was trembling, hovering there in the air above the
glove box. All he had to do was take a long drive and a short walk
and pull that trigger. Then run like hell, back to the car, lay rubber
down that fancy Terra Ceia street . . . and then what? Who would see
him there, a black man in a white Bronco driving too fast in the quiet
afternoon? Who would see him there? *Calm down, Blood, calm down. You
got a decision to make.*

He had talked to Tyrone about what Uncle Thurman was planning for Teach. The kid had told him about Teach going to his uncle's
office, pleading for his miserable white-man life. The way Tyrone
told it, the guy was already in a world of shit—laid off his job, his
friends at the country club turning their heads away out there on the
links or the greens or whatever you called those acres where white
people chased a little white ball.

Maybe the point here was that the guy had suffered enough. His
name in the paper, his reputation dirty, his job on the line. Maybe
Blood already had the revenge he needed. Maybe the thing to do was
stay cool, let this thing heal over. Get some scar tissue on it. Blood
had a good thing going, a good business. He was getting rich, and
the cops were leaving him alone. Going after Teach any more was
dangerous, could cost him everything if things went wrong.

Blood started the Bronco. He had to go down to College Hill,
the nasty side of town, the place where the street hos strutted their
butts. He had to because she'd be there and, seeing her, he'd know
what he had to do. Know if that .357 was coming out of the glove
box, or if he could just let this thing die away like a long, sad cry in
the night.

TWENTY

Holding a toolbox and a cooler, James Teach stood on the dock, under the high tin roof of the marina, admiring his thirty-two foot Hunter. The sailboat was named *Fortunate.* He'd bought her after his promotion to vice president and named her for what he felt. Now, he felt like a man returned from the dead. He put down the toolbox and the cooler and flexed his arms and shoulders. He planned to replace the sacrificial zinc on the boat's propeller shaft, change the engine oil, and give the cabin and head a good cleaning in preparation for a weekend sail with Dean. Across Tampa Bay to Egmont Key, then up to Caladesi Island. It would be a celebration of what he was calling—in his thoughts anyway—his new life.

It had been two weeks since Thurman Battles had dropped the lawsuit. In the press release, Battles had made himself look good and made Teach look like the luckiest man in the world. Battles had used some of the phrasing Teach had requested: merit on both sides of the case; Teach's actions understandable given his (obviously lamentable) perspective; both of them acting for the good of Tampa. But in subtle ways, Battles had left hanging in the air the heavy odor of the probability that a lawsuit would have proven Teach to be exactly the kind of white man who'd caused the stormy racial weather of Tampa. Teach's own statements had been terse. And, as agreed, he'd sent the negatives to Battles by registered mail.

He had talked to Marlie Turkel twice. The first time because it was necessary. The second time, as he saw it, doing the woman a favor.

She called early in the morning and asked the same question: why had Battles dropped the lawsuit? Teach could hear her fingers clicking on the keyboard, recalled the grainy photo of her narrow, news-hawk face that ran above her column.

"Did you meet with Thurman Battles?"

He figured she had already called Battles to confirm their meeting.

"Yes."

"Will you tell me what was said at this meeting?"

"We discussed the good of the community. We came to an accord."

Silence on the line. A big mouth, shut. Finally, Marlie Turkel said, "This whole thing smells like bad sushi, you know what I mean?"

"No. Tell me what you mean." He liked it, questioning her, urging her to commit herself to something she might later regret.

"You *know* what I mean."

Teach allowed himself the pleasure of dropping just one turd into her morning coffee: "Community harmony is good news, isn't it, Ms. Turkel? Why don't you write it that way? You folks print good news, don't you?"

Teach used the spring line to pull the Hunter to the dock and swung the toolbox, then the cooler, across to the cockpit. He jumped aboard, feeling the deck move under his old boat shoes. It was three o'clock and hot under the tin roof. He planned to spend a few hours with his mind on autopilot while his muscles did menial work. As soon as he was finished aboard, he'd strip, put on a mask and snorkel, drop the dive platform over the transom, and replace the zinc.

After the newspapers published Battles's decision, Mabry Meador had called.

"Jim, we've got a remarkably good outcome on this thing. Much better than I anticipated. Why don't you come in this afternoon, and we'll talk about the new sales campaign?"

Teach said, "Mabry, can you give me another week?"

We've got an outcome? My daughter hears that an honor student is a drug addict, I own a camera, and we've got an outcome?

Meador cleared his throat, emitted the dry laugh that meant he wasn't quite sure what was going on.

Teach waited, wishing he could say what he was thinking: *You gave me the tranqs for my wild mood swings and my gibbering anxiety. Maybe I'll take the pills now. Get blissed out of my skull and not come back for a month. If you don't like that, we can talk about a separation. Now that I'm not Tampa's own*

David Duke, the opportunities are rolling in. A guy who devotes his life to the good of the community has a lot of employment possibilities. I'm reviewing my options.

"All right, Jim. Take some time, relax. We'll talk next week. And Jim, I want you to know I'm genuinely happy to see you, uh, out of the woods on this thing."

A little control flowing back to Meador's side of the desk. *You were in the woods, Teach, you lucky rascal. Deep and dark in there, boy, deep and dark. Don't stay away too long.*

Teach took the cooler into the saloon and opened it. The six green bottles of Heineken sweated agreeably in their bed of ice. He had resolved to cut down on his drinking. Reluctantly, he had faced the possibility that things might have gone differently at Malone's Bar if he had not drunk so much bourbon. He was calling it a possibility, not a fact, and was facing it obliquely, not squarely. He had brought six bottles of beer and would consider the day a success if he worked hard, sweated out some of the poisons of the last two weeks, and brought home one or two beers. Cutting down was not quitting, it was harder than that.

Teach went back up to the cockpit and took in the quiet marina. Bright hulls rocked gently on luminous green water. Blue, maroon, and white canvas Biminis and sail covers glowed in the shadows. Outboards perched like long-necked birds on transoms, and dinghies swung from davits. This was the clean place, the place where Teach came to think about important things. He had always wanted to be a good man, and, like most, had fallen grievously short of the mark. Now he had resolved to take stock of himself, audit the internal accounts.

He had been good since Paige's death and the end of the affair with Thalia. He had recovered as much of himself as he could from that strange dream of Thalia's cinnamon skin. He had found the old, lost Teach, the man who loved his wife and daughter in the uncomplicated way all good things happened. He had given that man back to his daughter with a redoubled energy. When things got bad inside his head, he held to the idea that he had never left Paige. He had only lost his way for a time.

Teach went into the cabin, removed the steps that led down from the cockpit, exposing the engine. Better to do the hot work first. He studied the cooler, told himself he had not yet earned a beer, and crawled into the small compartment, curving his body into the space beside the Yanmar diesel.

As he changed the oil and filter, checked the hoses and belts, he thought about Dean. She had told him Tyrone's secret. Since that night, he had wondered what arguments she might have had with herself before exposing the boy. He knew her loyalties were divided. A part of her lived in the house of Teach, and some other part had moved on to the house of Woman, a dwelling he could never enter. In that house, Dean and Tawnya Battles had met and agreed that the offenses of Tyrone must be punished. *Us chicks hang together, Dad. Don't you know that yet?*

Teach resolved to know his daughter better. By some pathway still obscure to him, he knew this must lead to his telling her the story of him and Paige. He would begin by teaching Dean the things he knew, things that gave him pleasure: sailing, fishing, diving. Then maybe he could tell her the stories of his past. Let her into the world he had come from, the small fishing town on the Gulf Coast of Florida. Now was the time for them to learn each other. It was no little girl who had come to him in his study. A woman had come to tell him he drank too much and then hand him a camera. A woman should know her father.

TWENTY-ONE

Blood Naylor stood on the loading dock of Naylor's Rent-to-Own, watching the two hookers take up their positions under the jacaranda. The purple blossoms had all fallen and lay rotting on the ground. The tree had its full, dark-green growth now, but it wasn't pretty anymore. The two girls, Imelda and Mireen, one of them in cutoff jeans so tight they split her up the front, and the other in a gold miniskirt and red platform shoes, stood out there jiving to the tunes from a box propped in the crotch of the tree. Pretty soon the traffic would roll down the alley, white men from Suitcase City—college boys, rednecks from Lutz and Brandon—homing in on that booty.

Blood was sad tonight. For a week he'd been telling himself not to fuck up his good thing. Telling himself Teach had been punished enough, the guy running crazy all over town trying to save his job, his life. Blood telling himself to forget about Thalia, what the white man had done to him with her. Telling and telling. But something in there just wasn't listening. Blood looked back into the dark warehouse at the furniture shrouded in dusty plastic, the forklift, the office, the business he had built. Would he risk it all to screw this guy, and all for a woman? He'd asked himself again and again, the answer coming from way down there, some dark place like the bottom of a well: *Thalia Speaks isn't just a woman. She is the woman. She was your woman.*

Blood hated to admit he loved her. He was a pimp. He put women on the street, used them, cut them loose when they were used up, and never got close to them. Oh, he had convinced a good many that he loved them, would always take care of them, but when the time came to let them go, run his game on the next bitch, it was easy to get shut of Susie or Annie. Thalia had been different.

Blood knew that men like him never loved, or they loved just once. If it was never, they were safer in this evil world than if it was once. If it was once, and they were lucky, it finally wore out, went away. He had seen men turn fools for love and get over it. Time did that. The trouble was, Blood had gotten the heart thing for Thalia just before he'd done his five-spot in prison. If he and Thalia had been together another six months and things had run their course, maybe he wouldn't be out here now watching the shadows start to lean over the alley where the two hos were singing some drugged-out imitation of En Vogue's "My Lovin'."

He'd picked up Thalia on a College Hill street corner one afternoon, told her she knew him, knew he wouldn't hurt her, offered her a ride to wherever she was going. She got in his car, in those days a Sedan de Ville, looked around, approving, wiggling the prettiest little butt he'd ever seen on that soft leather, and said she wasn't going anywhere.

"What was you doing out there in the hot sun, girl? You wouldn't be selling it, would you?"

She gave him a sour look, that good-girl-with-the-wrong-man look. She opened the car door, got out, leaned back in. "This girl don't sell it. Anyway, *you* ain't got enough money to buy it. Not even with your rock empire." Referring to Blood's cocaine business.

Blood smiled. "Girl, you be surprised how much money ol' Blood got put away."

"Boy," walking away now, down that hot street, "you be surprised how much I don't care about that."

Well now.

It was a good start. He liked her. She had spirit, stone-fox beauty, and she talked that good trash. Blood found out where she lived and went over that evening. Her sister, one of the fat sopranos who fanned themselves and fell out with the vapors down at the AME Church, told him she might be visiting her Grandma Liston. Another old lady. This one half-blind and using one of them aluminium walkers.

Thalia was sitting on the front porch with this old lady, both of them fanning themselves and drinking sweet tea. Blood introduced himself to the old lady, and she said, "Humph!" and looked off down the street, that fan going like a hummingbird's wing. Blood asked

Thalia if she could come on with him, maybe go down to the Celebrity and let him give her one of them big margaritas, and she said, "No, but if you want to ask my granmon if you can come up on her porch, she might let you sit here with us and drink some tea and pass the time of day."

Blood smiled, laughed. He knew what she wanted. She wanted him to get up on that porch, sink his butt into that rattan rocker like some field nigger courting his Sophronia Marie after services on a Sunday afternoon. Blood was about to walk away, maybe throw an unkind word back over his shoulder, something about how there was plenty of pretty ladies down at the Celebrity that would suck his dick for a margarita and a rock of crack, but something happened just then. That voice from way down the bottom of the well, down where the water was sweet and clean, calling up. It said, *Stay*.

Blood stayed. Sat on that porch drinking sweet tea and eating fried plantains from a real silver platter, talking about the weather and the elections for city council and when, if ever, the city was going to pave the street in front of Granmon Liston's house.

Blood carried Thalia out for three months before he got busted, sent to Raiford. It was a sweet time. Blood was a bad man, that was how it was, but mostly he acted good with Thalia. She wouldn't have it any other way. He got hot-tempered with her, raised a hand to her, talked that nasty trash to her, brought around any of that criminal element, she'd disappear as quick as a chicken breast when the preacher came to eat.

And she made him wait a long time before she did the thing with him. When it happened, it was worth waiting for. Thalia had a powerful way with her pussy. But it wasn't really that, it was her whole self. When he made love to her, he knew he was crossing over into her and letting her into him, and, for a few seconds anyway, they were one glorious, flying black bird.

Blood had never had much to do with religion, not since his Auntie Mary, the woman who'd raised him, had died of a stroke scrubbing floors on the night shift down at the Citizen's and Southern Bank. She'd made him go to church with her until he was thirteen, and after she died facedown next to her mop and bucket, he'd never set foot in one again. But this thing with Thalia, it made him feel like he'd felt in church as a boy of seven or eight when the big black women had opened their throats and let roll that long, low moan that was a bridge to heaven. A bridge of sorrow and joy. When Thalia came for him, she cried out like that, some moan and song and prayer, and Blood had become as addicted to it as any fool was to the cocaine he peddled.

At Raiford, in the cells, when the mail came, it was a quiet time. Jabbering fools who never opened a book or magazine, couldn't tell you a damn thing about the news of the world, would sit quiet on their bunks and lower their heads into some letter from Mama or Sweet Little Sarah Jane, like it was the formula for the bomb that would blow down those prison walls. Blood would sit and watch them reading, their lips moving, hands scratching their heads or, often enough, going to their dicks, completely unaware of themselves. Men who would shank you for looking at them wrong out on the yard.

Thalia had written to him faithfully. At first, he didn't want the letters, didn't want any reminder of the life outside. This prison was going to be his life for a while. A man had to make it here, and he didn't want to be reminded of what was good outside. In the joint, you couldn't live like a kid passing the candy store window every day without a dime in his pocket.

But the letters became an interest and then a delight and finally an addiction. Blood loved them, waited for them, thought about them all the time. Thalia had a good way with words. She could tell a story, write how people talked, what they did, and put you there, make you part of it. Blood liked it, being pulled out of that cell back into her world.

When he'd first met her, she was what he called a good girl. She'd had her share of trouble, dropped out of high school, had some shit jobs, quit them, gone on to others. She'd lived with her fat sister, or stayed with her granmon on the old lady's Social Security. Her mother was dead. She didn't know who her father was. But she was a good girl because she'd never had any worthless nigger's baby, and she never did drugs, and she didn't shoplift or whore out her ass.

The letters were about her life, and what her and Blood were going to do when he got out. How she was going to reform him, get him going straight. But slowly they changed. Thalia got herself into some antipoverty education program down at the local vo-tech school. She wrote to him that the first time she rested her fingers on the keyboard of a computer, she was hooked.

Blood sitting in his cell thinking that the only thing he'd ever rested his hands on that had hooked him was that beautiful place between her legs. Blood not really able to understand it, but happy for her in his way. At least she wasn't falling into bad habits. At least she wasn't running the streets at night with that evil crowd that hung out down at the Celebrity. There were plenty of poontang pirates who'd like nothing better than to turn out Blood Naylor's good girl while he was locked down.

So Thalia wrote about computers, and about how she was learning word processing (her letters showing up typed and printed out), learning to program, learning spreadsheets and databases. She said she was going to get her GED now that she had this jones for computers and see if she couldn't get herself a decent job. She still made fun of the straight, white-man world, talked about what a joke it would be if she ended up in panty hose in some office saying, Yes sir, no sir, to a bunch of white men, but Blood knew she was changing. He could read it between the lines.

For one thing, she wasn't as interested in writing to him. Her letters seemed distracted and vague. She was hearing some voice he couldn't hear calling her into a world he didn't know. She wrote less often, and the letters got harder to read and full of people Blood didn't know. Thalia earned her GED, then took some classes in computer science and got herself a job waitressing at a country club. She didn't exactly say it, but Blood knew she was hoping to meet some people there who could help her move up, move away.

Blood had been in the joint for thirteen months when she got the job, and it was around Christmas when a nigger named Troyal Summers, another fool from the neighborhood, came to Raiford doing a dime for armed robbery and aggravated assault. Troyal Summers told Blood Naylor that Thalia Speaks was fucking some white guy. That she'd been seen with the guy in bars and restaurants where black people worked but didn't eat and drink. That it was a hot but secret romance, the guy being married and all.

Blood asked who the guy was. Troyal Summers didn't know. Just some white guy who belonged to the club where she worked. Well, Blood asked, where exactly is this club? Embarrassed by this, that he had to ask some dumb nigger who stuck up convenience stores with a chopped shotgun where his own woman worked on the outside. The guy said, "Some country club is all I know. Terra Ceia. You know where it is." And Blood said yeah, he knew where it was. (He didn't, but he would sure as shit find out.)

The thing was, it was humiliating. Blood Naylor had become a man of influence in the prison. He belonged to the unofficial committee that solved problems, did deals, sold favors, and kept a lid on the place. Kept it from blowing away in a storm of violence. If this thing got around about Blood's woman on the outside fucking some white man to keep her job, he would be considered a punk. He'd have to seriously fuck with any man who mentioned it, or even looked like he might want to mention it. It was just the way things worked here and, Blood thought, Thalia should have known that, should have given him a little more consideration. Respect.

But deeper still, farther down there in that well where the water was sweet and clean but getting muddier by the day, it was something else. It was the fact that Blood had sat in his cell at lockdown, in the quiet just before lights-out, and reread those early letters of hers, his hand sneaking to his dick, stroking it, making it large with his love for her, with the pictures in his head of what they were going to do when he got out. Blood was thinking of making the woman a permanent part of his life. Turning his addiction for her into something stable, something fortunate.

Now it had all turned into some nightmare of computers and country-club white men and moving up in a world Blood could never earn or buy or even kill his way into. So Blood decided some things. One was that he was going to get that white man, some guy who fucked little black girls so they could keep tapping their ignorant fingers on a computer. The other was that he was going to learn something about that white business world, get himself out of this prison and back onto the street in a way that was at least half legitimate.

That was when Blood stopped opening Thalia's letters. Started sending them back marked *Refused*. That was when he wrote to Lake City Community College about the business courses.

* * *

It was dark now and the two whores had stopped dancing to En Vogue. There hadn't been much traffic. Two or three cars had crept down the alley with their ambers on, nobody stopping to bid for tail. Poonhounds from Suitcase City just looking and rolling on. There were plenty of girls. Girls that looked younger, cleaner, not so crazy. Blood had to get out of here. Had to go see his addiction. His Thalia. *One last time,* he told himself. *See her one last time and you'll know what to do.*

TWENTY-TWO

At sunset, Teach anchored the *Fortunate* off the north end of Caladesi Island. The Hunter swung on generous scope in a gentle current running south toward the mouth of Clearwater Bay. Caladesi was deserted now. The park rangers cleared the tourists off at dusk, and the island recovered itself for twelve hours, becoming again a land of fiddler crabs, great blue herons, and raccoons.

A gentle breeze cooled the cockpit where Teach sat drinking a Heineken and watching his daughter swim. This time of day, the hot land pulled cool air in from the Gulf. He raised the cold bottle and drank to the breeze, then raised it a second time for a general thanksgiving. He was a free man again, relaxing in a seaworthy craft, and his daughter, graceful as an otter, was swimming in the sunset light.

Dean surfaced, threw back her head, tossing diamond ropes of spray. She held something up to him. "Daddy, look."

It was a horseshoe crab, about the size and shape of a German army helmet. It had a six-inch spike for a tail and ten struggling legs. Teach laughed, admiring her fearlessness. She just didn't have that *eee-ewww* reaction in the face of the slippery and the crawly.

"Will he hurt me?"

"Far as I know, he's harmless."

Treading water, she let the crab go, and Teach watched it bank and drift toward the sandy bottom. He remembered from his boyhood seeing the crabs congregate at mating time, knew they were not crabs but seagoing spiders. He remembered standing waist-deep on a mangrove flat, spin-casting for redfish and seeing the water around him for fifty yards go completely dark with sex-driven armies of these outlandish animals.

Memories. Teach had been having them lately. Feeling the strong pull of the places he had called home the first eighteen years of his life. He got up and stretched, looked out at the horizon. The line where the sky met the Gulf was fiery red. He said, "Deanie, I'm going forward to check the anchor lines. Why don't you come aboard in about ten minutes?"

Dean did a surface dive, her arms sweeping out, head plowing, legs rising perfectly aligned, slipping under. She came up with a sand dollar. Treading, she tossed it to him. "Come on, Dad. Let me stay in longer."

Teach tossed the sand dollar back to her. "Ten minutes," he said.

He went forward to the gently dipping pulpit. Earlier, he'd swum out to check the anchor line, found the Danforth buried deep, but he couldn't let darkness fall without checking again. His landmarks on the island showed him that the *Fortunate* was not dragging her hook. Teach glanced behind him and remembered making slow, sweet love to Paige up here on a bed of cushions while Dean, a child, slept in the V-berth below. Something about the proximity of the island, its primitive odors on the wind, the wildness of the Gulf stretching all the way to Corpus Christie, gave him a sudden, sad yearning for Paige and for their youth, for the time when all had seemed possible. The time when there had been plenty of time.

He looked north. The next coastal stop was Yankeetown, after that came Cedar Key where he had been born and had grown to a raw manhood. For him, it had been a place of beauty, family, and, finally, of trouble.

His father had captained a shrimp boat and had made a good living until one night from somewhere out in the middle ground, that vast chain of reefs in the northeastern Gulf of Mexico where the shrimp were plentiful but the weather was uncertain, the *Janey Anne* broadcast a distress call. Jimmy Teach's father gave his loran coordinates, and then said, "I am forced to . . ."

No one ever learned what the captain of the *Janey Ann* was forced to do. At sunset on the third day of the search, Jimmy Teach stood with his mother, Janey Anne, on the Cedar Key dock while a Coast Guard lieutenant commander told her he'd done everything he could.

After that, the Teaches, mother and son, were poor, and after five years of watching his mother come home at night from double shifts in a seafood restaurant, Jimmy resolved to do something about it.

One day at football practice, he was approached by an older boy, a varsity linebacker. Big and strong and looking older than his years, the linebacker took Jimmy Teach aside and asked him how well he knew the waters around Cedar Key. "Like the back of my hand," was Jimmy's proud answer.

"Good," the older boy said, smiling. "That's damn good, son. How'd you like to make some money?"

Teach was young, but no fool. He knew what the boy wanted. He considered it, thought about his mother falling asleep in front of the TV every night with her swollen feet in a tub of hot water, recalled what he'd heard people say about jail, then said he was interested.

So began the wild early days of the Florida marijuana trade. The older boys, together with some friends of theirs in the university city, rented trawlers from marinas in Homestead on the east coast and crossed to Freeport where they stuffed the boats to the gunwales with bales of spicy weed. They steamed back through the Florida Straits, skirting the ten thousand islands, always making Cedar Key at nightfall. Teach's job was to meet the boats offshore in a skiff and pilot them in through the narrow, treacherous channels to a spot where a rented U-Haul truck could be driven close enough to the bank for quick and quiet off-loading.

Teach carried bales with the other boys, then skippered the boat back out to deep water, untied his skiff from her aft rail, and waved goodbye to the boys who motored back to the east coast marina with plenty of time to clean the trawler of every trace of hemp. It was a good business for a while. There were no Guatemalans, there were no guns, and the federal authorities on land and water were under-staffed and slow to notice the rising style of life in the sleepy fishing towns. To fourteen-year-old Jimmy Teach, marijuana was nothing but a weed, and the money was a fantastic dream.

For a night's work, Teach was paid fifteen thousand dollars. The first time he took an envelope fat with cash to his mother, she was lying in her bedroom on a Sunday afternoon, listening to the Beatles sing "Norwegian Wood" on the radio. Teach knocked and entered quietly. He watched her lying there with her arm thrown over her eyes, her tired feet elevated on a cushion from the chair across the room. "Mama," he whispered, "I got something for you."

She didn't lift her arm, and Teach imagined the darkness in her eyes, what she saw in it, and how many times she had relived that night when the phone rang and Charlie Trimble, a local deputy sheriff, had told her the shrimper *Janey Anne* had sent a distress signal from the middle ground. He remembered his mother from the early days as a beautiful woman with light and love in her eyes, and a special, secret way of smiling when his father entered her kitchen in the morning. Now she was always tired, and she drank cheap wine when she sat at the kitchen table at night trying to balance the checkbook, pay the bills, buy her son the clothes the other kids were wearing to high school.

Teach walked across the dark room, turned down the radio, and put the fat envelope under his mother's right hand.

"What is it, Jimmy? Ain't you supposed to be working down at the Baybreeze by now?" She meant the restaurant where he bussed tables.

"Go ahead," he said, "open it, Mama."

She pulled her arm from her eyes, touched the envelope, and slowly sat up. She composed her face the way he remembered it from Christmas mornings when his father was alive. Her son had given her something and, even though it was probably some absurd trinket, it came from the altar of his love, and she would make big eyes and tell him in a girlish voice that it was the best gift a mother ever had. Teach watched her closely. When she opened the envelope, her eyes went small, then dark, then her mouth tightened and her jaw muscles jumped, and then everything that had been slow was fast. Her hand struck like a snake, and Jimmy Teach was backing away with the burn of her fingers across his face.

"Take it away. Get it out of here. I don't want it. And don't you ever tell me where it came from. I don't want to know." She stood over him in her rank, food-stained waitress uniform with *Janey Anne* stitched above her breast, her hands trembling at her sides, her face pale with anger.

"But Mama, I . . ." He wanted to tell her that she wouldn't have to worry now. That he wouldn't get caught. That the boys would make only a few trips. That they would be careful with the money, not flash it around. He wanted to tell her he'd done it for her, done it from his love, because he hated to see her so tired, so worried, muttering to herself about how much things cost. He wanted to say that he would take care of her now, just like his father had done.

Jimmy Teach didn't say any of these things. He backed out of the room touching the hot print of his mother's fingers on his cheek. A month later, he put the second envelope on the kitchen table in the morning and waited. His mother said nothing about it. She had said she didn't want to know, and Jimmy Teach took her at her word. At noon, the envelope was gone. It was from his mother that he learned to keep secrets.

She bought him school clothes and herself some new things too, and she stopped working doubles at the restaurant. When the old Ford Ranger pickup died, she bought a new truck in a town fifty miles away, nothing fancy, and after that life went on with no muttering over the checkbook, and bottles of wine with better labels on them. Teach and his friends made five trips in all, and his cut for maneuvering a big, sluggish boat in a tight spot at night was $75,000. His mother opened bank accounts in Trenton, Newberry, Bronson, Williston, and Archer. She kept her job at the restaurant, never dated, never remarried, and she and her son lived without want until she died of a cerebral hemorrhage during Teach's freshman year at the University of Florida.

Bloodworth Naylor, a boy from Rosewood, the black town not far from Cedar Key, joined the group of teenage smugglers halfway through their run. One of the football players brought him in, a boy who was considered smarter than most. The boy vouched for Naylor and said they needed a black kid to sell to his people in the university city. In Cedar Key, things were uneasy between blacks and whites, but this was business, and the young Naylor, who also seemed smarter than most, did his job well.

Teach knelt in the pulpit of the *Fortunate* and gave the anchor line a last tug for luck. He felt the boat move with Dean's weight as she climbed over the transom. He went aft and watched her towel off, marveling at the supple beauty of her limbs. She'd danced since she was six years old, and her flexibility was a thing that made Teach wince. She could stand on one foot next to a wall with the ankle closest to it pressed against her ear. Smiling. Her arms and calves were muscular without the bulk or excessive definition that, at least to Teach's eyes, seemed masculine. To him, she represented everything that was decent and fine about growing up healthy and disciplined in America.

She tossed the towel onto a cockpit bench and looked at the beer in his hand. "How many?" She put her hands on her hips, tilted her chin, and made scolding eyes.

"The first," Teach said, laughing. "Shall I write them in the log for you?"

"No need. I trust you. Can I have one?"

He looked at her. Paige had explained to him certain principles she considered to be European. Let the children drink with you, and you habituate them to alcohol in a congenial, responsible way. At dinner Paige had given Dean glasses of wine mixed with water saying it was what French parents did. Dean had drunk the mixture, smiled like a pirate's wench, and said she'd rather have half a glass straight up.

Teach went to the cooler and got her a Heineken. They touched bottles. "To getting away with it," he said, watching his daughter's eyes.

She thought about the toast, then gave him the look of mischief and delight he had hoped for. She drank and her eyes darkened. "Dad, do you think it's really all over?"

"Sure," he said, not entirely sure. "You want a freshwater shower?"

"Naw, it's only twelve hours till I go swimming again."

"That's my girl."

Teach went below to get some grouper filets for the grill and the things Dean would need to set the table in the cockpit. It was fully dark now, and he hung a Coleman lantern from the backstay.

"Daddy," Dean said, "Tawnya told me Tyrone's going to a special prep school up in Massachusetts. It's called Bede. They've got a football team, but it's nothing like ours, and the school's full of behavior problems. She said it's one of those places where the Kennedys and the Rockefellers send their kids that get the XYY chromosome or something."

"She said that? That Tawnya's some girl."

Dean set the table with paper plates and two more beers. She put out a container of potato salad and some apples. Teach looked at the beers, at his daughter. Dean smiled. "Come on, Dad, this is our getting-away-with-it cruise."

"All right, but that's it. You'll be swimming with a hangover in the morning."

"You think that school can really fix a guy like Tyrone?" She looked at him with hope in her eyes.

Teach had no difficulty reassuring her. "Sure I do, baby. They know what they're doing. In two years, they'll get him into Princeton. And Princeton's got a pretty good football team."

Dean was sitting now, watching him season the grouper filets. He wanted to protect her faith in the world. "Tyrone's lucky to have an uncle willing to invest in his future like that. Incredibly lucky."

In the lantern light, Dean's face was serious. "So," she said, "you could say we saved Tyrone. You and me and Tawnya."

Teach nodded, took her hand, and kissed it. "Yes, baby. I think we can say that."

"Good. Can I tell Tawnya that?"

"Sure, honey. Go ahead and tell her."

And why not? Maybe news of saving grace was in short supply for two young friends, a black girl and a white one, growing up in the last decade of the twentieth century.

TWENTY-THREE

Thalia lived in a duplex in Suitcase City. Blood knew she didn't have a roommate like most of the other girls did. They lived together for protection, for family. Better to have somebody with you, even if she's in the life. Better a ho than nobody. Blood wondered how many little ho families lived in the Suitcase. He was daddy to a lot of them himself. Thalia lived alone. Blood knew that much. He'd followed her home before.

The day he'd learned that Battles had dropped the lawsuit, he'd followed her all night, watched her do four tricks, watched her smoke crack behind a dumpster with two other girls, watched her stagger the streets after that, singing, muttering. One of the walking dead. One of the zombitches.

She had fallen hard since she'd been the good girl who'd taken Blood's heart. Her letters to him at Raiford, before he stopped reading them, had told him what it was like to rise up to that world of white people. In the last letter Blood had read, she'd told him how she loved the quiet at the country club. Nobody screaming, jiving, laughing, telling loud stories. She had written, *I love how it's just so peaceful.*

Thalia's place was like a thousand others in the Suitcase. A lime-green cinder-block rectangle that held two apartments. Paint peeling from the walls, the roof shingles blistering under the hammering sun, dead oleanders in the yard. Blood parked a half-block down and watched the street for a while. Two Harleys with rebel flags painted on their gas tanks across the street. A diesel tractor parked in the driveway of the house next door. Canvas awnings in drooping shreds from the last tropical storm. A half-dead Doberman lying in a sand hole near the curb where Blood was parked. The dog watched him, but didn't have the energy to come over for a sniff or a snarl.

But somebody was sniffing. A black man, wearing a purple shirt and green slacks, came out of Thalia's front door and stopped on her walk, looking both ways like his wife might be waiting out there. Dude looking down at his tight green pants, running his hand up the zipper, tugging it the last inch, then walking to his car. A new Mustang 5.0. Thalia could still attract a client with money.

When the guy drove off, Blood walked up to Thalia's apartment. Before knocking, he thought about it one more time, why he was here. It was some fool's combination of wanting her to quit the life and come back to him, and wanting to see her so fucked up he could forget about her forever. He could hear music from inside, Marvin Gaye singing "Sexual Healing," and see the soft light coming through the curtains. Thalia liked candles, little lamps with colored glass shades, mirrors that reflected light. She liked anything that smelled good— incense, flowers, candles that released a scent when they burned.

Blood tried the door and it opened. He moved across the dark living room to the bedroom. She was lying on the bed in a filmy rose-colored robe and black underpants. Her small, firm breasts were bare. She was smoking a cigarette and humming to Marvin's smooth, cool jam.

Blood watched her. He hadn't been this close to her in more than two years. The crazy thing was that she was still beautiful. She couldn't have weighed more than a hundred pounds, and her cinnamon face was gaunt. She looked like those Somalis Blood had seen on TV, so pretty in their starvation. Their copper cheeks scooped out, and their eyes burning bright with that need. Thalia had the large, surprised eyes of a doll, but her mouth was thin for a black girl, and her pretty little chin had a small cleft. It was a strong face, a face Blood had once thought had character. Now, with her eyes closed, her mouth moving, the cigarette coming and going from lips too tired to suck much from it, she looked like a woman singing in her sleep.

Blood looked around the room. A condom and two empty wrappers on the floor beside the bed, a hundred-dollar bill on the night table, a crack pipe and two rocks beside the money, and a pretty blue scarf thrown over the bedside lamp. The light shining through the scarf gave the room a blue wash. Scarves hung all around the place.

Scarves in wild colors and patterns, all of them silk, all expensive. Blood smiled, remembering the scarves.

Candles, twenty of them at least, burned on every surface. They stood in saucers and teacups and on pieces of colored paper, smoking, scenting, dripping in weird, tortured shapes. Quietly, Blood walked over to a candle on Thalia's night table. The hot red wax had run onto the tabletop, pooling around a tube of red lipstick. He righted the candle.

"You doing here, nigger?"

Blood jumped, concealed it with a pivot, a nod of his head. For all his thinking about her, following her, planning to come here, he had no idea what to say. No idea who he was tonight. Was he the man who had kept his evil friends away from her, who had never raised a hand to her? The man who had gone to prison planning to come out and make a life with her?

"Looking at you, woman. Watching you lie there singing to yourself."

Thalia threw her legs off the bed and sat up, bracing herself with both hands. She lifted a hand to her forehead, held it there, then reached for the crack pipe. In two big strides, Blood was there, twisting it from her fingers. She fought him for it. When he won, easily, she shrugged, laughed, fell back on the bed, her legs parted, the black panties wet between her legs.

Blood looked away from her. "Goddamnit, woman, you've had enough of that shit for one night."

"Listen to him." Her voice was a low slur. "Man sells it, promotes pussy with it, and he tells me I had enough of it."

"Never mind what I do."

Thalia looked up at him, smiled. "Long as you here," she said, "you might as well come on down here with me. Course, you got to pay just like everybody else. Thalia Speaks don't give it away no more. You got to *pay*."

Blood made himself look at her. She parted her legs a little more, threw her arms back, laced her fingers behind her head. "Come on, John," she said, calling him by the age-old trick's name. "What you waiting for?"

Blood reached down and threw one wing of the long, filmy negligee over her. It didn't cover much. That was the point of it, to tease. But he did it, then turned way. "I didn't come here for that, Thalia." Saying her name. Something important in that. He remembered it now, calling her just *Thale*. Using that name when they made love. She moved on the bed behind him.

"Answer my question then, Blood. What you doing here?" She was talking the street to him, talking the hood. Taunting him with it, making him remember how she had learned to talk like a white woman.

Blood made his own voice as correct as he could. "I don't know why I came here. I just wanted to see you."

"Why you want to see this ol' ho?" She was driving it in, giving him no room.

"I told you, I don't know." The anger in his voice surprised him. He was about to say he'd had to come, but he couldn't let her know that.

He turned. She was lying on her side with her head propped on her hand. One leg thrown over the other now, hiding that beautiful, slave-making pussy from him. Blood was thankful for that.

"Oh yeah," she said, "I got it. I know why you here." She pushed herself up and snatched the scarf from over the lamp on the bed-side table. The room was suddenly brighter, and Blood blinked like something soft that lived under a rock. A thing with no skeleton inside it. Thalia stood up unsteadily and walked across the room and turned on the overhead light. "You came here to see what you made me into. That's it. Well, here it is, look at it." She threw her arms out and stood in front of him, crucified, smiling.

"Bitch," Blood said, "I didn't make you anything. A white man did that. Mr. Teach. Mr. Drug Company Vice President did that." *And a howling hypocrite too*, he thought. *The man I smuggled with, the man who told me one night in a bar he had to disappear.* "And I advise you to do the same," Teach had said that night in Cedar Key. Teach's eyes narrowing with the pain under the bandage in his armpit. And when Blood asked what happened out there, what happened after Teach the pilot left with the shrimper and the three Guatemalans, and Blood drove the load to Gainesville, Teach would only say, "It's better you don't know that."

Thalia looked at him fiercely, took a step toward him, another, still holding her arms out straight. She knotted her fists, the muscles of her arms rigid. "No, Teach just a *weak* white man. You a fucking ho master. You a fucking pimp. You made me, not him." She coughed, staggered from the effort, the anger.

Blood went to her, took her by the shoulders, and lowered her to the bed. There she was again on her back, her legs spread, the dark eyes of her firm little breasts watching him. She was exhausted from talking to him, telling him her truth.

But she didn't mean *him*. She meant someone like him. Some other pimp who had turned her out while Blood was still in the joint. Some pimp who had put her ass to work after she'd fallen out of that country club and smoked her first pipe of crack. Some people smoked crack once, and it owned them forever. She was one of them. It was the way Blood had been the first time she'd let him inside, the first time she'd come to him with the song of her pleasure. No nigger would have dared touch her if Blood had not been locked down.

Standing over her again, observing her exhaustion, the pain she said was his gift to her, Blood understood it. Knew what he had to do. He let down his trousers and touched himself, surprised to find that he was already hard. The power she had. The thing that had to end here tonight. He tore open the wrapper of the condom and put it on. Then he knelt and slipped off her panties, opened her, pushed up her knees, stared into her eyes. They were smiling, they understood, they knew this had to happen. Blood put himself in, started working, long, slow strokes. Feeling it, that magic she had, that thing no other woman could do. Now he understood it—working, the sweat rising on him, the pleasure filling him—knew what he could do for her. The thing no one else could do.

He worked her, watched her until she started to feel it too. Until he knew she was past that working-girl-faking-it thing and into her own pleasure, feeling it. Until she was his again. Only a little, only a little, but his. When she smiled that tired, take-me-on, let-me-go smile, when she raised her hand to his cheek and slowly stroked it as he drove into her, Blood reached down to the floor where his feet struggled for purchase and felt the scarf come into his hand, the one she had snatched from the lamp.

He smiled at her, working, and threw a loop of it behind her neck. She lifted her head, helping, still stroking his cheek, those dark, bright, starving eyes telling him it was all right. Saying, *Go on, go on, it's all right.* She lifted her head and Blood threw another loop around her and began to draw it tight.

When she understood it, her hand froze on his cheek. He felt her nails dig at him for a second, the pain hot and sharp, then felt her stop it. Felt her seize his face in both hands and lock her strong, dark, starving eyes to his.

She let him do it. As he pulled the knot tight, he watched as she shuddered and gnawed her tongue, and her eyes filled with blood that doubled their size and mapped them with broken vessels, watched until her hands fell from his cheeks and her chest was still. And Blood came. It was glory and sadness, purpose and conclusion. The hot seed shot out of him for a long time.

Blood withdrew and looked at his hands. They were shaking, still holding the ends of the scarf, still pulling. *My God*, he told himself, *stop it or you'll cut her head off.* Quickly, carefully, he loosened the scarf, letting the blood escape from her eyes, looking into them. They were terrible, yes, but they thanked him, even in the terror. They said she had understood, that she had known what he could do for her, what only he could do. Blood stood looking down at her, loving her, hearing that voice from down in the well where now the water was fouled forever, that voice saying, *You released her. You let her go.*

TWENTY-FOUR

B lood sat in the little kitchenette, his back to the body on the bed until his head cleared, until he knew how stupid it would be to leave here without fixing things. He stood and turned to the bed, telling himself all the comforting things about how he had let her go, released her. A long, shuddering breath left his chest because now she wouldn't be staggering the streets, a zom-bitch with that accusation in her eyes.

And she moved.

The woman moved. She thrust her legs out, and a big, sorry sigh came from her throat like some insane imitation of Blood's own tired breath. His legs took him to the front door before his mind could stop them, tell him there was some reason for this. Something a doc-tor could explain.

He crept back to the bedroom, toward those flickering candles and sweet smells. He didn't know what to expect. Maybe she'd be ly-ing there on the bed like before, smoking, jamming to Marvin Gaye.

She lay where he had left her. Her eyes flamed with blood, their accusation fading, almost gone. He moved close and looked down at her. It must have been some last shock of the nerves, her body's final protest against this shitty life. That convulsion and that sigh. Now she was settling, sinking. He touched her cheek with the back of his hand. She was warm, but not human warm. His hand flinched from her face.

He tried to see himself walking into this room an hour ago. What had he touched? He went to the vanity and pulled the candle he had set upright from its pool of wax, blew it out, and stuck it in his pocket. He didn't remember his hands lighting anywhere else except on the front door latch, and he would wipe that on the way out. He didn't think they could take prints from a scarf. The condom wrappers, the crack pipe, and the money on the night table told the story. A hooker killed by one of her johns. The used condoms were gone, flushed. The guy Blood had seen leaving here was the prime candidate for a lethal injection at Raiford. His fingerprints were on the money, the condom wrappers. *Good*, Blood thought, *good*. Then he saw the photo album.

It stuck out from a neat row of cheap paperbacks in the small bookcase near the night table. Blood remembered how she'd liked to read romance novels, a chapter or two before she fell asleep. Blood lying beside her, asking her what it was about them she liked—a bunch of white women getting chased around by men who didn't know what their dicks were for. Thalia always smiled, shook her head at his stupidity. "They're sweet, that's all. You got to have something sweet in your life."

Blood pulled down a scarf that was draped over a curtain rod, covered his hand with it, and slid the photo album from the bookcase.

The album was full of pictures of Thalia—as a little girl on a sidewalk holding a skinny white dog, as a high school kid with girlfriends all trying to look like Diana Ross, as a granddaughter dressed for church with her grandmother, Old Lady Liston. Blood closed the album and put it back on the shelf.

Keeping his hands in the scarf, he searched the apartment. It didn't take long to find the cardboard box under the bed. A little black girl's pathetic stash of memories. She had saved papers from her job at the country club—pay stubs, a newsletter listing her as a new employee, a letter from the manager commending her for turning in a wallet she had found in the parking lot. But it was what he found next, that was the thing. Pictures of her and Teach. Teach and Thalia in a restaurant on a dock with boats in the background. Maybe Tarpon Springs, maybe Sarasota. Blue water, white sand, and Thalia looking like a *Jet* model in a yellow sundress. The restaurant table piled with food, the big smiling jock, Teach, using his money and his white-man sophistication to promote the pussy of Blood's good girl. In the pictures their eyes were drunk, the white man's and hers. Drunk with love and Bacardi.

It made Blood angry and sad, looking at the pictures. In the grimy

album of his mind, he could see pictures of himself at Raiford. Blood
Naylor pumping iron out under that hot tin roof on the yard (Teach
and Thalia sipping rum from tall glasses with little paper umbrellas
in them), Blood Naylor at counting-in, standing in a long line of blue
denim in the rain while the hacks checked names from a clipboard
(Teach and Thalia laughing with the sun shining out on the Gulf),
Blood Naylor sitting in the Rock cafeteria eating beans and greens
and greasy corn bread for the thousandth time (Teach and Thalia
eating lobster from that turquoise water), Blood Naylor working a
sheet-metal press in the tag plant, trying like hell to keep all his
fingers, stamping out plates that said, *Florida State Seminoles*. It made
him angry and sad. It made him want to know all there was to know
about Thalia's time with Teach. Teach, his old associate in crime, the
guy who had jodie'd him while he was in the joint.

Then, holy shit, it came to Blood that she might have saved his
letters. The ones he'd written her from Raiford before he'd heard she
was doing the white man. Sure enough, he found them at the bottom
of the box, tied with white string.

A dozen letters scrawled out on prison stationery with a pencil stub, letters that leaked from Blood's heart the strange, harmful
truth of his love. He imagined himself accused of this crime and his
letters read aloud in court by some smart-ass prosecuting attorney.
Just thinking of it made his head, his chest ache like they had been
beaten with a fist. His face burned at the thought of what she had
been doing while he was writing to her.

For one murderous instant, he saw her reading his letters to
Teach, both of them laughing. He stood up to leave. Go straight to
the man's house. Stick that stainless steel Smith into Teach's face and
keep pulling the trigger until there was nothing but blood and smoke
in the air. But Blood mastered this impulse. Mastered it because he
had noticed something else at the bottom of the box.

An envelope. Inside it, a bar napkin with some love words written on it and Thalia's crude drawing of what looked like Mr. Teach's
face. Such a saver Thalia had been, such a saver. And Blood found a
credit card receipt. On it, clear as the brightest day in heaven, was
the name *James Teach*. The date was a year ago, about the time she'd
stopped seeing the white guy, lost that country club job, and started

to fall, fall, fall. It was a receipt for dinner in a restaurant on Madeira Beach (smart white man taking his black girlfriend across the bay to eat).

And the idea came to Blood—the glorious idea. James Teach had been here tonight. The picture of what had happened here tonight formed in Blood's mind. Teach had paid with the hundred-dollar bill. Teach had used the condoms. Blood wiped the money and the two condom wrappers clean of prints. (The brother in the tight green pants was free and clear now.) Blood pulled the album from the shelf again. He opened it to the last page where there was an empty plastic sleeve. From the contents of Thalia's memory box scattered on the bed, he selected a picture. In the restaurant on the dock, Teach stood behind Thalia holding a scarf. There was an open gift box on the table in front of her, and there was Thalia's sweet, grateful smile. Blood fingered through the album again, taking the journey from Thalia's long-legged childhood, to her tender high school years, to that grandmother of hers, the woman who was supposed to keep her on the straight-and-narrow. Blood slipped the picture into the empty sleeve. He liked the story the album told. Teach was the last page. Teach who had been here tonight. He put the credit card receipt back into the envelope with the drawing of Teach's goofy love grin. He slid the envelope into the album, marking that last page. Sticking out so that a person looking at the bookshelf would notice it. He liked that too.

Blood went to the bathroom and looked at himself in the mirror. The scratches Thalia had made on his cheek were small, but he had seen his share of true crime TV; he knew about the forensic cops and the fingernail scrapings they did. He went back out to the bedroom and used toilet paper and nail polish remover to clean Thalia's fingers, careful to get way up there under the nails. He put what was strewn on the bed back into the memory box.

With the box under his arm, he stood in the middle of her little bedroom, in the glow of all those candles, looking at the story he had written. He wanted to throw back his head and crow like a big black bird. Stick his thumbs under his arms and flap his elbows like hell's own condor. He wanted to fly like a hawk, talons bare to the wind, because James Teach was a little rabbit down there on the ground, running from bush to bush. A rabbit with no earthly notion that the shadow of death soared above him.

TWENTY-FIVE

Aimes and Delbert parked the Crown Vic on the street in front of the dead woman's apartment. Aimes got out and looked up and down the street. It was night, quiet in Suitcase City. People with jobs had gone to bed tired, and the ones without them were sleeping off a day of beer, weed, and Oprah. This part of Suitcase City was almost bearable with the dew falling and the smell of the night coming on. Aimes had grown up in a place like this, and it made him shiver to think of decisions he'd made that might have kept him in it. Well, he'd made the other ones too, the decisions that got you out. Last night, somebody had decided to end the life of a prostitute named Thalia Speaks.

The speculation was that one of her johns had called it in. Some guy showing up with that special need, finding the door unlocked, going in, getting a scare that shrank his dick, then making the phone call—*Uh, you don't need to know my name, but . . .* Then came the march of official Tampa through the woman's apartment. Detectives handling the crime scene. Uniforms controlling the crowd, lab technicians, a guy from the medical examiner's office, and finally the city morgue attendants who'd taken the woman's smiling face away.

Yes, smiling. A good, careful look at the crime scene photos had assured Aimes of that. She'd been strangled and showed all the signs of it—the exploded eyeballs, blackened, swollen tongue, ligature marks at the throat—but her face held a sad, eerie smile. Aimes wondered about that. Some postmortem distortion of the facial muscles, something a pathologist could explain. Nobody got strangled and died happy.

Delbert went up the walk in front of Aimes, put on a pair of surgical gloves, and used his penknife to cut the yellow plastic seal that closed the apartment door. He opened the door and looked at Aimes. Aimes pulled his gloves from his coat pocket. The woman was their case now, the fifth dead hooker in six weeks. Aimes wasn't sorry he'd missed seeing her the night she died. Some guys got off on a crime scene. He didn't. The clanking of the chain of command, lots of people making sure other people saw them doing the right thing.

Inside, it smelled like candle wax, cheap perfume, the gray fingerprint dust that was smeared everywhere, stale food, and something else that made Aimes want to step back outside for a lungful of night air. He'd smelled death and sex mixed together too many times.

Delbert walked into the kitchen, opened the refrigerator, peered in. "Cheese," he said, "some kind of foreign shit. What is it, cum . . . membert?"

"Camembert," Aimes told him, rhyming the last syllable with *chair*. "It's what the French eat instead of Velveeta."

"Ah." Delbert went to the kitchen cabinets, opened them, poked a pencil between two teacups. He knelt and peered into the cabinet under the sink.

Aimes shook his head. "Come on, let's go to the bedroom."

"What you looking for?"

Aimes knew Delbert wasn't being impatient. Delbert knew better than that. He was just curious about Aimes's thinking. What could they possibly find here that hadn't already been bagged and tagged?

"Something. Anything," Aimes said. "We get the case, we look at the place. We're always thorough. We give the taxpayer an honest day's work for his hard-earned dollar."

Aimes was standing over the bed now. The sheets had been stripped, carried off to be vacuumed for hair and fiber. He was seeing the woman's face again, her smile. From behind him, Delbert said, "All these candles."

"Yeah, what do you make of it?"

"Some kind of mood, atmosphere thing? The guy did her with a scarf. Maybe it was, you know, one of those sexual-asphyxiation things. Maybe some game they were playing that got out of hand."

Aimes turned from the bed to the bookshelf. The fact that there was a bookshelf: that was the first thing. The kind of work he did, he saw a lot of shitty houses and apartments. Places that looked like animals lived in them and places that were clean but stupid. People from the bottom of life trying to imitate people at the top. You didn't see a lot of bookshelves in the apartments of dead hookers, and you didn't see books like these. Computer manuals, several of them. Some paperback romance novels and a whole rack of best sellers, mostly books about getting ahead in business. How to parlay a small capital investment into a fortune by using so-and-so's super system. This woman was different.

Aimes leafed though a computer manual, put it back on the shelf, and selected something else, a photo album. He opened it to some pictures of the dead woman and a fat woman who resembled her. A sister maybe.

Delbert was over by the window. He pulled aside the blinds, looked out, turned back to Aimes. "What's that?"

"What's what?" Aimes was trying to think, trying to find something here that made sense, because very little did. The woman had not been shot like the other four. She had not been hauled to a dumpster. She had been strangled with a scarf, one of her own by the look of things. Following the usual procedure, the department had withheld information about the manner of death. Aimes didn't think she'd been done by the guy who'd killed the other four. And the woman had died smiling.

"That . . . in the book there."

Aimes looked down at the photo album in his hands. Something, an envelope, had been placed between the pages like a bookmark. He pulled it out, opened it. Smiled. *Oh yes. Oh Lord, yes.* He handed the envelope to Delbert, watched him read, his lips moving.

Delbert smiled. "Teach. James Teach. I'll be damned."

Aimes thumbed through the pictures, stopped at the last one. He handed the album to Delbert. "Remember the pictures? Her face?"

Delbert studied the happy picture of James Teach and the dead prostitute in a restaurant somewhere on the beach. "I remember." Delbert's eyes going cool, his mouth tightening at the thought of the woman's face in the crime scene photos.

"What'd you notice about it?"

"You mean the smile?"

Aimes nodded.

Delbert tucked the envelope back into the album and closed it. "Our Mr. Teach with his condoms and his hundred-dollar bill and his credit card. He's some piece of work, that guy."

Aimes nodded. "Did you remember it?"

Delbert winced. Aimes knew he didn't like to be confused as often as he was. It bothered him. Delbert was going to be a good cop someday. Good cops resolved their confusions, got things straightened out.

Aimes said, "What you told me you were going to remember about Mr. Teach. The thing that wasn't football."

Delbert shook his head, serious, trying to retrieve that thing right now, whatever was lost back there in the gumbo and ham gravy of his memory. "Not yet," he said, "but I will. Now I know I will."

TWENTY-SIX

Dean was up in the bow with a flashlight, poking its long beam down the narrow channel between the slips. Teach had taught her to tie a bowline, and she was proving she could do it under pressure. Docking was always the dicey part of the cruise. Many a marina had rung with the angry words of husbands at the wheel and wives in the bow; marriages had ended with the sound of fiberglass tearing as big boats sailed inches too far in the last seconds of a long day.

Teach and Dean had had a good cruise. They'd trolled for sea trout and caught some. He'd taught her the rudiments of chart reading and some knots and splices. They'd taken the inflatable Zodiac ashore to explore an old Spanish sugar mill that was part of the state park system.

They'd had some good talks, mostly about what Dean wanted to do with her life. To Teach's surprise, his daughter had said she didn't want to dance in New York. Maybe, she'd told him, she'd go to law school after college. Teach cringed, and they both laughed. Dean said, "Well, if not a lawyer, maybe a cop. I'm interested in the crazy things people do." She looked at him, serious, questioning. Was this all right with him?

He smiled, showing her the face of approval while he tried on the idea of his daughter wearing a badge and a gun.

Teach turned the boat in its slow ponderous swing to the slip.

"Watch this!" Dean called. He watched her lean, strong legs run to the pulpit, her golden arms fend the bow away from a piling. Then she jumped to the dock with a mooring line, flipped it into a quick bowline, held the knot up for him. "Ta-DAH!" She fed the bight through the loop of the bowline, made a lasso, and slipped it over a cleat.

Teach shifted the auxiliary into reverse, gave the screw a rev that snubbed the line and brought the Hunter to a shuddering stop. He cut the engine.

Dean jumped back aboard, stood in front of him. "Dad, that was great. Let's do it again soon." She reached up, and he bent to her quick hard hug.

"Sure, baby," he said, struggling for more, the right thing. "You're growing up so fast now, and we won't . . ."

But she had already turned away to pick up some gear. *What the hell,* Teach thought, *you don't have to say everything. People know what you mean.* Still, picking up a tackle box and some dirty clothes for the walk to the car, he wished he possessed the skill with words he had with a boat, had once had with a football. And he wished Paige had been here for this, had shared Dean with him these few sunny days. She would have seen that his recent trouble had done nothing to damage Dean's spirit.

When all the gear was stowed in the car, Teach and Dean stopped in at the Stone Crab, a restaurant and bar across from the marina. On the way in, he bought a copy of the *Tampa Tribune.* Reading the paper was beginning to feel friendly again, now that he wasn't Marlie Turkel's daily meat and potatoes.

One headline announced: *Fifth Prostitute Murder Disturbs Black Community.* Teach's eyes drifted over the article, then lurched back to a name. It took him a second to connect the shock that lit up his nerves to anything that could be called recognition. It was like being stung—the blinding pain, then the realization that a wasp was driving its barb into the back of your neck. *Thalia Speaks.* Thalia Speaks was dead.

"What's the matter, Dad? You don't look so good."

Dean watched him from under a pinched brow, her mouth puckered around the straw that drew iced tea into her mouth.

"Nothing," Teach said, "I'm just tired, honey."

He put the paper down, lifted his coffee cup, set it back down, and looked at the bar. The glittering bottles were stacked in rows under an elaborate blue neon facsimile of a school of fish. Teach wanted a bourbon so badly that his throat ached. Someone put a coin in the old jukebox, and Jimmy Buffet started singing, "*It's been a lovely cruise . . .*"

And Teach thought, *Christ, that restaurant in Madeira Beach*. Some German tourist playing that song over and over again. Some Hans or Dieter at the end of a holiday, stretching out the last hours of the cruise. Teach and Thalia raising their eyebrows and laughing. Thalia happy with the gifts he'd given her, a scarf and a pair of pink coral earrings.

That afternoon, Thalia was beautiful and smart, and she was going somewhere because Teach had promised to help her. She had been a ghetto girl with about as much future as a stray cat when she had lucked into the job at Terra Ceia Country Club. Lucked into Teach. That day he had told her, promised her, that he would find a way to hire her at Meador Pharmaceuticals. The more they talked about it, the more Teach believed it could happen. He would be her Henry Higgins. He would reinvent her. Her beauty, brains, energy, and charm were beyond question. All she lacked was education and experience. If he picked her as his intern in the company's business opportunity program, gave her a shot at selling, who would question it? He would teach her business etiquette, sales strategies, show her how to use her gift for looking people in the eye, talking straight to them. She was a natural, and she'd be grateful to him, and she'd want him to know it.

Dean's straw gurgled at the bottom of her glass. "Daddy, are you sure you're okay? We can go now if you like. I'm not that hungry and—"

"Yes, honey, I'm okay. Like I said, just a little tired." *And thirsty*, Teach thought, *so thirsty*. "Deanie, why don't you go ahead and order that cheeseburger and another iced tea. I'm just going to have a drink. I've been awfully good with the beer and all."

Teach smiled, knowing the smile was rotten on his face, knowing she'd be disappointed about the whiskey. She knew him better now. But what the hell? Thalia, a prostitute? It couldn't be true. It was harder to believe than the fact of her death. There must be some mistake.

He waved the waiter over and ordered a double Turkey and a Heineken back. Dean looked away, out the window at the crushed oyster-shell road, the marina beyond. She looked so much like her mother now, Teach thought.

While Dean ate, he reread the newspaper article. Marlie Turkel had written it. He recalled that she'd been assigned to what the paper was calling a string of prostitute murders, but he hadn't paid much attention to her articles. A detective named Aimes (surely it was the same man) was quoted, giving the usual vague descriptions.

Police had found Thalia Speaks dead after an anonymous caller had alerted them. She had been murdered, but the killer's method was being withheld. She had been arrested twice for prostitution and possession of narcotics. A grandmother and sister were listed as surviving her. Teach searched his memory. Had Thalia ever mentioned them?

The article said that Thalia Speaks had taken community college courses and that she had worked as a waitress at the Terra Ceia Country Club. It occurred to Teach that right now people all over the city were reading about her death. The same people who had read about James Teach and an altercation in a men's room. Who could possibly connect the two people, a vice president and a prostitute murdered in Suitcase City? Teach knew with a certainty that hurt like a fishhook in his face, like a swallow of some evil poison, that two people would make the connection: Marlie Turkel was one, and a detective named Aimes was the other.

TWENTY-SEVEN

Aimes hung up the phone and glanced across the desk at Delbert. Delbert looking back at him like a kid about to open his Christmas presents.

"Was Mr. Teach surprised?" Delbert's eyes glittered.

"Told me he was."

"He sound scared?"

"He sounded tired."

"Tired will do for a start." Delbert got up and went to the bulletin board across the small office from Aimes's desk. The board was covered with memos and BOLOs and photos of dead prostitutes in dumpsters. Delbert started picking at the thumbtacks clustered in one corner of the board, his fingers jumping with that gerbil energy.

"Relax," Aimes said in a low, slow voice. "Be patient. We're just talking to the guy. We don't have anything that puts him in the woman's apartment on the night she was killed."

The hooker killings were big now. Thurman Battles had complained to the chief of police about the lack of progress in the cases. Major Crimes Bureau had put two more teams of detectives on them. Aimes and Delbert had been up and down Thalia Speaks's street in Suitcase City, talked to everybody who was home the night she died. Nobody had seen or heard anything. One citizen said Thalia Speaks must have known the guy. His Doberman would have barked at any stranger who came around that time of night. Aimes and Delbert had seen the dog, half-dead in a hole in the front yard. "He's a barker all right," Delbert had said to the man.

Delbert turned from the bulletin board, lifted his arms over his head, and stretched. That skinny frame shivering. He stared at the file on Aimes's desk like it was the big one, the major Christmas present. The one Mom and Dad hold back until the end.

Among other things, the file held the abridged version of the love story of James Teach and Thalia Speaks. Maybe Teach had killed the woman to keep the world from knowing that story. If he had, why hadn't he taken the photo album with him? Maybe he had panicked, left it behind. People did strange things when they killed other people.

After finding the album, Aimes and Delbert had reviewed the list of items from the crime scene that were stored in Evidence Impound. If there was one photo, somewhere there were more. (Who bought a roll of film and took just one picture?) Likely, there were other things too. Gifts, love notes, sweet sentiments a man wouldn't want other men to see. Women were keepers and savers, and Aimes thought maybe the techs who'd handled the crime scene had bagged and tagged some of the love story along with the condom wrappers and the money. But none of these things was on the list. Drugs were listed: crack, amphetamines, and painkillers. No surprise in that.

If Aimes and Delbert had not been assigned this case, if Aimes had not wanted to go to the woman's apartment when things were quiet, when he could think, the album with Teach in it would have stayed on the shelf, gone to the woman's next of kin or to a landfill.

Delbert said, "So, you figure she read about Mr. Teach in the paper and she asked him to come by and talk to her?"

"That's one way it might have gone. You see it another way?"

Delbert gave a nervous shrug. He went to the window, looked out at the sun-hammered parking lot, turned back, looked at the file on Aimes's desk. "No, that one suits me all right. The woman is living her shitty life. She's got her album of memories. She picks up the paper one day and reads about Mr. Teach, how he's up to his ass in trouble with the black community. Then he's out of trouble. Thurman Battles decides to drop the case, and—"

"Mysterious, that decision," Aimes said, "but go on."

"And the woman calls Mr. Teach, says she's got the picture and she'll show it to his daughter if he doesn't come across with a little casheesh."

"And that, my young friend, gives us motive."

Delbert was wound up now and running like a Christmas toy, batteries included. "Here's another one I like. Our Mr. Teach, he gets into a fight in a bar with Tyrone Battles, and we find his face in a picture in this woman's apartment. This guy really gets around with the . . ." Delbert stopped, his face going a little panicky.

Aimes knew what his partner was about to say. It was all right. It might even be true. Teach, a guy with some kind of thing for his colored brethren. A guy who liked to fight with them, fuck them, and kill them. He finished the sentence for Delbert: "With persons of color." He looked into Delbert's eyes, letting him know it was all right. "You might be right. It is strangely coincidental. We'll have to look into it, won't we?"

Delbert looked down at his shoes, up at the bulletin board, the pictures of Thalia Speaks's weirdly smiling face. "And there's Nate Means. Teach broke the guy's neck. Ended his career."

"And you think . . . ?"

"Part of the pattern. Teach taking it out on . . . people of color."

Aimes wanted to tell Delbert, *Go ahead and pick one, your favorite, and use it. Use them all. Blacks, people of color, African Americans, hell, Negroes even.* Between them, even *Negroes* would be all right. Martin Luther King Jr. had used the word and that made it all right with Aimes. He nodded gravely. "It's something to think about, but I like the blackmail angle better."

"The blackmail angle doesn't connect him to the other killings," Delbert said. Meaning that Teach was Delbert's number one candidate for Tampa Bay serial killer. Scourge of America's Next Great City. Well, better a name than no name. The name for now was Teach as far as young Delbert was concerned.

Still, Aimes wasn't convinced. Appearances could be deceiving, but Teach looked like a middle-class white man with one wing-tip shoe in the business world, the other in the country club. A guy who'd had some bad luck in a bar with Tyrone Battles. A long way from the profile of murderer and farther from serial killer.

"So," Delbert said, "how hard you gonna push on him?"

"First thing I want to do," Aimes said, "is make him lie to me. You think I can do that?"

Delbert looked at the file. "Sure I do."

TWENTY-EIGHT

Teach waited in the interview room that looked just like they did on TV—a steel table, four cheap steel chairs, puke-green walls, a dirty gray tile floor, and a large mirror built into the wall facing him: obviously a two-way mirror. If he got up now and walked over and pressed his nose to the glass, would he see an assistant DA and some mystery witness sitting in the dark waiting for the interview to start?

He had been sleeping soundly when the phone rang. Aimes inviting him downtown for a friendly talk. The policeman's voice quiet, calm, saying he was interested in anything Teach could tell him about Thalia Speaks. Teach protesting that he didn't know anything. Aimes getting firm: "You never know what you know until we talk, Mr. Teach. I've seen it a hundred times."

"Should I bring an attorney?" Teach had asked.

"With an attorney you'll be coming in the front door. And you might be walking through a crowd of reporters. I'm suggesting you drive down here, park in the back, and I meet you. We come in the back way, and we talk. That way, nobody has to know about it." Aimes's voice held no edge of threat, and no particular reassurance.

For a moment, Teach had considered calling Walter Demarest and asking what to do. But what could Walter say except that Teach would be a fool to go anywhere near Aimes without a lawyer? Some other lawyer. Teach had decided to take the detective at his word. He was helping the police. You didn't need a lawyer for that.

Aimes had met him in the parking lot and walked him to this room. Teach tried not to read too much in the eyes of the police officers they passed. Men who stopped talking, looked up from papers or computer screens as he walked by. Was there a buzz, or was it just

Teach's nerves? Aimes had left him alone in this room, said he'd be back in a few minutes.

Aimes and Delbert came in, both carrying briefcases. Aimes said, "Mr. Teach, how are you?" The black man held out his hand and Teach shook it, firm, brief. "You remember Detective Delbert?"

Teach shook Delbert's hand. "I remember him." Teach looked into Delbert's cold, excited eyes and recalled Malone's Bar, how he had hoped never to see these men again. He told himself to focus on what was happening now, not let his mind wander, but the image came to him of his toast with Dean in the cockpit of a sailboat on a beautiful sundown sea: *To getting away with it.* If he was publicly connected to this murder, he'd be finished in this town forever. There'd be no choice but to sell the house, take his severance from Meador, uproot Dean, and find a new place to live. A place where the name James Teach was as neutral as John Smith. Hell, Teach thought, there'd be no question of keeping the name. He'd have to have it legally changed.

Aimes sat down and opened his briefcase. Delbert put his on the floor by his chair.

Teach looked around the room. "Are you going to videotape or record this?"

Aimes removed a notebook and a file from the briefcase, smiled at Teach. "No sir, but I'll take a few notes if you don't mind."

Teach wondered if he could say he did mind. He decided to shrug. "Be my guest."

Aimes nodded. "Now, Mr. Teach, how did you know Thalia Speaks?"

"She was a waitress at the country club. A lot of people there knew her." He wasn't sure how much he should say. He'd never talked to anyone about Thalia, had tried not to think about her for a while now. There was a terrible power in his memories of her. Even here, in the presence of two cops, the past wanted out. He had to resist it. What was it they said about the courtroom? Answer only the questions you are asked? Don't volunteer anything?

Aimes smiled again, glanced at Delbert who had not taken his eyes from Teach's face. "How do you think she got to be a prostitute, Mr. Teach? A woman who worked at the country club?"

The question surprised Teach. All he could do was lower his eyes and say, not loudly enough, "I don't know." He forced himself to look up at Aimes, then at Delbert. They watched him carefully. He added, "It seems strange. I mean, that she fell so far."

"Strange to us too. In March '96, she's employed at your club, serving some of the most prominent people in Tampa, and in July she's picked up for soliciting."

Teach kept his eyes down. There had been no question.

Aimes rested his hand on the file. "How well did you know the woman, Mr. Teach?"

"I knew her as a waitress. She worked lunches. I saw her on weekends when I ate in the grille after playing golf. We said hello. Small talk, that's about it."

"She didn't work dinners? You and Mrs. Teach didn't see her when you had dinner at the club?"

"Thalia worked some dinners. She filled in sometimes when one of the other . . . I really don't remember her work schedule. Why should I?"

Teach glanced from one policeman to the other, hoping his smile seemed natural. He had tried to make it a smile of sadness for a death, and the good humor of a citizen doing his duty.

Aimes said, "You knew her only as a girl who brought you your food . . . and your drinks? Is that what you're saying? She was not a friend?"

"Yes. That's what I'm saying."

Aimes opened the file and removed a cocktail napkin. Holding it delicately by the corner, he set it in front of Teach.

It was like a thumb driven into Teach's eye. The napkin from the restaurant on Madeira Beach, Thalia's drawing of his happy face. Teach's head ached, his eyes watered. He had asked her to throw everything away. After it was over, after Paige died, he'd waited a decent time and asked her to throw everything away.

She had smiled, a little sad, a little remote, already moving away from him. She had said, "All right, Jimmy. Anything you say. See, all you have to do is tell me, and I do what you say. I'll go home tonight and have me a little fire. Will that make you happy?" Teach nodding, saying he'd be happy if she'd do that. But what was happiness to a man like him at a time like that? There was no happiness, and there would be none for a long time.

Aimes looked at Delbert, some message two cops understood. The black man said, "Mr. Teach, you lied to me. Are you going to keep on doing that? If you do, we'll have to stop this friendly talk and send you home. Who knows, maybe we'll come to your house later with a warrant, bring you and your lawyer through the front door, through all those newspaper people." Aimes's voice was low, careful, patient. He was waiting.

Teach wanted to rise and take the cop by his cheap tie and throttle him. Scream into his face, *You lied to me! You said just a friendly talk!* But how could he, a liar, do that? How could a man do that when his entire life since Thalia had been a lie? Teach stifled his rage. "I knew her better than I told you." The words come out lame, craven. "We were . . ." He couldn't say they were lovers. He couldn't claim that Thalia had loved him. Not after what he had done to her. So he said, "I loved her." It was true. Then he added, "For a while."

TWENTY-NINE

Teach told them the whole story. Why not? They'd caught him lying. Why not give it to them? Hope the story of a love affair convinced them that he had not killed a prostitute named Thalia Speaks.

He had met her the first day she worked at the club. She was a waitress in training, moving from table to table with Donna, the club's senior server, getting her education in how to take orders from rich white people. That day, Teach walked into the grille intending to hurry through a club sandwich before meeting Walter Demarest on the first tee. The new girl was a little over thirty, more than pretty, and touchingly formal in her white tuxedo shirt and black vest.

Thalia played her role. She folded her shapely hands in front of her black apron, inclined her head toward Donna when the older woman spoke in her wise and serious way about how to serve from the left and clear from the right. How to be personable but not personal. How Thalia must never cross certain lines with the members. Yes, Donna actually said the thing about personable and personal, and when she did Teach felt his face warm with a blush. To save the moment, he grinned and said, "Donna, you know I'm always the soul of propriety, at least in the dining room."

Donna, who could be a bit of a flirt herself, smiled back. "I've never heard the whisper of a complaint about you, Mr. Teach."

Implying? Well, that if there were whispers, Donna would hear them. And it would matter that she heard them. Teach glanced at Thalia to see how she took all this. Seriously was how she took it.

Waitresses, bartenders, clubhouse men, and cart boys came and went at Terra Ceia, and there were the legendary few who had been around forever. Dylan the Irish bartender who talked as an equal with the wealthiest members, Juan the seventy-year-old cart boy who told dirty jokes and still ran everywhere he went, and Donna, patient, serious, and exacting, den mother of the dining room. Training Thalia, Donna made the club sound like a big happy family. Of course the members had their flaws and eccentricities, but even so, the club was a good little world. And it would be a good world for Thalia if she minded the rules.

Was Thalia a rule minder? The day Donna trained her, she looked like one. And to Teach she looked like a million bucks. Her eyes were big, brown, and bright, and her smile was shy but generous. Her walk was graceful but fetching, and her skin was a seamless cinnamon poured over gorgeous bones like frosting on a cake. She was appeal and charm and energy—she was a woman in the last bloom of youth.

Donna's invocation of certain improprieties made Teach uneasy, but Thalia made him happy. He knew it was odd that he should feel a swelling happiness at this casual meeting with a waitress who might be gone in a week, but he did feel it, and he knew why. She was beautiful, and, as the poet had said, a thing of beauty was a joy forever. On that Saturday morning, when Teach felt joy in Thalia's presence, he had no idea what she felt in his, but he saw something playing in her eyes. Something that was not, *Please, God, let me keep this job*, or, *God, I'm bored*, or, *Let's get this over with as soon as possible*.

Later Thalia told him what had been in her eyes. She had recognized him.

She did not wait on him for a while after that first time, so one day he asked for a table she served, and what could the hostess do but comply? Soon he became Thalia's regular. He could say to anyone who asked (though no one would) that he wanted her to serve him because she was the best. She remembered what he liked and she took care of him. He tipped her lavishly. She never mentioned his largesse. He got the same polite "Thank you, sir" she gave to everyone. Either she didn't care about the money or she didn't want him to know she did. Time passed and he knew he cared about her, and he thought she, in her way, returned the sentiment.

Later, Teach tried to remember who had first touched. Probably he had congratulated her for some small thing and held out his hand for her to shake, loving the warm pressure of her slender fingers in his big hand, the half second of holding before they let go. With that handshake, he crossed a line. Thalia crossed it too. She let her hand rest momentarily on his shoulder as she leaned down to settle a plate in front of him. It was all simple and blameless, and after a while, Teach could not imagine going to the club without seeing her.

After a month at Terra Ceia, Thalia was confident, popular, and clearly bored with her job. She'd arrive at a table with a drink before it was ordered and say, "Your usual, Mr. Smith," and you could see that her mind was miles away from bourbon Manhattans and chicken tenders. Her mood worried Teach. He was afraid she would leave, just disappear as employees sometimes did, people whose coming and going caused not a ripple on the placid surface of Terra Ceia.

Then one day she approached his table, smiled at him frankly, and said, "What can I do for you, Jimmy?"

"Excuse me?" Teach liked this familiarity, saw it maybe as their next step.

She crossed her arms under her breasts and breathed a sigh. "So, you really don't know me. You don't remember?"

Teach squinted at her, trying. Finding nothing of Thalia in his memory, he shook his head. What was he missing?

"I knew *you* when you came in my first day."

Ah. Teach understood now. He said it with newsreel drama: "You mean you recognized Teach, the Gridiron Great?"

"Naw, not him. I recognized Jimmy the shirttail cracker from up that oyster-shell road in Cedar Key."

She meant that they came from the same place. She had known him, at least to recognize, to remember, when he was the Jimmy Teach who at twenty-four, football behind him forever, had returned to Cedar Key to tend bar in the sunshine and at night to pilot the shrimper *Delia B.* His second sojourn in Cedar Key had been brief, but Thalia knew him from that time. She had lived in Rosewood and she had sometimes helped her mother clean motel rooms in Cedar Key, and she'd seen him coming and going from the bar he tended. And so it followed that he had seen her too. Seen her the way you see the background of a picture.

After they had been together for a while, images drifted up from the silted channels of Teach's memory. He pictured Thalia, fifteen-year-old Thalia, dust whitening her bare summer legs, walking the few miles from Rosewood to Cedar Key to buy candy or ice cream, or maybe to talk somebody with a valid ID into buying beer for her and her friends. It was what kids did in the summer because there was nothing else to do if you were too young to work a boat or a kitchen. Searching back through the scrim that was half memory and half imagination, Teach saw her walking that road as a scene from Norman Rockwell, the adolescent girl still innocent, drifting along in the comfort of her own time, the thoughts and desires of a woman forming behind those sleepy brown eyes. *Don't burn your bare feet on the hot road, girl. Don't look up at the cars passing full of rich white folks from the university city like you want to be in there with them. Want to go home with them. There's something good for you at the end of this long, hot walk.* Back then, in that place, it was how things were. Too hot to worry much about the big things. Too poor to have the good things. Too young still for the things in between.

At the club, Teach couldn't stop watching her. He lingered over lunch and ordered drinks he didn't need. Then, watching her, he needed the drinks. Somehow knowing they were from the same place made this all right, his watching her, his drinking; made it all right that he drove through the employee parking lot thinking he might see her after a shift. Or promising himself he was driving through that parking lot for no reason at all.

One day he waited for Thalia. Sitting in his Buick a discreet distance from the back door of the kitchen, he read the newspaper and tried to look like anything but what he was, a club member waiting for a waitress. When the waitress appeared, she stopped in the late-afternoon sun to search her purse for her car keys, drew a long breath that said, *Free at last*, and then started her sweet, musical walk to a half-dead Toyota.

Stupidly, Teach had not planned his next move. Should he call her over to his window, get out and approach her, some third thing? He could not make up his mind. She was a block away in the smoking Toyota when he slowed behind her and blinked his lights, glad they were gone from club property. When she saw his face in her rearview mirror, she pulled over. Teach got out and walked to her window, painfully aware of what this would look like should someone he knew drive by or look out from a house here in Country Club Estates.

When he stood at her window, Thalia said, "So, you do remember me?"

"Yes, I do. It just took me awhile." He didn't know how she would take this. He knew it wasn't exactly a compliment.

He rested his hand on the windowsill. She reached out, took his hand, pulled it into the car, held it hard. "So what now, Cracker Jimmy?"

His hand warm in hers, Teach couldn't think.

She smiled, shook her head slowly. "I was fifteen and you were . . . ?"

"Twenty-four." His age the year of the *Delia B. And I was a smuggler.* A former football player, a failure, and a smuggler.

Still holding his hand, pulling it like she wanted him to climb through that window, she said, "You want to come home with me?"

Teach said, "No, I can't do that," knowing that he would do it, some time, if she would let him. He added, "Not today."

She looked at him now with a teasing reproach. "Better things to do, Jimmy? What you got better than me?"

Now that she was free of the dining room where she spoke like a news anchor, she was telling him, *If you go home with me, not today but someday, you'll be in my world. Different rules in my world.*

After that, and for a while, they went back to the rules, Thalia showing up at his table with burgers or sandwiches and beers and sometimes, on Friday afternoons after he had played nine holes with Walter, double bourbons with tall ice-water chasers. But Teach knew, and she did too, that someday he would go home with her. When their eyes had met that first day, she had made him hers. When her cinnamon skin was a liquid that flowed from her cheeks down her long neck into that stiff white collar to regions undiscovered. When the breath he caught of her perfume was like the air of a new season. When her eyes knew him from the long ago.

One afternoon, after she had placed a sandwich in front of him without resting her hand on his shoulder, he asked how she was doing. Standing with her hands folded in front of her apron, she said, "Well . . ." and let a long pause tell the story of her disappointment.

Teach knew what she wasn't saying. The work was mind-numbing. There was no future for her here; only more of the same. She was thinking of leaving.

Finally, she said, "There are lots of nice people here, and the money's all right, but I'm better than this job." When she said *better*, her chin lifted a defiant inch, as though Teach might dispute the point. She glanced at the hallway leading to the club's administrative offices. "I been thinking about an office job."

It was a question, not a statement. The grille was almost empty. A few duffers scattered here and there, sun-stunned and bourbon bent, ready to stagger off to the parking lot. It was safe for Teach to meet her eyes and consider what she was saying to him. He didn't want to think she was bargaining. *If you help me get out of this apron, help me down that hallway, then I'll help you.*

After a few seconds of silence, Teach knew he'd help her. And he knew he needed a change as badly as she did. He needed to go home with Thalia.

So it happened. The thing between them happened like fate, like it was ordained, inescapable. By a series of steps, phases, small actions, casual motions of eyes and hands, it happened, but these little things didn't really matter. There could have been other little things, because the big thing had always been as certain as death and taxes. And every time Teach let himself think about this, he imagined himself telling Paige, *It just happened.* The oldest, lamest cheater's line in the world. And those pale blue eyes of Paige's going from cool to cold to glacial, and Teach couldn't even imagine what happened after that. But what he always left out of his imagined confession to his wife was the *just.* There was a world of difference between a thing fated to happen and a thing that *just* happened. Just was accidental, fate was cosmic. Fate was written for you, not by you. And sometimes fate was tragic.

Their first time in her shabby apartment in Suitcase City—a place Teach had foreseen to its smallest detail, a place he knew represented to her a rising from worse places—was everything he hoped and feared it would be. Crossing over from watching, imagining, teasing, to touching, holding, and being inside, changed him forever. When the change happened, it was irrevocable. And from that vantage point of inevitability, he could see, far off in the future, the damage a new Teach might do.

One afternoon when he had stolen two hours from his job and they lay exhausted and sweating, inches separating them in Thalia's narrow bed, she said, low and dreamy, "You think I knew you back then as a redneck bartender, but I knew other things. We knew."

"We?" Teach muttered from the stupor of their sweet thrashing hours.

"Us black folks," she said not quite seriously, playing with the words to make herself sound like some voice of history, some radio wave of her people's consciousness. Teach reminded himself, *She's not from Cedar Key*. Thalia was from Rosewood, only a few miles from Cedar Key, where twenty-seven people had been massacred in 1923. Rosewood was a thousand miles from Cedar Key.

"What did you folks . . . know?" Teach's voice was no longer the low murmur of the postcoital dream. It was all his attention. It was his fear.

"You smuggled. We knew that."

"How?" He didn't deny it. Why bother at this distance, inches of sweat and miles of history, from this woman he trusted?

"Oh," she said, stretching, balling her fists like a child and rubbing them into her brown eyes. Turning to rest her head on his shoulder. "We had our ways."

"No, really. How?" Teach the professional, the former maritime consultant, wanted to know. He had staked his life on his secrets.

Thalia sat up in the bed and leaned over him. "White folks back there, back then, they thought we was completely separate. They wanted it that way. They thought they could do what they wanted to us, to anyone, anything, and they was safe. Well they couldn't, they can't. We knew. My uncle's friend, Edmond Curtis, deacon at our church, he worked for that old blind lady who let you keep your boat behind her house. He started out doing some roofing for her, and pretty soon he was there a lot cause she wanted more from him than roofing. Wanted him to drive her places. Wanted him to come pick her up when she fell down in the night. Get groceries for her. She talked to him. They got to be friends in their way. As much as they could be back then. He prayed for her in church, we all did when he asked for it, and he told my uncle about seeing you coming and going all hours, paying that old lady ten times what it was worth to slip your boat behind her house. You mighta fooled the white folks, but you never can fool the ones who do your dirty work."

She stopped, her eyes still hard. To him, she had been the background of the picture; to her, the background *was* the picture. The past meant more to her than he, naked beside her in his white skin, could ever know.

"Your uncle's friend, Edmond, he was taking a risk helping Mrs. Bye, wasn't he?" Teach said it with a kind of awe. They both knew it was a stupid question.

All Thalia said was, "He lived in Rosewood."

Later, back in his own world, the one he shared with Paige and Dean, the one that did not include Thalia except as a waitress, Teach wondered if there was another reason she told him the story of Uncle Edmond and Mrs. Bye, the blind woman he'd thought was as safe for him as a newborn baby. He didn't think Thalia would ever use what she knew against him, but he knew that in some possible world she could use it. He didn't like the thought, the feeling of it. Soon after that, he told her that he would help her get a better job.

Teach and Thalia were careful at the club. They didn't indulge in the small indiscretions and silly swoons of secret lovers. She stopped resting her hand on his shoulder because she could rest it where she wanted to at other times. They were friendly but not familiar. As much as he could, Teach kept himself from watching her while she worked. Every day, he cautioned himself to keep a level head. They used hotels, but never the same one twice. They took afternoon trips to the small towns near Tampa—Dade City, Lakeland, Bartow—but there was never enough time. Thalia wanted more of his time but there was never enough. He wanted more of her body, her mind, her secrets than she could ever give. As time passed, it became more than want. It became love, and it grew so large inside him it hurt. It moved his mind from things he had to do, and finally from things he had to love. When he began to think of a life with Thalia, when his fantasies at night became plans, when he began to think his way through the difficulties of it, and past them to the pleasures of it, Teach knew he was in trouble.

The day Paige put the scarf in his car, Teach knew exactly what had happened. He sat behind the wheel holding the scarf as a man would hold the head of a poisonous snake. He had borrowed Paige's car because his was in the shop. He had taken Thalia somewhere in it. Paige had found the scarf, had folded it neatly and put it on the seat of his car, had never said a word to him about it. And had never been the same to him again.

The scarf had become a silence, then a screaming silence, then it became a fourth person living with them. Some fetid, buried creature always there, sitting at the dining room table when they ate dinner, waving goodbye to them from the front porch as they both drove off to work, lying between them in bed at night.

And the inches between them in that bed had become miles, uncrossable, and then one day, witnesses said, Paige's Volvo had wandered out of her lane on the Veteran's Expressway, and her front wheel had become weirdly entangled with the rear bumper of a dump truck. Her car was flung into a spin across three lanes and she was hit broadside. Her gas tank exploded.

THIRTY

There was a knock at the door. Aimes put down the notebook and looked at Delbert. Delbert stepped out into the hallway, came back with a piece of paper in his hand. Teach looked at the paper the young detective held, then back at Aimes's hands. He had watched those hands while he'd told them the story of Thalia. He had watched Aimes write in the notebook, remembering how those hands had touched his shoulder that afternoon in the bar, hands that held the power of the state. Hands that took away your tie and shoelaces.

"One afternoon," Teach said, "when I was with her, with Thalia, my wife was killed in an accident on the Veteran's Expressway."

A fiery crash, the newspapers had called it. Paige's Volvo had burned so badly that the City of Tampa had to repave that section of the highway. Teach never drove that stretch of road anymore. He did not want to see that new concrete.

"So what happened to Thalia after that?" Aimes asked. He did not seem interested in the death of Paige. Maybe he thought Teach was angling for sympathy.

"There was terrible grief and guilt." The words fell dead from Teach's mouth. Words from eulogies and sermons. There were no words for what Teach had felt. "I didn't want to see Thalia, but I had to. We had to play our parts. To call those days awkward . . . well, there's no word for it. Thalia had religion, and she took her guilt in a way I couldn't. She told me she had caused Paige's death. She told me she prayed about it."

"She told you that?" For the first time, Aimes looked surprised. The cynical cop allowing his eyebrows to rise, his head to shake at the infinite mystery of human behavior.

"Yes, she told me. At the club we avoided each other, acted strange, exposed ourselves in ways we never had before. She came to me one day and said, *You're falling apart, and it's partly because I'm here, so I have to leave.* I told her that was ridiculous, but of course I was relieved. God help me, I wanted her gone. So one day she didn't come to work. She didn't give notice, never asked for a reference, never contacted the club again as far as I know. I think she wanted to burn her bridges so there would be no question of ever coming back. And—" Teach stopped, looked at both cops.

"And?" Aimes's dark eyes bored into his.

"And she took something from me when she left. Drugs. Pain-killers and diet pills. It was crazy the way she did it. I went to the men's room, left my keys on the table. She took the keys and went to my car in the parking lot. In front of the whole dining room. Nobody noticed. At least nobody said anything. She wanted trouble, wanted me to turn her in. Of course, I didn't."

"Of course," Aimes said.

Teach rubbed the back of his neck with both hands, then his eyes. "I told myself she'd be all right. With her brains and her . . . charm, she'd find a job." He looked at both cops again. They knew what had happened to Thalia Speaks. "I learned something from what she did. I always thought I loved her more than she loved me, but it wasn't true. She gave up . . . a life for me."

"You mean *her* life," Aimes said. It wasn't a question.

"Yes, I guess so. And maybe she saved mine."

"What'd folks at the club say? About her leaving."

"Just what you'd expect them to say. That it was strange. After all, she was popular. Nobody but me and Thalia ever knew about the af-fair." Teach looked around the bleak green interrogation room, back into Aimes's eyes. "And now you." He didn't look at Delbert. Delbert was an extension of Aimes. But now Delbert held the paper in his hands.

"And your wife. She knew." It was Delbert.

Teach couldn't see any method in the way the two cops divided the questions. Delbert listened mostly, jumpy, nervous, seeming to want something Teach hadn't said. Aimes's eyes gave Teach nothing. Throughout the long telling, he had watched Teach the way he might look at a television or the pages of a book.

Teach said, "You asked me how she got to be a hooker. The job market was bad, and she couldn't find anything. She couldn't make it. You know more about the rest of it than I do."

THIRTY-ONE

No, Aimes thought, *no, Mr. Teach, for a country club white man, you seem to know a lot about the rest of it.* But Aimes would say it to Teach anyway, just for the record.

"The rest is that a young black woman with a turd in her personnel file at the country club and no prospects for anything better than fast food or welfare starts to drink a little, starts to hang around the wrong people a little, snorts a little coke, and then she takes her first hit from a crack pipe, just a little one, and she just happens to be one of them who can't stop when they start, and then she's got a big habit, and she needs a whole lot of money, and she's selling her ass a little, and then a little becomes a lot, and then she's dead."

Aimes thinking: *And the question is, how much do you know about the last part? The dead part.* He decided to move on with it, see if he could get Teach to lie again. The past half hour, telling how a black girl had got her big chance with a white man and then lost it, Mr. Teach had seemed very truthful. Very sorry. Aimes wanted to see if Teach would keep on down the straight-and-narrow, or if the guy would swerve.

Aimes said, "So you lost touch with her after she left Terra Ceia?"

"I saw her a few more times."

"What'd you talk about?"

"Once I asked her to get rid of, you know, some things . . . She said she would." Teach glanced up at Aimes, smiled that betrayed-lover smile. Aimes didn't smile back. There was some betrayal here, but it wasn't a black woman saving her memories. Not unless she had used them to bring Mr. Teach to her apartment on the last night of her life.

Aimes picked up the cocktail napkin by its corner. He showed

Teach the woman's drawing again. She'd had some talent, Aimes thought. The drawing captured something. "So, you haven't seen this napkin since you split up with Ms. Speaks?"

Teach looked confused.

"Would you answer the question, please?"

"No, I haven't seen it."

Aimes watched him closely, didn't see any of that liar's squirm in the man's eyes. In fact, all he saw was Teach's wondering what the hell was going on. If Thalia Speaks had tried to blackmail him, those eyes would be different. There'd be some show-the-bitch-righteousness in there staring back at Aimes. Unless, of course, this guy was a better actor than Aimes thought he was.

"What else did you talk about?"

Teach held his hands out in front of him and flexed them. "We couldn't stay away from each other for a while after . . . after she left the club."

"You sleep with her then?"

"Yes, but it just . . . wore out, I guess. We tried not to talk about what had happened. She asked me to pray with her. I couldn't. I gave her money, tried to help her find work, but she was depressed. She missed some job interviews I set up for her. I'd go over, and we'd make love, and then she'd want to talk about the club, the gossip. It got . . . strange after a while. The sex was just . . . something we did so we could lie in bed afterward and talk."

"When was the last time you saw her?"

After a pause he said, "May. The middle of May a year ago. Things hadn't been good between us. I went over there, and she had some guy with her." Teach hesitated again. "A black man. The guy stayed in the backroom where I couldn't see him. Thalia talked to him through the doorway. He said he'd leave, but she insisted that he stay. Told him I'd be gone soon. What she said to the guy was, *Don't worry about him. He doesn't stay long.* Maybe the guy was a . . . client. Maybe that's when she started . . . getting paid."

Aimes said, "How'd you know he was black if you didn't see him?"

And Teach: "By his voice." Saying it in a way that let Aimes know he meant no offense.

Aimes said, "Mr. Teach, where were you on the night of May 25, between ten o'clock and midnight?"

Teach thought about it. "I don't know. I couldn't really tell you." Then Teach's head rocked back with a memory. "Wait a minute. I was on my boat at the marina. I did some cleaning and worked on the engine. After that, I fell asleep for a while. It was right after the thing with Thurman Battles was over, and I was exhausted, I guess. I was getting the boat ready for a trip with my daughter."

Teach looked at Aimes, at Delbert, like he wondered if he'd made some mistake mentioning Battles. Aimes gave him nothing back on that one. He said, "Anybody see you there?"

"Not that I know of. It's possible. Not many people around that time of night."

Aimes nodded at Delbert, said, "Mr. Teach, I'm going to ask you to wait here for a minute while I step outside with Detective Delbert. We'll be right back. Would you like a cup of coffee or a glass of water?"

Teach said, "No thanks." The big jock looking at the paper in Delbert's hand.

Outside, Aimes read it. The buzz about Teach had gotten around. One of the vice cops had knocked on the door, handed Delbert a report on the arrest of some high school kids out on the Gandy Causeway. The cops had confiscated everything from marijuana and powdered cocaine to crack. Nothing unusual about that, but the vice cop had interrupted Aimes's interrogation because of something else they'd found. Pharmaceutical methylamphetamine, diet pills. The pills were still in their wrappers. Meador Pharmaceutical wrappers.

Aimes and Delbert had seen drugs on the inventory of items found in Thalia Speaks's apartment, but the manifest had not mentioned the wrappers.

Aimes looked at Delbert, "You think?"

"Why not? She was an addict. Maybe he was smuggling the stuff home from work and she was selling it. It gives the guy another reason to do her. Criminal confederates have a falling out."

Delbert bit his thumbnail and shrugged, that nervous jump of the shoulders again. Aimes wondering if his partner didn't have a little too much of a hard-on for Mr. Teach. Aimes handed the arrest report back to Delbert. "Take it inside but don't mention it."

Delbert nodded.

Back inside, Aimes saw Teach's eyes go to the paper in Delbert's hand. "All right, Mr. Teach. I think that's all we need for now. I want to thank you again for coming in."

Aimes didn't see what he expected in Teach's face. He expected relief. What he saw were questions. Well, sometimes it went that way. You had to drag a guy in kicking and screaming to do his duty as a citizen, and when you were finished, when the guy looked at his thumbs and didn't see any screws on them, he wanted to know what you were thinking.

Teach gave a tight little smile. "From what you've asked me, I could conclude that you think I killed Thalia."

Aimes shrugged, looked at Delbert, whose cool blue eyes said that he had Teach measured for nailing to the barn door. "Like I told you on the phone, Mr. Teach, we're covering all of the bases." Aimes gave it a tired, memorized sound. He wanted Teach to think: *Routine. It's just routine.* For a while. Then he said, "Now that's my view of it, Mr. Teach. I see us still in the information-gathering phase. But my partner here, Detective Delbert, he thinks he might know how you fit into this. He thinks Thalia Speaks got a little down on her luck, had a little negative cash flow, and she reads about you in the paper, the trouble you had with Thurman Battles, and she thinks why not call you up and say she never did burn those . . . *things*, and she wonders if your daughter would like to see them, or would you rather come on over and talk about it? . . . And bring your checkbook. That's what Delbert thinks could have happened. Delbert's trying to convince me, and I'm trying to keep an open mind."

"So I killed her to keep her mouth shut. Is that it?"

"Delbert thinks it might have gone just that way."

"And you're not sure?"

Aimes nodded.

"Why didn't I take that napkin with me after I killed her?"

"Delbert thinks you panicked." Aimes took a crime scene photo from the folder and put it on the table in front of Teach. A photo of Thalia Speaks smiling in death, her eyeballs the size of hard-boiled eggs, the ligature marks at her neck blue and crusted with blood.

"After what you did to that poor woman, you panicked, and you ran like a scalded dog. That's what Delbert thinks."

Aimes watched Teach's reaction to the picture. The man was upset, very upset. His throat worked for a few seconds like he might vomit. Aimes was ready to push back from the table, away from the stream Teach might spew, but the guy got hold of himself and reached up with a shaking hand and wiped a tear from the corner of each eye. It was damned good acting, Laurence Olivier stuff. Or it was real.

Teach looked at Aimes out of those wet, red eyes. "How was she killed, Aimes? Does Delbert know how she was killed?"

Aimes pulled another photo out of the file and put it down in front of Teach. It showed Teach and Thalia Speaks in a restaurant on Madeira Beach. There were pretty boats and pelicans, tourists and tall drinks with paper umbrellas in them. Spiny lobsters and rum drinks on the table. Thalia Speaks was seated and Teach stood behind her, leaning down with his chin almost resting on her shoulder. That happy love-dog look in his eyes, the face in the drawing on the napkin.

Thalia Speaks had a scarf around her neck, and James Teach held both ends of it as he leaned down over her, his strong hands resting at the sides of her neck.

Delbert said, "She was strangled, Mr. Teach. With a scarf."

THIRTY-TWO

Teach stepped out into the hot white light behind the police station and squinted at the tall royal palms that bordered the parking lot, the gleaming black-and-white police cars with their blue signal lights and City of Tampa crests. Meeting him here an hour ago, Aimes had been all smiles and good public servant. Ready for a friendly little talk. After Teach had given them everything that was secret about Thalia, Aimes and Delbert had left him sitting at the green steel table wiping tears from his eyes. Left him to find his own way out.

Those pictures, those soul-maiming photos of Thalia's dead face. He started walking. Walking would settle him, help him forget. He crossed the lot, vaguely aware that his head was hunched down into his collar as though something might fall from the sky and crush him. He told himself to stand straight, quicken his pace, get out of here, and hope that he did not hear from Aimes and Delbert again. Hope that they solved the crime and moved on to others, their miserable lives a procession of brutalities.

Teach lurched when he heard voices to his right, from the rows of police cars. He walked faster. The gate was twenty yards away. After that, the anonymity of the streets.

"Mr. Teach! Wait a minute, Mr. Teach! Please!"

He heard the tapping of heels on the asphalt. He turned to his right. Two uniformed policemen were getting out of a cruiser. Between them and him, coming fast in a long black skirt, white blouse, and black blazer, was Marlie Turkel. When she saw that she had his attention, that in all likelihood he would not bolt, she turned back to the two cops. "Thanks, fellas. We'll talk again, okay?"

One of the cops waved to her. His partner was already heading toward the station. Marlie Turkel turned to Teach and asked the inevitable question. "Mr. Teach, what brings you to the police station?"

Many things occurred to him at once. He could simply walk on. Ignore her. He could lie: *My little niece Emily lost her bicycle.* He could jump on the woman and commit the act Aimes thought him capable of. Joyously, quickly, brutally, he could strangle her. Teach bought time: "I could ask you the same question."

She stood in front of him frowning . . . at what? His stupidity. In a cold, flat voice she said, "I got a call, a tip you were here."

Jesus, Teach thought, *a tip*. Probably one of cops he had passed on his way in. Some guy doing quid pro quo with Marlie Turkel. His tired brain told him it was time to tell the truth. "I talked to Detective Aimes about the murder of Thalia Speaks. He thought I might know something that would help with the investigation."

"Do you?"

"Do I?" Teach was confused, wrung out. It was hot here on the asphalt. He was sweating and Marlie Turkel in her blazer was not.

"Do you know anything that can help Detective Aimes?" Keeping her eyes on Teach's face, she pulled a notebook from her purse.

It came to him. Something he had often read in the paper. "He asked me not to mention anything about our talk. You know, official police business. He said leaks could compromise the case." Teach knew this wouldn't stop her from writing that he was connected to the inquiry. Unless. Unless she thought it would anger Aimes.

"Have you read my pieces about the prostitute murders?"

Teach had never met the woman, had only talked to her on the phone, seen her picture in the paper. But there was always something grimly intimate in her voice. It frightened him even more than her newspaper job, the license to destroy it gave her. Why did she want to know if he had read her articles? Was it simple vanity? Some strategy to get information from him? A lie here would not hurt him.

"No," he said.

Of course he had read them, long, artfully constructed meditations on the misery of lives spent in the world's oldest profession. Interviews with prostitutes (names changed), stories of childhood abuse, school failure, running away, shoplifting, drugs, and finally the sale of the body. And all of it, as Marlie Turkel saw it, the fault of men.

Teach had parked a block down and two blocks over on Cass Street, thinking that distance from the police station might somehow provide a measure of anonymity. He started walking again, and Marlie Turkel fell into step with him. He slowed. He wasn't running from her. He was walking to his car, and he couldn't prevent her from accompanying him if she wanted to. She carried the notebook low at her side. It reminded him of gunfighters concealing revolvers in the folds of white dusters.

After they had walked a block, she said, "I still think there was something funny with you and Thurman Battles. How that whole thing just suddenly went away. And that kid going off to prep school. You two must have discovered some very powerful common interest." That voice, in the dark, in the alley, hot breath in your face. That hurry-up-and-do-it voice.

Teach slowed a little more. "We discovered the good of the community, Ms. Turkel. I told you that on the phone."

"Forgive me, but . . . bullshit. There's something going on between you guys." Beside him, she was breathing a little raggedly. "Whew," she said, "slow down there. I've had a long day. You're walking my legs off."

And I've had a long month, Teach thought. He decided to risk it, ask her what she planned to do with his life. Get the news now rather than waiting for the morning paper. He stopped on Franklin in front of a bar, smoked-glass windows and a neon beer sign. Some country tune on the jukebox inside. "Are you going to put this in the paper, Ms. Turkel? That you saw me at the police station? That I talked to Aimes about the murder of a prostitute? Who wasn't a prostitute when I knew her as an employee at the country club."

Marlie Turkel stepped in front of him, reached up, and loosened the large white bow at the throat of her blouse. Breathing hard, her face flushed, she said, "*Only* as an employee, Mr. Teach?" There it was, the implication her readers would find in her next story. She wouldn't come out and say it, but the careful reader would not miss the suggestion that Teach had frequented Thalia Speaks as a client. It occurred to him again that he would like to reach out and seize the bow at this woman's throat and draw it tight until . . .

Teach closed his eyes, rubbed them. He couldn't do that, wouldn't do it, because he was a good man down where it mattered, and good men didn't. But he had to take hold of something. The world he had guided back into orbit, the world he had blessed for its goodness as he watched his daughter swimming in the sundown Gulf of Mexico, was spinning into the dark again.

"Look, Mr. Teach, why don't we step inside here and have a drink? I haven't said I'm going to write about you."

"Jim," Teach said, "call me Jim, and I'll call you Marlie."

Inside the bar, two things surprised him. The bartender nodded to Marlie Turkel the way he'd nod to a beat cop or a fireman from the station down the street. She wasn't just known, she was a regular. The second thing was the shot of bar whiskey and the beer she ordered. She knocked back the rye without a wince, chased it with two bites of cheap draft, and tapped her shot glass on the bar. "Another bump, Henry." The bartender brought the bottle of generic whiskey over and poured a second shot. He glanced at Teach's untouched Wild Turkey and went back to the baseball game on the TV behind the bar.

Marlie Turkel led him to a booth. There were no pleasantries. Teach's mind had been going like a blender, always churning up the same question. He asked it again: "Are you going to write about seeing me today?"

She knocked back the second shot, sipped the beer. She leaned back and rested her head on the red leatherette, watching him like she was trying to make up her mind. Her face was long, and her undershot jaw was narrow. There were acne scars in the swales under her cheekbones. She wore her wispy dishwater-blond hair in a pageboy that only made her jaw seem keener. Her teeth were large, chalky, and coffee-stained. *No wonder she practiced that purring voice,* Teach thought. He could write her biography. She'd grown up poor, been abandoned either emotionally or in fact by parents, then later friends, and, finally, men. She'd discovered journalism as revenge but had convinced herself it was a social crusade. She used the voice to get information which was revenge. The voice was sex, and sex was abandonment, the thing to be revenged.

She tilted her head to the side a little, smiled, and answered his question: "I don't know yet. I think you're news, don't you?"

Before she could remind him of the public's right to know, Teach said, "Why am I news? Why now? Tomorrow Aimes could find out that some drooling perv in a house full of pickled human remains in Suitcase City killed those women. Tomorrow the fact that he talked to me could mean nothing at all."

"You're what I've got today, Jim. All I've got."

"So, it's a slow day, and you've got to feed the beast, and I'm the food?"

She drank some beer, looked into the glass, glanced at her watch, then at the bartender whose back was to them. "You could put it that way. I wouldn't. I'd say that a vigilant free press is the cornerstone of a vital democracy. I'd say that the newspaper comes out every day and nobody waits to see if President Lincoln dies before they report that President Lincoln was shot by a man named Booth. The difference between murder and attempted murder doesn't stop the presses."

Teach took the first sip of his whiskey, obscurely pleased that Marlie Turkel was ahead of him on the alcohol highway. "But isn't there some principle of proportion? I didn't shoot a president. I knew a woman a year ago, and somebody killed her, and a detective talked to me about her."

"Sure, but why you? Why not a lot of other people at the country club? Is it because Aimes knows you, Jim? And how does he know you? He knows you as the guy who beat the crap out of Tyrone Battles. The guy who paralyzed Nate Means. He might even think he knows you've got some serious violent tendencies."

Jesus, thought Teach. *Jesus Christ, look at the way this woman's mind works.* He leaned forward, made his eyes as friendly as he could, tried to look like a good man with a reasonable question. "Look, Marlie, I need to know. Are you going to write about this or not?"

She smiled again, sipped. "I don't know. I'm thinking about it." She was using that voice. The not-very-pretty girl who had to be a little aggressive, had to have something the other girls didn't have.

He wasn't sure where the next thing came from. From desperation, from a sudden vision of Dean swimming, of him and Walter Demarest standing on the first tee at Terra Ceia, the sunrise just breaking over the dewy grass. "Will you wait if I can get you something good? Something better than me talking to Aimes?"

Marlie Turkel had been sitting with her head back, turning her beer glass slowly on the table. Now she lowered her gaze, her eyes boring at him. "What? Get me what? Something Aimes told you?"

Teach nodded. "I can't tell you now. I've got some things to . . . confirm."

"When?"

"A week, two at the most. What do you say?"

She looked at him with skepticism and a ravening interest and, Teach thought, a little hatred. Because she would have to agree, because, as she would see it, in his way he had won again. She leaned forward, put her hand on the back of his. "You can't tell me anything now? Not even a hint?"

"Not yet, but you won't be disappointed."

She pushed back from him, turned to the bar. "Henry, another round here, please."

She thought about it till the drinks came, making him wait. Finally, she knocked back her third generic and said, "All right. It's a deal. I don't usually do this, and I want you to know that if you don't deliver, I'm going to be, let's say, very interested in you for a very long time. But I'll do it. Neither of us mentions this talk to anyone. And remember, there's a time limit. It's one week, not two." She wrote something in her notebook, tore out the page, and handed it to him. "Here's my home number. Call me anytime, day or night."

Teach took the paper and looked down at his whiskey. Knew he couldn't drink it now without gagging because he had no idea what he could possibly dig up for Marlie Turkel. He'd had to do something, say something. He had pulled this crazy idea out of that fading vision of the good life, of Dean dancing and sailing with him and growing up good and straight and tall. Out of Hope itself. But what, in God's name, could he give Marlie Turkel to keep his name out of the paper?

He was about to head for the door, when she said, "You're a charming bastard, aren't you, Teach?" Her voice was grim and a little slurry. "You've always gotten your way with the charm, haven't you, Teach?"

She was hitting his name with extra emphasis now, saying *Teach* like it was a curse or a bad condition. The whiskey had hit her harder than he'd expected it to, or something else had hit her. She seemed to be having some sort of realization about him, and that could be a good thing. Surely a charming Teach was an improvement, better than a racist Teach or a violent one. Seeing people and things in a new light, he had been told, was the meaning of life. They'd taught that in college. It was what all the important books said. The books he had read on team buses and planes when other people were thumbing through comic books or puzzling out articles in *Sports Illustrated*.

Teach offered to walk her to her car, hoping the gesture would bank him some good will. She'd had three shots and two beers, and this wasn't the best of neighborhoods. When she didn't argue with him, he knew she wasn't herself. When she stopped, spun a three-sixty on the hot sidewalk, and said she couldn't remember where she'd left her car, Teach got a little worried. He figured the police station was the place to start. His hand under her elbow, he said, "You were talking to some cops when you . . . stopped me."

"Naw," she replied, "they don't let me park in that lot. I'm some-where on . . . Zack, I think." She leaned on his shoulder for balance. "It's my blood pressure. These things . . . just hit me sometimes. I get . . ." She twirled a finger in the air between them.

When they passed Teach's car, he said, "Let's get out of this heat. I'll drive you to your car."

"You're not all right to drive," she muttered.

"I'm all righter than you are."

"It's a Taurus, white. Well, it used to be."

But he couldn't find her car. He drove up and down the grid of streets, farther and farther away from the police station.

Teach said, "Look, you're not feeling well enough to drive. Maybe you need to see a doctor."

A look of panic came into her eyes. Her face was gray. "No doc-tors." They passed a motel. "Take me . . . there!" She hooked her thumb back at the motel. "I need to lie down."

Teach slowed the Buick and thought it through. If he took her to the ER, she'd be in hands other than his. Good hands. If they stopped at the motel and something bad happened, fate or Turkel could as-sign him the blame. Probably she was shy of the ER because they might draw blood and she could imagine the headlines. *Local Reporter*

Collapses, Blood Alcohol Level Higher Than IQ. He couldn't take her to the hospital against her will.

He registered and paid cash in advance. The clerk insisted on a credit card impression. The room was in the back, away from the street. Teach helped her out of the car and into the plain, clean room. She stared at the bed like it was a boat on a stormy sea, and her knees buckled. He caught her and laid her on the bed. He took the liberty of tugging her skirt down to cover her knees. She lifted an arm and rested it across her eyes.

"Shoes off?"

"Yeah," she said, "I think so."

You think so? Teach undid the straps of her medium-heeled sandals, revealing feet that were dainty and strangely young. Weren't members of the fourth estate known for pounding the pavement until their feet bled?

"Do you need something to eat or drink?"

She closed her eyes. He waited, standing by the bed.

When he was sure she was asleep, Teach searched her purse for her car keys. He drove to a bar, ordered coffee, and watched thirty minutes of baseball. How long would it take her to sleep this off? What would she want when she woke up?

Teach left the bar with a diet soft drink, a carton of orange juice, and a ham sandwich. He found her car on the only street he hadn't searched. He drove the remarkably cluttered and dirty white Taurus back to the motel and let himself in as quietly as he could. She was in the bathroom with the door closed.

Marlie Turkel emerged looking somewhat refreshed. She lifted her hand to the collar of her blouse, ran it down her bosom, and he saw not just embarrassment but anger in her eyes. Teach thinking, *Christ, somehow I've blown it again.* "Look," he said, "I'm sorry . . ." But what was he sorry for? He couldn't think of a damned thing.

She shook her head as though he ought to know how to finish his sorry story.

He shrugged and dangled her keys from his forefinger. "Found your car. It's out front. Can you take me to mine?"

She snatched her purse from the bedside table. "You were in my *bag?*"

"Well, yeah, I . . ."

He offered her the two drinks and the ham sandwich. She took them, tossed the soft drink on the bed, swallowed half the orange juice, and took a bite of the sandwich.

Teach made his voice as neutral as he could: "Do you take pills for this, uh . . . ?"

"Yeah, but like a lot of things in this world, they don't always work." She took another bite and mumbled through the food, "What do you care?" She finished the sandwich and the orange juice, looking at Teach like he was bad wallpaper. As he opened the door for her, she took out some bills from her purse. She handed him two twenties and a ten. "For the room," she said.

"You don't have to—"

"Take it."

He took it.

When she let him out of the dented Taurus, he could feel the blazing concrete through the soles of his shoes. Before she drove away, Marlie Turkel said, "Don't think this changes anything. You've got one week."

The house was empty when Teach got home. He found a note from Dean in the kitchen.

> *Dad,*
>   *Practicing cheerleading at Missy Pace's house. Check your messages.*
> *Weird!*
> *XXXOOO,*
> *Deanie*

He went to the answering machine. The first message was from Walter. "How are you, old buddy? Still on that phony medical leave? Some guys have all the luck. What about an early round next Saturday . . . if you can get your lazy ass out of bed. Let me know. Ciao, buddy."

What Teach heard next made his hackles rise. The same message, three times. It was music, a verse from an old '50s rock tune. He remembered the song, but not the title or who had sung it.

A plaintive teenage boy soprano sang, *"You don't remember me, but I remember you. T'was not so long ago, you broke my heart in two. Tears on my pillow, pain in my heart, caused by you . . ."*

The first call had come in the morning just after he'd left for the police station. He imagined Dean waking up with those words drifting up the stairs. The other two calls had come at ten and eleven o'clock. Each time the same verse.

"Caused by you . . . whoo . . . whoo . . ." That was where it ended. Dean was right, it was weird. Teach played the messages again. It was a scratchy old 45 RPM record, and the eerie effect was doubled by echo and background noise, some machine with a big engine. He saved the messages.

The phone rang. He waited while his greeting played, James Teach in his salesman's voice saying no one could come to the phone, please leave a message. Then the long beep. Then the song started again: *"You don't remember me . . ."*

THIRTY-THREE

Blood Naylor had bought the little record player in a pawn-shop. He'd set it up in the back of the warehouse where he'd met with Tyrone, given the boy his portion of Blood's Special Reserve. It was quiet back here and private. Once in a while you could hear the forklift engine whining or one of the trucks pulling into the loading dock, but mostly it was calm and still. Blood owned a collection of old '50s tunes. He had played them for Thalia, trying to interest her in the Drifters, Sam Cooke, Martha and the Vandellas, all that. She had listened with him, smiled, said she liked them. They'd even had some good, dreamy slow-dances to the tunes, but Thalia was just jiving him along. She loved the music of her own young years.

He had decided to play Little Anthony and the Imperials for Teach because of the message: *You don't remember me, but I remember you.* Teach, the guy who had picked up Thalia at the country club like she came with the dues he paid. The guy who had told Blood one night in a bar after closing time that they were going to stick to their bargain and he was going to disappear and Blood, if he knew what was good for him, would do the same thing. Well, Teach had disappeared for a while and then he had reappeared and he had prospered. He had forgotten about Blood, but Blood had not been so lucky or so smart. Blood had gone back to the university city where the load of marijuana waited for him in the rented U-Haul truck, where it had to be distributed before anybody could disappear. And before he could disappear, he had been busted. Not caught with the entire load of product—in those days he would have done life for that much dope—just caught in the act of passing a modest consignment to a couple of fraternity boys. But caught was caught, and Blood did his first jail time for possession-with-intent-to-sell at the Glades Correctional Institution. And he spent a lot of that time wondering why James Teach had shut down their operation so abruptly, and how the guy had earned that wound under his arm. That bloody bandage he'd tried to hide. Blood's mind eventually ran to the possibility that Teach had highjacked the Guatemalans, taken money from them, and that some of that money was owed to him, to Blood Naylor, because the other part of their bargain was a fifty-fifty split of everything, every last dime.

Wearing out his first jolt in prison, Blood figured that Teach had double-crossed him. If there had never been a Thalia, never been anything between her and Teach, Blood would have found him eventually and asked him about the sudden ending of a very sweet deal. But there *was* a Thalia, or there had been, and Blood had gone to prison a second time, and she and Teach had done their thing, and Blood had two good reasons for getting back into Mr. Teach's fortunate life.

Blood had been using every day for a week. Using his own product like it was food and water, and he was running out of it. He'd started with a little, and with a promise that a little was enough, and then like every other fool he'd moved on to a lot. That was bad enough; it was worse that he had none to sell. His customers were finding other sources, and he was in arrears to his suppliers. Up at Raiford, out in the yard where he had pumped iron and gone to crime school, the better-informed inmates had described what Blood was doing now: *Might as well put a gun to your head.*

There were always bad cops, cops on drugs, cops on the take, cops who looked the other way, and Blood knew his share of them. One of them had told him that Detective Aimes had called Teach in for a little talk. So Blood knew the story he had told with Thalia's photo album was working. And now he was playing Little Anthony for Teach, that beautiful song about how one person remembers a thing, how it becomes everything to that person, and how the other person doesn't remember because something has disappeared. Little Anthony was letting Teach know it wasn't just Old Bad Luck that was fucking with him. It was *somebody*. A person. Some guy Teach didn't remember. Blood liked to think of the guy standing in his big house in Terra Ceia (he had been out there, scoped the place), standing there with blondie girl child listening to that song and trying to explain it to her. Hell, the man had no idea what it meant. Not yet. But he was going to know. He was going to remember.

Blood cut himself a line with the edge of his Visa card and sucked it through a rolled twenty. The drug was everything they said it was, and worse. High was not where it took you; it took you to another planet, and every time you did the drug that planet drifted farther away from the system where you had started your fucked-up trip. Coming down . . . that was right. Coming down was just one thing—paranoia. When the drug stopped burning your nerves, you didn't land, you crashed. What took its place in your nervous system was the certainty that everyone and everything in the world was out to fuck with you. Paranoia was an addiction too. You started thinking that way, you couldn't stop.

When you were high, you needed something that tied you to the old reality, the place where you had started, and for Blood vodka was that thing. So he drank when he did the blow, and when he came down to land on planet paranoia, he drank to ease the fall.

He had told himself to sit tight, do nothing, wait to see what happened after Thalia, so he sat in the recliner in a corner of the warehouse and comforted himself with the Visa card, the rolled twenty, the vodka, and the old 45s. He told Clara in the office out front that he was doing inventory, meditating on ways to better the business. He needed quiet. He needed to be alone. She looked at him like she knew what he needed and it wasn't quiet, but she nodded and went back to the green glow of her computer screen. What she knew was what he paid her for, how to run the 25 percent of his business that was really cheap furniture and vig from the fools who couldn't make their payments on time.

Blood knew he had to stop using before he looked like he was using, before people saw the changes, the weight loss, the skin going from brown to yellow, the sag under the darting eyes, the twitching hands, the clenching jaw. But all he could manage was to promise himself to stop tomorrow, to stop after his next fall to earth, after this high was over.

Twilight came to the loading dock and the parking lot, and the two zombitches came to the jacaranda tree in the alley, and the john cars rolled in, pricing poon and talking the dozens with the two half-dead girls. Blood watched and smiled sadly and said to himself, *Nigger, you might as well walk on down there and sell something. You ain't no different from them girls now, and you need the money.* When he remembered to do it, he dialed Teach's number and played Little Anthony, but now there was little pleasure in it. He needed something else. More.

Finally he knew what he had to do. He had to see someone. Someone who had known Thalia.

THIRTY-FOUR

Sitting in his study, Teach heard Dean come home. Whispers and giggles told him she was not alone. She turned on the message machine, that weird male falsetto singing, *"You broke my heart in two . . ."*

Teach called out, "Deanie, can you come here a minute?" He was holding the thin hope that one of her friends was playing a prank.

He had drunk one bourbon and poured himself another. He sat with the glass in his hand, sighting through the amber liquid at the shafts of afternoon light cutting through the shutters Paige had installed. In honor of Teach's nautical past, she'd decorated his study to look like a captain's cabin on a clipper ship. A lot of brass and polished mahogany. On their last anniversary, she'd presented him with an antique sextant in a glass bell jar. "To steer the ship straight," she'd said, raising a glass of chardonnay to him.

He spent a lot of time in the study, most of it working, some of it imagining himself a man of another time, a rover, a seagoing romantic whose ties to the land were no more substantial than the light that filtered, honey-golden, through his bourbon glass. But Teach had been a real seagoing man once, and it had not been romantic. Of course, he had never told Paige the truth of his life on the water.

Dean stuck her head into the office, saw the glass in his hand, frowned. "How many?"

"This is the second, and the last tonight." Music started upstairs, a black man's voice, some mellow R&B. Teach pointed at the ceiling. Dean gave him her melt-Daddy's-heart look. "Can Tawnya sleep over? We need to practice some jumps." She did an effortless pirouette. "Ballet girls conquer cheerleading."

Ah, Teach thought, *cheerleading.* His policy on sleepovers was liberal. They meant pizza delivery, which meant he didn't have to cook, or more accurately subject healthy young people to his dubious kitchen skills. And they meant no boys. He considered briefly the question: *Why does Thurman Battles allow his daughter to sleep under the racist roof of Teach?* His mind churned up answers ranging from the man having a change of heart (unlikely but possible) to the man's daughter simply not telling him about it, or (more likely) the daughter striking the sleepover deal with Mrs. Battles (the old divide-and-conquer).

"Sure, she can stay. You girls are getting really . . . tight, huh?"

"Yeah, Dad." Her face said, *So?*

Teach told himself not to worry about Dean and Tawnya. The forces that made friends were as mysterious as those that bound lovers. Tawnya Battles was no more likely to hurt the house of Teach than Dean was to hurt the house of Battles. They were two girls who liked each other, had things in common, could giggle and whisper. Two girls floating free in the time-out of youth. They didn't care about two hundred years of race relations; they had a relationship. It was a good thing.

"Uh, listen, Deanie, do you know anything about those messages on the machine?"

"Know anything?" That teenage privacy kicking in. The instinct to give as little as possible to the parental question.

Teach smiled. "Come in and sit down." His daughter walked in a little warily and sat down. "Maybe it's one of your friends. A prank. You know anything about that?"

She pursed her lips and scrunched up her face. "Not that stuff. That's *way* retro."

Faintly, Teach heard the words *"sexual healing"* drift down the stairs. He sighed, sipped, tried to think. "Okay, Deanie, thanks." Meaning she could go.

She stayed. "Dad, is somebody leaving those messages for you? I mean, are you in trouble again?"

She looked scared, her face a little pale, her hands smoothing the thighs of her razored jeans. Teach wanted to protect her, to jolly her out of the room, buy time like he had done with Marlie Turkel. See what developed. Then he thought: *She's my daughter. She has some rights here. And what do I have, what do I have but her?* He set the bourbon on his desk, pushed the glass away from him.

"Deanie, I think somebody wants to . . . hurt me. I don't know who it is. I don't know why." He had begun, and now, seeing her widening eyes, the hands that started to tremble, he felt panic. What could he tell her, what would she understand? Certainly not all of it. Not yet. Maybe never. He stumbled on: "Honey, we have to be strong, and . . . and careful, you and me. We have to take care of each other and get through this."

And suddenly there was anger in his daughter's eyes, a hard, impatient anger. She shoved up and stood in front of him. "Bullshit, Dad. Tell me what's going on. You can't just give me, *We gotta care, we gotta love.* Is Tyrone doing this? Is that what it is?"

Teach's mind was tired. He wanted rest, but he couldn't stop here. "Deanie, I just don't know. It's possible." A part of him wanted to say: *A woman is dead. A woman I knew. The police talked to me today.* But he could see too clearly all of the questions that would follow, and he wasn't ready for them.

Dean turned away and walked over to the shutters where a buttery light poured in. She bent and peered through, like she thought someone might be out there. She closed the shutters. When she turned back to him, a calm, cunning smile came to her face. "Wait a minute, Dad," she said. "I'll be right back."

Her footsteps receded in the hallway that led to the garage, then after a minute she appeared in front of him holding a manila envelope. "Damnit, Deanie," he said, "I hid those. How did you find them?"

"I know, Dad." Her face was resolute. "I'm sorry if you're mad at me, but I had to look at them."

She had snuck into his darkroom, found the photos of Tyrone where he had hidden them at the back of a cabinet. And how could he be angry? The photos had been her idea. She had saved him. Of course she was curious. She opened the envelope and sorted through the shots. Teach waited.

She found the picture she wanted. "Look at this one, Dad."

Teach took it from her. It was the first shot he had taken, Tyrone talking to the man who had driven up in the white Bronco.

The driver was only a grainy image. His left cheekbone and one eye caught some of the light from a pole on the Gandy Causeway, but the right side of his face was in Tyrone's shadow. Teach remembered the man's arrival and his quick departure.

He handed the picture back to Dean. "What's the point, honey?"

She was excited, her blue eyes large and bright. "Dad, can you enlarge this? Can you get this guy's face to come in a little clearer?"

"If I can't, somebody probably can. Why, honey? What's this about?"

She looked straight into his eyes. "It's about that song, Dad."

Teach was catching her excitement now and losing his patience too. "Damnit, Deanie, what are you trying to tell me?"

A face appeared at the study door. Tawnya Battles said, "Hi, Mr. Teach, I—"

Dean turned to the doorway. "Um, Tawnya, maybe . . ."

Teach said, "Come in." He walked to the door with his hand extended. Tawnya Battles shook with him. She was taller than Dean and her pretty face already held some of her father's stern bearing. She wore ripped Levi's like Dean's and a white T-shirt that she had scissored off five inches below her breasts. Her midriff rippled with muscles a man would envy. Teach pictured her ten years from now—an attorney like her father, and a society wife, dignified, vital, and a little grave . . . How long had she been listening out in the hallway?

She stood in front of him barefooted like Dean, her skin a little darker than Thalia's, looking him in the eye. "Tyrone gets his drugs from the guy in the Bronco. The guy is his, whaddayoucallit, *connection*. People laugh because the Bronco's so, you know, O.J."

Teach liked that she didn't know what to call it. He didn't know the current term. *Pusher* was probably out of date. He kept his voice fatherly, measured. "What about the song?" Something was wrong here, he could see it in Tawnya's eyes. Something was stealing her courage.

"Mr. Teach," Tawnya said, "the guy in the Bronco always plays that '50s rock. It's his thing. He's way nuts about it. That song, it's his favorite."

Listening, Dean rubbed the slashed denim at her thighs.

Teach said, "And you know this how, Tawnya? That he *always* plays that song?"

He saw the grim decision come into the girl's eyes.

"I was out there one night, on the causeway, and the guy came, and Tyrone talked to him, and he played that song. It's not a song you forget."

Dean shook her head and wiped at her eyes, suddenly red and swollen. "I swear, Dad, we didn't do any drugs. We just had a beer, and we left right after that."

We. Of course. *Us chicks hang together.*

Teach turned to her, a war going on in his heart. What should he say, what should a father say?

He took a deep breath, sighed it out. "Thanks for telling me the truth, Tawnya, Deanie. I'm not happy to hear you were out there, but I'm glad you were honest with me." *And*, Teach thought, *maybe someday I can be honest with my daughter.*

"Sexual Healing" had ended upstairs. Out in the foyer, the phone rang and Teach's voice answered, saying nobody could come to the phone. Then the kid sang it again, "*You don't remember me . . .*"

PART THREE

THIRTY-FIVE

Blood put Thalia's box of memories on the porch behind him, knocked, and called out, "Granmon Liston? You in there? Please come to the door. I got something for you."

It was his mournful voice, a complaint searching for sympathy. He'd drunk enough vodka to tie himself to earth, but the coke was still confusing his nerves. He thought he could cover his condition with the look and the sound of his grief. And who could blame a man for using a little at a time like this? He knew exactly who could blame him. She was shuffling across the floor inside, probably wearing those slippers that looked like two dead rats.

"Who is it?"

"It's Bloodworth, Granmon. You know my voice. It ain't been that long. I want to talk to you."

"Nigger, what you want here this time of night?"

Blood could not keep his voice from changing, something bent, a little crazy coming into it. "I brought you my con . . . condolences for Thalia. My sweet little Thalia. Can't you let me in, Granmon?"

"Just a minute then."

Blood listened as she released two dead bolts. She opened the door six inches, and he tried to read her face in the narrow slice of light, wondered what his own fucked-up face said to her. The old lady's one good eye was hard black, the other one the color of egg custard. Her back was straight, her jaw clenched. She opened the door and stepped out of his way. He remembered Thalia telling him her grandmother had cataracts, needed surgery, but wouldn't or couldn't pay for it.

Blood had never liked Mary Lena Liston, but he had stopped short of hating her. Stopped there for Thalia's sake. He picked up

Thalia's box, smiled sadly, and walked in. Standing on the worn living room rug, he put the box down again and pulled the old lady into a hug. She was like nothing in his arms, a weightless bony nothing. When he let her go, he saw that her face had not changed while he held her.

She said, "It's too late at night for you to be in my house. Say what you want to say and go. I'm old and I'm tired."

The worn pine floor groaned when Blood walked to the sofa. He sighed. "Ah, Granmon, I just come to tell you how sorry I am about Thalia. I miss her so much, and I know you do too, and—"

"I miss her now and I missed her then. When you took her away and shown her them evil nigger ways. All that drinking and running around. Newspapers say she was a ho. If she was, you made her one. Now you tell me you miss her. What kind of fool you take me for?"

Blood didn't say anything, but he could feel his anger like the swelling of a bruise. It occurred to him that maybe he had come here to finish something, end the story of Thalia and all that went with it. This old woman knew more than anyone else about Thalia and him. She hated him. He could see it in the black light of her good eye, and he knew she could tell the cops plenty about him if she wanted to. She could point them in his direction like an old quail dog pointing a covey before she dropped to her belly with the crack of the shotguns behind her. His voice was sullen when he said, "It wasn't me made her a ho. It was that white man she run with when I was in the joint. You ask anybody around here about that. They tell you."

The old lady sighed. "I don't believe she had no white man. No man but you, and I ain't sure you a man." She waved her hand in front of her like someone shifting smoke in the air. "Anyways, I'm too old to care. You done told me how you feel, now go."

"I brought you something. I know you love boiled peanuts. I brought you some, just like I used to when I come here to see Thalia."

Blood sat on the sofa and the old springs complained beneath his weight. He took the bag of peanuts from Thalia's box and held it out to the woman. She eyed it carefully. The gift changed hands. She gave him a grudging, "Thank you, Bloodworth. Now . . ."

"All right. All right. I hear you." He shifted toward her on the sofa. "I just wanted to see you, Granmon. Nothing bad in that, is it?"

"Nothing bad in that," she muttered. "Plenty bad though, plenty bad all around."

"All right. All right." His heart's sadness in his voice now. "You still got that picture of Thalia in there? In your bedroom?"

The old lady shook her head. "You ain't going in my bedroom, and I ain't letting you have no picture."

"No, no," Blood said. "You don't understand me. I come to trade. I got some pictures. Thalia give them to me. You take as many as you want, and I'll take that picture in the bedroom, the one where she a little girl. So, it's a trade, not . . ." He let the words die in the silence. He shifted the box to his lap, took out the sheaf of photos, and handed them to the old woman. "I think Thalia wanted you to have these."

Not even that hard eye could resist the envelope. *Ah, curiosity,* Blood thought. *It killed more than the cat. Killed everything alive on earth one time or another.* He watched her sift through the pictures, tried to read her as she took in the story of Thalia and James Teach, businessman, vice president, husband, and father.

Finally, she looked up at him, the eye full of sadness. She shook her head. "Why you bring these here? I don't want see this."

"So you see your little angel was a ho while I was up at Raiford where I couldn't hurt her one bit, couldn't hurt nobody. She hoing with a married white man, man lives in Terra Ceia with his blondie wife and his blondie daughter. Man has everything, and he still take your angel, my angel, my Thalia." Blood could feel his eyes swelling, getting wet, and he didn't want the old lady to see it. See him like that. He cleared his throat so loud it was almost a scream. "So, which ones you want keep? You decide yet? Take your time. I got plenty time. Keep some so you remember your Thalia like she really was. Not like that picture in your bedroom."

Mary Lena Liston walked to the front door with the sheaf of pictures and the bag of boiled peanuts and threw them as far as her feeble hands could out into the night beyond the porch.

Blood followed her to the door. She stepped aside for him.

"Well . . . Granmon, I'm glad I came by. It . . . did me good to see you. We both loved her. We loved Thale, didn't we?"

The old lady looked up at him, pure hatred in that one dark eye. "I loved her, Bloodworth, and I know what you did. Now, good night."

Standing on the porch, he heard the door shut behind him. He said to the night, the darkness, "I loved her . . . but I let her go." He turned back and said it to the closed door. "Want you to know that. I released her." He knew she was listening. He said it again, louder, "I released her."

He collected the pictures from the dewy grass, picked one, and left it on the porch for the old lady to find in the morning.

THIRTY-SIX

t woke you up?" Aimes stopped the Crown Vic at the traffic light on Kennedy and Armenia and looked over at Delbert.

"I shot right up in bed." Delbert stared straight ahead into the intersection. "I don't know why it came to me when it did, but I told you it would."

"It wake her up too?"

"Who?" Delbert looked over at Aimes, confused.

"Her. Betty Sue. Ellie Lou. Fanny Blue. Cindy Clueless. The one you go line dancing with down at Zichex. The one who bought you that whole case of Cholula hot sauce for your birthday. It wake her up too?"

"I was sleeping alone." Delbert going sulky, unappreciated. "And they don't line dance at Zichex. Zichex is a disco for '70s burnouts. Travolta wannabes, I don't know. You ought to get out more often, get your nose in the wind, see what's going on out there in the land of the living."

Aimes hadn't been out, had his nose to the wind, since his wife died of cancer a year ago. He had stayed home, watched TV, read books on military history, and worked out on his treadmill, trying to control his weight. He knew Delbert didn't mean anything with his reference to the land of the living. And now, nose to the wind or not, he was glad Delbert had finally remembered.

After Delbert had remembered it, Aimes had cajoled his way into some supposedly sealed records. Back in 1979, James Teach had been convicted, sentenced, and incarcerated on a charge of drug-related activity. He had served eleven months of a two-year sentence in the Federal Prison Camp at Eglin Air Force Base. After his release, Teach had had the record of the felony conviction legally expunged. It was one of the weird anomalies of Florida law. If you had money for a lawyer, and the lawyer knew the right judge, and you kept your nose clean for a year, you could eliminate every trace of the offense from the public record. From all records except the mind of a persistent policeman.

Delbert had told Aimes there was something about Teach, and it wasn't football. Well, this was it. Back when Delbert was a kid, his uncle had been a sheriff's deputy in Gilchrist County, and before that his uncle had played for the Gators. Third-string tight end. The uncle and the boy, Delbert, had been watching a Gators game one Saturday afternoon, and the uncle had shown the boy an arrest warrant for James Teach, ex-Gator great. "Remember him?" the uncle asked. Young Delbert nodded, said he remembered. "Well, they don't all end up in Hollywood," the uncle had said.

So Teach had been a drug smuggler, or had known them, had run with them. The information Delbert had obtained by the magic of the mainframe did not specify the exact nature of the offense. But Mr. Teach would specify it in their next conversation. It and a lot more, and if the specifics didn't sound right, maybe Teach would not leave the police station this time.

Delbert said, "It's all part of a pattern, you ask me. Those kids out on the causeway get busted holding pharmaceutical speed. Thalia Speaks had the same kind of crank in her apartment. Mr. Teach, who used to be her sugar daddy, he's done some time in the shade for drug-related activity, and you know what that means. They wanted him for something bigger, but they couldn't make the case. So they slapped him with the catchall charge."

Aimes nodded, smiled. He knew what it meant. It meant Mr. Teach just got more and more interesting all the time. He wondered if he could get Teach to come in again without a lawyer. There was still nothing to put the guy in that apartment on the night of the murder, but murder cases had been successfully prosecuted with less than Aimes and Delbert had right now. Still, he could see the city prosecutor giving him the old litany: *It's all circumstantial. Bring me something that puts him there that night.*

But, Aimes would say, *the guy has no alibi. Says he was asleep on a boat in a deserted marina when the woman was killed. You buy that?*

I don't buy it, but a jury might. They might call it a reasonable doubt.

Fucking ADAs, Aimes thought. They wanted you to put the fish in the barrel, put the gun in their hands, aim it for them. They wanted you to say, *Okay, go ahead and shoot now.*

Aimes said, "What about the other girls? You still like our Mr. Teach for all of them?"

Delbert shook his head, impatient. "I like him for Thalia Speaks so much I don't care about the others anymore."

"Easy now. We got to get as much out of this as we can. If Teach did the others, we want him for them too."

Delbert looked at Aimes like he had a sudden gas pain, that redneck bile rumbling in his flat belly, all hot and corrosive. Teach was Delbert's meat.

Aimes said, "*Some time in the shade?* Where'd you get that from?"

Delbert put a hand gingerly to his belt buckle, pressed it there. He looked thoughtful. "My granddaddy used to say that. It means you been in prison. You're all pale. You know, you been in the shade."

"Your granddaddy ever do time, Delbert?"

"No. He was a mortician, but come to think of it, he had a light complexion."

Ah, culture, thought Aimes. *The different ways people construct meaning.* He saw humanity as comprised of two tribes: the evildoers and the law-abiders. He was a man on a long march and his living reason was to bring down as many from the evildoing tribe as he could. It was practical for him, without theory. It was a thing he did for his wife, because when she was alive she had admired him for it, and now he lived on memories of her admiration. Delbert was a curious kid. Under all that energy, all that earnest, hard-working, up-by-the-bootstraps ambition, Aimes thought there might beat the heart of a true believer in Justice and the American Way. Sometimes the kid scared Aimes a little.

"Delbert, something I never asked you. Did you play football?"

Delbert looked at him, wondering where this was going. "No, I was in the band."

"In the band?"

"Yeah, I played the clarinet."

"You marched up and down the field in that uniform that looked like the army of Bolivia?"

"Yeah, I did. So?"

"So, nothing. Just curious."

Maybe Delbert's hard-on for Teach had something to do with football. Teach being the big star. Whatever it was, it was strong. It wasn't clarinet music. It was a big bass drum.

THIRTY-SEVEN

Teach spent the evening in his darkroom working with the enlarger until he was sure of the Bronco's tag number. He could do little with the shot of the man who drove it. Blown up and cleaned up, the face looked like half of a hockey mask, or the Phantom of the Opera. When Teach finished, he went out to his study and picked up the phone.

"Sorry to call so late, Walter, but it's important." By the unspoken rules of Terra Ceia, eleven thirty was too late for a phone call. But Teach was buzzed by the darkroom work, and he wanted to keep the momentum going.

"That's all right, old buddy." Walter's laugh was not entirely one of mirth. "What can I do for you? Not, God help us, another barroom altercation, is it?"

Teach put into his voice what there was of obligation between him and Walter. There wasn't much. "I need a favor. Do you know anybody down at the Department of Motor Vehicles? I need the name that goes with an auto tag."

Walter was silent. Teach heard in the background the sounds of the Demarest household. Letterman on TV. The thump of rock music, Walter's teenage son, Peyton.

Walter finally said, "I, that is, *we* retain an investigator with contacts at the DMV." Now his voice was reserved, a lawyer's voice. "He runs things down for us occasionally. Nothing Sam Spade, you understand. Mostly vehicle registration numbers for probate cases. I'll ask the guy to see what he can find. What's going on?"

Teach had anticipated the question. "I'd rather not say, Walter. I can promise you it's nothing that will ever come back and bite your butt." *It could take my butt in one great, bloody crunch, but not yours, old buddy.*

Walter thought about it. Letterman told a joke. Peyton Demarest's brain death by heavy metal floated across the wires to Teach. "Hokay, buddy, but I hope there's green grass on the other side of this rough patch you're going through."

Teach gave him the tag number. Walter Demarest explained that he could have the information by midmorning tomorrow, then he said, "By the way, Peyton tried to call Dean, and your phone was out of order. Thought you'd want to know."

"Thanks, Walter. Some malfunction over here. We'll fix it." He had unplugged the phones. The messages had been coming every hour on the hour.

Teach had saved the brief obituary of Thalia Speaks. It listed two survivors: a sister, Bennie Marie Speaks, and a grandmother, Mary Lena Liston. He found the two women in the phone book. He didn't know much about the College Hill section of Tampa, only what he'd seen on news programs: night scenes of drunks in handcuffs, splashes of blood on sidewalks, anguished faces strobing on and off in the blue-and-red lights of police cars.

He went to the foot of the stairs and called up, "Dean, I'm going out for a while." He waited.

His daughter's sleepy voice called down, "All right, Dad." The TV murmured up there.

Teach drove through College Hill with a city map on his lap. The houses were frame and cinder-block boxes. TVs glowed in barred windows. Porches owned pairs of gleaming red canine eyes.

Teach stopped at the curb across the street from Benny Marie Speaks's green and brown bungalow and opened the window of his LeSabre. The warm night air flowed in, carrying the sounds of sirens. Only a few blocks away, the worst of the ghetto began.

He wasn't sure what he was doing here. It was too late for a reasonable knock on anyone's door. But he had that buzz in his chest and the weird feeling that if he didn't keep going tonight he'd just return to the waiting, waiting for Aimes to call him in again, waiting for more of those falsetto messages about not remembering someone. Thalia's sister's house was dark. Teach moved on to her grandmother.

Driving slowly through the night streets, he thought about connections. He had bloodied Tyrone in a bar, and Tyrone was connected to a man in a white Bronco. The man in the Bronco was calling Teach's house leaving a message about remembering people. He had left the first message the day Teach had talked to Detective Aimes about the death of Thalia Speaks. Was Thalia connected to the man in the Bronco? Was Tyrone somehow connected to Thalia? They had both done drugs. The man in the Bronco had been out there on the Gandy Causeway feeding Tyrone's crack habit. Teach had to assume that drugs connected all three.

Suddenly, it occurred to him that maybe meeting Tyrone in a bar was not an accident. Not a thing that had happened to him, but a thing *done* to him. By someone. For a reason. A thing that had stalked him, caught him there happy, drinking, telling football stories. *You don't remember me.*

He drove past Thalia's grandmother's house twice before stopping. Mary Lena Liston lived in a bad place. There was a burned-out convenience store at the end of the block, and a house across the street stood in a weed-choked yard, its windows covered with plywood. Teach passed two groups of hard-eyed young black men. From one of them, a boy had run a few yards after Teach's car shouting, "What you doing here, bitch?" The challenge, fading behind him, seized his chest like a cold fist and made him slip down in the seat waiting for a rock or a bullet to shatter his window.

He waited in the car for fifteen minutes, watching Mary Lena Liston's house, trying to make up his mind about what to do. Finally, the porch light snapped on, and a frail old black woman stepped out and peered up and down the street. She held a bowl in her hands, and carried a newspaper. As Teach watched, she went stiffly to a white rattan chair and sat, smoothed the newspaper out at her feet, and rested the bowl on her knees. He drove the Buick down the block and hid it in the mouth of an alley. He got out and walked back toward the old woman's light.

Close enough for her to see him, he slowed his pace. He didn't want to scare her. He had no idea who else was in the house. Closer, he saw that the bowl on her lap held field peas, and that her busy fingers were shelling them, dropping the shells onto the newspaper.

He stopped on the sidewalk and waited for her to look up. She didn't. "White man, what you doing here this time of night?"

Teach said, "I'm looking for Mary Lena Liston. I have something for her. Something of value." He had planned this on the drive over. It was cheap, tawdry, but it was all he had, and it might work.

"You found her." The old woman kept her eyes on the peas in her lap. She broke the pods with a pop, then ripped her thumb through to sprinkle the peas into an old porcelain basin. "But she don't let no white man call her Mary Lena. You call me Mrs. Liston, or you get on out of here."

Teach was about to apologize, start again, when she muttered, "Coming here in the middle of the night telling an old lady you got something for her."

Teach blundered on: "I'm from the . . . Dixie Fidelity and Trust Company. Your granddaughter had an insurance policy with us, and she named you as beneficiary. I'd like to talk to you about it if you've got time." *Forgive me*, Teach thought.

The old woman looked up for the first time, revealing the milky film of a cataract across her right eye. The left eye was aimed at him like the black dot at the end of a gun barrel. "When you white mens start doing the insurance business at night?"

Teach stood ten feet from her in the porch light, letting her see him. He tried to seem small and harmless. "I think I can smell a thunderstorm coming. Does it seem that way to you?"

She looked at him, at the peas in her lap, set the bowl aside, and wiped her hands on her apron. "Might be right about that. I didn't think you young'uns noticed the weather unless it blown your hair out of place or destroyed some of that nasty crack rock you always consuming."

Teach made his voice earnest. "Mrs. Liston, I don't use drugs, and I notice the weather, and I wonder if you might invite me out of it so we can talk."

She stood up, groaning, touching the middle of her back. She picked up the bowl of peas. "I give you five minutes, white man, but you better not be wasting my time, and you better not be selling no aluminum siding. I done run off more aluminum siding mens than you got teeth in you head."

She gave him more than five minutes. In the cramped kitchen smelling of bacon and soap they sat under a bulb shaded by a large plastic sunflower. She offered him a glass of cream soda, took one herself, and asked if he had a cigarette. He told her he had given up the habit, and she explained that she had cut herself down to bumming. In an ungenerous world, it was a good way for an old lady to suppress a vice.

Teach knew enough about insurance to make the thing seem plausible. After setting the hook, a ten-thousand-dollar benefit, he guided the talk to Thalia. He explained that he needed information about her to file the claim. The old woman looked at him sharply. "Thalia had her a policy with you. Ain't you got all the information you need?"

Teach moved the talk to the past, to Thalia's life before she'd worked at the country club. He asked about her education, what she'd done in high school, the community college, hoping the old lady would warm to him, to the past.

After a while, it began to work. The woman's good eye misted as she talked about a dead granddaughter. "She was my baby. I raised her. She'd try to live with that sister of hers, but she kept coming back here to me. We got along good, and she never disrespected me. Then she got involved with that Naylor. All her trouble started with that evil nigger. When she saw the life them crack mens live, the way they throw money around and turn women out like dogs. She got shut of him when he went to the jailhouse, and things was good with me and her again for a while."

Naylor. *Naylor?*

Teach kept his voice quiet, easy, the voice of a man representing an insurance company. "Did you say Naylor, Mrs. Liston? Was that the name you used?"

"That's right, Naylor. Nigger was her boyfriend before he went to Raiford. She made him come here, get out of his big ol' fancy car, and sit on my porch and court her like a man ought to. He was good to her for a while. She told me she was gone make something out of him. Get him out of that crack life. But he got lawed and sent to the jailhouse. Thalia wrote him letters, and she got herself educated and went to work at that fancy white folks club, and she dropped him. Stopped writing to him. It was a dangerous thing to do. I told her that. Bad as he was, I told her she ought to stick with him while he

was doing time. Them mens, they get out of jail and they come looking for the girl that runs around on them while they locked down."

Teach cleared his throat, looked away from that one bright black
eye. "Did she, uh, did Thalia take up with another man while this
Naylor was in prison?"

The old lady looked at him hard. "Some white man. Met him
at that club where she worked. You go to that club? You know that
man?"

"No, no ma'am, I don't know him." He watched her, hoping she
believed him. It had been a while since anything had been said about
insurance. She had grown soft remembering Thalia, but the talk of
Naylor, and of a white man Thalia had gone with, had made her hard
again.

"Thalia told me she loved that white man. *I love him, Granmon*, she
said to me. I think she was drinking that night, else she wouldn't
have said it. She known I don't hold with white and black together
like that. You know what I said? I told her lots of little black girls
loved white mens, and lots of them got babies from them. That's how
you get high-yellow niggers, I told her. But you go over to the white
side of town and see how many them little black girls is living with
them white mens in them nice houses. You go look, and you come
back and tell me about it."

Teach saw the thing getting dangerous now. He decided to be
quick, surprise her. He took the photo of the man in the Bronco
from inside his jacket and held it in front of her. "Is that him? Is
that Naylor?"

He saw immediately that she knew the man, even the phantom
likeness Teach's camera had captured. She pushed back from the table. Her voice was tired when she said, "You ain't here 'bout no insurance policy, white man. You after him, you after that Naylor, ain't you?"

She got up and shuffled away, her back to the ancient claw-foot
gas stove with its blackened burners and smell of lard. Teach moved
toward her, holding his hands up in front of him, trying to calm her,
trying to find the words to tell her why he was here. Tell her that love
was a part of it.

The old lady put her hand to her bony chest and sucked a sharp
breath. He tried to read her face, struggled for something to say. She

clenched her jaw and took a step past him toward the door. He had to do something. He took her by the shoulders, firm but gentle, and looked into her good eye. When she focused on him, he whispered, "Don't tell him I was here." She looked at him with more anger than he thought one eye could hold. He added, "Please."

Her old arms like sticks in his hands, she shook her head at the shamelessness of men.

She knows, he thought. *She knows it all now.*

She put her bony hands on his chest and pushed him back toward the kitchen table and whispered, "He was here. Bloodworth Naylor. Came in the middle of the night, just like you. Said he had something for me, just like you."

God, Teach thought, *Bloodworth. Blood Naylor.* He felt the small house grow crowded, dangerous with so many secrets. He wondered what was between the old lady and Naylor that she hadn't told him.

"He said he loved her, told me how he missed her. Said he . . . released her. Told me it wasn't him who made her a ho. It was that white man."

Teach imagined the scene, Naylor and the old lady in this room, felt his anger growing. Naylor might have hurt Mary Lena Liston. He might still do it because she knew about him and Thalia. Teach would have to do something now. Maybe this was what the whole thing was really about. A second fight between Teach and a black man. A man from out of the past.

The old lady crossed her heart with her hands: "He showed me a box of pictures. Said Thalia give them to him. Now you come here trying to fool me. Telling me 'bout some insurance policy. You ought to be ashamed of yourself."

Teach looked at her, glad she was so still, glad she wasn't up and on him, beating him with with a broom like a dog. He said, "I am. I am ashamed."

Groaning, she walked into the living room. When she returned, she placed a photo on the table in front of Teach. He and Thalia in the restaurant in Madeira Beach. Their smiles a little sad. The empty gift boxes on the table and the scraps of their meal. This one had been taken at the end of that afternoon when they were beginning to think about the hard return to separate worlds.

The old lady sighed. "I don't care no more. Too old to care."

Teach knew what he had to do. It might not matter here, or any-where, but he had to do it. He had to promise. "I'll find out who killed Thalia," he said. "I'll find out, and I'll see he gets what he deserves." He was at the door now.

"Thalia said she loved you." Her voice was quiet, brittle as the heart she held. "She said it one night sitting here in this room. She never said that about him." She looked at the door, letting him know it was time to leave. "I suppose that matter for something."

THIRTY-EIGHT

Teach woke up at midmorning with a pounding headache. After his talk with Mary Lena Liston, he had come home to a dark, quiet house. Full of guilt, full of a crazy resolve to get Thalia's killer, full of shock at the discovery that time and fate and Thalia had connected him again to Bloodworth Naylor, he'd had three stiff bourbons and fallen asleep on the sofa in his study.

The silence of the house told him Dean had gone to school. He wondered if she had checked in on him before leaving. Her whiskey-reeking father lying in his study, his face tortured by evil dreams. His night hadn't been all cringing self-accusation. In the lucid hour before first light, he had done some clear thinking. Bloodworth Naylor had to be the man behind all his trouble. He had been Thalia's lover. He had killed her in jealous revenge to destroy James Teach. And he had arranged her apartment so that Aimes would find the napkin and the photograph.

My God, Teach thought, *that paper Delbert left the interrogation room to get. It must hold more of what Naylor gave them.*

He sat up carefully, waiting for the nausea to pass and the headache to sink its grim talons deeper into his brain. The phone rang. Teach walked to it unsteadily and snatched it from its cradle. He would talk to the man, talk to him before the message played (*"You don't remember me, but I remember you . . ."*). He would tell Naylor he did remember. Say he knew more than Naylor could ever imagine, and he was ready to deal with it now.

Walter Demarest said, "Teach, old buddy, I've got the information you asked for. And a little bonus for you . . . Anybody home?"

Teach's hands were trembling, his head throbbed like some demon homunculus was jackhammering rocks inside it. "Sorry, Walter. Go ahead. I'm all ears."

Walter Demarest gave him the name and address of the man who owned the white Bronco. Teach knew the name already, but not that the Bronco was registered to a business: Naylor's Rent-to-Own in Suitcase City. Walter said, "Our investigator threw in some extras for us. He's a zealous fellow. It seems that your Mr. Naylor is a convicted felon. Two prison terms, the last one at Raiford for aggravated battery on a prostitute and living from the earnings of prostitutes. Not a nice man, apparently." There was a pause, then Walter said, "In keeping with our usual drill, I'm not asking why you want to know about this lowlife."

Lying for a good cause had always come easily to Teach. "Some guy ran into Dean's car. He took off, but she got his tag number. I just wanted to find out who he is, see if it's worth pursuing. Sounds like the scumbag is better left alone."

"Sounds like that to me."

Teach could hear the office business humming behind Walter. Walter's billable time ticking on the clock. "Thanks, Walt. I owe you one."

"You owe me a round of golf. How 'bout Saturday morning, bright and early?"

"I'll have to call you back on that one, Walt."

"All right, buddy."

When Teach hung up, the doorbell rang. He wanted badly to go upstairs and sleep for an hour, ignore the bell. Ordinarily, he endured his hangover headaches until the dinner hour when he gentled them with a little wine. This one needed aspirin and rest.

The bell rang again, and Teach went quietly to the dining room window. A young man in a cheap sport coat stood on the front porch. Teach didn't recognize him, but his military bearing and the white Crown Victoria in the driveway told him the man was of a tribe he had seen too often lately. A policeman.

Teach wondered if you could just ignore a cop. Go upstairs and take that nap. If he had not looked out the window, he would not know who was there. The bell rang again and the man called out, "Mr. Teach, it's the police. Open the door, please."

Suddenly, Teach's ears became those of his neighbors, and he moved quickly. Mrs. Carlson next door was often in her yard at this time of the morning, fussing with her daylilies. He imagined her saucer-eyed look as she struggled up, dirt falling from her fat knees, craning to hear the young cop call out Teach's name. He opened the door six inches and peeked out, shading his bleeding eyes from the sunlight.

"Are you James Teach?"

What could he say? He admitted it.

"Detective Aimes would like you to come downtown."

"What for?"

"Just an interview." The cop smiled, but it was the smile of a man approaching a child with a needle. *This won't hurt much.*

"An interview?" Teach opened the door a little more. The policeman looked at the clothes Teach had slept in, his unshaven face. The man's eyes said that his words had been perfectly clear. An interview was an interview. Teach looked at the City of Tampa car in his driveway. Mrs. Carlson was not, blessedly, rooting in her yard. Across the street, one of the idiot sons of a neighbor was mowing the lawn. The boy wore earphones, jiving as he followed the mower. Teach was not sure why he said, "Wait a minute. I have to leave a message for my daughter."

He closed the door just as the cop stepped forward, apparently expecting to wait inside. Teach stood behind the closed door waiting to see if the man would demand to be let in. Nothing. He felt panic rising from his stomach. He tried to push it back down. Tried to remember those Saturday afternoons when the job of football was before him, and his head was as clear as a hawk's, flying high above a field with prey in its eyes. Standing, waiting, Teach felt some of the calm come back. Enough of it.

He picked up his wallet from the table in the foyer and found his shoes where he had stepped out of them the night before at the foot of the stairs. In the kitchen, he opened the refrigerator and grabbed a half-eaten turkey sandwich wrapped in cellophane. He put it in his pocket, drank some milk from the gallon jug, and went to the bay window that let onto the backyard. Gently, he lifted one of the miniblinds and looked out.

A second policeman stood by the back door. He looked and dressed like the first, a young man with short blond hair and a tough, cool face. He rocked on his heels, his right hand resting on the pistol clipped to his belt. He checked his watch, looked up at the hot sun, and tugged at his collar.

Jesus, thought Teach. *Jesus Christ. This is it.* He went to the garage, to the darkroom. He found the photos where he had hidden them and tucked the manila envelope under his shirt. The garage had a side door that opened to a narrow passage between Teach's house and the Chelms's place next door. As Teach put his hand on the doorknob, he remembered that the door was rarely used, that it might groan when he opened it. It did.

And Teach was out in the hot morning, running.

He had no idea where he was going, knew little of why he was running. He just knew he had to. Had to stay free for a while longer. And if he were to lose his freedom, then it would have to be on his own terms, whatever those might be. He ran between the houses, toward the backyard. He heard the cop from the front yard shout, "Look out, Ray!" Heard the running footsteps of the cop in the backyard.

Teach lowered his shoulder as the blond cop loomed in front of him, the man going into a crouch, sweeping his jacket aside to expose his service revolver. Teach hit the man at midchest and went up the middle of his face. Two more strides and a leap at the stuccoed wall that enclosed Paige's garden, and Teach was dropping down onto the pool deck of the Hollingsworths, an old couple recently retired from Maryland. They had a rottweiler, a beast whose deep, angry voice Teach had often heard beyond the wall. He crossed the deck, dancing to miss a fall into their blue pool. He skirted the lanai and ran for the space between the Hollingsworths and the Dyes. Behind him the dog growled then barked, and Teach heard, "Ray!" shouted twice more, but there was no sound from the wall he had just scaled. Apparently the shoulder Teach had learned to use during his year on the Atlanta special teams had laid Ray down.

Running, a good sweat breaking on his face, his headache loosening its hot ring around his skull, Teach hoped he had not hurt the man seriously. He broke into the open, angling across the Dyes' front yard just as the rambling wreck of Angel Morales's yard-work truck and trailer pulled out of the driveway across the street. Teach did not know who owned the house. Many people in the neighborhood em-

ployed Angel Morales. The trailer, half a pickup truck divided from
its cab and fitted with a wagon tongue, was piled with royal palm
fronds, their long green tails trailing ten feet behind. Angel Morales
and his son, Romero, were inside the cab of the old Ford pickup and
probably, Teach thought, sharing the six-pack of malt liquor Angel
brought with him every day.

Teach heard running feet on the Hollingsworths' deck, then a
bark, a shout, and a splash. He dove for the bed of palm fronds in the
makeshift trailer.

He landed soft and burrowed hard. He did not stop worming and
digging until his hands hit the rusted metal of the truck bed. He lay
there panting, feeling the trailer rocking on its old leaf springs, feeling the cool wet of the palm fronds which had been cut and stacked
when the dew was heavy. Teach held his breath, waiting for the truck
to stop, to hear the cop's order: *All right, Mr. Teach, you can come out of
there now.* Teach imagining himself crawling out from under the pile
of cuttings, his clothing soaked with dew and palm sap, his face covered with sawdust and the embarrassed expression of a feckless ass.

All he heard was the song of the tires on the asphalt, the *crank-
clank* of Angel double-clutching as the truck accelerated. Teach tensed
when it stopped a moment later, but he heard the whistling of traffic
and knew they were at the intersection of Sunset and Westshore.
And he knew that if the cops were going to stop Angel they would
have done it by now. Teach lay happy in the cool and dark of getting
away with it. Of running and breaking out. He lay as the miles rolled
under the trailer, wondering where Angel would dump the cuttings.
He lay in the cool, the rumbling, the engine sound, wondering what
he was going to do now. Now that James Teach was a fugitive from
justice.

THIRTY-NINE

When Angel Morales stopped his truck at the Manhattan Avenue yard-waste dump, Teach scrambled out and hid in a stand of Brazilian peppertrees. Angel and his son unloaded and left. Teach watched from hiding as the commercial yard-work rigs came and went. Finally, he caught a ride in the back of an empty one with a Pinellas County tag. At the traffic light on the Gandy Causeway by the Derby Lane greyhound race track, he jumped out and waved to the surprised driver. "Thanks, Bobby. See you at Susie's wedding." A little method acting for the commuters waiting at the light.

Teach called Bama Boyd from a phone booth in front of an adult bookstore. He was exhausted and dirty and every car that passed made him turn his face away as men did in the movies. Men on the run. Men who might be recognized and ratted out by decent citizens.

The receptionist at the Isla del Sol Yacht and Country Club told Teach she'd have to page Ms. Boyd. Teach waited, exposure cold on his hunched back, listening for the crunch of tires, the crackle of a police radio.

"Samantha Boyd. How can I help you?"

Bama's voice was good to hear. "Hey, Bama, it's Teach. Whaddya say, darlin'?" He waited.

He needed a friend. Right now, all he had were the few dollars in his wallet, half a sandwich, and a soggy envelope full of photographs. And an old friend, Bama Boyd.

Finally, Bama said, "Hey, how's it going?" Her voice was professionally warm. Golf-professionally so. People were listening.

Teach looked out at Gandy Boulevard. The stream of cars, and beyond, a couple of shabby seafood restaurants and a bedraggled driving range. He had never phoned that apology to her. "Look, Bama, I'm . . . I'm in a bit of a tight. I need your help."

Again the quiet. A murmur of talk in the background. The pro shop? Bama standing there trying to sell the latest driver to some fool who didn't know a tee box from a pot bunker.

"Hey, Bama, you there?"

"I'm here, Jimmy. Where were *you*?"

"Darlin', I'm feeling kind of . . . exposed where I am right now. Can you come get me? I need a ride."

"*Get* you? Right now? Hey, buddy, I'm in the middle of—"

"Bama!" Teach said it too loud. A man had stepped out of the adult bookstore with an unsatisfied expression on his face. He looked at Teach. The guy wondering if Teach was, well, fun. Teach gave the guy a fuck-off look, dug his face farther into the plastic cube of the phone booth, and whispered, "Look, Bama, I'm in trouble. I know you're pissed at me. You've got every right to be. I'll apologize for a long time somewhere else. You pick the place."

Bama sighed into the phone. "Sorry, Jimmy. If you're in trouble, I'm there for you. Just like you always were for me."

Teach gave her his location and went inside to hide among the rubber penises, vibrators, and a very large selection of movies. He eyed the merchandise and not the people, and they, kindly, did not look at him. Where better to hide a fugitive face than a porn shop?

On the twenty-minute ride from Tampa to St. Petersburg, Teach apologized for stranding Bama and her two friends at the Terra Ceia Country Club. He explained his trouble as best he could and asked again for help. "I need a place to stay for a while. I need to use a phone. I need to borrow your car if you can let me do that. And Bama, more than anything else, I need you to be—" Teach quit. He was about to say, *quiet, discreet, trustworthy.* All insults to the past they shared.

He looked at Bama's pretty, earnest face, permanently blushing from hours on practice tees. Her strong, slender hands guiding the ancient Alfa Romeo along Interstate 275. She had bought the car with money from her first WPGA victory, and she had never won again. She had not become the next Nancy Lopez, or the next anything but a club pro, a woman in a man's profession. Teach knew she would never give up the car, and that she would give him what she could and more.

She looked at him with those wide, bright blue eyes. "Hey, Jimmy, maybe they weren't going to arrest you. Maybe they really did just want to talk."

Teach took the half sandwich out of his pocket, ate it with the hunger of fear and exhaustion. Maybe she was right. Aimes just wanted to sweat him again with pictures from Thalia's apartment. Maybe he and Delbert would do another charade with a knock at the door, Delbert coming back like a good dog with a mysterious paper in his paw. Teach didn't want to sweat for them anymore.

"If they just wanted to talk, why'd they put a cop at the back door?"

Bama thought about it, squinting into the sun. "Maybe the guy was just checking things out back there?" She laughed. "Then you come through like Mike Alstott and the guy just reacts." She looked over at Teach. "You really go up the middle of that cop's face?"

Teach nodded. "And then some. The other one fell in the neighbor's pool. Or jumped in to avoid the rottweiler."

"You're a piece of work, Jimmy. Always were."

"Christ, maybe you're right. Maybe they just wanted to talk." But he didn't think so, and he had a promise to keep. Justice for Thalia. He had promised Mary Lena Liston. His own justice, not the state's.

Bama parked in the lot between the golf course and the marina. They waited until a foursome teed off and a big Bayliner pulled away from the dock hauling a party of retired inebriates. Bama hustled Teach along the dock and aboard a Morgan 45.

Below deck, she said, "The owner's gone till November. I've got maintenance contracts on a lot of these boats. I keep the ACs running, start the engines once a week, and get the bottoms cleaned when they need it. The extra money comes in handy." She looked at Teach and pinched her nose. "Man, *you* need some maintenance. There's a shower in the head. I'll bring you some clothes from the pro shop."

Reflexively, Teach reached out to hug her.

She stepped back. "Don't go there. That would confuse both of us."

Teach showered. Bama returned briefly with clothes and the promise of food at nightfall. He found a couple of bottles of Pilsner Urquell in the galley refrigerator, crawled into the V-berth in the bow, and lay there listening. The air conditioner hummed along, fed by a cable from the marina. Boats passed on Boca Ciega Bay to the north. He heard voices from the marina, hands who worked for the dockmaster, an occasional owner checking his boat. Cars came and went in the parking lot by the first tee. But mostly he heard his own heart beating and what he imagined to be the fuddled sound of his brain trying to think.

He watched the falling sun through the frosted glass of the hatch above his face and listened for the first cop's foot to hit the deck. He tried to think about his problems, tried to make a plan, but the more he tried to think the more he remembered. Thalia, the spicy scent of her cinnamon skin, the way he'd let himself plan a life with her. Paige and the love they'd made, the daughter they'd made, and the slow increments by which a good life had begun to slip away. And lying in the V-berth with only a few feet of space between his body and the hatch, he remembered the shrimper *Santa Maria* and the fetid few inches of bilge where he had hidden three bodies.

Teach had left Cedar Key the morning after sinking the *Santa Maria*. He had gone back to Atlanta and lived rough, worked landscaping, worked off the books when he could, never staying in a job long. He'd changed addresses when he'd changed jobs, and he'd kept a packed suitcase by the door of his motel room or trailer or apartment. He'd planned to live as a permanent transient for six months. If nobody showed up at his door in a tight suit speaking Spanglish through a smoke-stained smile, he would go back home, dig up his money, and start thinking about real life again.

On the thirtieth day of the sixth month, the FBI showed up at his door. The suits were from Brooks Brothers and the smiles were brief and very white. Bloodworth Naylor had been busted wholesaling weed. In Naylor's car, the government had found an envelope with Teach's name written on it. The envelope was full of money. The agents were clear about what they wanted from him. They wanted the story of Naylor's life. If Teach gave it to them, the money was just money. Or it was Teach's, and they might let him keep it. Yes, they might even do that. When he refused to give them the story, the money became drug-related activity.

"All you've got is money," Teach told the government. "In an envelope with my name on it." He thought a smart lawyer might argue the separation of the money and the envelope. Somebody had put money in an envelope with Teach's name on it, but that didn't mean the money was intended for or belonged to Teach. "Maybe the envelope with my name on it was just lying around and somebody needed an envelope."

"That's all we need," the government said. "An envelope."

Teach was charged, and on the advice of a public defender opted for a trial by judge alone. His lawyer figured that a sophisticated legal mind might see Teach's argument about the envelope better than a jury who might remember Nate Means. The judge convicted Teach and sentenced him to two years in the Federal Prison Camp at Eglin Air Force Base. He never forgot the moment after the verdict, when the bailiff walked over to him and put his hand on his shoulder. "Let's go, bud." The man led Teach to a holding cell and ordered him to remove his tie, belt, and shoelaces. For a long time, Teach surrendered things to the state, but he never gave up Bloodworth Naylor. There were items in a few newspapers about Teach's fall, but only a few. He was football trash, and trash was discarded.

His first day in the general population at Eglin, in the cafeteria line, Teach was approached by a big man with a whore's smile. The man's body was hard but his eyes held something soft, and Teach could see it. It was the thing he'd seen in the eyes of Carlos, the gangster who had loved boats. The man put one hand on Teach's tray and the other on Teach's ass. He said, "Both of these are mine. Now come on over and sit with me, sweet baby." Slowly, Teach lifted the man's hand from his tray, kissed it, and tore the forefinger from its socket. The man stumbled back, his eyes howling but his mouth closed.

Teach said, "Put some ice on that. To control the swelling."

It wasn't so much the finger as it was the kiss. After that, Teach was considered crazy, a bug. He chose his own friends and did his time as quietly as he could. With gain time for good behavior, he walked out of Eglin eleven months later. He was twenty-six years old. He'd done a lot of reading, some vocational rehabilitation, and a lot of thinking. He'd met a lot of men like him, men who'd suffered reverses and convinced themselves that evil luck was an entitlement to someone else's money, some woman's body, something in a bottle or a capsule, something at the other end of a fist or a gun. They were men who'd never read the maps of a moral landscape, or who, for one sorry reason or another, had decided to leave the maps behind on their way to money, women, or revenge. Teach believed he was the second kind, a man who knew the maps but had strayed from them.

Like an addict, he admitted to himself that he had loved being lost in the secrets. That he could relapse if he was not very careful. He decided to find the maps and follow them, never stray from the lines they gave him. And he knew what he wanted from life: to be a good man again. To make the good man as simple as he could be: a husband and a father.

Teach drifted down to Tampa and took the first job he could get, humping boxes on the loading dock at Meador Pharmaceuticals. When he had saved some money, he hired a lawyer.

At Eglin, in the jailhouse law school, he had learned about the Florida statute that allowed a man to expunge a criminal record. The lawyer did his job, took cash for the work, and after a year on the loading dock Teach was promoted to forklift operator, then warehouse manager, and then he moved to sales. His boss, Mabry Meador, took him out to dinner one night not long after Teach began selling. "Jim," Meador told him, "you've risen fast in this company, and I think the sky's the limit for you. I think you exemplify everything that's right and decent about the free-enterprise system."

The night before, Paige had accepted Teach's proposal of marriage, and she sat across the table from Meador giving them both her cool, ironic smile. Where Paige came from, money was not discussed at the table. Teach knew that much. And he knew she was running from that place, and maybe even then he knew she would go back to it. He wanted to go with her.

Later that night, Teach took her home to his apartment and undressed her in the dark bedroom. He traced the hollow of her long, perfect neck with his lips, and told her he loved her. A tipsy Paige giggled and said, "Oh yes. The sky's the limit, Jim."

* * *

The sun was setting when a foot hit the deck and roused Teach from a half-sleep of dreams and memories. He lurched out of the berth and stumbled across the dark saloon feeling for a way out.

"Hey, turn on a light."

Christ, it was Bama. Teach remembered now. Bama Boyd bringing food and friendship. Teach found a light switch. Bama's sunburned face was worried in the sixty-watt glow. From an L.L.Bean canvas bag she pulled out two cheeseburgers and a six-pack of beer. Teach stripped off a beer, opened it, and took a long, cold pull.

Bama said, "There's nothing about you on the radio or TV. If the cops want you, they ain't telling the media. What do you plan to do? Just wait here till they catch the guy?" Her eyes said she didn't like the wait-here scenario.

"Did you bring the phone?"

From the bag, Bama retrieved a satellite phone she'd taken from one of her boats, handed it to him. "Can they trace these things?"

Teach tried to smile. "I don't know. I'll keep it brief."

"Who you gonna call?"

"Hey, girl, it's better if you don't know."

Bama stiffened with hurt, then thought it over. "Sure," she said, "you need anything else?"

Teach thinking: *A lot of luck, more brains than we've got between us, and friends in high places.* "Just the keys to your car."

Bama looked at her watch, reached into her pocket for the keys. Teach opened the paper bag, pulled out a cheeseburger, and took half of it in one bite.

Bama stretched, yawned, and bumped her head on the saloon roof. Rubbing it, she said, "I left the car in the lot out there. I can walk to my condo." Teach nodded. She turned away, but he called her back.

"I owe you, darlin'."

"No you don't," she said. "We're buddies."

When Teach could no longer hear Bama's footsteps on the dock, he dialed his home number. His message played, invited him to record something. Then Dean said, "Hello."

"Hello, baby. How you doing?"

"Dad, where are you?"

"I can't tell you that, honey."

She sighed. "Are you all right? You're not hurt, are you?" Something strange in her voice. A quiet, cautious thing Teach had never heard before.

"I'm tired and a little scratched up for reasons I'll explain later, but otherwise I'm fine. How are you?"

"I'm worried . . . about you."

He waited. She waited. Something was wrong with her. Teach wondered if somewhere, someone possessing marvelous technology he did not understand was monitoring this call, homing in on this sailboat thirty miles from the house where Dean stood holding a telephone.

Finally, she said, "Dad, the police want to talk to you about a . . . a prostitute. What's going on?"

Teach said, "I didn't kill anyone, Dean. You have to believe that. I'm going to find out who did."

"Dad, why don't you come home and talk to them? They won't hurt you. They just want to hear your side of it. This is all a big mistake and . . . it can be worked out."

"How?"

"How? What do you mean? I—"

"How, Dean? Did they tell you how it can be worked out?"

"No, Dad, but—"

"Listen, Dean . . ."

"Dad, there's . . ."

Teach was about to tell her she could contact him through an old friend named Bama Boyd, but he had heard the strange thing again in her voice. He waited.

"Mr. Teach, how are you, sir?"

There was no mistaking Aimes's voice, that low, musical rumble. Teach remembered thinking it was a voice for hymn-singing in a country church. He felt an unchurchly anger rising in his chest. What do you say to a cop who has hounded you out of house and home, run you through a truckload of palm fronds to a porn shop, then to this hideout in some rich man's sailboat? Well, Aimes had asked how Teach was doing.

"Better than I'd be in your damned jail, Aimes. That's how I am."

"Mr. Teach, the young man I sent to your house told you I only wanted another interview. I don't know why you had to run like that."

"And I don't know why you put a policeman at my back door if the one at the front only wanted an interview."

"And I don't know why you had to knock that young fellow down and break his collarbone. That's a painful injury, Mr. Teach. I know because it's one I've had myself. We have a law against assaulting police officers in the City of Tampa. Did you know that?"

"Are you tracing this call?"

Aimes laughed, a raspy baritone. "No, no sir, Mr. Teach. The paperwork on a thing like that would take me a week. If you were as important as you think you are, maybe I'd be doing that, but the truth is, I just wanted to talk to you. Why don't you come on in and talk?"

"I'll think about it. I really will. In the meantime, I want you to talk to somebody. His name is Bloodworth Naylor. Look him up in the phone book. Hell, you can look up his criminal record if you want to."

"Mr. Teach, I don't want you to hang up. I want you to keep talking to me. I think you might do something you'll regret. You might be getting into a mean frame of mind, and—"

Teach said, "I'll be in touch," and pushed the *off* button, imagining the evil demons of technology sniffing out his location on a sailboat in Boca Ciega Bay.

FORTY

Aimes handed the phone back to Dean Teach, a rich girl whose dead mother had been what Aimes's own mother had called "a society lady." Aimes knew he had to be careful with this girl, at least for the time being. And with her friend too. Tawnya Battles sat on the sofa in the living room watching Aimes, Delbert, and young Dean Teach with a somber, speculative expression that reminded Aimes of her father. She was a pretty girl whose ways of moving and speaking were beyond her age. So far she hadn't said anything, and he wondered if there'd be any profit in asking her some questions. And he wondered how much of what was happening in the Teach house today would go straight to Thurman Battles.

Delbert was at the bookcase in the foyer, pretending to inspect the titles, running his finger along the spines like he might ask to borrow a volume. Aimes felt uncomfortable in this house, sorry for the girl caught between her father and the police. The part of him that was not a cop was glad she had a friend with her today.

Tawnya Battles got up from the sofa, walked past Delbert without a glance, and stood next to Dean Teach. Aimes knew her from the family gatherings he attended, had watched her grow up from that distance, always noticing how she observed people, how her eyes knew things she didn't say. She'd seen him eating barbecue in Bermuda shorts. Now she looked at him like she wondered who this big man was with the badge and the gun.

Aimes decided not to ask these girls what they knew about Bloodworth Naylor. Not yet. Of course he knew the name. When a prostitute was murdered, the computer coughed up a list of local men who had been convicted of violent crimes against working girls. Bloodworth Naylor had done time on pandering and aggravated battery charges. He had been a seriously bad man, but had come out of prison and, apparently, turned himself into a citizen. The guy running some rent-to-own furniture outlet over in Suitcase City. There was only so much time in a day, so Aimes and Delbert had crossed taxpayer Naylor off their list. But how did James Teach know the guy? What connected them? Was it Thalia Speaks? Aimes decided he would have to visit Mr. Naylor.

Aimes said, "Ms. Teach, are you sure you don't know where your father is right now? We'd sure like to talk to him."

The girl shook her head.

Apparently, James Teach kept his child in the dark about a lot of things. Among them, his affair with Thalia Speaks. To Aimes, the loyalty of a daughter was a beautiful thing.

He offered the girl his card. "If you think of anything, will you let us know?"

She took the card, read it. Tawnya looked at it too. Dean Teach said, "Detective Aimes, what do you think my dad did . . . to this woman?"

"We don't know if he did anything, Ms. Teach. She worked at the country club a while. He knew her there. Of course, that was before she got into the life. Excuse me. I mean before she became a prostitute. Maybe your father knows something that will help us find the man who murdered her."

Suddenly the girl's face resembled faces Aimes had seen in the cancer ward where his wife had spent her last days. Her skin turned a blue-white, and her eyes seemed to look through him to some faraway place. The girl must have spent time at the club, seen Thalia Speaks there. Maybe she had her own suspicions about her father and the waitress.

Aimes said, "Ms. Teach, we have other leads. Your father's connection to the case is just one of the things we're interested in."

At the word *connection*, the pretty daughter winced as though something sharp had gone in deep. Her eyes opened wide, then tightened to a darker blue. Aimes could see she loved Teach and she didn't want a policeman to see it. Like an animal, she hid what made her vulnerable. But she didn't hide anything from Tawnya Battles. The two girls shared a long, searching look.

Mr. Teach had been stupid to step out on the mother of this child. And now Mr. Teach was getting smart in a very bad way. Smart enough to outrun two cops half his age and disappear into thin air, or so they had said. Smart enough to hide where Aimes couldn't find him, to have a plan that included Bloodworth Naylor.

The two girls watched from the front porch as Aimes and Delbert drove away. Tawnya Battles put her arm around Dean Teach's shoulder and guided her back into the house.

Aimes pulled the Crown Vic out onto Rome, turning toward the Old Hyde Park shopping district. Fashionable Junior Leaguers and young lawyers in love strolling under the oaks and royal palms, past the shops—Godiva Chocolatier, Banana Republic, Laura Ashley. White men with pink sweaters thrown over their polo shirts; white women in plaid shorts and leather flip-flops. *Uniforms*, Aimes thought.

His wife had started her career in a starched white nurse's dress and a funny white cap with a badge, those crepe-soled white shoes. Later, they'd let her wear green scrubs, even jeans and running shoes.

This was the time when Aimes missed her most. When he'd given the city more than it deserved, and other men were going home to drinks and dinner with women whose eyes had held the secret of their yearning all day long. Aimes turned to Delbert. "I guess we don't find Mr. Teach today."

"Naw, not today." Delbert gave a quiet sigh. "Some house that guy has." He meant the antiques, the books, that wealth and culture.

Aimes and Delbert were separated by a lot—skin color to begin with, and a long history of people hanging other people in trees, putting signs around their necks that said, *Nigger Beware*—but they both lived a long way from Mr. Teach. He was from the top of life's money mountain.

It was painful to see the girl hurting, but hurting was Aimes's job, stopping it for the good people and starting it for the bad ones. Healing had been his wife's job, and she had done it well until the cancer had tripped her, laid her down with the awful hurt inside her and no one to stop it. For a while after her death, Aimes had been the kind of cop no cop wanted to become. He had worked like a man possessed, then begged other cops, men who still had lives, to go out

and drink with him. He had sat with them in bars and talked shop,
a wild man with eyes full of a lost wife and a head full of cop knowledge he could talk about only with other cops. It had finally ended
one midnight when Aimes had looked at his Glock nine-millimeter and
wondered what it would feel like to put the barrel into his mouth.
What it would feel like to sit in his favorite chair, the one his wife
had given him for his fortieth birthday, and suck first from a bottle of
vodka and then from the barrel of the Glock, one and the other, until
he was so numb he didn't know which was which. And then just see
what happened.

Aimes never put the pistol in his mouth. He never got that low.
He bought the treadmill and got demonic with it, and started a relationship with the main branch of the Tampa Public Library. They had
hundreds of books on topics of interest to him. It would take the rest
of his life to read them all.

He stopped at the signal at Howard and Kennedy. He and Delbert
had gone to talk to the girl, tell her that her father was hiding out,
that they only wanted to talk to him. Tell her they knew Teach would
contact her. When he did, she should let them know. Some kind of
luck, Aimes and Delbert being there when he called.

Aimes turned onto Howard, heading toward Kennedy. "How you
see it now?"

Delbert said, "Vice presidents and scumbags don't usually know
each other. Maybe they were all involved—Thalia Speaks, Teach, and
Naylor. Teach did drug-related activity, and Naylor beat up a prostitute. Teach gave us Naylor, so he knows the guy from somewhere."

"So what do we do?"

Delbert looked at Aimes like it was too late in the day for another
question.

Aimes smiled, thinking of going home to his treadmill, two shots
of Stolichnaya, and then his biography of Hap Arnold, of Delbert going out on the never-ending quest for the perfect barmaid. "Humor
me," he said.

Delbert listed the possibilities for a day's work: "Watch Teach's
house, see if he visits the daughter, see if she goes to meet him somewhere. Find Teach and he tells us what he knows about Naylor.
Check Naylor's prints against anything found in the woman's house.

Go see Naylor." He cleared his throat. "You think the other girl's in this some way?"

"Tawnya?" Aimes kept his voice neutral, but some combination of laughter and sadness was mixing in his chest. "Naw. That's . . . that's a little far-fetched, my friend." He could almost hear Delbert telling himself to back off from Tawnya Battles. "Tomorrow we go see Naylor."

"Tomorrow's another day," Delbert said.

FORTY-ONE

When Teach called Missy Pace's house and she answered, he heard music and the languid chirping of teenage girls. They were practicing cheerleading. He asked to speak to Dean.

"So, how's it going, Deanie? You going to make cheerleading?"

Dean was quiet for a moment, the music playing. Some teen love tune. Then she said, "Actually, Dad, I think I've got a pretty good chance."

Teach liked it, his daughter going for what she wanted. He hoped she made the squad, hoped he could see a game, watch her perform the awesome rite of cheerleading.

She said, "Missy invited some girls to sleep over tonight."

Teach didn't tell her that she might need to stay at Missy's for as long as they would have her. Well, Missy had slept at the Teach house more times than he could remember.

"Is Tawnya there?" He found it comforting to think of the two girls together.

"Yeah, she's here. She jumps higher than anybody." Teach waited, listened to his beloved daughter's breathing. The music in the background seemed farther away when she said, "Dad, is it bad?"

"It's not good, Deanie, but I don't want you to worry. Actually, I think I've got a pretty good chance of straightening this thing out soon."

"You ever going to tell me what it's all about?"

"That depends, honey."

"On what?"

"On how it turns out." He gave her the number of the satellite phone, told her to keep it secret, not to call unless she had to.

"Daddy, I *know* that. You need me to do anything?"

"No, honey. I love you . . . Uh, just, stand up, sit down, fight, fight, fight."

"We don't do that one anymore, Dad. That went out with leather helmets."

Teach called Marlie Turkel and asked for a meeting. He would be driving Bama's Alfa, and, as far as he knew, the police had no idea he and Turkel were in touch. Still, the skin on the back of his neck prickled with the thought of returning to Tampa.

Marlie Turkel said, "Why don't you meet me at Hugo's? It's a little Cuban place on Howard. Nobody but students and drywall guys. We can talk there."

Teach had called her home number, and he could hear a small dog yapping in the background. He told her he'd need thirty minutes.

Marlie Turkel said, "It's almost eight o'clock. They close at nine, but what the hell? I know the owner."

When Teach got there, she was sitting in a back booth with a plate of black beans, rice, and fried *platanos* in front of her. She was drinking beer. Teach was too buzzed to eat, but the beer looked good. Crossing Tampa Bay he'd held Bama's Alfa to the speed limit and kept one eye on the mirror. Looking for a white Crown Victoria with Aimes and Delbert in it, or maybe the military twins who'd come to his front and back doors only a few hours ago.

While Teach ordered his beer, Marlie Turkel looked around the restaurant. An old Cuban couple sat in a booth at the front windows. Across from them, a slumming yuppie couple were paying their check. That left four guys from a softball team back by the men's room. They were drunk and arguing a slide into home plate. Marlie Turkel leaned forward and put her hand on Teach's. "So, what you got for me?"

He had thought about this a lot, and it wasn't simple. It put both of them into deep and turbid waters. But it seemed to him that he had to do it. He pulled the manila envelope of photos from inside his shirt and passed it to her. While she opened it, Teach considered his risk.

He had promised Thurman Battles no one would see the pictures. There was no telling what Battles would do if this got out. Teach feared the man's wrath, but he feared Bloodworth Naylor more. Battles was ruin, Naylor was death.

Teach also risked a simple sniff of contempt from the woman who was carefully reviewing the pictures now. Maybe she'd just hand them back, tell him they proved nothing about the murders of five prostitutes. Teach waited.

Marlie Turkel examined the last photo in the stack, the one of Tyrone and Bloodworth Naylor, for a long time. Finally, she paired it with the one of Tyrone raising the crack pipe to his lips and turned both to face Teach. When he saw her eyes, the curiosity jumping out of them, he knew he had her.

She said, "I knew it. I knew there was a reason Battles dropped that action against you. You two assholes and your public spirit. Jesus H. Christ, I knew it all along."

Teach just looked at her, knew she was enjoying this beyond measure. Knew it was what made her who she was. She had just turned over the fallen log, revealed the slimy larval things that lived under it. She reached into her purse, took out her notebook, a pen, and a pint of bourbon. She poured some bourbon into her empty water glass, knocked it back, chased it with beer, and looked a challenge at Teach. "They don't have a liquor license here," she explained. "Wine and beer only. It's a damn shame."

Lots of things are a shame, Teach thought. "You were right," he said, "there was a reason Battles dropped the lawsuit. His beloved nephew was a crack addict and that," Teach pointed to the hockey mask of Naylor's face, "is the man who supplied the drugs. His name is Bloodworth Naylor. He owns a place in Suitcase City called Naylor's Rent-to-Own."

"Charming." Marlie Turkel was writing it down.

"He's also the man who killed Thalia Speaks."

"Thalia Speaks. Wasn't she number five?"

Teach nodded.

"Did he do the others too?" She stopped writing.

Teach shrugged to her question.

She put down her pen. "How do you know all this? Are you sticking to what you said before about helping Aimes with the investigation?"

"I can't tell you how I know. I can't even tell you why I can't tell you. But it's the truth. The absolute truth."

He put his hand on the photo of Tyrone standing at the window of Naylor's white Bronco. "Pictures don't lie. The man is obviously a drug dealer. He was Thalia Speaks's lover before she worked at the country club. He killed her."

"What's your proof of that?"

Teach shook his head again. He watched as the light of Marlie Turkel's excitement started to go out. He decided to give her the rest of the bad news. "You can't use Tyrone's name."

"Why not?" Pushing her face toward his. Her voice loud enough now to stop the drunken conversation behind her about the endless slide into home. The Cuban couple by the windows rose in stiff dignity and left, the man giving Marlie Turkel a look of old-world disapproval.

Teach leaned forward until they were almost kissing, put a finger across his lips. "Why hurt the kid? He's up north in a ritzy prep school getting his life back together. And Battles is paying for it. Why smear the good uncle with the blood of a bad nephew?" As he spoke, Teach wondered if these things meant anything to her. She had to slop the beast its daily diet of news. Did she even notice the gruel of ground-up human lives she threw into the trough?

The woman's belligerent eyes told him she wasn't buying his putting the Battles family off-limits. Teach said, "If you want anything more from me, you'll leave them out of it. They aren't central, anyway. The important thing is murder, isn't it, not some kid messing with drugs?"

She leaned back, opened her purse, took out the pint again, and offered it to Teach. He waved it away, sipped his beer. She poured herself another boilermaker. "I could leave them out and put you in," she said, smiling, but without mirth. "Are you willing to make that trade?"

Teach had seen this coming, had placed his faith in the ravenous appetite of the beast. "You do that, and you lose me as a source, and you piss Aimes off. Permanently." When he mentioned Aimes, he put his hands on the photographs, hoping she'd get his message.

He watched her think it over, the heat of resentment finally giving way to a cool pragmatism. "All right, but when do we meet again? When can you give me more?"

Again, Teach shrugged, and loved the feeling of it. The loose, carefree rise and fall of his arms and shoulders. "I don't know, but I'll be in touch as soon as I can. And believe me, there's more where this came from."

Marlie Turkel pulled the photos from under Teach's hands and put them into her purse. "Walk me out to my car."

When it came to masculine courtesies, Teach took orders from women. This woman was tough in a restaurant with her pint of whiskey, but a little unsteady in a parking lot at night. He opened the door of the beat-up white Taurus for her, and watched her taillights disappear down Howard toward Tampa Bay.

FORTY-TWO

Marlie Turkel had been up late the night before writing her column. Working hard but the words not coming. Not like they usually did, like they used to. Before Teach and the prostitute murders had come along, she'd been in a long slump. Now she had something big and she had to milk it as hard and as long as she could. She had to because she had heard from loyal sources that there was talk among upper management of replacing her with some kid fresh out of J-school, some size-six with cleavage like a knife, a nose for news, and the lean young legs for running it down. Girls like that were pouring out of Northwestern, Emerson, and Indiana, knocking off internships from sea to shining sea, and winking their tits at managing editors who would hire them for the scenery alone. Marlie Turkel had seen them come and go with résumés and smiles that aimed to please. And she could see bad news in the eyes of her bosses. Their eyes said she was getting tired, losing that go-for-the-groin instinct that had made her Tampa's toughest woman reporter. One of these days the girl with the résumé and the smile would arrive and stay.

Marlie Turkel had come up the hard way in a man's profession, and she had done it without the usual comforts—marriage, children, real estate. She lived in a cluttered and drab apartment, drove an aging Ford, and had no friends. She'd worked so hard for so long she had lost her friends to neglect and she'd forgotten how to make new ones. Instead of friends she had a thousand sources and a dog. The dachshund was older than the Ford, and his bowels worked about as well. She had taught him to defecate on a stack of newspapers in the bathroom, but the poor thing had his accidents. On good days, the apartment smelled like Lysol.

She had slept later than usual after the long night of writing for her deadline, and she had risen to the dust and clutter of the apartment, an empty refrigerator, and the dog sitting beside her bed whining for something she could not give him—her time. She got up, showered, dressed, considered the day before her, and decided that she would have to rethink Mr. James Teach. She had made a bad deal with him. Why should she wait for more information from him when some reporter from the *Times* might already be ahead of her, might be writing the story of the prostitute murders while Marlie Turkel was searching her pantry for something to feed a dachshund with a spastic colon?

The animal whined and raised a paw to scratch at her, ripping her panty hose at the ankle. "Down, Pulitzer!" she snapped. "Damn it, look what you've done!" The dog shrank out of kicking range, watching her with sad, disappointed eyes. "I'll go to the store, I'll get you something and bring it back." The dog lay down with his head on his forepaws. She had lied to him before.

She grabbed her purse and car keys. She shouldn't have given in to Teach. Should have told him she was going to revisit the story of Thurman Battles, James Teach, and the deal they'd made. She didn't believe the photos Teach had shown her came from Aimes. Police photos had laboratory markings on them, warning labels identifying them as evidence. Teach had taken the pictures himself, had used them to get Battles off his back. Now he was using them to keep her from writing about his connection to the murder of Thalia Speaks.

Somewhere in the tired, restless night she'd spent after finishing her column, Marlie Turkel had decided to break her bargain with Teach. She had decided to write it all up, a long, complicated, fascinating story about a prostitute, a drug dealer, an honor student, a civil rights attorney, and a corporate vice president. She had even come up with a title. She was going to call it, "The Five Shall Meet: How a Wealthy Businessman, a Community Leader, a Pimp, an Honor Student, and a Prostitute Became Entangled in a Drama of Drugs and Murder." Hell, maybe there was a book in it. The kind of true-life crime story that could hit the best-seller list and make Marlie Turkel the name and money she had always wanted.

Sitting in her car, happy to be away from the dog's demonic

whining, she found in her notebook the address she had written down after talking to Teach at Hugo's. Naylor's Rent-to-Own was out on the edge of Suitcase City. It was a nasty place, but she was going there. She couldn't write her piece without seeing Mr. Naylor face-to-face. Asking him exactly what it was that connected him and Mr. Teach and Thalia Speaks.

FORTY-THREE

When the newspaperwoman called, said she was nearby and wanted to talk, Blood Naylor told her to come to the back of the shop. He'd meet her on the loading dock. He took her into the warehouse, the room where he had sat with Tyrone, giving the boy drugs and talking to him about their plan. The old record player was there in the corner with its stack of 45s. Little Anthony. *Tears on my pillow . . .*

When she flashed the picture of him and Tyrone, Blood was surprised and very angry. And of course he concealed it. The white woman, big and ugly and dick-sure of herself, whipping the picture out of her shoulder bag along with a notebook. "Mr. Naylor, I'd like to talk to you about your relationship with Tyrone Battles."

He was glad she hadn't come in the main entrance, done this in front of his salesmen and their moron clients. He imagined the salesmen stopping their bored sermons to the Barcalounger idiots, looking over at the boss and this pushy white lady. Wondering what the hell was going on.

Blood handed the picture back to her. "That's not me. You can't see it's me from what you got there. It's only half a face."

"It's half of *your* face, Mr. Naylor. Anybody can see that."

She walked over and stood near the forklift, looked around the warehouse, taking it all in. Blood always cleaned the residue from the little table where he cut his lines, and he knew you couldn't smell cocaine, but the half-empty bottle of Stolichnaya and the bleary glass were there for the woman to see. It didn't look professional.

"Looks like you do quite a little business here. In *furniture*." The woman smiling at him. Suggesting that something going on here wasn't furniture.

A crate of damaged Taiwanese table parts rested on the fork-lift's hydraulic elevator. The woman picked up a broken table leg, dropped it back into the crate. She looked around for something to wipe her hands on, looked at him like he might be the thing, then she frowned and wrote something down. Blood had to laugh. What in the hell was she writing about a forklift?

"Look," he said, "you kind of took me by surprise with those pictures and all." The woman smiled. Blood could see that taking people by surprise was her thing. He didn't know where he was going with this. He had not anticipated this at all. "Where did you get those pictures?" he asked her.

She only smiled. "I can't tell you that, Mr. Naylor. But I can tell you I'm doing a piece on the murders of several prostitutes. You knew one of them, Thalia Speaks. You obviously know Tyrone Battles, and I have reason to believe you know a Mr. James Teach. I'm wondering what connects the four of you. Would you care to comment on that?"

There was something Blood needed to know. He needed it very badly. He had to be careful now, ask her the right questions. He said, "The newspaper send you over here? The police think I did these murders?" Maybe she was just some crazy woman, trying to sell a story about him to the *Trib*. What was it they called them? Stringers? If no one knew she had come here, maybe he could do something about this.

"I told you I represent the *Tribune*, Mr. Naylor. I'm surprised you haven't heard of me. Do you read the paper?" Blood thinking: *Can you read, Mr. Naylor?* It made his hands shake with anger. She said, "Haven't you seen my columns on the murdered women?"

Blood walked over to the crate of parts, reached into it, and took out a table leg. It was about the size and heft of a baseball bat.

"Look," the woman said, getting impatient, "it's hot back here, and I had a long night last night. If you aren't willing to talk to me, I can just print what I have now. I think you'll be happier with what comes out if you give me your side of it, starting with Tyrone Battles. Then maybe we can talk about your relationship with Thal—"

The table leg hit her in the mouth. Blood had accelerated the blow because he did not want to hear her say Thalia's name. She fell back against the crate, stunned. Blood climbed aboard the forklift, started the engine. He needed the noise. When he stepped off the forklift, she was holding the notebook to her bleeding mouth. Her eyes were crossed, and she seemed to be trying to focus them on the notebook, trying to say something. When Blood hit her the second time, just above the right ear, the light went out of her eyes.

He knelt, grabbed her knees, and tipped her into the crate, tossing the notebook and the table leg on top of her. Then he got back aboard the forklift and raised the elevator to its maximum height. He set the lift lever in the locked position so that the crate would stay up there, and turned off the engine. "Sleep tight, baby," he whispered. "No more tears on your pillow."

Blood had to think. For the life of him he had to plan. He went to the little table where he cut his lines, grabbed the vodka, and swallowed until his eyes teared. He hid the bottle and the glass behind some crates and looked around, trying to see the place through the eyes of a stranger.

"Mr. Naylor!" Someone was calling from the front of the warehouse. Blood moved into the long aisle and saw two silhouettes against the windows of the lighted showroom. "Mr. Naylor?" one of them called again. "Your man out there told us we could find you back here."

Aimes didn't like Bloodworth Naylor. He knew that right away. There was something creepy about the guy. He was supposed to be a nonrecidivist case, a big success for the criminal justice system. Ghetto rat goes to prison for pimping and battery, does his time with a clean record, gets out and goes into business for himself, makes a success of it. But where did he get the money to start the business? Aimes figured Naylor had stashed his pandering proceeds before he was busted. Black women had bought this place—on their knees and on their backs.

And where was the business? The showroom looked shabby, nobody but a couple of hangdog salesmen and some scratch-and-dent furniture. This warehouse wasn't any better. A lot of dusty crates and boxes, sofas and sectionals wrapped in plastic. Aimes wondered how long it had been since anybody had fired up that forklift behind Naylor, moved any of these goods onto a truck for shipment.

Aimes looked at Delbert. Their signal. Delbert showed Naylor his detective's shield and said, "Mr. Naylor, we're investigating the murders of some prostitutes here in Tampa. One of them was a Thalia Speaks. We understand you knew her."

Naylor looked sad now, and it pissed Aimes off. It was that phony sadness scumbags pulled into their eyes when they needed it. Next thing the guy would be crying the tears of an alligator.

Naylor said, "I knew her around the neighborhood, but, you know, it was a long time ago. I don't remember her much."

Blood Naylor was standing under the crate, so close he could feel the heat from the forklift's engine. He felt, also, the powerful urge to look up at the crate. He wasn't sure why. He tried to concentrate on this cop's face. Tried not to grind his jaws like the drug wanted him to do. He had heard of Aimes. They'd grown up about the same time, not far from each other. Blood getting into trouble early, running with the bad dogs. Aimes turning himself into a white man's nigger. Football hero at Middleton High, then at A&M. Aimes one of the first black men to make detective in Tampa, twice the white cop's age and letting the little cracker do the talking. *Yassuh, boss. Yassuh, boss.* Blood wanted to break into a buck and wing, sing a few bars of "Camptown Races." He didn't. What he did was go humble, stare at his feet, scratch the concrete floor with some shoe leather, and say, "I don't remember her much." *Oh, Thalia.*

The little white cop said, "Do you know a Mr. James Teach?"

Blood let them see him think about it hard. He pursed his lips and squinted, reached up to scratch his head, and . . . that's when he felt it, something wet. "Name don't ring a bell. Was he a friend of Thalia's?"

The white cop frowned, glanced over at his partner. Aimes didn't look at him. He walked over to Blood's left, into the corner where he kept the old record player, the stack of 45s. Little Anthony. Sam Cooke. Martha and the Vandellas. Blood turned his head very carefully and watched as the big black cop picked up some records, sorted through them, and put them back down. Aimes walked back over and stood beside the white cop.

Carefully, Blood rubbed his thumb and forefinger together, feeling the sticky wet. He knew what it was. He could smell it. Soon, the two cops would smell it, see it. Blood felt another warm drop strike the top of his head.

The white cop said, "We found some drugs in Thalia Speaks's apartment. They came from Meador Pharmaceuticals. Mr. Teach works for Meador. We were wondering what would happen if we got a warrant and searched this place. Maybe we'd find some of the same stuff here. Maybe bring a dog in here, let him sniff around. You used to sell some drugs, didn't you, Mr. Naylor? I mean, back before you became a taxpayer and all."

Another drop, and this time Blood felt *and* heard it. It hit with a little *pat*. Sounded like that first big drop of rain slapping your dusty sidewalk on a summer afternoon. Those drops that come cold from high up in a dark cloud. Only this wasn't water. It was warm. It was that woman up there. Blood Naylor didn't know what to do. If he stepped away, the next drop would hit the concrete. The two cops would see it. If he took them out to the loading dock, they'd see the newspaperwoman's car out there. If he walked them back into the showroom where the light was brighter, they might see the blood in his hair, see it run down the back of his neck, or worse, down his forehead.

The white cop looked angry now. Blood wasn't taking this serious enough for him. *Concentrate*, Blood told himself. *You can pull this off.* He said, "I did the crime and I did my time. I don't have nothing to do with drugs no more."

"What about the ladies, Mr. Naylor? You still sell back?"

Blood shook his head, but not too hard. "I sell furniture. You can see that, man. I don't have nothing to do with selling no back." Blood looked an appeal at the black cop, Aimes. *Get this cracker off my ass, man.* Aimes looked back at him like he was a hole in the air. Not there.

The white cop said, "When was the last time you saw Thalia Speaks, Mr. Naylor?"

"It was a long time ago. Back before I went to Raiford, I think."

"You think?"

"Oh, I might of seen her once or twice right after I got back. We might of talked then, but I don't remember. She wasn't no friend of mine after I got back."

"Where were you on the night of May 25, Mr. Naylor? Do you recall that?"

"Yes sir, I was at a bar over in Ybor. It was a big crowd in there that night."

After arranging Thalia's apartment for the cops, Blood had gone to the Celebrity to show his face.

"Anybody see you there that night?"

"Sure, I imagine so. Imagine you could find somebody saw me in there. If you look for them. You gone look for them?"

"We're gonna do what we have to do, Mr. Naylor."

Blood smiled at the cop, and another drop hit him. He could feel the warm blood pooling on his scalp. He tilted his head back an inch and it crept toward the back of his neck.

It surprised Blood when Aimes spoke. "We've got your fingerprints on file, Mr. Naylor. We're going to check them against the ones we found in the woman's apartment. You're telling us you were never involved with the woman, never had sex with her?"

Had sex? Jesus Christ, Blood thought, *I lived inside her body for a year. She was my eyes opening in the morning and my last waking thought at night.* "No." He shrugged, smiled. "I knew her around the neighborhood, you know. She was just some girl, that's all. I don't remember much about her."

"All right, Mr. Naylor," Aimes said, "we'll be in touch."

"I'm happy to help whenever you need me." Another drop hit the top of Blood's head. A warm rivulet ran into his collar, down the back of his shirt.

The two cops started walking toward the front of the store, leaving Blood standing very still under the forklift. He sighed his thank you, then Aimes stopped, turned back. "You used to be an evil man, Mr. Naylor. You sold drugs and women. You beat up women and you went to prison for it. Now you're a good man. Is that what you want me to believe?"

Jesus, it was a crazy question. Blood held his head very still. "It happens," he said. "Believe it."

The black cop smiled, shook his head, and walked away with his little white partner.

* * *

Walking across Bloodworth Naylor's empty parking lot, Aimes turned to Delbert. "Nervous," he said.

"Scared," said Delbert.

"Lying his ass off about not knowing the woman. Her not being his girlfriend."

"The man has no ass," Delbert said. "Lied it completely off."

"Complete crock of shit about being in the bar?"

"Remembered it way too quick. Didn't even have to think about it."

"You interested in Naylor now?"

"I'm a blind dog in a meat house, and he's a pork chop wrapped in bacon."

FORTY-FOUR

After the two cops drove away, Blood Naylor fired up the forklift and lowered the elevator. The woman's purse was still slung over her shoulder. He put on some work gloves and opened the purse, found her car keys. He tore a sheet of plastic from an old sectional and went out to her car, lined the trunk with it.

Back inside, he jumped onto the forklift and drove it out to the parking lot. He stopped beside the woman's car and lowered the lift. It was late afternoon and quiet in the back lot. Mook and Soldier were off in the truck delivering furniture. Down the alley, the jacaranda tree where the two whores plied their trade stood on its carpet of purple petals. They'd be coming soon.

Blood reached into the crate and put his arms around the woman's body. She was big, and it took all of his strength to lift her. As he raised her out of the crate, her head lolled against his, and he felt her hair brush his cheek and smelled her thick, musky perfume. This, and the warmth of her body and the odor of whiskey that rose from her, sickened him. As he turned and dropped her onto the bed of plastic in the trunk, his stomach turned. He stepped back, closed the trunk, and held his heaving stomach until it steadied.

Blood looked around again, saw no one, accepted his luck. He drove the forklift to the dumpster and lowered the elevator. He climbed up, stood on the forks, and shoved the crate into the dumpster. It fell among the scraps of plastic and cardboard with a hollow rumble and a geyser of dust.

Inside the warehouse, in the small bathroom used by the deliverymen, he washed the blood out of his hair. With a wad of wet paper towels, he followed the trail of blood drops from the crate out of the warehouse, down the ramp, and across the lot to the woman's car. He wiped up the drops and went back into the warehouse to flush the towels.

Blood tried to remember when the city truck came to empty the dumpster. It was tomorrow—yes, tomorrow morning. His luck was holding. He walked across the parking lot and unlocked the door of his Bronco. He took the stainless Smith .357 from the glove box and put it in his waistband.

Inside the office, he told his secretary he was going out for an early dinner. The woman turned her face from a stack of invoices and gave him the usual response, "Unh-hunh." Her way of telling him he didn't spend enough time around the place. Blood smiled, waved. He had an errand to run.

Teach drove Bama's Alfa past a big jacaranda in the alley behind Blood Naylor's Rent-to-Own. The white Bronco was parked at the back of the lot, by the dumpster. Ahead of Teach, a dusty Ford Taurus moved across the lot and turned into the narrow lane that led to the front of the store at the corner of Fletcher Avenue. The slanting afternoon sun gave Teach a glimpse of the face behind the wheel. It was Naylor. The years had changed him, but underneath the work time did to faces, Teach saw the same guy he had said goodbye to that dark morning in a bar in Cedar Key. *I'm going to disappear. I advise you to do the same.*

Naylor turned left and headed toward I-275, and Teach saw the *Tampa Tribune* parking sticker on the Ford's rear bumper. What was Naylor doing in Marlie Turkel's car? Teach had come here thinking he would try to get into the warehouse, find something that linked Naylor to Thalia Speaks. He followed the Taurus.

Blood Naylor was heading north on 275, toward the open country out around Lutz. Plenty of pastures and pinewoods, sinkholes and abandoned farmhouses up that way where he could leave the news-paperwoman. Places where nobody would ever find her. He wasn't sure why he had picked up that table leg and smacked her mouth with it. It happened so fast. The way she pulled those pictures out, stuck them under his nose. A smart-ass white lady asking him if he'd read her stories about whores. Like she wondered if he *could* read.

It wasn't until he had her in the trunk of her car that he'd placed

her name. She was the woman who had written about Teach thumping Tyrone in that men's room. She had done a good job on Teach.
Blood remembered laughing his ass off reading it. Well, he had killed
her without planning it, but it was a good thing she was dead. She
was going to write Blood Naylor like she'd written Teach. Call the
cops back into his life.

The Ford's air conditioner cooling his face, Blood felt himself
relaxing a little. He had been thinking about just running. It was all
over. He had killed the woman. The cops had come and they would
be back. Now he was thinking maybe he could get away with this.
Maybe the woman hadn't told anyone where she was going today.
The two cops, Aimes and his little white dog, had just been fishing,
stirring up the mud to see what crawled out of it.

When the idea came to him, and he saw its brilliance, he pulled
the Taurus over. He pounded his gloved hands on the steering wheel
in jubilation.

It took Teach by surprise when Blood Naylor jerked the Taurus off
275 and stopped, idling there on the shoulder. What was the guy doing? Teach was going too fast to stop behind Naylor, so he drove on
past and pulled over just before the Lutz exit ramp. In his rearview
mirror, he could see the man sitting there, a half-mile back. Then
the Taurus pulled out into traffic, cut across two lanes, and bounced
across the grassy median. Teach gunned the old Alfa down the exit
ramp, turned left under the overpass, and headed back south. The
Taurus was nowhere in sight.

Teach cursed and beat his fists on the steering wheel. Traffic was
thick, and it was dangerous weaving through the gaps, searching
ahead for the Taurus. Finally, he glimpsed the Ford's rear end swerv-
ing between a Winnebago and a city bus. The Taurus took the Westshore exit, and Teach was stuck six cars back from the intersection,
waiting for the light to change.

Teach told himself to calm down. Some traffic signal up ahead
would stop Blood. He would catch up. He looked over at the pistol
on the seat next to him. It wouldn't do for him to be caught speeding
in Bama's car with a stolen handgun, an old Navy Colt .38. Teach
had found it under some charts in a locker on the boat Bama looked

after. He had to be careful. His felony conviction was old, but the cybershadow of his past was somewhere in a computer. He had always lived with the fear that some cop, stopping him for a traffic violation, might call in his name and get a report on his record. He had paid a lawyer a lot of money to have the record expunged, but he had always believed more in Santa Claus than in the promises of the State of Florida.

The speed limit was thirty-five on Westshore and Teach was going fifty. He'd glimpsed a white Taurus crossing Kennedy. It resembled Turkel's car, but there were a thousand like it in Tampa and a hundred just as dirty. He reached over and put his hand on the revolver. What the hell was Naylor doing in Turkel's car? Were the two of them together now in some scheme? Up ahead, the Taurus crossed San Rafael, still heading south.

When Teach crossed the intersection at Westshore and Sunset Boulevard, he was only a few blocks from home. He'd lost the Taurus, but a cold dread had crept into the pit of his stomach. It seemed that Bama's Alfa turned of its own will onto Sunset. It would be stupid to drive to his own house, the cops could be there watching for him, but Teach had to do it. He could not shake the ugly thought that Blood Naylor was in this part of town for a reason. And the reason was Teach.

He coasted past the house. The Taurus was parked two houses down from his, in front of the Winstons'. Teach felt the sickness of fear sap his strength as he turned into Mrs. Carlson's driveway, backed out, and stopped at his own curb. He looked up and down the street. There was no sign of Naylor. Maybe he had left the car on this street as some weird message or threat. Left it for the cops to find, and walked away. But a black man like Naylor would stand out in this neighborhood. Just seeing him, someone might call the police. Teach slipped the Navy Colt into his waistband and walked to the Taurus.

In the front seat, he saw nothing but dust, coffee stains, scraps of paper with notes scrawled on them, and credit card receipts. Nothing in the backseat but old newspapers. He stepped back and looked at the car, at his house. A strange quiet came from the house, and the weak sickness in Teach's limbs grew. He felt exposed standing here, like some night creature forced out into the daylight. He opened the car door and pulled the trunk release lever.

Seeing the face through the wrapping of dusty, blood-smeared plastic made Teach sink to his knees. Holding onto the bumper, he closed his eyes, steadied his head, and peered into the trunk, unable to identify the face that stared up at him through layers of dust and blood. He thought of Dean, of safety, of a good life lived in quiet and reason and law, and he peeled aside the smeared plastic.

"Oh God. Oh my Christ," whispered Teach. "You poor, poor woman." All she had done to him, all he had hated her for, left him now as he looked at the mess of her face. Someone had dealt her two huge strokes with a heavy weapon. Strangely, the phrase *blunt trauma* came to him, and with it a curious calm. He reached into his waistband and drew the Navy Colt. He released and spun the cylinder, rested the hammer on the chamber he had left empty. There they were, five messages for Mr. Naylor.

FORTY-FIVE

The man held her hard, and Dean stood in front of him trying to give her body a calm compliance. To tell him with her limbs what she had already told him in words. She would do anything he asked of her if he would not hurt her father.

Her father was here somewhere. He was close. She had heard nothing, and she knew from the way the man held her mouth, from the way his mouth breathed against her neck, that he had heard nothing. But she knew Teach was here. She could feel his secrets in the air, hear his mind whisper that he was coming. She wished she could send to him what she knew, that he was walking into death in his own house. She closed her eyes and, breathing as calmly as she could, wished her message to her father: *Look out, Daddy. Beware, my dear Daddy.*

Blood held the girl's mouth, pressed the gun barrel to her throat, and whispered to her, "You be quiet, you understand me? You don't say nothing when he comes in here. I only want to talk to him. You make noise, anything could happen, you understand me? Anything." The girl moved her head in his hands, trying to nod.

Out there on the road, the plan had hardened in Blood's mind. He had decided not to take the body to a sinkhole, not to run. How the hell could a man who owned as much as Blood did just pull up and run? It would be like calling in a confession. So he had turned around and driven to Teach's house. The plan, the beautiful plan, was to leave the car in Teach's neighborhood, not exactly at his curb, but near it, then get one of the whores to call the cops, talk in a snotty white-lady voice, tell them there was something suspicious in her neighborhood, a car that didn't belong there. She thought something might be wrong. Then the cops come, and they look in the trunk, and there's the poor dead newspaper bitch, and they want to know who killed her. Who in this nice white neighborhood has a motive? James Teach, the man whose life she pissed on in print.

But then Blood had seen the girl come home. Her girlfriends dropping her off. They had driven past and she had looked at him. She had looked right into his face, that white-girl surprise in her eyes. *Nigger, what are you doing in my neighborhood?* So Blood had to change his plan. He had to park the car and go into the house and take the girl. Because now, now that she had seen him, it had to be different. It had to be a murder-suicide thing. Teach losing his mind over all the trouble that had come down on him, killing the newspaperwoman, driving her car to his house, and shooting his pretty little daughter, then himself. Blood knew he could do it. He could hold the gun to the girl's head, and make Teach kneel. Get him to take the barrel of the unregistered Smith in his mouth.

Blood felt the girl move in his arms. She had been good, but now she was beginning to panic. He whispered to her in his sweetest voice, "Be still now, baby. He'll be home soon. I told you I ain't gone hurt him. I'm just gone talk to him a little. Then you two can go back to your nice little life."

The girl stopped struggling, went calm in his hands. Blood Naylor had a way with the ladies.

A few minutes later, he heard Teach downstairs, the guy calling out, "Dean? Dean, are you here?" It didn't sound right, not like Father Knows Best coming home, calling his little daughter. The man sounded scared. He must have seen the car, maybe even looked in the trunk. Blood held the girl's face hard. Teach calling out again, "Dean? Deanie, are you here?"

Blood whispered to the girl, "I'm gone take my hand off your mouth. You tell him to come upstairs. You mess up, and I kill you where you stand. You understand me?"

She nodded. Blood could hear Teach down there creeping through the house. Going room to room. The phone rang. Christ, Blood didn't want the guy answering it down there. He crossed the bedroom, pulling the girl by the arm, and whispered to her, "Stop it ringing. Don't answer it, just turn it off."

She picked up the phone, hit some buttons. The phone stopped ringing. The girl's hands were trembling. She'd almost knocked the phone off its little table onto the floor.

Blood whispered into her ear, "Get him up here. Tell him he's got a phone call."

Aimes grabbed Delbert by the arm. "Come on."

"What the . . . ?" Delbert shrugged out of his grasp, a fighting cock with his ruffle up. Aimes had made him spill a forkful of grilled Cajun sausage.

They were sitting in a booth at the Green Iguana. Aimes had gone to the men's room, then stopped at the phone booth in the hallway to call Teach's house. See if the daughter was there, if she knew anything.

They ran out of the restaurant, leaving their food behind. In the car, Aimes caught his breath, thanked his treadmill, and told Delbert the story.

The answering machine at Teach's house had malfunctioned, or someone there had done it on purpose. Instead of James Teach's cheery salesman's voice with the usual message, Aimes had heard a song that he remembered from his youth. Little Anthony and the Imperials. "Tears on My Pillow." A very pretty tune, a very sad story.

Aimes pushed the Crown Vic through the traffic on Westshore. Delbert held onto the hand strap. "What does that mean? That song. I don't get it."

"It means Bloodworth Naylor. You remember that little record player we saw in the warehouse? That song was on the turntable." Aimes thinking, *It means blood on somebody's pillow.*

Teach heard Dean call down, "Father, you have a phone call." It was never *Father,* always *Daddy.* But nothing else seemed off. Her voice sounded normal, and if it were not for the car out there at the curb, a dead woman in the trunk, Teach might have walked up the stairs to ask his daughter why she had called him *Father.*

He stood at the foot of the stairs with the pistol in his hand, its grip slippery with the sweat of fear. Naylor was up there in his bedroom with Dean. Some mad revenging symmetry working in the man's brain, doing to Teach what Teach had done to him. He would not let himself think of what Blood might have done to Dean already. It had only been minutes since Blood left the Taurus at the curb, but a man with his hate could do a lot of harm in minutes.

Teach put his foot on the first riser and remembered how the moon had come out that night, leaving the sea and the boats that ran on her open to the sky. How he had pushed the shrimper, the *Santa Maria*, hard to the shore, and how glad he had been with the fisherman, Carlos, standing beside him when the moon had hidden behind the clouds. Teach saw the flames that had consumed Frank Deeks. Heard the great breath of combustion and smelled the burning boat and flesh and boiling seawater. Then he saw the pistol rising in his hand toward the side of Carlos's head. He had known it for a while now. You never escaped. Some men could never find their way back to the maps. The charts of a good life. You were always what that time had made you do. Well, Teach had put a gun to the head of the best of three bad men and pulled the trigger. He had painted the man's brains onto the wheelhouse window, and then things had gone from bad to worse.

Teach checked the load in the pistol again and called up the stairs, "Blood! Blood Naylor! You don't know what you got yourself into! You fucked with the wrong man!"

Dean had never heard that voice before. She didn't know what was coming through that door, but she knew her daddy wasn't coming unwarned. She was glad of that. For that, she had called him *Father*. She would die now, she thought, and in dying she would miss him. But she would do what she could before the man who held her hurt her daddy.

Running up the drive, Aimes pointed to the side of the house, said to Delbert, "Get the back door."

A car pulled up and some high school kids poured out onto the street thirty yards from the Ford Taurus. One of them was Tawnya Battles. The trunk of the Taurus was still open. Aimes had found it open and wished now he'd closed it. He hoped the kids didn't look inside. They didn't need that. Tawnya Battles saw Aimes and Delbert with guns in their hands, and started walking toward Teach's house. Then she started running. "Deanie!" she called out. "Is Deanie all right?"

Delbert tackled her in the middle of the front yard.

"Damn you, let go of me!" The girl screaming, kicking, scratching at Delbert, and the cop whispering, "Police! Police!" Trying to show her his shield.

The last thing Aimes saw before going gun-first through the front door was Delbert sitting astride her, holding her hands and talking into her ear about the danger inside the house.

Teach came through the bedroom door with the Colt out in front of him, centered it on Blood Naylor's eyes, those cold black eyes beside Dean's cheek. The man's big hand covered her mouth, but her eyes told Teach it was all right. She loved him. Everything was all right. He could do what he had to do. Teach took two more steps into the room, sighting the Colt at Blood's right eye. The bed looked untouched. Dean looked scared but not hurt.

Blood Naylor said, "We got something to do here, Mr. Teach, Mr. Wrong Guy I Fucked With, and we got to do it right. You gone kneel down right there in front of your daughter. You gone apologize to her for what you did with Thalia Speaks. What you did to her and her mother. You killed Thalia. I want you to kneel down there and tell her about it for me."

Teach kept the pistol aimed at Blood's eye. "What did you mean, Blood, when you said you *released* her? You said it the other night to Grandmother Liston. Tell me what you meant."

The sick surprise in Blood's eyes made Teach happy. Some of it going back the other way. Somebody watching you, knowing what you did, what you said when your heart was in your hands. The words made Blood's gun move an inch away from Dean's neck. Maybe this was the time. Maybe it was time for Carlos.

Creeping up the stairs, hoping the old wood didn't sing under his weight, Aimes heard Blood Naylor say it again: "Kneel down there, Jimmy Teach. I want you to apologize to your daughter, and then I'm gone put this gun in your mouth and stop you talking."

Aimes was outside the bedroom door now. It was quiet out in the yard. But soon, he knew, the street would be all noise. The neighbors seeing the police car, looking into the trunk of the Taurus, and puking in the street.

Aimes didn't hear any of that yet. What he heard was Teach in there: "Fuck you and your kneel-down, Blood. Don't you understand what I'm telling you? You fucked with the wrong man. I know you killed Thalia. I can prove it. There's a cop downtown named Aimes who knows you did it too. He thinks you *released* her, Blood."

Aimes heard nothing for a second, then Naylor's voice sounding as cold as the bottom of a well: "She had to die. She was in too much pain. You gave her the pain, and I took it away for her. I did a kind thing. But you, white motherfucker, you gone die for it. Now kneel down."

When Dean saw Aimes's face at the door, she opened her mouth wide and bit down hard on the hand that covered it. She tasted hot blood, heard the man behind her scream. Aimes leveled a gun at him.

Blood's eyes jumped to something behind Teach, and Teach fired at his forehead. Then the world went white light, screams, and shooting.

Aimes's first shot missed. He shoved into the room, stood beside Teach, and saw Naylor already falling backward, pulling the girl with him by a hand clamped across her mouth. Naylor's gun went off twice beside her face, and Aimes felt the smack in his chest. He dropped to his knees and put a bullet into Naylor's armpit. Naylor spun, firing as he turned, filling the air with plaster dust and pillow feathers. As he turned, the girl spun with him, blocking Naylor from Aimes's view. He saw Teach lunge forward, push his pistol to Naylor's spine, and fire twice. Then he saw the bright spurt of blood from Teach's ribs. Aimes thought, *Yes, the wrong man. Mr. Teach was the wrong man.*

FORTY-SIX

Aimes sat on the mezzanine in the public library looking over the new biography of Harry Truman. It was long, and political biography wasn't his usual fare, but Truman had fought in World War I, as an artillery battery commander, and he could look forward to that part of the story. His head was beginning to ache from the fluorescent lights, and he was hungry. His evening session on the treadmill had burned up his lunch. Maybe he'd walk up to Franklin, see if CDBs was still open. Get a pizza.

A black woman about his age, a librarian, walked over to him. Aimes had seen her in here before. She stood in front of him holding a book against her pretty chest. When he closed the biography, she said, "I thought you might like this. It just came in."

He took the book from her. It was a study of the Grenada invasion. He felt something he had not felt in a long time, years maybe. It was that confused tremor in some unnamed organ a man felt when a woman came nearer than was proper, did it for her reasons. His palm was suddenly moist holding the book. He thanked her.

She stood looking down at him for a beat, then two, and he knew he should say more, but didn't find anything in the confusion to say. She said, "Well, I hope you enjoy it," and walked away. She went into a little glass-walled office, and Aimes could see her talking to another librarian, a thin young white man. Aimes took a deep breath, wiped his hands on his trousers, and opened the book, pretended to read.

Things had been quiet at work since the shooting at Teach's house. Aimes and Delbert had been assigned to the murder of a cab driver in Ybor City. The guy shot for a few dollars, money that had probably bought drugs. The case of the serial killer had been cracked, but not by Aimes and Delbert. Since the day Blood Naylor died, Aimes had been tired and something else he could not name. That day, Aimes and Delbert had been the center of attention, for a while anyway.

The two of them had sat in the middle of the squad room and for thirty minutes, cops had stood around them, looking at Aimes's vest spread out on a table, the bullet stuck in it, upper-left, over the heart. The cops making him show them the purple bruise on his left pectoral the size of a cocktail coaster. A couple of guys cracking on Delbert, asking him to show his wounds. Delbert showing them the scratches on his forearms where Tawnya Battles, who had been running to help her friend, Dean Teach, had got him. One of the cops saying, "So that was your contribution to the gunfight, Delbert? You sat on the dancer?" Another guy looking at Aimes: "You sure know how to break in a detective. Make him sit on a ballerina."

And then the cops drifted away, back to offices, computer screens, the coffee room. It's quiet and Aimes picks up the vest, examines it again, sweat breaking on his forehead. Then there's noise out in the hall, and a detective comes in with a little Asian guy in handcuffs, and suddenly the squad room is like the locker room after the Super Bowl. Winning team.

This detective, a guy named Orin Smithers, has the serial killer. The scourge of Tampa, America's Next Great City, is a five-foot-two, forty-three-year-old Korean. Aimes and Delbert join the crowd, but the suspect is hustled to an interrogation room. He wants a lawyer. The watch commander calls for one. Smithers comes out for a minute to get a cup of coffee. He looks like a kid at Christmas. His face is the color of Santa's hat. Here's the story he tells:

"The weird thing about the dead women, you guys all know it, was how calm they seemed, and the way the blood ran down from their head wounds to the front of their bodies. Some of us were talking about how they might have been stood up in a closet after they were shot, something like that. Well, I went to New York last week to see my sister's daughter get married, and I took a walk through Central Park. And I saw this Chinese guy giving massages, ten bucks for fifteen minutes, and he's using this weird chair. You sit in it leaning forward with your face in this oblong slot, and he stands behind you, and you're almost upright. It stuck in my mind. So, I get back from New York, and I'm out talking to some people about the Vietnamese girl, Phuong, and I see this guy in a little storefront place off 7th Street, giving a massage in one of these chairs.

"I don't know, something about the guy wasn't right. I figured I'd go in, ask him if he's got a license. I walk in the door, and this woman's getting her neck rubbed, and she's Korean or Chinese, and she takes one look at me, and she pays the guy and leaves. The woman is in the life. I can tell by the way she's dressed, the way she makes me for a cop the minute I walk in. And I can smell something. I look down. On the table by the chair, there's a bottle of oil—peanut oil.

"I show the guy my shield. I'm about to ask for his license, and I notice there's a back room. One of those bead curtains, no door. So I ask him if it's okay if I look around back there. The guy gives me a big smile, says, *Of course, officer.* And Jesus, what do I find? The guy's got a bulletin board, a regular trophy case with newspaper articles about the killings, and thumbtacked next to each article is a little plastic baggie with something in it. Well, this is getting creepy, so I draw my weapon, and I lean close to one of the baggies, and I see it's got hair in it. They all do. And I'm no expert on hair, but I can see it's all black and some of it's fine and some of it's coarse. At which point the hair goes up on the back of my neck like a rottweiler, and I'm thinking, *Holy shit,* and I hear the bead curtain behind me, and I turn and here's this little Korean guy holding his hands out to me palms up. *I confess,* he says, and I can smell the oil on his hands. *I killed them all,* he says. *I killed them while they were very relaxed. And I only kept one thing from them. I only kept a lock of hair.*"

The captain comes out of the interrogation room wanting to know where the hell the public defender is. The excitement in the room is higher than Aimes has ever seen it. While Smithers is telling the story, Aimes buttons his shirt. Nobody interested in the bruise over his heart anymore. He turns to Delbert. "The guy sure doesn't fit the profile. Supposed to be an angry white male, reclusive, intelligent, socially maladroit."

Delbert nods at him, touches the scratches on his arms. "Teach didn't fit either."

Aimes wonders what this means. Is Delbert trying to say his hard-on for Teach was the right thing? This Korean guy, a guy as far from what you'd look for as shit is from ice cream, proves Delbert's point about Teach? Aimes lets it go. "Well," he says, "it's all police work. And it's all interesting. Isn't it, my young friend?"

Delbert nods, that ambition of his making him crane his neck in the direction of the interrogation room where the senior detectives are all crowding around the door. Aimes decides he isn't going to call his partner his *young friend* anymore. Just *friend* will do. Delbert's been at it long enough for that.

Aimes lifted his eyes from the puddle of blurry words about Grenada and snuck a look at the glass-walled room where the nice-looking woman had been sitting. She wasn't there anymore. Well, it was all right. There were ten reasons she was the wrong one: She wasn't any Whitney Houston to start with. She was Aimes's age at least, and her backside was bigger than it had been last year. She looked like she was hiding herself in that librarian's dress. He could see her going to church three times a week (Sunday and Wednesday night services, and once for the Covered Dish Supper Preparation Committee). One of those sisters who had lost a man or three and settled for a dull life here, and the promise of harps and white gowns hereafter. Aimes went downstairs and checked out the book.

He was getting into his car when she walked past him on the way to hers. Something made him get back out and walk over to her. She was settled behind the wheel, had the engine running. It scared her when Aimes showed her his shield. "You ought to get one of your male colleagues to walk you out here at night. It might be the best thing." Holding his voice low, calm. Smiling.

She looked at him for a long time out of those big, dark eyes, a little mischief sparkling around in them. "I wish I had a male colleague in there. But it's just us ladies."

Again, Aimes didn't know what to say, damning himself for coming over here, bothering her if he wasn't going to do it.

She helped him: "I see you checked out the book."

He looked down at it, heavy in the hand that was sweating again. He looked up at the high royal palms that bordered the parking lot. A warm wind from Tampa Bay was blowing up there, making the palm fronds rustle and rub together. It sounded like a man rolling over alone in bed, groaning, an unhappy man. What was it Delbert had told him? *You ought to get out more, get your nose in the wind.* Aimes looked into the woman's eyes and said, "How would you like to walk over to CDBs with me and get some pizza?"

She pulled her key out of the ignition and opened the door. "Detective Aimes, I thought you'd never ask."

FORTY-SEVEN

Dean waved from the coppery water. "Dad, I'm gonna swim to the beach." She tossed back her hair and gave him that wet devil grin.

Teach called after her, "Careful. And be back before dark."

The *Fortunate* was anchored off Caladesi again. Continuing north in the morning. Teach was taking his daughter to Cedar Key, and on from there to wherever the wind blew them. He had quit his job. The house in Terra Ceia was up for sale. Somewhere up north where the coastline bent to the west, a new life waited for them. Maybe it was Panama City, maybe Pass Christian, maybe it was all the way to Corpus Christi or inland somewhere from there. America was full of cities, and there were phone books full of names to choose and lawyers enough to make the changes legal.

Teach and Dean had decided to leave after Teach had shot Blood Naylor dead in his bedroom, but not because they had to. Their names were in the papers and would be for weeks to come. Teach was persona non grata at the club, and most of Dean's friends had drifted away, though Tawnya Battles had remained fiercely loyal. Teach was pretty sure Mabry Meador would fire him if he didn't quit first. He and Dean couldn't go to the grocery store or to a restaurant without seeing heads dip into whispers. They had lost almost everything, and James Teach felt better than he had in years. There were no more secrets. They didn't have to leave; they wanted to.

The first night after Teach had shot Blood Naylor, he had sent Dean to sleep over with Tawnya because that was where she had asked to go. The Battles had taken her in without question. It was a kindness Teach would never forget. When he got back from the emergency room, he slept in his study and in the morning went upstairs to clean up the blood and sweep up the feathers and the plaster dust. The neighborhood was quiet. Teach could hear televisions murmuring the morning news through open windows. Somewhere a mother called to her children to come inside. A few streets over, a dog barked at the whining of a garbage truck. Since dawn, there had been a steady stream of Teach's neighbors, gawkers driving by in their Benzes and Jaguars to look at the house, but it had slowed. From the outside, there was nothing much to see.

As Teach worked, ignoring the pain from his second superficial gunshot wound, he repeated to himself the simple instructions of a physical act: *Sweep the floor, collect the fragments in the dustpan, put them in the plastic bag.* Sometimes his hands shook on the broom handle, then they steadied. He was living one simple act at a time. When he had the place clean, he called the Battles's house and asked Dean to come home. He had to talk to her. Tell her.

Dean stood in the bedroom doorway staring at the stained oak floor, the bloody Persian rug folded on the little balcony that overlooked the walled garden, the wall above the bed riddled with bullet holes that revealed sixty-year-old wood lath.

She said, "Jesus, I . . ." She sagged against the door frame, and Teach hurried over to fit his hands under her arms and steady her. When he did it, the pain in his own ribs made him grunt. Dean looked up at him. "Look at us, Dad. A couple of basket cases."

He let go of her and felt the pain ease under his right arm. She stood in front of him, using both sides of the door frame for support. "Dad, you're bleeding."

Teach looked at himself. The mopping and sweeping had started the bleeding again. Maybe he'd ripped out a suture just now holding Dean. It hurt.

"I want to look at it." Dean put her hand on his chest and pushed him back toward the bed. She went to the bathroom for gauze, scissors, some hydrogen peroxide, a roll of surgical tape. With the scissors, she cut away the bandage they'd applied in the emergency room. When she saw the wound, she drew back a little, her brow knitted, her lips locked tight. She looked hard at Teach. She reached out to him, but she didn't touch the new furrow torn by Blood Naylor's bullet.

She touched the old wound, just above it. She rested two fingers there like she was closing someone's lips. Someone who must not speak now. "Dad, what is this? Tell me. I have to know what it is."

Teach remembered the first night he and Paige had been naked together in his shabby apartment, back in the time just after prison, the time when he was humping boxes of drugs on the loading dock and talking to a lawyer about burying his old life. Teach had figured maybe the first time it should be dark, but Paige had asked him to leave a light burning while he took off her clothes. Teach had liked it, thought it was bold, sexy.

So he'd gone to the kitchen and found the stub of a candle he used when the big thunderstorms came through and the power went out. He put the candle in one of his mismatched saucers and brought it out to the bedside table. When Paige took off his shirt, she placed both hands flat on his chest and kneaded him a little, her discoveries making her sigh. Then she gave a sharp little gasp, and one of her hands went to the scar under his arm. The scar was a word Esteban had written on him, the first word of a story Teach could never tell.

"What's this?" the young, naked Paige asked him.

Teach told her it was something that had happened to him on his father's fishing boat. An accident with a gaff. He had practiced telling her the story, knowing he'd have to answer this question. He had even stood in front of a mirror looking into his own lying eyes until they seemed natural, truthful. He had invented details of weather and fish and people to give the story a needed authenticity. The young Paige had believed him, sighing for her lover's old pain. Saying in her sweet, sexy voice, "You poor, poor boy. It must have been so awful. Out there on the ocean so far from land." She had leaned forward and kissed his scar and told him she loved him, and then James Teach, lucky Jim, had bent to take one of her nipples into his mouth.

Now his daughter touched the old scar three inches above the new wound and repeated, "Tell me. I have to know."

Teach had to tell. There was a map somewhere that led out of the land of secrets to the new place where they would live if they were to live at all. And he knew the thing would pull out of him like a hook buried deep in the guts of some savage ancient fish yanked up from dark cold depths. It would pull out with a lot that was rotten and a lot that hurt.

Teach told her his father's death and his mother's poverty. He told it lean and cold, how he'd done the smuggling as a kid trying to stop some deep, deranged sorrow in his mother's eyes, and later as a young man with a broken compass and a fatuous belief that losing a good life entitled him to a crooked one.

Then he told her about Thalia. The story stuttered and almost stopped. But Dean, listening with her eyes closed, put two fingers on the old wound again and pressed them there, and Teach disgorged the time in prison and brought up the outlaw love affair, and once it started it came out fast because he was afraid he would start to lie again. The savage old fish would dive deep, even with half his guts pulled out, and die down there alone and rotting in his secret hole.

He told Dean about Thalia, about his past with Bloodworth Naylor. He told all that he could surmise, and all that he had learned from Aimes about what Blood had done or tried to do to James Teach and his daughter. He finished with the day Aimes had called him in for a friendly talk, and his own pursuit of Blood Naylor and what Dean had guessed already about Blood's revenge invasion of this bedroom. His daughter cleaned and bandaged him while he told the last of it. Finished with her work, she stepped away from him and went to the window that overlooked the garden he had built for her mother.

"I knew it," she whispered. "I guess it was when you read the newspaper after we sailed up to Caladesi. Or maybe even before that. I don't know how I knew, but I did. Did Mom know?"

"Yes, I think so. We never talked about it. I want you to know something, Deanie. I chose your mother for my life, for you, and I never would have left her."

"I know." She turned back to him. "I know that too. But did you love her?"

"Yes," he said without hesitation. He hoped she wouldn't ask him how this could be. How a man could love two women. No one could answer that question.

"Was she a good person?"

"Until I made her a bad one."

Dean said, "Do you love me?"

"More than ever."

"Is there anything you want to ask me?"

Teach thought about it. He had no right to any knowledge of her secrets. Not now, not yet anyway. He said, "I want to know if you want to go on. With me. I don't know where it goes from here. But I want you with me if you'll come."

She smiled, moved toward him. She didn't hesitate. "I'll come. I don't care where it leads. As long as I'm with you."

Fifty yards away, on Caladesi Beach, Dean was a tanned torso and legs, bisected by two bright yellow pieces of cloth, walking a slice of sand so bright that it burned Teach's eyes. He knew that she could feel the protection of his eyes on her and liked it.

Teach dozed and then awoke to the boat sway of Dean pulling herself aboard. When it was almost dark, he lit the charcoal cooker that swung out from the rail and put on two tuna steaks. He opened a bottle of good chardonnay and poured two glasses. He looked at Dean. Still in her bathing suit, she sat with a towel around her shoulders. He said, "This is not to getting away with it. It's to starting over."

She touched her glass to his. "To starting over."

They drank and Teach said, "So, you're not going to be a cheer-leader now, I guess."

Something complicated, a thing he supposed would always be there, happened in Dean's eyes. She said, "I don't know. Maybe they'll have cheerleaders where we end up. Wherever that is. Any-way, my ultimate goal is to become a lawyer or a policeman. I know that, at least."

Teach looked out at the robe of purple spreading along the hori-zon. He saw a quiet, somber curtain coming down on their old life. The high-dollar life no one ever leaves. He and Paige had built walls between them because they'd had too many things to protect and only secrets to protect them with. Behind their walls, they had built separate lives. Those lives were over now. Two people had died to end them. Maybe where he and Dean were going, somewhere be-yond that purple curtain, they would not tell people who they had been. They would try to answer better questions. *Who do we want to be? What do we really want to do?*

* * *

At midmorning, they were off Cedar Key, and Teach could see the low shapes of the pier, old clapboard houses, and the hotel he had known in his youth. And the newer, taller buildings, condos and apartment houses. He gave Dean the wheel and stood behind her. He leaned close so that she could hear him in the wind.

"We've got to decide. We can dig it up, use it for the new start, or leave it where it is. Hell, maybe it's not there. Maybe somebody found it." Teach doubted it. Like the pirate he had been told was a distant relative, he had buried the money carefully and deep.

Dean glanced back over her shoulder at him, happily steering. "I thought about it all night. I still don't know what to do. Who knows how long it'll take you to find a job you like?"

"Tell me what you want to do."

"No," his daughter said. "It's up to you."

Teach had thought about the money all night too, lying in his berth unable to sleep. A night of pictures: the *Santa Maria*, rotting sticks and bones now in a mangrove hole somewhere not far from here, the faces of the three Guatemalans, Blood Naylor, and those nights of running contraband on a moonlit sea. Teach had left prison and worked for money to buy a clean record from the state. He'd left the stash buried to prove something to himself: that he could work his way up from a loading dock to the good life on sweat and invention. That he was a good man, after all. He didn't know, now, if digging up the money, using it for a new start, for Dean, was right or wrong.

"I don't know," he said to Dean. "I'll decide when we get there. When I see the place." He looked at the resolving shapes of his hometown. "They know me here, you know. There'll be somebody who'll walk up to me in a bar or a restaurant and say, *Why, ain't you Jimmy Teach? Why, I remember when you thrown that pass that beat Auburn back in—*"

"Promise me something, Jimmy Teach."

He leaned back in the wind and sun and said to his daughter, "What's that?"

"Don't tell any more stories."

Teach laughed. "All right, baby. I won't."

Also available from Akashic Books

FIGHTING IN THE SHADE
by Sterling Watson
320 pages, trade paperback original, $15.95

"High school football mixes with Faust in this blitz of a novel from Watson . . . the novel avoids slipping into morality tale excess as it spins out a big Dennis Lehane–like story of society, opportunity, and consequences, revealing Watson as an accomplished storyteller." —*Publishers Weekly* (starred review)

"Honor, loyalty, even life and death form the core of this wrenching story."
—*Kirkus Reviews* (starred review)

"Watson's visceral descriptions of the physicality of sport are more than matched by his knowing depiction of small-town corruption in this fast-paced coming-of-age story." —*Booklist*

"A sleeper that sneaks up on you. Pitch it to old school readers who appreciate intelligent and hard-hitting novels that are more than sports books."
—*Library Journal*

THE DEAD DETECTIVE
by William Heffernan
320 pages, hardcover, $24.95

"*The Dead Detective* is William Heffernan's first novel in seven years, and wherever he's been, he hasn't forgotten how to write a good, gritty police procedural . . . This edgy police drama succeeds in capturing the hysteria the grips Tampa residents when a celebrity criminal . . . is found dead in a cypress swamp with her throat cut and the word 'Evil' carved on her forehead."
—*New York Times Book Review*

"*The Dead Detective* is a meaty story that offers an intriguing and conflicted protagonist, a darkly fascinating victim, solid police procedural detail, a knowing look at the Tampa Bay area and its politics, an unlikely murderer, and a creepy denouement that hints that Harry [protagonist] will be back."
—*Booklist*

"In his first new novel in seven years, Edgar Award–winner Heffernan delivers a readable, tidy police procedural that echoes any number of popular television series, from *The Mentalist* to *Criminal Minds*, whose many fans will find this series debut enjoyable." —*Library Journal*

BLACK ORCHID BLUES
a novel by Persia Walker
320 pages, trade paperback original, $15.95

"Walker's exuberant third Harlem Renaissance mystery [is a] dark, sexy novel." —*Publishers Weekly*

"[T]he tale is strengthened by plenty of period detail and a fine feel for both the gay underworld of Harlem in the 1920s and the sociopsychological dynamics of her characters. Best of all, [protagonist] Lanie has the makings of a strong series heroine. Walter Mosley fans, in particular, should look for more from this promising crime writer." —*Booklist*

"Put a Bessie Smith platter on the Victrola, and go with the flow on this mystery/romance/history mix." —*Library Journal*